From Now Until Forever

ROWAN COLEMAN

HODDER &
STOUGHTON

First published in Great Britain in 2023 by Hodder & Stoughton
An Hachette UK company

1

A CIP catalogue record for this title is available from the British Library

Hardback ISBN 978 1 529 37650 0
Trade Paperback ISBN 978 1 529 37651 7
eBook ISBN 978 1 529 37652 4

Typeset in Plantin Light by Manipal Technologies Limited

Printed and bound in Great Britain by Clays Ltd, Elcograf S.p.A.

Hodder & Stoughton policy is to use papers that are natural, renewable and
recyclable products and made from wood grown in sustainable forests. The log-
ging and manufacturing processes are expected to conform to the environmental
regulations of the country of origin.

Hodder & Stoughton Ltd
Carmelite House
50 Victoria Embankment
London EC4Y 0DZ

www.hodder.co.uk

For
Noah Peter Devitt Brown
23 April 2003–8 August 2022

Because I could not stop for Death –
He kindly stopped for me –
The Carriage held but just Ourselves –
And Immortality.
                    Emily Dickinson

XII

Hours fly,
Flowers die:
New days,
New ways:
Pass by!
Love stays.

Henry van Dyke

2

Chapter One

When it happens, it's almost like a memory, or a rehearsal for one. Like something I've half-imagined a hundred times. Not quite real and not quite true, but immovable.

'Is there anyone with you?' she asks. Ten minutes ago I was staring through the window, watching the rain and planning what I'd make for dinner, and now for the first time ever since I turned 18 she is asking me if I brought anyone with me.

'Nope,' I say. 'Just me, Doc.'

'Right.' Her hand reaches across the desk and briefly covers mine. A tiny break in the cool professional exterior that I have always known, that tells me everything. 'It's not good news, Ben. As you know from previous treatments, aneurysms have been a symptom of your Marfan syndrome. Over the last few years we've dealt with a few. However, the most recent scans show a new one in your brain, right next to the brain stem. It's large – 5 centimetres in diameter – and the cause of your headaches and the increase in blurred vision.'

It dawns on me that this is about to be the worst moment of my life, yet I can't feel it. Everything seems to be happening in slow motion.

'Right,' I say uncertainly. 'But most of the time I feel pretty normal really. Maybe I made too big of a deal of it?' She says nothing. I hear her swallow. 'So, you can clip this one too, right? Or stick a balloon in?'

Mrs Patterson shakes her head minutely.

'I'm afraid that the location of the aneurysm means that to attempt to treat it as we normally would is extremely dangerous, with perhaps a 3-per-cent chance of a total recovery. It is much more likely that you wouldn't survive the surgery, or if you did, you would be severely brain-damaged. As such, I cannot recommend this course of action in good conscience. If we do nothing, aside from mitigating the symptoms, the quality of your remaining life will be good.' She pauses, frowning deeply, and then looks at me. 'You will have symptoms but not debilitating ones. You will be able to enjoy the rest of your life, though it will in all likelihood not be a long one.'

'How long is not long?' I ask her slowly, waiting for what I'm hearing to materialise into a tangible reality that I can touch and feel.

'With the size it is now, and the extreme pressure of blood flow through the vessel, it will rupture at some point in the coming months, weeks or…' she hesitates, 'it could be days, Ben. There is no way of knowing exactly when. When it happens, it will likely be very fast – you won't experience prolonged pain or suffering.'

'There's always that.' Thunder rolls outside; it sounds like a bag of rattling bones. I look at the photographs of her daughter in her graduation gown on the desk, and think about my mum sitting at the kitchen table I grew up eating at. About my sister Kitty doing a job that bores her rigid to keep a roof over her kid's head. My dog, Pablo, sleeping by the front door, waiting for me to return to my drafting desk where the engineering project that is – was – going to make my fortune lies almost finished.

'I'll give you medication for the pain and nausea,' Mrs Patterson says, coming around to my side of the desk. 'You'll be discharged from my care and a district nurse will be in touch with all the information you need on the drug regime. There are very good support groups and counselling available. She will have all the information you need. But I'm not going anywhere. You have my phone number. You can reach out, ask me any questions once you've had a chance to process this.'

'Thanks, Doc.' I nod. 'You're the best.'

'Good luck, Ben.'

All that stuff I didn't do, because I thought it wasn't the right time. The women I walked away from. The parties I missed to study. Never really travelled; never danced until it felt like my heart was bursting; never jumped out of an aeroplane or learnt how to surf. Never joined Instagram or skinny-dipped. Never really fell in love. The late, lonely hours building up my business, because I had all the time in the world to actually live. Or at least I thought I did. I will never be a dad.

I try to shake her hand as I stand up, but she pulls me into a tight hug. I feel her shoulder shaking, and this should be the moment it hits home, but all I feel is sorry for her. Sorry for this brilliant woman, who cares more than she probably should about me.

'Sorry.' She takes a step back, smoothing down her skirt. 'Not very professional.'

'Don't be sorry for caring. We've known each other a long time,' I say. 'Thank you. Thanks for everything.'

***

I walk out of the hospital and into what happen to be the last chapters of my nothing-special life. Turning my face up to the rain, I let it soak me through, running down my neck, under my collar and ice down my back. Not tears.

Thing is, I thought I was in the middle, not at the end. And now? Now seems impossible to navigate.

'Never rains but it pours, does it?' an old lady mutters next to me when I walk out of the rain and into the train station. Clear plastic rain bonnet tied under her chin, a face etched with a life lived and eyes that sparkle with more yet to come. 'You want to get home and get dry, lad – you'll catch your death.'

I laugh. The station steams up as more and more people stream in, seek shelter from the rain. Puddles from hurriedly shaken-out umbrellas reflect the lights overhead.

'Need help with your bags?'

'No, job's a good 'un,' she says. 'Got my trolley, see? Now you go and get something hot in you. Look white as a sheet, you do.'

'I'm heading that way now,' I reply, looking up at the live train times. My rucksack weighs heavy on my shoulders, packed with essentials for overnight stays in case I need a hospital admission at short notice.

Scanning the departures board, I see that the next train to Hebden Bridge leaves in five minutes. I think of my mum sitting at the kitchen table alone, reading a book and having a coffee. Of my sister Kitty, at work at the garage, or maybe she's got the day off with my nephew Elliot, all blissfully unaware of the bomb I'm about to drop into their lives. And I think of all the things I will need to get sorted: my optical-engineering business, the project I've spent years on that is almost finished, unpaid bills, that walk I promised Pablo just before I left. All of those things I thought could wait a couple of hours, before a couple of hours seemed so precious. I have no idea how to do this.

The train just above mine begins to flash, last call to board. A fast train to London, a city where I know no one and have never been, leaving in three minutes.

Something instinctive takes a grip of my heart. Maybe it's fear, maybe it's desire. I don't know anything except that I need to try and find a way out of my own skin so that I can think. So that I can feel.

Breaking into a run, I scramble on to the London train just as the doors are closing, and tumble into the first empty seat I find. For the first time in my life I don't have a plan and I'm terrified.

Chapter Two

I've dreamt of this moment for almost the whole of my whole life. Now that it's here, I'm terrified it won't work. On the other side of the huge, gilded, rococo double doors is the hum of excited conversation and the clink of champagne flutes. They open on to what was once the ballroom of one of the most lavish and fashionable addresses in London, now the Bianchi Collection, named after the wealthy widow who bequeathed her home and its contents to the people of London in perpetuity. This is the place where I work so many hours. I all but live here. This is the place to which I have pinned my fragile hopes. And if they crumble away to dust once again, then I will finally know that I've reached the end of *looking for the end*. After that I cannot imagine.

The opulent, golden-mirrored ballroom is brimful with the great, good and not so good of the art and museum world, their otherworldly reflections shimmering in the polished floor – as above so below. All of them are here for the preview night of the exhibition that I have spent years bringing to the Collection. At last Leonardo da Vinci's surviving portraits are here.

'Are you going in, Vita?' Anna, my boss smiles at me. 'You look beautiful, by the way. Is that genuine Dior?'

'What, this old thing?' I gesture down a vintage Fifties gown of dove-grey silk and tulle that fits as if it were made for me. 'What can I say? It was just hanging about at home.'

'How do you have such an impressive array of made-to-measure fashion through the ages just hanging about at home?' Anna asks incredulously. 'You could exhibit your wardrobe at the V&A.'

'Comes from a long line of hoarding predecessors,' I tell her with a smile. 'We never can bear to throw anything away.'

Anna takes my hand.

'Are you nervous? You're hovering around out here like Cinderella,' Anna decides. 'You know you can go to the ball, darling, don't you? It is your party. You are Princess Charming. The rest of us are the fawning admirers of your amazing achievement.'

'I know you're right,' I say. 'It's just a lot, you know? It feels like there's a lot at stake. More than I realised.'

Years planning and negotiating, and begging and bargaining with all the great museums and galleries of the world to bring almost all the remaining Da Vinci portraits to the Collection in one single exhibition. All that work and time has come down to this moment.

Anna nods. 'After tonight, the whole of London will know your name,' she promises.

The thought makes me shudder.

'I'm not sure I like the thought of that,' I half joke, obscuring my true fears. 'But it's not even that.' I choose my words carefully. 'I have a lot of questions about these works. And I hope that while I am their custodian, I will finally be able to answer them.'

'I'm sure your research will be a triumph.' Anna squeezes my fingers. 'Come on, Princess Charming,' she says, smiling at the footmen who open the doors in unison. 'Come with me and see what wonder you have created.'

'It was Da Vinci who created the wonder,' I say. 'I just follow in his wake.'

***

By midnight the very last of the guests have left and I am almost completely alone, comforted by the balmy embrace of peace and quiet. It was a wonderful evening, a 'resounding success', Anna told me, though I can't seem to recall any single detail, just a whirl of smiles and congratulations bubbling constantly like the champagne in my glass. Now almost everyone has gone it feels as if the museum is suddenly alert, as if the occasion has woken her from a hundred-year sleep. Memories seem to dance just a few moments out of reach, as if I could turn a corner and find the echoes of revellers descending the grand staircase.

It feels like a wonderland. It feels like home.

'Mo, would you mind?' I ask our security head as he conducts final checks before heading back to the control centre in the basement. 'Can I have five minutes alone in the exhibition before you turf me out?'

'Go on, then,' Mo says. 'As it's you.' He is a father to five girls, kind and sweetly patient with the romantic whims of his superfan daughters, who have given him a surprisingly in-depth knowledge of Korean Pop that he likes to brief me over whenever we happen to be in the coffee room at the same time. 'But if you try to leave with the *Mona Lisa* under your coat, I'm nicking you.'

'We haven't got the *Mona Lisa*,' I remind him. 'The Louvre wouldn't part with her, not for anything.'

'I never liked that one anyway,' he says, winking at me. 'You enjoy them all to yourself. You've worked hard on this, Vita. You look like you just fell out of the stars.'

'I don't exactly know what that means, but I'm taking it as a compliment,' I tell him.

★★★

The paintings glow like gemstones in the dark, each one lit so that they appear to levitate. Their images are so familiar that they are almost commonplace, and yet to see them here together never fails to give me a frisson of shock and awe. Eyes seem to search out mine, lips poised, as if at any moment they might say my name.

I stop in front of *Lady with an Ermine*, or Cecilia Gallerani as she was known in real life. Eternally capricious and coquettish as ever, the favourite mistress of the Duke of Milan, she could always light up a room with her wit and grace. Then I move on to

Ginevra de' Benci, the poor sallow-faced young woman painted on the eve of her marriage to a man she did not love. So much sorrow and fatigue in her tired features, as if she is already ready for the death that came for her just a few months after the painting was completed. At least I have known love in my life. Ginevra de' Benci's sad gaze always reminds me of that.

These portraits are exquisite, they are each marvels, but they are not the work of art that makes my heart pound with excitement and affection. That likeness waits for me near the very end of the exhibit; her ivory complexion glows in the dark.

La Belle Ferronnière, or Portrait of an Unknown Woman as she has also been called. A serious oval face, framed by dark, straight hair, her head tilted just a fraction. She seems to watch me as I approach her, as if she has been expecting me. It's been a long while since we last met.

Standing face to face, eye to eye, we reflect one another's gaze as I wonder at her secrets. The world lost her name hundreds of years ago, historians still argue about her identity. It's not her name that matters to me though. It's who she is now; every lost woman caught for ever in that moment between smiling and weeping. And, somewhere hidden behind that almost smile, almost sob, are secrets only her creator knows.

Chapter Three

I was almost 16 when I found out that I happened to have been born with a rare genetic condition.

I'd been having headaches, blurred vision, for weeks, and I'd brushed them off. Mum made me go to the optician and they suggested I saw a neurologist. At no point did either of us think it was anything to worry about. I was totally oblivious on the train to Leeds. Mum talked the whole way there, and I pretended to listen as I looked out of the window and thought about girls and football.

That's when I first met Mrs Patterson, who told me the secrets my body had been keeping from me. Marfan syndrome. Rare, genetic, possibly inherited, though we found out later that my genes just decided to mutate in the womb – no one could really explain why. It was the reason I was the tallest kid in the year, the reason I was double-jointed and short-sighted. 'Nothing to worry about,' Mrs Patterson told us. Yes, it would need managing, monitoring, but 90 per cent of Marfan sufferers lived into their seventies these days. That had seemed like forever away to me. It still did.

'What about the other 10 per cent?' Mum had asked.

'There is an increased risk of complication with heart function or aneurysms,' Mrs Patterson had said. 'But treatments are improving all the time. Try not to worry. We'll take care of you.'

'So, what does this mean then?' I'd said to Mum on the way home.

'Nothing's really changed,' she said. 'You heard her – 90 per cent of people live a normal life. That's almost everyone. We've just got to keep an eye on you is all. Try not to think about it, love.'

I returned my gaze to the window, and even though everyone told me that everything was fine and there was nothing to worry about, I remember having the half-formed thought that *someone* had to be in that unlucky 10 per cent. Someone had to get the rough end of the deal so that the 90 per cent got their chance. Every year I went for a check-up, and every year it was fine until eventually I stopped worrying about it and the fear faded away. It never occurred to me that I didn't have all the time in the world to start to really live; it was always *after* one thing or another that I'd made my mark on the world that I'd lift up my head and really look around at it.

Fifteen years later and I'm standing in King's Cross, London. The evening has turned to late night. A guy drives a sweeper around the platforms and people come and go from the tube station all in a hurry to be somewhere. I feel like I am in a hurry to be somewhere too. The trouble is I don't know where.

When I got on the London train it was because I knew, before I even really understood, that I had to *do* something, right now or never. An instinct propelled me away from everything and everyone I knew. Sitting down next to the window, I turned off my phone without reading the waiting text from my mum. I got the notion that I should take off my watch and leave it behind. If I lost track of time then perhaps it would lose track of me, at least for a little while. It was a good watch. I had bought it for myself the first year my business turned a profit. So I tucked it into the space between the seats and wished luck to whoever found it. Whatever came next, I decided, had to *matter*. No more time to half-arse it. The only excuse I had for running away from home, friends and family was to make something happen, to *feel* something before the last second of my life got there. I couldn't let one piece of untested, unknown equipment sitting on the desk in my shed be my only legacy in this world. As the train rushed me through the landscape at 100 miles per hour it felt like my heart was the needle of a compass, pointing towards an impossible hope.

Now I recognise the Post Office Tower jutting out of the skyline, a relic of a futuristic age that never seemed to happen. It seems like something to aim for at least, and so I start striding purpose-fully towards it. It's gone 11 p.m., but the streets are still busy, traffic stops and starts, sirens sound, bass thumps behind closed windows. A pub door bursts opens; I catch a burst of laughter and the scent of beer. It's tempting to feel like one of those archetypal kids with their noses pressed against sweetshop windows, longing for something they can't have, but I can have it if I want. I came here to lose myself in this labyrinth of a city, made up of myth and more questions than there are answers for. I came here, because I'm not willing to give up. I came here to find a way not to die, but to live.

Chapter Four

Walking home through central London on a summer's night like tonight is always a bit like walking on a cloud of grit and stardust. There's a comforting, never-changing familiarity existing simultaneously with something always new, always unexpected. I don't think I could exist anywhere else but in this timeless city of constant evolution.

It's still not quite dark and the air is humming with life. The walk to the top of the Mall, where Madame Bianchi's mansion house is tucked away behind the Institute of Contemporary Arts, to my Soho hideaway, is full of colour, memories and so much history, both mine and this city's, much of it snaking along together like the slow-moving Thames. Trafalgar Square is always thick with bustling crowds so I take the Charing Cross Road way home. It's a slightly longer route than through Chinatown, but I like to catch the theatregoers tumbling out on to the street, exhilarated and heady after a performance, not knowing that they walk over secret tunnels built by dangerous aristocrats, or hidden rivers that flow deep under the city that feed into the pools of long-forgotten Roman temples. Weaving in and out of the crowds of after-work drinkers exchanging jokes and phone numbers, I am both part of it and not, and that's exactly how I like it.

On the corner of Wardour Street I pick up my pace a little, happy to be almost home, moving in and out of flurries of extravagantly good-looking men flirting with one another like there will be no tomorrow. A hen party bursts into the middle of the street singing tunelessly but enthusiastically at the top of their voices.

I love London with all that's left of my heart.

It was the first place I ran away to, long before Dominic, and it was a beacon in the darkness. London can be cruel and it can be brutal, but it is honest too. It saved me then, and has kept on saving me ever since.

I turn a corner. If anyone were watching me right now it might seem to them that halfway down Poland Street I step into the shadows and vanish. That's because the place I live is something like a run-down urban Narnia, often accessed by shoving aside an industrial dumpster. Most of the world doesn't know it's here at all.

As I emerge from the alleyway that leads to the tiny courtyard, I'm greeted by the scent of pizza floating into the night, and just a few lights illuminating the dark little courtyard at the centre of which, built into the listed cobbles and dated 1770, is a sundial that hasn't seen sunlight in about 200 years, not since most of the original row of houses was knocked down and redeveloped by industrious Victorians. Our one streetlight throws a spotlight over my elderly neighbour.

'Hello, dear!' Mariah is sitting on her front step, tan-stockinged legs crossed, smoking a long cigarette, taking the air as if she were on the Amalfi coast and not in a Soho back alley, a gin and tonic at her feet. Eighty-six and as elegant as Audrey Hepburn. 'Lovely night for it, don't you think? You are still coming for dinner, aren't you, darling? I've sent the help home – couldn't be doing with them tonight.'

The help are Viv and Marta, Mariah's day and night carers, who look after her around the clock. Marta waves at me from the doorway with a shrug. I motion for her to go to bed and let me look after Mariah for a few hours. It's something I often do. Mariah is very dear to me. One of only two people in the whole world that I don't have to hide from, she is the closest thing I have to family now.

'Did we make plans?' I say, leaning on the narrow, wrought-iron railing that separates the stone steps that lead up to both our front doors. We didn't make plans, but Mariah's memory is a fleeting thing that can pivot her backwards and forwards for days, months, or even years at a time. I always just follow her lead, fitting into whatever reality she is walking through – it's easier that way. 'It is rather late. It's almost one in the morning.'

'Nonsense! Young folk like us don't worry about bedtime,' she says. 'And what about you? What have you brought me?'

I reach into my pocket and drop a handful of brightly coloured boiled sweets into her hand. She smiles in delight.

'I'll save them for after dinner,' she says.

'What are we having, Mariah? I'll pop into mine and fetch a bottle of wine.'

'Spaghetti, Evie. Spaghetti hoops on toast and custard after. Isn't that grand?'

'Perfection.' Mariah often calls me Evelyn, my predecessor's name. Evelyn was brave, boisterous and permanently undaunted. I wish I was more like her now.

'I'll just have one more cig,' Mariah mutters as I go in to fetch the wine. 'Then I'll get the toast on.'

My house is the perfect twin of Mariah's, ours the two last remaining narrow Georgian townhouses, with pot-bellied bay windows looking out on to nothing. Deep Cut Yard is far too dirty to be called a mews and too small to claim the status of a square. Our neighbours are the back entrances of restaurants and offices, which is fine by us. I like our secret corner of the city that only a handful of people know about.

Letting myself in, I switch on all the hall lights and watch them flicker unsteadily up two flights of narrow stairs in uncertain bursts of magic, illuminating decades of clutter, room after room stacked one on top of the other over four floors and the attics, filled to the brim with books and trunks of clothes and hats. Paintings, sketches and the entire history of photography is crammed on to every inch of wall space, and every surface is crammed with mementos: physical reminders of moments long lost to history.

When I first walked into the house after Dominic had died, I thought about moving out everything that had been left behind, making the house entirely new, along with myself. But I couldn't do it; this house isn't just the walls and the roof. It's every second that's been lived in here. I can't bear to sweep that out with the dust and the mice. This house is my loyal companion, it's the shield that makes me brave.

Dumping my bag at the foot of the narrow stairs, I descend quickly into the tiny, spidery cellar and extract a bottle of wine that was probably considered vintage when Mariah was a girl.

On my way out the door I catch a glimpse of my wedding photo, the hall light winking off its silver frame. And just for a moment a memory of Dominic leaps vividly into life, his hands on my hips, his breath on the back of my neck. The sound of laughter and cheers as we danced on the banks of the Dordogne drinking from bottles of champagne. With one inward breath it is broken, a memory as fragile as the webs that lace the door frame.

Chapter Five

'Where are you?' Kitty asks urgently the moment I answer the phone to her. It took me until this moment to switch it back on again and it rang at once. 'Mum's going spare! You sent her a text asking her to pick up Pablo and keep him for a few days, and no other explanation? What's going on, Ben?'

'I had a bit of a moment,' I understate, opening the door to my hotel room with a key card and walking in. I had somehow got myself lost between here and where I started, arriving at a nice-looking hotel well past midnight, which I suppose is maybe why the only room they had left was a junior suite.

'I was on my way home when I saw the London train and I thought why not live a little? Is Pablo all right? Did he eat his tea?'

'Your dog is fine, Ben. Your humans are not. Wait! You're in bloody London?' Kitty exclaims, before lowering her voice, presumably in a bid not to wake up my nephew, Elliot. 'You went into Leeds this morning and you're in London tonight?'

'I went to the hospital for my annual check-up,' I say slowly, looking around the room. It's ultra-modern and high up enough to make me catch my breath at the view from the window. I can see right across the rooftops towards Trafalgar Square. The room is large with a deep-blue, velvet sofa in front of a huge TV, and in the bathroom there is a huge freestanding bath. But it's the TV that rises out of the foot of the bed that really pleases me as I let myself sink on to it and the toll of this strange empty day starts to weigh heavy in my tight, exhausted body. I'm using every second I can to delay getting to the point because I don't know what the point is yet. That's what my life is all about now.

Days, minutes, hours and seconds. Each one must be used precisely and with purpose.

'And?' Kitty asks cautiously. I don't know how to tell her. They are just words and yet they're the end of everything. This isn't something you do over the phone. This isn't something I want to say ever. So, I don't.

'Yeah, the usual, you know.'

I don't know that I am going to lie to her until I do.

This morning I was eating cornflakes and thinking about bingeing a new series over the weekend, maybe messaging that girl who gave me her number in the pub a couple of days back. Tonight, I'm avoiding delivering news of my imminent demise at all costs. It is surreal to say the least.

'So, everything fine?' she says, picking up on my evasiveness at once.

'Yep, good as gold,' I say.

There's a long silence in which I know that Kitty is trying to navigate where to go next. Does she press me for more detail, or let it go? I pray for the latter.

'Well, you've got to call Mum, Ben,' she says eventually. Her voice feels full of all the distance between us. 'Tell her you're clocking in on your midlife crisis a full decade early.'

'I know,' I say turning my head towards the window. Suddenly the city outside feels very big, and I'm just this one insignificant dot of existence in the grand scheme of things. A heartbeat that won't be missed when it stops – nothing special. 'I don't want a drama. Maybe you could...'

'No chance,' Kitty says, just as I knew she would. 'I'm not copping the grief for your mental breakdown. So, why London of all places?' she asks.

'Why not?' I say, infuriating her.

'Because everything costs 18 times more and it's full of Londoners?'

'It was a spur-of-the-moment thing.'

'Are you going to take loads of drugs and get strippers?' Kitty asks.

'I don't know. I always wanted to go to the Tower of London.'

'You've got the lamest idea about living it up,' Kitty says, but her tone is soft. Suddenly I miss my little sister fiercely. Was it stupid to come here, to head in the opposite direction from the people who love me? Of course, it was stupid, but it felt like I had no choice.

'When will you be home?' she adds.

'When I've spent all my money,' I say. 'Ages. This is just a little break, that's all; a chance to get my head together.'

'Jammy git.'

'Yeah, I know,' I say.

Grief pools in the spaces in my chest at the thought.

'Ben?' Silence follows my name, stretching all the way across the country and all the years she doesn't yet know that she will live through without me.

'What, Kits?' I ask.

'I think you're a right daft bastard,' she says.

'I love you too,' I reply.

Chapter Six

'This reminds me of that time in '41. Do you remember?' Mariah asks me as she pours herself another glass of wine. Her kitchen is small and cluttered, but this is where she always likes to eat. I watch her light a short, stubby candle, melting a little wax on to a saucer to secure it.

'I remember,' I say.

'Remember how scared I was?' Mariah goes on, undeterred. 'Mum couldn't get home because of the raid and the bombs were coming down like it was raining hell. You came, remember? To try and take me to the shelter? But I wouldn't go – I was too scared of the noise and the fires. We sat under this very table with a candle just like this one. You held my hand and told me stories and sang to me. What did you sing now?'

Mariah's hand reaches out for mine and grips my fingers hard, her eyes meeting mine. 'I can't remember. Perhaps something nice and cheerful like "We'll Meet Again"?'

'I remember!' Her eyes light up. 'It was "Run, Rabbit, Run"! Over and over again you sang it, in all these silly voices and accents to make me laugh. We were still here at dawn when Mum came home. It weren't long after that that you disappeared. Where did you go, Evie?'

'I got married to a very handsome man,' I tell her. 'He had black hair, the darkest eyes and an absolutely wicked smile. The kind of smile that told you he was always up to no good.'

'Ooh la la!' Mariah laughs. 'I have always been drawn to the dangerous types. My Len could be a right one when he wanted to be. Was he marvellous in bed?'

'Well, it is true that he was an expert lover,' I say, only partly to see the delight in her eyes. This is not the first time that I have told her about Dominic, but I don't mind repeating myself. Not on a night like tonight, when I find myself longing for all that I have lost.

'Enough about me,' I say. 'Tell me about meeting your Len.'

'Oh, my Len.' Mariah's face softens and she is 20 years old again, blue eyes glowing, her cheeks flushed with pleasure. 'He had this lovely wavy hair, like a film star. His mother didn't approve of me but Len told her I was the only girl for him and she'd better like it or lump it, so we were married and that was that. I *loved* Soho in the Fifties. It was like the world had suddenly burst into colour and everything happened right here – not all of it good, mind you, but so thrilling.'

I lean back in the rickety kitchen chair with my glass in my hand and listen as Mariah strips away the passing years to lead me through dance halls and picture houses to the day of her marriage to Leonard Hayward. Oh, to be like Mariah. Here she is near the end of her life and there isn't a moment of it, good or bad, that she hasn't lived with all her heart.

I can see that in artefacts of her past. The nicotine-stained wallpaper is covered in photographs pinned directly on to the wall. On the shelves among a dusty collection of mismatched crockery are the things she wants to see every day. An art-deco vase she once told me had been her mum's pride and joy and a lace-trimmed baby's bonnet, made with long pink ribbons that have faded almost to white.

Even the bowl belonging to long-departed dog, Kip, still sits next to the fridge as if he might come back hungry any day. Sometimes, if Mariah is having a particularly bad morning, she'll fill it with food and take it to the front step, call his name again and again until I gently guide her in. Despite all she has lost, Mariah has never lost hope.

She leans against me, a little tipsy, as we squeeze our way, side by side, up the narrow staircase to her bedroom. Appearing out of her room, Marta comes to help Mariah into bed.

'I'll put her to bed,' I tell her.

'You sure?' she asks. 'I feel bad just sitting around reading.'

'Yes,' I reassure her. 'Get some sleep. She's bound to get up later for a wander.' I turn on the dusty, tassel-fringed lamp and find her nightdress folded neatly under her pillow – pink chiffon, of course. Mariah often says the day you let your standards slip is the day you might as well give up.

'You're a good girl,' Mariah says, as I tuck the blankets around her. 'I wonder – if I'd have had children, if my little Rosie had lived past her first week, would she have been as kind to me as you are?'

'Everybody loves you. You have that effect on people. Everyone who works round the yard would do anything for you.' I smooth the covers over her small frame, brushing her fine hair back from her forehead.

'But it wasn't God's plan for me, was it?' Mariah sighs, closing her eyes. 'I only had the shortest time with my Rosie and it wasn't long enough. What's it like to be a mum?'

The question stills me for a moment and I don't know how to answer. As I watch her breathing steady, the lines in her face ease.

'Tell me one of your stories, Evie.'

'Which one would you like?' I ask.

'The witch. Tell me about the Tyburn witch,' Mariah says.

'Poor Elizabetta Sedgewick. Of course she wasn't really a witch at all,' I say softly. 'She was just different. Spoke differently, with an accent, seemed to know a lot more than a woman should. And she lived alone with no husband or children, making a very good living importing goods and scents from as far away as Turkey and even Egypt. People didn't trust her one little bit, especially not the other merchants. They feared the strange-sounding woman, who was too young and too unmarried to be doing so well. They decided it had to be the devil's work. Elizabetta knew she was in danger but she didn't leave or move or try to hide herself away.' I smile slightly. 'She was a very stubborn person. The fact that she was fearless made them hate her all the more.'

'And what happened to her?' Mariah murmurs.

'Well, they executed her at Tyburn,' I tell her, knowing that this is her favourite part of the story. 'Or at least they tried to. They accused her, found her guilty and took her to the gallows and hanged her. But do you know what happened?'

'Tell me,' Mariah says. A smile peels the years away from her skin and she looks exactly 6 years old again.

'Elizabetta did not die. Her neck didn't break, she didn't choke. She just hung there. They threw rocks and stones at her, but still she just swung on the rope watching them all with alert, open eyes, muttering curses. She said if anyone came near, she'd drag them down to hell with her. The local people, the soldiers and lawmen were so afraid they ran away inside to let the devil claim her. At dawn, when they summoned up enough courage to look again, she was gone; entirely vanished.'

'Although...?' Mariah whispers.

'Although some folk swore blind that they saw her the very next day at the prow of a boat with a fellow so handsome it had to be the devil himself come to take her away.'

Mariah breathes out, a long, slow, contented sigh. She's sleeping.

I sit on the edge of her bed for a while longer before returning home. As I open my front door I pause, looking up into the city sky, searching for any trace of a familiar star, perhaps the very same that looked down on Tyburn gallows the night that Elizabetta Sedgewick did not die. But there are none there tonight.

I

Life is but a shadow: the
shadow of a bird on the wing.

Traditional sundial motto

Chapter Seven

'How about a pair of braces?' the sales assistant Amelia asks me.

I thought I should probably get some new clothes, to avoid a worst-case scenario. No one wants to die in supermarket jeans. Still, I have my limits.

'There's no way they'll let me back into Yorkshire if I buy them,' I tell her. 'I just want to look, you know, smart. Presentable. Like you'd take me seriously.'

The thing about impulse decisions is that I had packed hardly anything. I wandered out on to the Charing Cross Road and came across this boutique. I'm normally a two-t-shirts-from-Asda sort of bloke, but not now. Now I am going to give a fuck about everything, just in case anything makes a difference. Besides, once I'd caught the eye of Amelia all hope was lost. She came out of the shop and invited me in. I tried saying 'No, thanks', but it came out as, 'Yeah, all right then'.

'Well, then,' Amelia looks me up and down. 'How about this? Look, it exactly matches the colour of your eyes!'

She holds a sky-blue, short-sleeved shirt under my chin and I stare at myself in the mirror, frowning at the deeply disconcerted man looking back at me.

'Oh yes, very handsome,' she says. 'And if we team that with some dark jeans and a crisp white t-shirt underneath, I think that will do the trick. Why don't you try them on?'

Once I have the clothes on though, I see that she is right. I look...not bad actually.

Amelia smiles as I come out and gives me a miniature round of applause. 'You need shoes to complete the look. How about these? Handmade in Italy; very stylish, but comfortable.'

'Go on, then,' I say. 'Can I...?'

'Wear them now? Of course.'

After she's taken my card Amelia crosses her arms and appreciates her handiwork.

'Good luck,' she says. 'You look great.'

There's a moment, right after Amelia smiles at me, when I'm pretty sure that I could ask her out for a drink and she'd say yes. After all, that's why I'm here in London, to take chances and live it up. But the moment passes without me doing anything except taking the bag and saying goodbye. I'm waiting for something. Only I don't know what – or who – it is I could possibly be waiting for now.

★★★

I launch into the hectic street, almost stumbling to find a place to put my feet among the constant flow of people. Bike messengers hop on and off the pavement, a string of girls with linked arms suddenly looms, breaking loose to pass me with a gale of giggles. The smell of a hundred different kinds of fried food hangs in the air and nausea rises in my throat. I can't remember the last time I ate. The street tilts suddenly and I stumble forward. Lights swarm my vision and I'm reaching, groping for something solid to grab hold of. I suddenly realise with a jolt of panic that I forgot to take my meds.

'Watch it, mate.' I hear a man's voice. 'Bit early to be pissed, isn't it?'

Someone barges into me and I reel to one side, slamming into a wall. Pain darts down through the crown of my head. What little I can see swims and fractures. If I can just hold on to this wall until everything stops...

My forehead is pressed against something cold and smooth. I lean into it, grateful for the support. The glitter of the lights begins to dim and the pain subsides. Opening my eyes, I hear the footfall of people flowing back and forth around me as if I'm invisible.

Something catches my eye. As I pull back, a pair of sad brown eyes looks back at me. A poster of a painting, of a woman from a long time ago. Her grave, dark eyes are steady and uncompromising. I know exactly what she is feeling, trapped in a weighted sorrow that sits as heavy as a rock right inside the rib cage; a burden that can never be set down. Pressing my palms either side of my face, I rest my forehead against hers and wait until my vision focuses.

I know this image; it's so familiar that it's become one of those things you stop seeing over time, until suddenly you come across it out of context and it's made brand-new. This face is on the cover of a big heavy book that my mum bought in Paris when she was a young woman way before she met my dad. *The Art and Work of Leonardo da Vinci* is what she said it was called, except all the text was in French. That didn't matter to me though. I loved that book when I was a kid. Not the paintings so much, but the drawings and notebooks and inventions. I'd sit at the table and make dozens of kid-level copies of his drawings, of giant slingshots or half a dissected head, whereas Kitty coloured in endless versions of the *Mona Lisa.* The three of us spent a lot of time together exploring the world through Mum's passion for art and colour.

Looking at her face, which had always been incidental before, I remember vividly how getting lost in the details of Da Vinci's drawing absorbed me. Now just looking into these sorrowful, familiar eyes comforts me. Like I've bumped into a long-lost friend, a connection to my past that points me in a firm direction at last. I need to go and find this painting.

Chapter Eight

I unlock the little-known and very old door that leads out on to the roof of the Bianchi mansion. Not only am I the only person who has a key to open it, I'm the only person who knows the door is there at all, hidden away in a dark corner of the attic, as yet untroubled by restoration. Behind the low, narrow exit is something like the Red Queen's Kingdom from *Through the Looking-Glass*. The stone balustrades stand in for the chess pieces; the gables and turrets that make up the landscape of the roof, the perfectly symmetrical topiary: a secret kingdom that I can be queen of as long as I stay out of sight of the security cameras in this one blind spot.

'You know if I get caught up here, it's a sacking offence?' I tell Jack, who has brought sandwiches and half a bottle of chilled rosé for our *skyline picnic*, as he likes to call these periodic transgressions. That's the problem when your oldest friend in the world is a bad influence. You find yourself taking silly risks just for the sake of seeing his smile. And Jack does suit the majesty of the London backdrop.

'I very much doubt that,' he says, gazing out at the streets that surround us, his hands in his pockets, as I pour the wine. 'You are the darling of the art world, or the museum world, or whatever it is they call it.' He looks to me, raising his glass in a toast. 'And I am so proud of you. You did it, Vita. You brought her here at last. Aren't you excited?'

'I don't know how I feel,' I say, as I stand beside him. From up here London looks like the kind of miniature you find in eccentric people's gardens. A hundred thousand streets spread out beneath the sky: avenues, crescents, roads and high rises growing in every spare square inch of the city that has not already been claimed. There are millions of lives down there, but just in this moment they are all far enough away for none of them to seem real.

'Try,' he says, turning to look at me, his brown eyes full of light.

'Terrifying, exhilarating, devastating,' I tell him. 'I look at *La Belle*, and I see how very young she is. It breaks my heart. But this is the closest I have come to being able to study her for myself instead of reading other people's research. To find out what she is hiding. I hope she will forgive me and show me the answers I've been searching for so long.'

'All of them?' Jacks asks, his smile faltering. 'You're sure?'

'I'm sure I can't go on like this anymore,' I say. 'Always wondering, never knowing anything for certain.'

'Knowledge is very overrated in my opinion,' Jack says, and I hear the sadness in his voice and an undercurrent of something more elusive. 'Zero mystery soon gets dull, trust me on this.'

Tilting my head to one side, I examine him a little more closely. 'Why are you *really* here persuading me to contravene about a hundred health and safety laws?' I ask him.

He sighs deeply, leaning forward on the balustrade. His glass, now emptied, dangles precariously, poised to fall at the merest loosening of his elegant fingers.

'I'm working up the courage to go and see your exhibition,' he says at length. 'I can't not when it's the culmination of your life's work, can I? I thought I'd start up here and gradually work my way down. Perhaps I need a whole bottle of this stuff... or two.'

'You don't have to go,' I say. 'I get it. It will be painful.'

'We never would have met if it wasn't for him,' he says. 'And he's been dead for so long, I can't let him have so much of a hold on me from beyond the grave that I can't even go and look at a Da Vinci. It's pathetic. I don't even love the memory of him anymore, that's long gone. And yet, I suppose I'm afraid it will remind me of how much I loved him once. That I used to be that young, adventurous heart filled with...' he pauses, searching for the word. 'Faith, I suppose. I haven't spent this long carefully crafting a distant cynicism to throw it all away just like that.'

He looks at me. 'I don't want to suddenly be showing the whole world the secret contents of my heart. I guard them closely.'

Smiling, I reach for his hand, covering it with mine.

'How about you come back after we're closed and I'll walk you round, just you and me?'

'Not today.' He gives me a long look and a small shrug. 'I'll work up to it with varying-percentage-proof types of alcohol. Perhaps a nice cognac next.'

'I'm here,' I say.

'You are always here,' he says looking around him. 'At least I'd like you to be.'

'You know what I mean.'

'I know, but you could be part of it all, like you used to be,' he says as he has so many times before, nodding at our town. 'Living your life right in the middle of it, instead of observing from the outside. You could have all that back, if you wanted it.'

'I don't. I'm not like you,' I say. Jack loves lovers; all varieties of men and women. Difference thrills and delights him, and so do the sex and chaos that come with those things. But I am done with all of that. I have been since Dominic. I am allowing myself to grow old in my heart and I don't mind it at all. If anything I ache for it. 'Don't worry about me. I'm OK.'

'I'm not suggesting you throw yourself into a life of hedonism,' Jack says. 'It is exhausting, and too often rather lonely, no matter how much I hope it might compensate for the things denied me.' He looks away from me for a moment. 'No, what I'm saying is that OK is not a good enough state of being. Existence is meant for extremes of emotion not for… pottering through life.' He suddenly grips my hand, pulling me closer to him. 'Come dancing with me again. Just us, like the old days, but better. Let me make you happy again.'

'I'm afraid I relish the pottering rather too much,' I tease, pushing him away with the palm of my hand. 'Pottering is my calling.'

'You are impossible,' he says, with a deep sigh.

'Not impossible, just so very tired,' I tell him. 'I need it to end, Jack. I need it to end.'

'Everything does eventually,' he says. 'And some things never even begin.'

The sorrow in his voice surprises me.

Chapter Nine

I'm so lost in my thoughts that it takes me a moment to realise that I have come to a standstill outside St Martin's Crypt Café. I wait for a moment. No new pain; no new dizziness. I can still see pretty straight, even if my glasses are a bit wonky. I'm hungry though, and thirsty. I take the stairs down into the cool, darkly arched space for a cup of tea and a grilled-cheese sandwich.

It's unnerving to find what would once have been silent, sombre chambers of the dead filled with chattering people, walking back and forth over the decommissioned headstones that are set into the floor. I find a corner to hide in. I still haven't called Mum. I don't know how to call her and lie to her. I don't know how to tell her the truth. It's not fair, not on Kitty or Mum, but every time I try and picture the words I'd have to say I lose courage. I need to do something though, so I send her a text.

> *Don't worry about me. Just getting my head together. Call later. Don't forget that Pablo likes his teddy at bedtime. x*

I press send and turn off my phone before she calls me.

Chapter Ten

Our memories make us necromancers, bring back the dead, day after day. Perhaps we should let them rest, but how can we when all we have of them is their ghosts? After my rooftop picnic with Jack and all his talk of the old days, Dominic's ghost has come to walk beside me as I navigate the busy traffic on the short walk back from the National Portrait Gallery. He appears suddenly out of nowhere, as memories do. One moment he's laughing, dark eyes flashing. The next I picture a nebulous replica of the way he would suddenly catch hold of my hand, bring it to his lips and make my heart stop.

My image of him is so clear that I almost trip over a little girl of about four with red ribbons in her braided hair. Unconfined joy lights up her lovely face – A bus! A black cab! A pigeon! – full of wonder at every commonplace thing. Her mother sends me an apologetic look as her daughter skips in front of me again, tugging her arm, telling her with a great sense of urgency that she must have her photo taken while sitting on a lion's head.

'*Maman, lion!*' she shouts in French, pointing at one of the great bronze beasts.

Disaster unfolds in an instant.

The little girl breaks free of her mother's grasp and runs right into the path of an oncoming bus. Time speeds up and slows down. Only I can save the child. I know this to be a fact I cannot turn away from. Stepping into the road, I scoop her up into my arms and hold her tight against me, taking a step out of the path of the bus and into the narrow space between the two lanes of traffic, making us as slight as possible. Brakes howl and screech; a cab slams on its horn. Around us the world unravels into long ribbons of frayed colour and noise. I feel death's hot breath on my neck and turn my cheek towards it for a kiss.

Someone is screaming. It seems that I can't move my feet or exhale the breath of pollution and car exhaust sucked deep into my lungs. I'm not at all certain that if I took even one step there would be road under my feet to greet me.

Then there is a hand under my elbow and for a moment I think, *Dominic*. I see him, guiding me gently to safety on the square. For a second two forms seem to occupy the air and then he is gone, replaced with another, a real-life man, tall, slender and fair.

The little girl cries for her mother, who rushes to take her from my arms, scolding her while kissing every inch of her teary face. Entwined, they sink down on to the pavement, the woman trembling as she rocks her, murmuring into her hair.

Then it's just me and him, standing looking at one another. The sound of the traffic falls away. In the air between us there is only silence. Unsteady, I sway closer to him, my hand touching his chest briefly. Who is this man who shares a shadow with my lost love?

'That was quite something,' he says breaking the spell, at least a little. 'You OK? You could have been killed.'

'I didn't have time to think about it,' I tell him. As the sensation gradually returns to my hands, I turn them over, flexing my fingers as if I have never seen them before. Collecting myself I look at him again, suddenly shy. Blue eyes behind glasses, a slight smile. 'It was you who stopped the traffic, wasn't it? Thank you.'

Mother and child are gone, the threads of our lives unravelling as quickly as they became tangled. I catch sight of the little girl's ribbons dancing as she charges into a flock of pigeons, her brush with danger forgotten

'Well, I should get back to work,' I say.

'That's so London,' he laughs. 'Face down death and then get back to the spreadsheets!'

'Is it?' It's my turn to laugh. 'I'm not really sure what else there is to do.'

'Shouldn't you have a cup of tea at least? You nearly died there!' He then catches sight of my brochure. 'Have you been to that exhibition? Is it very busy? I'm going there now. I was hoping I could buy a ticket on the door.'

'Seriously?' I exclaim. 'It's my exhibition. I work there, put the whole thing together. It took years and I will shut up now, otherwise I will never stop talking about it.' I hold out my hand. 'I'm Vita Ambrose.'

'I'm Ben Church,' he says. Our fingers enclose each other. 'Our meeting must have been written in the stars, or something rational and intelligent sounding,' he adds self-deprecatingly.

'Oh, I believe in fate.' I smile.

Chapter Eleven

I give Vita Ambrose a long sideways glance as I walk beside her. We're used to quirky folk in Hebden Bridge, but even there, where every third person is an artist, she would stand out on the eccentricity scale. The top of her head is about level with my shoulder. Her dark hair sways down to the middle of her back, contrasting sharply against her bright yellow dress, printed all over with tiny white flowers. With her green Converse and neon sunglasses she's an explosion of primary colours, and I have never felt so monochromatic before.

People greet her with warm smiles as we walk into the cool marbled hallway of the Bianchi Collection. Inside, the pillars are gilded with gold, there's a painting on the ceiling of birds and angels and a huge portrait of a woman who looks like Marie Antoinette, in a powdered wig and gown, who I am guessing must be the aforementioned Madame Bianchi.

'I'll grab us a table,' she says as I stand at the counter in the café. 'Usual for me, please, Remi!'

The trouble with being about to die, as I am fast discovering, is that every second of every day feels like it must be loaded with significance, including meeting Vita Ambrose. I'm expecting a revelation or an epiphany when really I'm just having coffee. I glance over at her, already lost in some book she is reading, making notes on the pages in pen, which, according to my sister, would make her a psychopath. Her mind is very much elsewhere.

As I approach the table, she smooths her hair back from her face and closes the book, using the pen as a bookmark.

'So, you were on your way to see my exhibition,' she says. 'Are you a Da Vinci fan?'

'Who isn't?' I say. 'I mean, yeah, I was when I was a kid, and I'm an engineer now.' I pause, thinking of my drawings at the kitchen table. 'His notebooks, his inventions and ideas are mind-blowing. But that's not really why I came. I didn't even know this was on until I saw her,' I say, nodding at the image of the portrait on the front of the brochure. 'Then I knew I had to come and say hello.'

'Really, this portrait in particular?' Vita says, tilting her head slightly. 'What is it about her?'

'She looks…' I falter, shaking my head. 'It's stupid.'

'It's not, I promise you,' she says. 'There isn't a wrong way to feel about art, any art, not just great paintings by Old Masters.'

'Well, when I looked at her, I didn't see a Da Vinci, or even a portrait of a girl,' I say. 'I saw me.'

Vita sits back in her chair, her lips parted slightly.

'I told you it was stupid,' I say.

'No, what you said isn't stupid at all.' She takes a sip of her tea. 'It's exactly how I feel when I look at *La Belle Ferronnière.*' When I frown, she adds, 'That's what she is often called – the girl in the portrait – after the band around her head. No one can remember her name any more.'

'That's sad,' I say. 'I wonder how many years a person has to be dead for no one to remember that they ever lived.'

'Well, just look at Da Vinci,' Vita says. 'He will live for ever. And perhaps no one remembers that girl any more, but she is still the subject of a lot of fascination. I've been trying to discover her secrets for most of my life.'

'What secrets?' I ask, intrigued.

'Now it's my turn to sound stupid.' She lowers her voice as she inches a little closer to me, glancing around as if she is worried that we will be overhead. 'But at the time that Leonardo made this portrait he was also working to discredit the alchemists. He thought they were a load of conmen and liars. But there is a legend, one that is mostly forgotten these days, that he actually did exactly the opposite. He accidentally made the very discoveries the alchemists had been chasing for centuries. Some people believe that Da Vinci uncovered the secret to eternal life, the cure to all ills;

everything you've ever read about or seen in a movie. And that the discovery, the power that came with it, is in *La Belle*'s portrait.' She pauses. 'I don't know why I'm telling you this. I never tell anyone this, but I am one of those people looking for that secret. In other words, a lunatic.'

'You believe there really is a secret to eternal life?' I ask her, suddenly feeling the thud of my heart loud in my chest.

'Let's say that I believe he did make an earth-shattering discovery of something that modern man still thinks of as impossible,' she says. 'His work is littered with secrets, signs and symbols. So why not this one? I would really like to be the one to find out. I'm conducting a review of all the data and research right now, while I've got her under my roof, so to speak. So far there's nothing new to report. Every surviving Da Vinci has been analysed, X-rayed and photographed, and to the nth degree, so it seems unlikely I'll find Leonardo's secret to the elixir of life hiding in the folds of her gown now.' She sighs with what seems like genuine regret. 'But I can't stop trying. In fact, don't tell anyone, but the main reason I brought her here is the hope that just by looking at her, in the flesh as it were, I will be able to invent a new way of looking that will actually *see*. It's an obsession. You see, I wasn't joking when I told you I was a lunatic.'

There is a silence in which I work very hard to work out what to say. I must be careful. I can't let my desperation tip into madness. If I had all the time in the world I would check myself; slow and repress my sudden fascination, temper it with all the prosaic reality I can muster. But I can't, so I don't.

'I've never really believed in fate,' I tell her. 'But I might actually be exactly the person you needed to bump into after a near-death experience. I work in the business of seeing what others cannot.'

'Really?' She looks sceptical. I like that about her.

'I'm an optical engineer,' I tell her, 'and design specialist lenses for labs. You said the painting has been imaged with all the latest high-spectrum tech?'

'It has,' Vita nods slowly. 'But nothing has been found hiding there, not even any significant repainting. It seems like Da Vinci knew exactly what he wanted to paint and how, at least when it came to this portrait.'

'Huh,' I say.

'Huh what?' she asks.

'For the last few years I've been working on a new generation of lens design that might be exactly the kind of new tech you are looking for – a high-spectrum lens paired with an entirely new software I've written. It is designed to separate out individual elements on a molecular level, and image layers of any given subject in order to reveal how it is composed and when. I've been designing it with astrophysics and research chemists in mind, but it would see your painting like no one else ever has before. I don't know... maybe I could leave you my card and you could always get in touch with me lat—' I stop myself from finishing the word. 'Maybe I could send it down for you to try out if you like.'

I don't know how I expected her to react, but her expression is unreadable.

'That's so kind,' she says at last. 'But it's not that easy unfortunately.'

'Isn't it?' I say, dropping my gaze from hers so she won't see my disappointment.

'There are all these protocols we'd have to go through for you to be able to use any imaging equipment here – not to mention that *La Belle* is on loan from the Louvre. It took years of negotiating to get her here, and they have already studied her comprehensively with the most advanced technology we have. And...' she frowns deeply. 'It's not that I'm saying that you haven't got something different or new, but they aren't going to let you test it out on their Da Vinci – not until you've collated a lot of data and have the right credentials and connections. We could work towards it, but it would take years. Everything moves so slowly in this world. We are about two centuries behind everyone else.'

I nod. 'Sorry, I must seem like an idiot,' I tell her, shaking my head at myself. 'I didn't mean to seem like I could just waltz into your museum and tell you how to do your job.'

'No,' Vita says with feeling. 'No, you are not an idiot. I'm so glad we met today, Ben. The way you feel about her,' she touches the cheek of the girl in the portrait on the front of the brochure, 'is like a gift to me. Thank you. Thank you for the tea.'

I have to make a determined effort not to collapse under the weight of anticlimax. So, I sit perfectly still as Vita Ambrose briefly presses her palm on the back of my hand in goodbye, and then she is gone.

Chapter Twelve

'**W**ait. Tell me again what happened,' Jack asks as we sit in the bar over the road, waiting for the Collection to empty of stragglers so I can take him to see the exhibition free from 'the public' as he likes to call everyone who isn't him or me.

'He was just there,' I say, as the barman hands me a large glass of wine, which I drain half of at once. 'I stepped out in front of a bus, and then he was there and we talked and he loves *La Belle* and it was just really refreshing, you know, to meet someone who really sees her the way that I do.'

'I can imagine,' Jack says sipping his Martini. 'Tell me about the bus part again.'

'The bus part isn't important,' I continue quickly. 'The important thing is that somehow this man turned up out of nowhere, told me that *La Belle* reminds him of himself and offered to help with my research. And that he has this new tech that can read and analyse images like never before. That's just weird, isn't it? It has to be some kind of scam, right? I mean, he sounded like he knew what he was talking about, but of course I had to say no.'

'Why?' Jack asks, his voice level as he regards me over the top of his glass. His expression is inscrutable. 'Because it sounded too good to be true?'

'Actually, I really think he was legit,' I say after a moment's thought, remembering the expression on Ben's face and the sincerity in his voice. I've met more than my fair share of fly-by-nights and he didn't read like one. 'But modern museum protocol and insurance demands are terribly dull when it comes to this kind of thing.'

'So, what are you planning to do then?' Jack sets down his glass and signals to the barman for two more. 'You have what you want: you have the portrait and all her associated history and research under your roof. What do you think you will find now that no one else has in the last 500 years?'

'I don't know,' I admit. 'I am hoping that by gathering all the data in one place and examining it all with fresh eyes, by looking her in the eye, it will somehow all fall into place. I'll get that eureka moment.'

'You worked all these years to put together this exhibition in the vague hope of a eureka moment?' Jack asks. 'I don't buy it. You are a brilliant woman. I assumed all this time that you had a fail-safe plan.'

'Not really.' Now I say it out loud it does seem insane. 'My plan was to get her here and that was hard enough. Now all I can do is to apply the new research data to everything we already knew and hope *something* becomes apparent. Good old-fashioned academic legwork. It's how all the best discoveries are made.'

'So then perhaps the gentleman who was so keen to show you his lens was the mystery factor you were hoping for,' Jack suggests. 'Fate put him in your bus lane.'

'You don't even believe in fate,' I remind him, wondering about the nagging feeling that I've had ever since we parted that I made a terrible mistake when I passed on Ben's offer.

'I don't,' he says. 'Meeting this fellow is just the predictable result of a very high probability that when you bump into someone outside the Bianchi Collection, they are going to the Bianchi Collection; considering that you've got posters plastered all over London.' He takes his glass, ignoring the barman's rather obvious attempt to flirt with him, his expression set in a frown. 'It's not fate that brought you together. It's marketing.'

'Exactly,' I say.

'And yet...' Jack teases me with a long slow smile. 'The chances of you meeting someone with exactly the kind of technology you need to progress your research is less predictable. That's more of an opportunity, and I do believe in those.'

'An opportunity I can't do anything about if I want to keep my job,' I say, rubbing my forehead. 'I honestly think that I'm finally losing my sanity.'

'You are only as insane as you need to be to survive,' Jack tells me calmly. 'Look, why don't we take a break after the exhibition, go to the other side of the world like we used to, but fly first-class this time. I'm sure we can get you back into fighting shape again, no matter what happens with *La Belle*. Just you and me. I miss those days sometimes.'

For a moment I consider the idea, remembering the times when it used to be possible to run away from it all and start again. The adventures we had, back when it felt like the whole world belonged to us. I've changed so much since those days. The one thing I know now is that it doesn't matter how far you run when *you* are the problem you are trying to escape from.

'I can't leave the Collection, not now,' I tell him, seeing the regret in his face. 'And anyway, wherever we go, whatever we do, nothing ever changes. It's all so arbitrary, all so stupid and pointless.'

'Do you really feel that way?' Jack asks quietly. 'Even about me?'

'I... sometimes,' I admit, seeing that I've hurt him. He is always so good to me, so kind and steadfast. And I have been a shadow friend to him for such a long time. It isn't fair.

'It's not you, not really. You are the one thing keeping me going,' I tell him. 'If I didn't have you then—' I shake my head, unable to articulate what a world without Jack in it would be like.

'Look, I know you are struggling. I'm not blind,' Jack says. There's a sadness in his voice. 'I suppose I hoped the exhibition would lift your spirits and if it didn't, you would let me make you happy.'

'It does, and your friendship does make me happy.' I don't even sound convincing to myself.

'Then perhaps you should worry more about finding the answers you are so desperate for and less about keeping your job,' Jack tells me, leaning forward so our faces are inches apart, his voice a whisper. 'Track down your lens fellow and tell him you've reconsidered. It would hardly be the most scandalous thing you've ever done.'

'Perhaps you're right,' I say slowly. Jack sways away from me, catching the barman's eye and a charming grin. I suspect that the plans we made are about to be postponed while he does his best to chase away the shadows of a broken heart. 'But I'm not sure I should drag him into my obsessions. Hardly seems fair.'

'How do you know that?' Jack asks. 'Perhaps you represent an opportunity for him. To get his tech on the map, by fair means, or slightly underhand ones. After all, in the end it's the results that matter, right?' His expression softens as I scowl, annoyed that Jack still has the clarity I have lost somewhere along the way. 'Sometimes it's OK not to think, just to do. That's how I get through life, and it seems to work out pretty well for me. In fact it's always better when I stop thinking altogether. It used to work out pretty well for you too.'

'But then there was Dominic,' I say. 'Dominic was the love of my life, the very last love of my life. That is how it is meant to be.' That is how it must be and now all I can do is think about how different things should be.

Chapter Thirteen

The hardest thing to deal with when you know you are going to die, I think to myself, as I sit in the hotel bar drinking steadily, is the end of possibility.

Closing my eyes for a moment I imagine another universe, the one where I meet an interesting woman, someone a bit like Vita Ambrose, with another 40 years on the clock – all that time to take for granted. I'd ask her if she fancied a drink later and maybe she would say yes. And maybe we wouldn't hit it off; maybe we would. But I will never know, because there are no maybes any more.

'Top-up?' The barman reappears, hovers the bottle of house red over my glass. I nod, grimacing, and knock back a gulp of wine. This is not exactly what I had in mind when I ran away to London, but then what did I have in mind? I thought once I got here it would all become clear. For one gloriously naive moment I thought that it might. In reality all I've done is buy a load of fancy clothes that won't get enough wear and embarrassed myself in front of an art historian.

'Ben? Earth to Ben?' A familiar voice that sounds so strange in this setting breaks the moment. My first thought is that it is an auditory hallucination. 'Are you in there?' She speaks to the waiter. 'I'll have whatever he's having, please.'

I open my eyes and somehow Kitty is standing there looking at me, her eyebrows furrowed in a scowl.

'Kitty?' I say her name like a question. 'What are you doing here?'

'You're on Find a Friend on your phone, aren't you?' she says, sliding into the booth next to me, dumping a large duffel bag at her feet.

'No, I mean why have you come to London?'

'Because you had that tone of voice on the phone,' she says.

'What tone of voice?' I ask her, knowing exactly what she means.

'You remember after you first found out about your Marfan syndrome and went through your emo stage, reading Shelley, Keats and Byron, and wafting around in leather trousers and frilly shirts, having a permanent existential crisis and getting yourself into stupid avoidable messes, seemingly intent on embarrassing the fuck out of your cool 12-year-old sister? That one. You sounded like you were in dead-poet mode when we talked on the phone, and that has never been good in my experience.'

'Ah,' I say. 'You know me too well.'

'So, what really happened at the hospital?'

Kitty holds my gaze, her pale eyes rimmed with too much eyeliner.

'Aneurysm,' I tell her. 'Big one, near the brain stem.'

'Fuck! So what's the plan?' she asks. 'How long until we can bin Goth Ben and get Boring Engineer Ben back?'

'There is no plan,' I reply, edging my way ever closer to getting to the point. The thought of saying it out loud makes me feel sick.

'Because it's OK and it's not going to do you any harm?' Her words slow down with the weight of realisation. 'Or because it is not going to be OK?'

'It's not going to be OK, Kits,' I manage to say, unable to look at her.

'Are you sure they've got it right?'

'Yes,' I say, recalling the look on Mrs Patterson's face. 'Yes, they got it right. Maybe I shouldn't tell Mum. Maybe that would be better – for her, I mean. Maybe it will hurt less if she doesn't have to expect it.'

Kitty shakes her head.

'How... how long?'

I shrug. 'Not that long.'

'We need to go home. We need to tell Mum. We need to get second opinions and look for treatments that might not be on the NHS. We need a crowdfunder and a... and a... We need to get mobilised so we can beat this shit.'

'I'm not going home yet, Kits. I'm not ready.'

'For what?'

'Anything,' I say with a hopeless shrug. 'But especially not seeing Mum's face when I tell her. Or having her look after me, when I don't need looking after. Wondering if every time I walk Pablo or have a pint with Danny if that will be the last. I don't want to take this,' I gesture at my head, 'back home to where everything is so familiar. I need everything to be strange and different, because I'm strange and different and I need to get to know this last version of me before I take him home.'

'Right,' Kitty says, fear and shock showing just beneath her bravado. 'I get it. So, tell me, how's that going?"

There's a pause then. I could try and explain this void where my heart used to be, where the only thing approaching to fill it are the fluttering wings of leathery fear. Or we could just have a laugh, and for a little while everything could be all right again. She looks at me for a long moment.

'Yeah, pretty standard,' I say with a shrug. 'Your run-of-the-mill apocalypse.'

'Ben,' she says, 'don't piss around with me. Could it really happen any time?'

'Yes,' I nod. 'Also, it might not. So, let's go with that, shall we? Let's err on the side of everything being fine for the foreseeable. Tell me what's going on with you.'

'Well, I saw you two days ago, so not a lot,' Kitty says falteringly. 'Everything was pretty much run of the mill and then... this. Remember when we used to go up the hill and fly a kite, and there was nothing to think about except keeping that kite in the sky? Or when Mum had us making psychedelic dyes for her heat-sensitive, rave t-shirts, and we'd end up with multicoloured faces? Everything seemed so simple then.'

'I remember,' I say with a smile. 'Those were good days, weren't they? We've been happy, right?'

'We have. We are.' Kitty looks at me, her smile quivering. 'I can't imagine a life without you there. What will I do without—?'

The waiter brings our drinks and Kitty buries her face in her bag until he is gone.

'Kits, you OK?' I reach for her hand and she shakes her head, warning me off being too nice to her.

'I don't know what to do,' she says. 'But I need to do something.'

'So, let's just have a drink, shall we?' I ask.

Kitty's eyes search my face intently, looking for something, any little crack that might let her in to what I am really thinking. And then tears brim and she shakes her head, furious.

'Why the fuck not?' she says.

'It's good to see you, Kitty,' I say. 'I mean it. Thanks for coming. I'm glad you're here. I didn't realise I didn't want to be alone until I wasn't.'

'Course. I've always got your back, you know that.' She manages a smile. 'Besides, I need to doss in your room tonight.'

'I'll get you your own room,' I say. 'I've got money to burn.'

'Well in that case,' she says, 'we'd better get another round in.'

Chapter Fourteen

M y father raised me to believe there was a great plan in which my whole life had been mapped out for me by God, and all that was required of me was to follow and obey – that choice was an illusion. Even though I left all that behind long ago, indoctrination still lingers entwined with every thought and feeling. Which is why, even though I hate even the lingering notion of some universal puppet master pulling all my strings, I am not surprised when I walk into the foyer of the Collection and see Ben Church standing there. He is gazing up at a larger-than-life, full-length portrait of Madame Bianchi in all her powdered-wigged and silk-satin-gowned glory that has presided over the comings and goings of her beloved home ever since it was hung.

Backing up a little, I step into the shadow of the deep doorway to look at him for a moment longer. He is standing perfectly still, arms hanging loosely at his side, eyes drawn upwards towards the coquettish, questioning position of Madame Bianchi's head, the elegant poise of her hands.

'Ben,' I say as I approach him.

'Vita.' He turns to the sound of my voice and smiles. 'I was hoping to see you here. Listen, I wanted to apologise. I feel embarrassed about offering you the lens I made in my shed,' he says. 'When I say *shed* I do of course mean home-lab, NASA-standard, clean room, but it is at the bottom of my garden, so...'

'You have a clean room in your garden?' I say. 'That's cool.'

'Having a clean room isn't usually most people's definition of cool.' Ben smiles. 'But thank you.'

'I'm really not like most people,' I say.

'I can see that.'

The day is bright, the mansion glitters, pretty reflections and refractions dance and bounce off every surface. An idea springs to my mind.

'Did you get to see the exhibition yesterday?'

'No. I had to go and see my sister, who arrived in London as well.' He gestures vaguely.

'Well, we've got 20 minutes until the Da Vinci exhibition opens – plenty of time to get ahead of the crowds. Will you let me give you a private tour and introduce you to *La Belle*?'

'Really?' He looks delighted at the suggestion. 'I would love that. Thank you, Vita.'

I notice how he makes my name sound like it belongs to me.

'It must be amazing working in a place like this,' Ben says, his gaze roaming around as we walk. 'All this magnificence and beauty. I do a lot of work in my bedroom, and all I get to look at are the moors out the back of the house. Not that they aren't magnificent too.'

'Which moors do you look at?' I ask.

'Wadsworth, mostly, Heptonstall and Stoodley Pike,' he says. 'Brontë country – wild and wuthering and all that.'

'I spent a week or two in the area once,' I say. 'It is really beautiful up there.'

'What were you doing up my way?' he asks me.

'Staying with some sisters I met in Brussels. They had this mad, loud, loving family – it was something of a revelation. I was so jealous of how much they loved and hated each other. I always felt like a virtual stranger in mine.'

'Ah, you were the family weirdo,' he says. 'Me too. I was a very dedicated Goth for quite a while. Wore eyeliner and everything.'

'Bold choice,' I say, giving him a sideways look. 'I suppose I was, though I kept it hidden until I ran away from home and never went back.'

'Wow,' Ben whistles. 'There's a story there.'

'A long and depressing one,' I assure him. I'm surprised at how easily I've confessed to this. Outside of Jack, and Dominic of course, it's been a long time since it felt this natural to talk about my past. Perhaps it's because he's a compatriot, not of a country, but of minds. But that sounds dangerously like a sonnet. Jack would have a lot to say about that.

The light is very low, dark almost everywhere except for the portraits that shine out of the darkness, a procession of beautiful phantoms.

'These are amazing,' Ben draws in a breath as he walks into the middle of the room looking at the first portrait. 'This is breathtaking.'

'Thanks,' I say, as if they are all my own work.

'You should be proud. I mean, this is incredible.' He walks over to the first portrait, *Ginevra*. 'She looks so sad.'

'She was sad,' I say, walking to his side. 'You can feel her pain, can't you? That's what Leonardo could do better than anyone: capture an emotion, a thought and feeling, and somehow make it live for ever.'

He nods pensively, as his eyes wander her face.

'Come and see *La Belle* before the public get here,' I say with a smile, gesturing for him to follow me. 'That way you can have some time with her alone.'

'I could get used to this VIP treatment, you know,' he says grinning. 'Oh, there she is.'

He takes a few quick steps towards her. Holding her gaze for a moment or two, he moves closer, bending so close to the surface of the painting that for a moment I think he might be about to kiss her.

'One millimetre more and you'll set off the alarm,' I warn him with a smile.

'She's everything I feel.' He sighs without taking his eyes off her.

The way he looks at her, the way he talks about her, it's almost as if he knows her secrets already.

'Do you really believe that the secrets of life and death, immortality and cure-alls are hiding somewhere in there?' he asks, turning to look at me, suddenly intense. 'In a portrait of a woman whose name no one remembers anymore?'

The world tilts dangerously on its axis.

'I know they are,' I say. 'But a cure for everything comes at a cost. Would you want to live for ever?'

I expect him to laugh and make light of the idea, but he considers the question so seriously that I can almost see the weight of it pressing on his shoulders.

'Yes,' he says eventually, 'I would give anything for the legend to be true, to have that much time. Yes, I would.'

He sighs so heavily I feel the weight of it in the air. 'Really?'

This time he laughs, but there is no humour in it.

'I have an inoperable aneurysm, you see,' he says quietly. 'I'm not sure how much time I have left, but I do know it isn't long enough for everything I want to do. Everything that I've been putting off since I was a kid and all the things that I didn't even know I longed for until now.'

Our eyes lock. Instinctively I catch hold of his wrist, as if my grasp alone can anchor him to this world.

'Ben, I'm so sorry.'

Those words are so small, so meaningless, but they are all I have. Gently he pulls his wrist loose from my hand.

'No, I'm sorry. That's a lot to lay on a stranger,' he says. 'I didn't mean to blurt it out.'

'I'm glad you told me,' I say, moving round him to find his gaze and meet it.

'So, if you do find any mysteries hidden in her portrait, try them out on me, OK?' He shakes his head, embarrassed. 'I suppose that's why I came here to ask you that dumb question and make a fool of myself. To say that if on the off-chance you happen to find the secret to eternal life, then I'm your perfect test subject.'

'And you wouldn't be afraid?' I ask. 'To find out the truth and realise it's not the answer you want?'

'I don't think I have anything left to be frightened of,' he says.

I used to think that once too.

Chapter Fifteen

We are silent as we walk out of the soothing, private dark of the exhibition. I should feel devastated, embarrassed, but somehow, I don't. I assumed that Vita would be afraid or uncomfortable after I told her what I told her. Instead she took it in her stride, with the kind of grace and gravitas you don't see very often. She didn't turn away – if anything, she turned towards me. And that in itself is more than I could have hoped for.

As we walk into bright, gilded hallways, the dazzling light seems to fire right into my brain. The horizon tilts and swivels, my head spins, atoms explode and refuse to recombine. Pain blots out everything else.

Stumbling into a wall, I slide my back down it until I'm sitting on either the floor or the ceiling – I'm not sure. My hands tremble.

Take deep breaths, count seven in, eleven out. The pain is everything. It's the whole world and all of me.

Vita's voice suddenly echoes all around me. 'What can I do?' she asks. 'Ambulance?'

'No, no, don't do that. Can you just stay here?' Eyes closed, I reach around me for anything that might distract me from the pain, pressing my palms into the icy marble tiles.

Now all I can do is wait for it to be over.

Colours explode, the waves of agony throb against bone. But in the midst of it I can feel the cool touch of Vita's hand on my forearm.

Try to focus on it.

I'm not sure if I slump, or the floor comes up to meet me, but I'm aware of my cheek pressed against marble, the connections of my hips and knees to the tiles. The tide of pain recedes in slow, tortuous increments. The world returns in small, disorganised pieces, except for one constant: her hand on my arm.

'Ben?' Her voice forms out of the senseless noise, and with it, footsteps, other voices; the distant din of traffic and chatter through an open door; amazingly, birdsong.

'Sorry,' I whisper.

'Can you sit? Should you sit? Do you want water?' I try opening my eyes and see she is bent over me, her hair screening my face from the other people circled round me.

'It's passing,' I say. 'Could you make them go away?'

'Nothing to see here.' Vita shoos them away as though they are a flock of geese. 'Just a migraine. Please go and look at some works of art! Mo, can you give us a hand?'

'It's all right, son. I've got you.' I hear a male voice, feel an arm under my arm. Vita grips my hand. Somehow, I'm on my feet and in another cool, dark room, sitting on a chair. Someone – Vita – presses a glass of water into my hand. When I don't quite grip it, she presses her fingers around mine and raises it to my lips. I feel it travel through my body, cool and calm.

'How you feeling, fella?' I focus on a man dressed in a security uniform, with a long beard and kind eyes. 'I should get you an ambulance, yeah?'

'No.' I speak and my voice sounds out loud. This is progress. 'No, honestly there is no point. I don't want to spend any time in hospital when I know that already I'm feeling better. I'm really sorry about this.'

'It's fine, mate,' Mo assures me. 'Nothing on having to remove a bloke fiddling with himself to the naked ladies paintings, I promise you.'

'Anything else we can do?' Vita asks. She has taken a seat next to me. Behind her a series of screens flashes black-and-white scenes of the museum rooms.

'What you've done is great,' I assure her.

Then a door opens, a slice of bright light penetrates the dark and a very elegant woman steps through it.

'Is everyone OK?' she asks Vita anxiously.

'Yes, everything's fine now,' Vita says. 'Ben is just taking a moment. He thinks the heat got to him.'

The woman, who I guess is Vita's boss, bends over to look at me.

'Are you quite sure we can't get you medical help?' she asks me.

'I am. Thanks though,' I say. 'I feel like a bit of a plank. A grown man forgetting to hydrate.'

'Vita, stay with him until it passes,' she says. 'I'll make sure someone from the café brings down some water and something to eat.'

'I'll get out of your way for a moment,' Mo says as the door closes and we are alone.

'Thank you, Vita,' I whisper. 'Telling you that I might die any minute and then acting like I am in fact about to die this minute was more dramatic than I usually am.'

'You have nothing to be sorry for. I'm glad I was here to help you.' Her heart-shaped face is very serious, her dark eyes full of concern.

'You have, so much. I think I'd better go.' I so desperately want her to watch me walk out of here like I am just a normal bloke in his thirties. 'I'll be fine.'

'I can't leave you like this.' Vita shakes her head. I see a stubborn streak in her eyes.

'I'm OK, honest.' I stand up. 'I'm a Yorkshireman – it takes much more than a headache to stop me in my tracks.'

'But...' She hesitates, her eyes dropping, a small horizontal frown line appearing between her eyebrows.

'I'm going to go now,' I repeat. 'I'm fine, truly I am. Goodbye, Vita. It really was great to meet you.'

'Goodbye, Ben.'

We embrace, her arms tighten around me, and for a moment I feel the beat of her heart underneath the soft warmth of her body. When I let her go, everything around me has intensified into vivid living, all my feelings are beginning to crash towards me at the speed of a tsunami.

I walk away as fast as I can.

Chapter Sixteen

'How are you, Vita? Still upset about that poor chap?' Anna asks me. She's been talking for the last few minutes and I haven't heard a word she's said.

The truth is I am shaken by how much my brief meeting with Ben has shaken me. We embraced for a moment; I felt his warm body, I could see his pulse racing in his neck, feel the rhythm of his heartbeat. It seemed impossible, like it always does, that in one moment, all that can stop, and that man can be entirely gone... vanish. It seems impossible, even though I should know more than anyone that it is not.

'Sorry, yes, I am a bit.' I drag my attention to Anna and force a smile. 'I am paying attention. I promise.'

'You've worked so hard, these last few weeks especially. Take a bit of time off if you need it,' she says gently. 'I know you won't want to go on holiday when the exhibition is on, but the odd after-noon here and there won't hurt. She gestures at the large image of the *Burlington House Cartoon* on the whiteboard that I am due to give a talk on for the National Gallery. 'After this talk's out of the way there will be a bit of a lull. You should make the most of it.'

'Thank you, Anna.' I smile wearily.

'We all need a break sometimes,' Anna says, patting my hand as she gets up to leave. 'You know you can talk to me if you need to, Vita.'

'I know.' I nod. 'I'm grateful for that.' After one more long look from Anna, I have the room to myself. It's all I can do not to rest my head on the square of sunlight falling on the tabletop and weep.

Ben has churned up the calm waters of my life and reminded me of all those I have lost. It's a dangerous thing to feel and remember: it peels away carefully layered defences until I have no choice but to hurt. But since I said goodbye to Ben an hour ago it is all I can do.; I find that I want it. The pain reminds me that I *live* and I suddenly feel grateful for that gift after the longest time of begrudging it. Grateful, because more life is all he wants, and he can't have it.

It's a relief to be alone in the white-painted, panelled room, silent except for the hum of the traffic outside the long window and just the image of a mother and child for company. It's Da Vinci at his best, somehow spontaneous, tender and timeless. It's a masterful drawing – not a cartoon as most people would understand it at all, but a preparatory sketch of the Madonna, the Christ Child on her lap, and Mary's mother Anne sitting beside her as the baby plays with his cousin John. The figures are conjured up out of charcoal and chalk on pieces of stitched-together canvas – three simple materials that have created this portrait of Christian significance, yes. But, as always with Da Vinci, it's so much more than that. This is a portrait of motherhood: Anne gazing at her daughter, knowing that her child will need to endure the most terrible losses; Mary's tender smile full of sweet sadness, a foreshadowing of what is to come – the loss of these little children to the will of God and man. Hers is the expression of a mother who knows her child will not be hers for long.

I know loss. A long time ago, in another life, before I set myself free, I was that woman, holding on to what she could not keep.

Abruptly I turn off the white screen and turn my back on it. I have survived that part of my life by never thinking about it, doing my best to forget what God and man did to me, because I had no choice but to survive and keep breathing.

Long before Dominic I gave birth to a baby boy. My son, who was taken from me before he was a day old.

Something about the expression on Mary's face causes memories to rise from the darkest depths. All at once I am able to recall my baby's face in the minutest detail: the burnished coppery hue of his skin, the down of dark hair. The way his hands curled into the gentle fists; his eyes resolutely closed against the dawn of his life.

The hour of his birth came in the blueish light of an early morning, long grey shadows washing over my room, the burnt-umber countryside tumbling away outside. I was so young. Nestled in my arms was my son, so small but utterly perfect, a coiled spring of possibility. I can remember the weight of him, settled against my breast, seeing the Fibonacci curl of his ear. The deluge of love I felt for him washed away every painful, desperate, cruel act that had caused his creation. My precious baby, who I had loved even before I knew him. Who I had prepared myself to say goodbye to even before we met.

The deepening shadows crept across the room, the rising sun igniting motes of gold in the air to briefly bathe my boy and me in balmy warmth. The sky ran with rivulets of molten copper as the day headed towards night.

My legs cramped, my bladder protested, my back screamed in pain and I bled steadily between my legs. Still, I would not move, would not put him down for a second, because I knew that all too soon the last moment in which I would be allowed to be his mother would arrive.

The moon was high when she came to take him from me.

'Where will he go?' I'd asked her, turning him away from her outstretched arms.

'To a good place,' she'd said, 'where he will be loved and safe.'

Her words were no comfort. The last of the last of my minutes of motherhood had come and I was not ready.

'Can't he stay with me?' I begged her. 'I swear, I will do everything right. Please just let him stay with me.'

'He can't,' she'd said simply. 'It's time.'

I pressed my lips to his face, over and over, and whispered promises to him.

'I will never forget you,' I told him. 'I will be with you all of your life, even if you can't see me or know me, I will be with you, I swear it. There won't be a day I don't think of you and think of how I love you.'

Then he was gone, and there was only the cold night air on the skin of my empty arms.

What I have not told anyone, not since I lost Dominic, is that my baby was taken from me on a clear spring night in a convent just outside Milan in the year 1498 – more than five centuries ago. That the secrets hidden in Da Vinci's portrait of that sad, lost girl matter so much to me because I *am* her. I don't know what happened to me that night – I don't know how or why or what.

All I know is that I have spent hundreds of years looking for a way to undo what was done to me without my consent. Hundreds of years of seeing the world turn all the way back to the beginning again and again. Centuries of love and loss and the end of hope. All I know is I cannot stand this world anymore, but that no matter how many times I have tried to escape into death at my own hand, it will not let me go. That somehow my fragile heart was made invincible against my will.

Leonardo hid so many of his secrets in his artwork. My very last hope is that he hid the secret to setting me free inside the image he painted of me, an immortal woman, looking for a way to die on the day she meets a dying man who only wants to live.

II

While self-dependent power can time defy,
As rocks resist the billows and the sky.

The Deserted Village
Oliver Goldsmith

Chapter Seventeen

'What happened?' Kitty asks immediately as I let myself into my room. I had booked her a room of her own last night, but she's obviously been waiting for me. As I walk through the door she drops her phone on the bed and sits up. 'You look awful.'

'Have you been here all morning?' I ask her. 'There's a whole massive city out there and you've been in here looking at your phone?'

'Ben, I'm a single mum, I've got some time off work and you are paying the bill for this five-star hotel. Not doing anything at all is the lap of luxury, my friend. Besides, I've been to London before and it's basically like everywhere else but bigger and more expensive. I came here to be with you, not go day-tripping and anyway, stop deflecting. What happened?'

'Nothing, like always. Nothing happened,' I lie. Telling her about my 'turn' will only result in me being made to sit down and Mum taking a train. 'I went to the Bianchi Collection, to see a painting – a Da Vinci.'

'The *Mona Lisa*?' she asks.

'No, one of the other ones. It was beautiful.'

Going over to window, I pull back the slatted blinds to look out at the street below. Something about this afternoon has set my heart in motion and everything that seemed so unreal before is now terrifyingly close.

Kitty comes to stand beside me.

'There's something you aren't telling me.' She takes my hand, examining my face. 'Ben, what happened? You look like you saw a ghost.'

'There was something about her, the girl in the portrait. She seems so sad, so lost. The expression on her face made me want to reach out to her, to tell her that everyone is going to be OK. But of course, I can't do that. Her portrait is nothing more than a ghost of a sad, young woman, and no one is even sure who she is any more. I don't want that to be me. I don't want to die and fade away until no one ever thinks of me again.'

'Ben…' Kitty puts her hand on my arm.

'Don't.' I step away, shaking my head. 'I have to keep it together. I don't want to spend my last days sobbing in some pitiful heap. I can't waste another minute.'

'Then tell me what you're thinking, how you are feeling. Tell me,' Kitty says, her eyes tracking my every movement. But I can only think about one thing. One person.

I think about telling her about meeting Vita, and how she told me about the paintings and how one is supposed to conceal the legends of eternal life. I want to explain how it felt like divine intervention, for someone like me to have such a strange conversation precisely now. But how can I tell Kitty that it felt like it had to *mean* something when it didn't – it doesn't? That we really are all alone in the universe grubbing about desperately? That when it comes right down to it, the universe clearly doesn't go by the happy-ending playbook?

'It's just all so arbitrary, Kits, all so stupid,' I say. 'I wanted answers, a why and a what for. But there aren't any. It hit me for the first time that I am fucked, Kits. I am pretty much done. And I'm scared.' My voice breaks a little at this.

Kitty puts her arms around my neck. 'Please, don't be scared. I've got you. I will be at your side all the way, if you want me.'

I pull back a little to look at her, her eyes looking up into mine.

'Don't be wasting time looking for meaning,' Kitty says, taking my face in her hands. 'You are alive *now*, in this place *now*. That *is* the meaning. I know that's easy for me to say. But I've got you, Ben, I've got you. Try and keep your head out of the dark and keep it right here with me now. As you know, I have two ways of dealing with stress: first, drink; second, reside firmly in a river in Egypt.'

'Denial?' I deliver the punchline just like she wants me to.

'That's right,' Kitty says. 'You're fine until you're not. So, let's do this thing. I'm going to have a shower and then we are going out to spend all of your money on stupid, overpriced tourist attractions, OK?'

'It's a plan,' I say, making myself smile for her sake.

Chapter Eighteen

Mariah is sitting on her doorstep when I turn into the square. She sits, basking in the small patch of summer-evening sunshine that graces the front of our houses at this time. Her compression stockings are rolled down around her ankles, her skirt drawn up over her knees, her face tipped up to meet the light as a long cigarette burns down between her fingers. She is the image of serenity; an example of someone who somehow knows just how to live each moment of her long life, even as parts of her drift away. I envy her.

'Evening,' I say, greeting her with a smile. 'Have you had a good day?'

'A great day. Did you bring sweets?' she asks, opening her eyes. The cigarette falls to the ground and she's 10 years old again, clapping her hands together, eyes wide. 'Mum sent me out to get out from under her feet, so I went down the river and hopped barges all day. Got all the way to Greenwich, I did!'

'I did manage to lay my hands on some,' I say, dropping a hand-ful of boiled sweets into her cupped palms. She looks at them, bright as jewels, as if they were just as precious, and puts them in her open handbag. 'I'll save them for a special occasion.'

'Weren't you scared?' I ask her, taking a seat on my half of the steps. 'Going all that way on your own, hitching lifts with strangers?'

'No, why should I be?' Mariah asks me, eyeing her bag before diving in to retrieve one sweet, which she promptly pops into her mouth. 'Were you scared, running away from home and crossing the sea to London?'

'I was terrified,' I say, thinking of that first perilous journey across the sea to a place so unlike anything I had ever known.

The timbers of the ship groaned and creaked like a dying man. And the smell of sickness and sweat was so thick in the acrid air I could taste it. Hungry eyes followed me at every moment, so intense I hardly dared to sleep. Such easy prey, a young woman alone. More than one could not resist the temptation of trying to make me theirs. What they didn't know was that I was more than 80 years old when I boarded that ship. That in those eight strange decades I had taught myself how to fight out of every corner and never let another man lay a finger on me that I did not wish for. They did not know that I carried a knife under my robes, and I knew how to use it. Once they did, they let me be.

I knew it was time to leave when I heard my son was dying. While he lived, I had hidden in the cloisters of a convent as close to him as I could get. Watching from afar as he grew into manhood. Witnessing with pain and pride the fleeting sparks of joy and triumph that marked out his life, the tragedy and loss that showed his courage. I watched as he bent and twisted into age, and at the very last I was able to go to his side.

My boy, my son. I held him at the end, just as I had at the beginning. He knew me then, in that final hour, as I whispered a lullaby to him against the sound of the falling rain. He recognised my touch somehow. I believe that. In death I was able to give him the maternal comfort that I had been prevented from giving him in life. It was when he was gone and I was truly alone that I found the courage to leave. The world I knew, the life I had believed would be my entire existence, had turned to dust under my feet and all there was left to do was live.

'Well, if you could come across the sea on a boat all on your own, then I don't suppose me hopping a few barges was of very much consequence,' Mariah says, drawing me back through the years to her side.

'You were so small back then and the world was so dangerous. I don't know why I didn't worry about you more.'

Even then, with bombs falling out of the sky the world had seemed a safer place, somehow.

'Different times,' Mariah says, her expression settling as she sucks on the sweet and 80 years return to claim her. 'I suppose I was lucky. Maybe everyone was too scared and too exhausted by war to worry about a little scrap like me. I've had a lucky life, I had Mum and Dad, and Len and you. There's been sorrow and loss for sure, but nothing bad was done to me, not in the way it was to you. Those hard years you've lived, all the people you've seen die… I don't know how you are still standing, Evie.'

I don't have any secrets from Mariah. I have never needed any. When she was a little girl, she loved my fairy tales, just like her mother did at the same age. And now that she is very old, all of the stories and the memories I have shared with her only exist in her particular present. There is no past or future for Mariah. She only lives in now – a place where anything is possible.

'You are one reason,' I say touching her cheek. 'My beautiful girl, I know you had your mum, but I like to think I was your favourite aunt and best friend. You are a beloved daughter to me.'

'And you are like a daughter to me,' Mariah says with a chuckle. 'Ain't it funny! I missed you something awful when you weren't here. But I was glad you had found someone, like I found my Len. I was glad about that, Evie.'

'Is there anything I can get you?' I ask her.

'Tell me a story,' she says, resting her head on my knee. 'The one about that Isaac Newton feller.'

There are traces of the little girl I knew still in her face, the twinkling eyes, the dimple round her mouth. Often, when she was afraid of the planes overhead and her mum was still on shift, she'd come and find me, and put her head on my knee just like this. I'd plait and unplait her braids, stroking her hair and telling her stories until the danger was gone.

'Oh, Isaac was a fascinating man,' I tell her. 'But when I knew him, he almost went completely mad. I don't *think* the two things were connected.'

'What happened?' Mariah asks dreamily.

'He wanted to discover all the secrets of the universe himself. He really believed that what the alchemists had studied centuries before was possible.' Dear Isaac, always frowning, ever angry, always on the verge of something miraculous or devastating, and I was never quite sure which. He was, for a short time, a most brilliant friend. 'I went to find him in Cambridge because I heard he was looking for the impossible, and I thought he might like to meet someone who was evidence of the mysteries of the cosmos. That he might be able to help me understand what had happened to me.'

'Did he?' Mariah asked.

'No, though it was a fascinating attempt,' I say with some regret. 'I've never known a man so obsessed as he was then. Every hour he was awake he studied alchemy. Pages and pages of notes, experiments and inventions he thought might help him become the master of space and time. I think he was perhaps even quite close. But either his obsession or working with mercury, or both, made him gravely ill. I wrote to his family, which he hated, and they summoned him home. He was so angry with me, he could never forgive me, but I didn't want him to die on my account. He recovered, of course – the rest is history. But he never admitted to his studies in alchemy again during his lifetime. And he never, ever wanted to see me again. He never forgave me for sending him home.'

'Well, I don't care how clever he was, he's an idiot,' Mariah says and we both laugh.

'Shall we get you into bed?' I ask her.

'Oh, no, thank you. I'm happy,' Mariah replies. 'I'm happy as a lark. My Len will be home in a bit and then he's taking me dancing. What about you, Evie? Where's your chap tonight?'

It's tempting to fall into her world of memory and effortless time travel, to go back to the time of dashing and daring Evelyn, dancing the night away in case there is no tomorrow. But I am nothing like I was when Evelyn was my name – I wear my cares heavily now.

'I haven't seen him for a long time,' I say sadly. 'He's away.'

'Fighting, is he?' Mariah says, looking up at the faultless sky. 'Will there be a raid tonight?'

'No,' I assure her. 'They said on the wireless there are no air raids tonight.'

The door opens and Viv emerges with a bag of rubbish that she drops into the wheelie bins.

'That's me done then, Mariah!' she says, 'Marta will be here in a bit. I'll see you tomorrow. Try not to get into trouble, OK?'

'I'm going dancing,' Mariah tells her happily. 'There's not going to be a raid tonight, Evie says.'

I look at my narrow little front door. Just for a moment I savour being on the sunny front step with Mariah, where all of time happens all at once and nothing hurts, because nothing is lost.

'Mariah, how have you stayed so happy?' I ask her.

'Because I am not like you,' she says breezily. 'You have to live with it all, Evie. All I have ever been is a blink in the eye of God.'

***

Sitting on my bed I open my laptop and search for Ben's name. I don't know what for exactly, or why, but it doesn't take long to find his website, which tells me that he works, in his words, 'creating optical design solutions for small businesses'.

There's a photo of him sitting on a doorstep with a cock-eared dog at his feet, his long fingers buried in its coat, his mouth caught in the moment before a smile.

Seeing this version of him, before he knew how bad things had got, stings like a sharp slap. I should be revelling in my good fortune, in my dozens of lives that have allowed me to heal a terrified, broken girl and turn her into the woman I am now. My experience, my pain should be my reason for going on, not giving up. During war, famine and plague I endured, evading even the most determined efforts to end me. I always suspected that I could not kill myself, although it was only after Dominic died that I knew how much I didn't want to live on this earth without him. One evening I ran a warm bath, took two dozen tranquillisers with a bottle of good red wine and cut my wrists open with the same knife I had kept at my side since leaving Milan. Lying there, watching my blood curl and coil into water with a distant fascination, I felt glad that it was finally over at last, felt the promise of rest for my aching body. Until, that was, I woke up in a tub full of cold, pink water the next morning without even a scar to show for it.

Then I knew there was no escape.

I'd been searching for answers to understand what had happened to me because I wanted to die. But what if it could help someone who so wanted to live?

But if – *if* – I contacted him again, who would it really be for? For his sake or mine?

Closing the laptop, I reach under my bed and take out a shoebox-sized mahogany case; the last memento I have from my friendship with Isaac. Opening the lid to look inside I find myself wondering.

What if there is the smallest chance that I am the only soul in the world that could save his life?

Chapter Nineteen

'Now what?' Kitty asks me as we get off the bus and look around us. 'Where even are we?'

I squint at the map on my phone. 'I think we are in… Wapping. I think maybe we got the right bus, but we're going in the wrong direction.'

'Wapping.' Kitty narrows her eyes at me.

'Look, you were on board when we ran for the bus. I didn't hear you say it was the wrong one! And anyway, I've never been to Wapping. Why don't we just ride this wave and see where adventure takes us.'

'In Wapping,' Kitty repeats. 'OK, not *totally* what I had in mind for the evening, but find me a pub and buy me a drink and I'm in.'

'Oh, look, this is great,' I say, showing her my phone screen. 'The Prospect of Whitby is a five-minute walk. Let's go there. Apparently it's the oldest pub in London. Tons of cool history. Pirates, smugglers, cut-throats, the lot.'

'Excellent,' Kitty says, not entirely convincingly. But she hooks her arm through mine and we follow the map towards the river until we come across a rather decrepit-looking Georgian building of dark bricks and black-painted bow windows.

'It says that a pub has existed here since the 1520s,' I read aloud to Kitty as we go in through the entrance. 'Somewhere in here is an original flagstone!'

'Just as long as the booze is still flowing,' Kitty says. She is about to head into the bar when I spot something and grab her arm.

'Look at this!' I say, gesturing at an A4-sized poster that catches my attention, pinned between news of pub quizzes, five-a-side football sign-ups and darts matches. 'This started five minutes ago upstairs. Shall we check it out?'

Kitty comes back to read the poster at my side, looks from the low-resolution image and handwritten, badly photocopied poster to me in frank disbelief.

'Are you insane?' she says. 'We have the whole of London at our feet, all of your money at our disposal and you want to spend the evening with some group of losers called the *Last Supper Club*? What the hell?'

'It says they are a group of people into the Renaissance and Da Vinci. He seems to be figuring quite significantly in this trip. Maybe it's a sign? Kitty, stop rolling your eyes.'

'I'm sorry, it's like a little-sister reflex,' she says. 'Go on, I'm listen— Oh look, it's happy hour.'

'No, I've got a feeling about it,' I say, making her meet my eyes.

'A feeling,' Kitty says, her reassuring sarcasm nowhere to be seen.

'Yeah.' I shrug.

'Ben, we talked about your feelings before. Now we are drinking.' Kitty looks up at me. 'You think you are going to find your answers and reasons to this impossible, unfair and totally tragic situation in a pub in Wapping. But you aren't. So I beg you, please don't do this.'

'Do what?' I ask her, although I already know the answer.

'Start up with the quest stuff. You'll only end up hurting yourself.'

'Quest stuff?' I ask.

'The stuff where you are Don Quixote and I am the fat bloke on a donkey.'

'Am I a dead poet or Don Quixote? Make your mind up.'

'You are all the tragic heroes,' she says gently. 'I can't save you from your brain, but I can try and save you from wasting your time looking for miracles in places where they don't hide. Like in the seedy upstairs room in a pub.'

'I wasn't...' I lie.

'Don't make me follow you around like when we were kids and I'd have to trail after you to that bookshop every Saturday, keeping a lookout for those kids at school who wanted to beat you up while you sat on the floor reading. That's not an ideal weekend for a 12-year-old, you know. I should have been down Boots shoplifting lippie with my mates. Life is too short for you to be chasing shadows, Ben.'

'I just want to check out this geeky club, in my capacity as a geek,' I tell her. 'Anyway, I always thought you liked looking at books too,' I say.

'No one interesting likes looking at books, Ben,' she says. 'I faked it for your sake. Except for Jilly Cooper, I learnt a lot from Jilly Cooper – credit where it's due.'

'Kits.' I put my hand on her shoulder. 'I don't want to go to this thing to tilt at windmills, I want to go because I am a nerd and I get a very strong feeling that the Last Supper Club are nerds too. And that's my idea of a good time. And yes, you'll let me, because you are loyal and kind. Plus, imagine how much fun you'll have taking the piss out of us all after.'

'That would be fun,' Kitty says, deadpan. 'But don't go in there like a lost little dead poet on a donkey.'

'If anything it's the opposite,' I say. 'Somehow… somehow, I feel like I've been found.'

Kitty enveloped me in a deep hug.

'You realise I'm never going to stop taking the piss out of you for saying that out loud, don't you?'

★★★

About a dozen men fall silent as I open the door to the room where the club is meeting.

'It's not too late to back out,' Kitty whispers loudly from behind me, even though it definitely is.

'Hello. Hi!' the first of the group to notice us says. 'Sorry, as you can see, we weren't expecting you to join us. We do put posters up, but no one ever comes to the Last Supper Club. Ever.'

'It's virtually the first rule of Last Supper Club that no one but us ever attends,' another young man says with a chuckle.

'Is it OK?' I ask them. 'We don't want to put you out.'

'We really do not,' Kitty adds emphatically.

'No, god, don't go,' another says. 'Seriously, we need new blood.'

'Not that we do ritual sacrifice or anything. Hi, I'm Dev,' another adds, with a charming smile directed at my sister.

'We *are* up to full capacity though,' the first one says. 'So technically...'

'Full capacity?' Dev asks.

'Thirteen. There are 13 of us, the number of disciples at the...'

'Well, our thirteenth member hasn't been for ages and anyway, no one said that was a rule,' Dev says. 'If that's a rule, why do we advertise? We aren't affiliated to any religion!'

'It is not a rule,' the oldest of the group chimes in, a man of about 40 with a greying beard and close-cropped hair. 'We are a group of enquiring minds and there is never a limit on curiosity, I'm sure you agree, Ian.' Ian sits down with a shrug. 'Welcome to the Last Supper Club.'

'I'm Ben and this is Kitty,' I tell them as I take a seat next to Kitty. 'I'm an optical engineer, specialising in lens innovation. I'm getting into Da Vinci.'

'Who isn't,' Ian mutters, like I just brought up S Club at a thrash-metal convention.

'And I'm just his hapless companion,' Kitty says.

'We are all very pleased to meet you,' the older guy says. 'I'm Negasi. My interests are astrophysics and ancient astronomy. You've met Dev, mechanical engineer, and Ian is an industrial chemist.' He goes on to list the names of the others and I forget them all at once. 'We always partake of red wine, unleavened bread and a selection of cheeses at our meetings. Can I interest you in any of that?'

'A glass of wine, thanks,' I say.

'Large one.' Kitty smiles at Dev, suddenly seeming much happier to be here.

'So how did you hear about us?' Negasi asks as he pours us two glasses of wine.

'Just chance really,' I say. 'We got on the wrong bus, ended up here, saw the poster downstairs. Right place, right time sort of thing.'

'No one ever says that about the Last Supper Club,' Negasi jokes.

Before I can reply, the door opens, and a woman, dressed in a long, dusky-pink velvet dress that almost sweeps the floor with its hem of lime-green beading, and carrying a large wooden box, comes walking in.

Little cheers and salutes, and good-natured cries of 'Look what the cat dragged in' sound from the group.

'I know, I know, I haven't been for ages, but I think you will forgive me when you see what I've—' Vita's eyes widen when she sees me, the round O of her surprised mouth quickly spreads into the most beautiful smile.

'Ben,' she says.

Chapter Twenty

My cheeks are approximately the shade of my 1960s Biba dress as I take my seat next to Negasi and my friends greet me with friendly complaints over my failure to turn up for the last few meetings and show a decided interest in my mysterious box.

'I wouldn't mind, but you are the founder of this group,' Dev says with a teasing smile.

'I know, I know,' I say. 'Da Vinci kept me a bit busy.'

'Totally worth it though,' Ben says. 'Vita's exhibition is amazing.'

'You two know each other?' Ian asks.

'Not exactly. We met yesterday,' Ben says. 'Kitty, this is Vita, a curator at the Bianchi Collection.'

'Cool,' the girl says with a smile. 'I'm Ben's sister.'

'You have the same smile,' I say.

'What's this all about then, Vita?' Ian asks, as I glance at Ben. I hadn't noticed until now the breadth of his shoulders, or the grace of his hands. The heat rises over my chest and neck as his eyes meet mine.

'Well, my next project is looking at where scientific discovery and alchemy intersect. Those early scientists predicted so many of today's known discoveries, what else might it be possible to learn from the past?'

'Well, this is exactly our bag,' Dev says. He rubs his hands together in anticipation. 'Are you going to open it?'

I set the box that I retrieved from Isaac's lab before it was dismantled on the table, pushing it into the centre. Everyone leans in to examine it.

'I found this *instrument* a few years ago,' I tell them, 'in Cambridge. The box is good quality and has been made to fit the *device*, and dates from around the late 1600s. It was obviously designed to do something, but I can't quite fathom what. The puzzle has driven me mad ever since I acquired it. But what if it might unlock the key to some modern advancement? A slim chance, I know, but nothing is impossible.'

'Except time travel,' Ian murmurs.

'What do you mean, *found it*?' Dev asks. 'Did it fall off the back of a lorry?'

'Would you believe I found it at a flea market?' I ask.

'I will if it helps.' Dev shoots a charming smile at Kitty.

Carefully I open the box and remove its contents mostly in one piece. Made of brass, the object is expertly tooled with hand-ground glass lenses of varying sizes and thicknesses set into the mechanism. 'I thought at first it was a failed design for a microscope.' I take the last part of the object out of the box and slip it out of its velvet bag. Carefully I set the hand-cut prism into its cradle at the top of the mechanism. 'Or some kind of optical experiment. But as to what it's for, I'm at a loss. Any ideas?'

'I say,' Mike says, peering at it over his glasses, as an excited murmur travels round the table.

'That is a conundrum,' Tom says, reaching for it and then hesitating. 'May we?'

'The period is too late,' Ian says. 'For our special interest I mean. We are meant to be focusing on the early Renaissance period.'

'Oh, Ian, do shut up,' Dev says. 'It's fascinating.'

'Yes, but everything about it reminds me of the many objects and inventions in Da Vinci's notebooks,' I tell Ian. 'Not that I can find one that precisely aligns with this. But I feel that the person who made this knew Da Vinci's work and perhaps was familiar with his thoughts on alchemy.'

It's normally at this point that people smile or outright smirk, but no one in this room does, which is partly why I founded the club in the first place. I wanted a way to collect like-minded people who, when all together in a room, might just solve the most impossible riddle, even if they didn't know it.

'I would agree with that assessment,' says Negasi, as the others murmur their own thoughts.

Everyone around the table moves in closer to peer at the device. Ben holds back a little, but I see his gaze roving over the instrument, searching out every detail with intense fascination.

I came here tonight thinking about him, and here he is. I don't know what this is, but it makes me cautious. Serendipitous coincidences and causes for hope always come just before the greatest loss; that's something you only know when you have lived as long as I have.

'I'll go and get some more wine while you look,' I say.

'Don't worry, the landlord will bring some up in a bit,' someone says, but I pretend I haven't heard them, hoping that somehow Ben will find a reason to follow me so we can marvel at the oddness of our meeting together.

When I founded the Last Supper Club I chose the Prospect of Whitby because it's one of those places that has been familiar to me since I arrived in London all those centuries ago. From time to time it's been more than a friendly landmark; it's been a refuge too. I even lived and worked here once, sheltered by this small rock of ages that stands stalwart-still against the ever-turning wheel of the city.

The main bar has changed a lot since I worked and lived here, but I still recognise some of the lines of the room, know that I've touched my hand to the sturdy beams that support the ceiling more than once, and walked across these flags before. One thing hasn't changed recently: my former boss standing behind the bar, one hand on a pump as he chats to his regulars.

'Hello there, Hew,' I say with a small smile, 'Sorry I've been AWOL, work's been mad.'

'Nice to see you, love,' Hew smiles, and, taking down a glass, he pours me a neat measure of gin, dropping a couple of ice cubes in as an afterthought. Just the way I like it.

'I thought you might need a hand,' Ben says, appearing at my side. I turn to him and forget what I was talking about.

'Oh, is this the new fella?'

'Oh no,' I blush. 'This is Ben. We just met yesterday.'

'Right,' he says, raising his eyebrows as he puts another four bottles of wine on to a tray with some fresh glasses. 'I thought maybe…well, you know. It's been a while since Dominic passed.'

An awkward silence follows.

'Tell you what,' Hew says after a while, 'you two go ahead and I'll bring these up. And say goodbye before you leave, promise me?'

'I promise,' I tell him, glancing at Ben over my shoulder as I lead him into the quieter hallway at the back.

Once alone we fall into an expectant silence.

'Well this is unexpected,' Ben speaks finally.

'Yes,' I say. 'Really is.'

'I'm glad though,' he says.

'I'm glad too,' I tell him, carefully touching my fingertips one to the other in sequence. 'I found your website and I thought about getting in touch, but I wasn't sure if it would be right to or not.'

'You thought about contacting me?' Ben laughs. 'I can imagine that most people would never want to see me again after seeing me like that. I wouldn't blame them either.'

'I'm not scared of death,' I say. 'I was with my husband when he died.'

And so many others.

'Oh, god,' Ben says, his face falling. 'I'm sorry.'

'Thank you. His name was Dominic,' I say. 'It was… Time has passed.'

'Vita, this may not be a—'

'Ben, I was thinking—'

'Oh, there you are,' Kitty says as she comes down the stairs. 'I was just looking for the ladies.' She must have missed the huge sign for the bathroom right outside the room where the club meets.

'Sorry, sis,' Ben says, smiling. 'Did I leave you with the nerds?'

'You did. Luckily the one called Dev is also pretty cute. What's going on here then?'

'Nothing, just chatting. I met Vita the other day at the gallery. Mad to see her here tonight!'

'Mad!' Kitty says. She is smiling, but I can see the grief etched just under the surface of her skin.

'Well, shall we go back up?' I ask. 'The ladies is up there.'

Kitty heads up the stairs. Ben and I look at each other, I can feel something in the air change, as if the cogs of time are turning once again.

Chapter Twenty-One

It makes no sense, but I knew Vita was going to be there for several seconds before she came into the room. As if when you meet someone at a particular time, in such an extraordinary way, there is some kind of universal friction that refuses to leave a story half told, even when it hasn't been written yet. At the moment I saw her I somehow knew that even at the very end, there can be a beginning. I'm not sure yet of what, but I knew that it had already begun.

Now more wine has been drunk, and the 13 members of the Last Supper Club are arguing about Vita's device with deep, pointless joy. Against all expectation I feel so close to happiness that I can almost touch it. A few minutes ago Kitty asked Dev what he thought the strange object was, and now they are talking, shoulders touching, looking only at each other, and I can see the curve of her cheek, round like an apple; it only looks like that when she is really smiling.

'A banana peeler?' Kitty guesses, as Dev strokes his beard.

'An interesting proposition,' he says. 'I was thinking more of a prototype mobile phone.'

'I know!' Kitty puts her hand up like she's in class. Not that she was ever this enthusiastic at school. 'It's a time-travel machine.'

'Impossible,' Ian says.

'Wouldn't that be brilliant,' Dev replies contemplatively.

'Oh, you don't need that to travel in time,' Kitty says casually. 'I've always found that a really good kiss can make you feel like you're 20 again.'

Dev turns to her.

'Do expand on your hypothesis,' he says.

Hoping to talk to Vita again, I pull the odd object towards me, pick it up and turn it over in my hands. The weight of it is satisfying, the craftsmanship still more. Every perfectly handmade component that joins and interacts with its sister parts gives my engineer's heart deep satisfaction. The lens would have been hand-ground; the precision and finish are things of beauty.

'Do *you* know what it is?' Vita asks me from across the table, as if I really might have the answer.

'No, not really.' I look at it for a moment more. 'Although, in my very limited knowledge, a prism and a lens are two different things, right? One is to split light waves and one to magnify. So maybe it was meant for getting a close look at... different light waves? Not that it would ever work in this combination, or any. But it could have been an early half-right attempt at something like the Lumière camera, a way of seeing under layers of paint almost like...' A thrill of excitement runs down my spine as I realise what I'm looking at. 'A very early protype of the same technology that I've been developing myself.'

Vita's lips part a fraction, her eyes widen.

'That's really interesting,' she says, leaning towards me. Around us the table erupts into a discussion of multispectrum cameras, layer-to-amplitude method and signal-to-noise ratio, and why I, a humble engineer, have to be wrong. But in the midst of the noise, I feel a silken thread of awareness of the physical proximity between me and Vita.

Kitty's hand on my shoulder makes me jump.

'I'm going back to the hotel,' she says. 'Coming?'

'Not yet,' I say, glancing at Dev, who is standing behind her, pretending not to notice as his friends all stare at him. 'But you go on. Have fun.'

'Thanks for a lovely evening, fellers,' Kitty says, blowing me a kiss as she walks out of the door.

'Well, I'm still none the wiser, but it's been a delight. I have to go too,' Vita says a few minutes after Kitty leaves. A chorus of groans and pleas rises from around the table as she starts to pack her strange artefact away in its marvellous box.

'I have to. I've got an early start. But I'll definitely come next time.' Everyone cheers. It seems the Last Supper Club are very taken with her too.

'Shall I escort you?' I offer hurriedly. Escort? Who do I think I am, Sir Lancelot?

After a split second of hesitation Vita nods.

'Thanks,' she says. 'This box does get a bit heavy.'

Disproportionately pleased with myself, I hold the doors open for her as we leave the pub and emerge on the night-cooled streets.

'You promised to say goodbye to the landlord,' I remind her.

'Oh, Hew? Yeah, I know, but I think I've done enough small talk for one night. I'll see him next time.' She shifts the box from one beautifully cushioned, rounded hip to another. 'You don't have to take me home if you'd rather not.'

'I rather would,' I say. Bloody idiot. Vita's answering smile is worth it though.

'You have no idea where I live.'

'Everywhere is far away from Wapping. Anyway, where do you live?'

'Soho.' She smiles.

'Perfect. I'm getting the same train as you anyway. I could sit in another carriage if you'd prefer?'

Vita chuckles.

'I like you,' she says. 'And I hardly ever like anyone.'

'Is that a compliment?' I ask her.

'Yes,' she says. 'You have no idea.' She glances at the box in her arms. 'So, are you are carrying this box then? It weighs a ton.' She then catches herself. 'Oh, unless…'

'I can carry boxes,' I tell her. 'Boxes will not speed up my demise. And I really hope I don't drop dead on the tube. Imagine all those pissed-off Londoners. Although, actually, that might be a positive.'

She laughs this time, and her eyes sparkle with streetlights as we walk into the tube station.

'I am sorry about your husband, by the way,' I say. 'He must have been young. Not that you have to talk about it if you don't want to.'

'No, that's fine. I think sometimes it's easier to talk about the really serious stuff to strangers,' Vita says as the DLR pulls in. 'But I'd rather not talk about him tonight. Tonight, I want to sit at the front and pretend we're train drivers.'

'Really?' It's my turn to laugh. 'You don't look like the sort of person who's into playing trains.' I slide into the seat next to her, putting the box on my lap, adding, 'Besides, you don't feel like a stranger.'

To this she gives me a slow smile, one that looks like it's been woken from a long sleep.

'It's not really the trains I like so much as the electricity,' Vita tells me. 'It's been around so long I think we forget that it is basically magic.'

'Magic?' I laugh. 'You really do fit in with those Last Supper blokes, don't you?'

'Five hundred years ago all of this would have been seen as sorcery,' Vita says, gesturing at the neon skyline. 'And in the grand scheme of things, 500 years is just the blink of an eye.'

'And what about 32? What's that in the scheme of things?' I ask her.

'Ah, well, that's the beauty of time,' she says, her eyes following the tall, brightly lit buildings as they march by, soldiers of progress. 'Mortality means you can slow down its passing almost to stopping if you want to.' She turns to look at me suddenly. 'If you practise hard enough you could make one moment last for ever.'

'How?' I ask.

'Just hold on to it.' Her dark eyes fix on mine. 'When you're happy, when things are good or you are full of expectation, just feel that moment and hold on to it for as long as you can. Remember every little bit of it: how warm it was, the scent in the air, the feel of the train moving beneath you. Memorise it all, and then hours, days from now, whenever you want, you will be able to say, *I was there, I was so happy, and it was real.*' She takes a half-breath. 'The funny thing is, meeting you this week has reminded me how to do that.'

'Me? Why me?' I must have asked that same question a thousand times in the last couple of days, but this time, it means something different. Something hopeful.

'It's just you,' she says. 'I had forgotten how to do it. Thank you for reminding me.'

Neither one of us says more until the train draws into the station where we have to change lines. That perfect miraculous moment has gone into the past, but it is still mine. The rush of warm air, London a city of sparkling glass standing tall against the soft, purple sky. The sound of Vita's voice, soft and clear, the tilt of her head, the sweep of her hair and the light in her eyes. I've got all of that here in my pocket, and now I always will.

For the rest of the journey we sit next to each other in comfortable quiet. In the reflection of the tube-train window I can see the shape of her, the tumble of her hair, the pale oval of her face, and how we are connected at the shoulder. There is no way of knowing whether it is fate bringing us together or something random that has made our paths cross again. But for now that doesn't matter. For now it is enough the way that Vita leans towards me as we sit in silence on the train.

Chapter Twenty-Two

My father was strict and devoutly religious, but not out of love or faith. His devotion came from fear. He was so afraid that he would go to hell that he spent most of his life paying for a place in heaven, giving money in exchange for life eternal; giving his 14-year-old daughter to a man of influence in payment of a debt. Somehow it all made sense to him; from this great a distance, it is impossible to understand how his brain worked.

Who I am, what I am prepared to accept from other beings has grown and stretched over what feels simultaneously like infinite time and the blink of an eye all at once. There have been a few glorious moments in the last 500 years when I've hoped and believed that humans had reached a point of progress that was irreversible. Then each time all the beauty laboured for by one hand would be burnt to the ground by another.

If I live another 500 years, what fresh horrors will I bear witness to? What new miracles?

I barely knew my father when he was alive. If you'd asked me when I was a child, I would have told you I loved only him and God, even after I was made an old man's mistress at his behest.

As for my father, no amount of money or prayer could prevent my father from turning to dust. And as for God, if there is such a being, then He must be duty-bound to hate me, for I am an affront to nature. I am the monster that stalks dreams and nightmares. I am the Undead.

Sitting beside Ben on the train, I wonder. If he truly knew me, would he – could he – have the will and courage to want to know me as Dominic did?

We slow to a halt at the place where our paths diverge, on the corner of Lower John Street and Brewer Street. The evening is warm and bathed in a rosy glow, and the streets are still busy. People flow around us, travelling their own paths, but somehow still united. The warmth of the day lingers in the pavements.

As Ben transfers my wooden box into my arms, his forearm brushes against the inside of my wrist. In that brief moment of exchange my years-lonely body leans into the longing.

Neither one of us moves.

'Can I ask you something personal before you go?' he asks me, eyes low, hands in pockets. I nod. 'Did your husband know he was going to die?'

It took me a while to know how to answer.

'He was a man who always expected death,' I say eventually. 'He took risks with his life all the time when he was healthy and strong. It drove me mad with worry. He was never afraid, even when any sane person should be. I suppose I always knew I wouldn't have him for nearly long enough.' A flash of pain forces me to close my eyes for a moment. 'When he became ill, he was bitterly disappointed that the end wasn't in battle, but at home with me at his side, holding his hand.'

'I can understand that,' Ben says.

'He was so ferociously alive.' I smile at the thought of Dominic, his black eyes sparkling with laughter. 'And he was gentle and funny and romantic.'

We both fall silent again for a moment.

'And how did you cope afterwards?' Ben asks suddenly, before checking himself. 'Say if I'm overstepping the mark. I just... I just find you so easy to talk to.' He sticks his hands in his pockets, looking at his feet. 'It's like nothing seems to shake you. I know I'm not doing a very good job of explaining myself here.' He looks up at the deepening sky. 'The thing is, I'm worried about Mum and Kitty. I worry about how they will cope.'

'They will cope badly,' I tell him, 'because they love you. And then they will find a way to go on, and even eventually be happy again... because they love you.'

'I'm not sure I want them to be *totally* happy,' he says with a rueful smile. 'Seems a bit rude. I was thinking like a good old cry at least once a month seems about the right level of grief.'

Suddenly we are engulfed by a gaggle of tipsy young women singing Adele. For a moment it rains glitter on the street, and then they are gone, their voices echoing around Golden Square.

'And what about you?' Ben asks, picking a piece of streamer paper out of my hair. 'Are you happy again?'

'I have been content,' I say. 'And that's why…'

'And that's why?' Ben asks tentatively as I make a choice.

'I haven't told you everything.' Even as I say it, I am unsure that I am doing the right thing. Our eyes meet. 'I don't want to give you false hope. I know I said I was sure there was probably nothing else to discover about *La Belle,* but that wasn't exactly true. I still think she is the key to eternal life, to curing all ills. I… I really believe she has the answer to immortality and how to harness it. And I'm looking for it.'

'You are?' he says, not with mockery or disbelief, but with wonder and hope. The expression on his face, the longing to believe and the fear of being wrong twists round my heart. If we go one step further together then I will be holding his heart in my hands. Even so, I am more afraid of not trying.

'If you wanted, we could look together.'

'Are you serious?'

'Maybe it's not impossible,' I say carefully. 'Maybe it's knowledge that was lost or hidden; something known but that has not yet been understood. It's like I was saying about electricity – so many of the things our ancestors would have thought of as flat-out sorcery are facts of our everyday life now. So many things we think of as being science fiction today will be commonplace in the future. And as far as I know, no one foresaw more of what could be possible than Leonardo da Vinci.' I stop talking and take a breath.

'What I'm saying is, if you are OK with understanding that we will almost certainly fail, then come on this quest with me. And maybe,' I adjust the weight of the box again, 'maybe, just maybe, I can find a way to get your lens in front of *La Belle.*'

He takes in a sharp breath and wraps his arms around himself in a bid to stifle an involuntary shudder.

'So, shall we meet tomorrow?'

'Yes.' He shudders.

'Are you OK?' I ask him.

'Yes, I'm more than OK,' he says. 'I'd just never realised before how frightening hope can be.'

Chapter Twenty-Three

London spirals around me, neon-lit arms of a galaxy that I am at the centre of and nothing else matters but now. Not all of the rehearsal years that led up to this moment, or all the years that may not come. There is only now. If there is one thing I can leave to the people I care about, then I hope it's some understanding of that.

When I raced for the London train I was trying to run away from something inescapable. When it pulled away, I left behind versions of me standing on the platform, watching me leave.

The wilfully lonely man described as distracted and remote by all the women who have dated him. The man who didn't trust relationships because he grew up in the wreckages of one. The man who planned and worked for a future with a single-minded dedication that never questioned if it would one day come into being, even if his goal was always another year, another month, another week away. The man who removed himself from most of life's networks and connections, willingly self-secluded in clean rooms and vast empty skies. I don't know what I was waiting for to make me live, but death coming up fast on the horizon has certainly done the trick. That and meeting Vita.

I must be so careful not to make a fairy tale out of all of this. Not to fall into fantasy after a lifetime of prosaic practicality. I can't allow myself to connect the dots of my impulse to come to London and finding the poster that led me right to Vita, who is perhaps the only person in the world who believes there really might be a cure to death in a fantasy picture where I am saved.

Desperate as I am for it all to be true, ready as I am to fall into rabbit holes and become a fully paid-up citizen of Wonderland,

I must pull myself back from the brink and remind myself that, as convincing and compelling as Vita's faith is, none of this can possibly be true. There is no last-minute, miracle rescue for me, which is OK, because somehow that's not the reason I'm so ready to follow Vita.

This is what Kitty called one last quest, and as far as I'm concerned a more than fitting way to spend what might be the last days of my life. An esoteric pursuit in an unfamiliar world, that whatever the outcome, I know I won't regret. Because if I am honest, if Vita had invited me to attempt to fly to the moon with her in a home-made rocket fashioned from the insides of toilet rolls and empty washing-up bottles, I probably would have said yes.

I can't say that if I had met Vita a year ago she would have had such an impact on me as she has now. I know I would have found her beautiful, and might have wondered about asking her for a drink, but in all probability I would still have withdrawn from any connection before I got to know her too well like I always do.

I do know I have never met another woman who is so unafraid, and that her courage seems to be transmissible. It's as if all the awkward discomfort that people have around the broken and the wounded runs right off her. She looked me in the eye and listened, with open empathy that was not weak or needy. She is not fazed by anything I've told her, and that has grounded me. In the middle of her wild claims about the secret to immortality, she has helped me see that death, even mine, is nothing at all. Nothing more than an essential component of life.

So yes, I will follow her gladly now. Wherever she might lead me, I will go.

III

Time takes all but memories.

Traditional sundial motto

Chapter Twenty-Four

When Jack comes to walk me to work he seems to be made of the golden morning that is waiting for me outside my door. White shirt, faded jeans that suit him perfectly. Jack is just one of those people that could live in any age of history and fit in perfectly yet stand out for being so beautiful at exactly the same moment.

We dawdle through the narrow streets of Soho, stopping to pick up coffee and pastries on the way.

'Did you take that barman home?' I ask him.

'No, I rather lost the impetus after you left,' Jack says. 'It's almost as if I want something more meaningful.'

'Are you ill?' I laugh.

'Just sick,' he replies looking at me sideways. 'You have a spring in your step. What happened to you?'

'The strangest thing. I went to the Last Supper Club.'

'You found the meaning of life in Wapping?' Jack asks.

'Ben was there, the guy I told you about – the man with the lens. It was so random and also somehow *not*.'

'Oh,' Jack says. 'Really. Was he stalking you?'

'No, he had no idea that I had anything to do with the club. He was just there at the same time as me and it was weird, because I'd seen him earlier in the day and he told me...'

I pause for a moment, trying to pin down the feelings I have about what Ben told me into something translatable.

'What?' Jack prompts me.

'He is dying,' I say. 'Not dying, exactly. He will die shortly as a consequence of a catastrophic event in his brain. He doesn't know when, but it could be very soon.'

'I see,' Jack says. 'Poor fellow.'

'The day after he discovered this information in Leeds, we met in London, because of *La Belle*. Because of the very object that proves that death can be conquered. Don't you see?'

'I see,' Jack answers warily. 'I see that you are being seduced by the notion of fate.'

'And you're not?' I ask him. Jack shakes his head.

'I can see the pathos and irony in the situation without having to attribute it to some overarching universal purpose,' he says. 'Do you remember when we first met?'

'Hard to forget,' I say. 'I did nearly kill you.'

He grins.

'You were so fierce and brilliant, more than I hoped you would be,' he says. 'Our first years together set the world alight.'

★★★

I had lived in, loved and left London half a dozen times or more on the night that I met Jack.

There always came a point in any life that I built, any field I excelled in, when I would draw the wrong sort of attention from the constantly circling men And once they had seen me, they would never let me out of their sight until I would have to withdraw, regroup and return with a new name and new story. By then I was 200 years into discovering who I truly was and what I was capable of, in a way the merchant's daughter from Milan would never have had the time or strength to do. I knew that I was strong, that I was brave and, best of all, that I was clever.

The London that I returned to again and again still belonged to men, but she and I entwined like secret lovers over the years, parting ways only to come back together even more passionately. Together we were magnificent, making trades that wrapped around the globe, buying and building streets of properties, filling our coffers with gold and more importantly power, a little more each time until the men I refused to marry or go to bed with determined to make me pay for saying no.

The night I met Jack was soon after my return to London from a few years in France flirting with Paris and all the danger and opportunity she had to offer. I had come home in another guise, with another name, but this time I was determined to put down roots that would last, that would always be there for me to return to in one way or another. I was a wealthy Italian widow, young and vivacious, with a delight for society and impeccable taste. I called myself Madame Bianchi.

The night was warm and full of stars. The torches in Vauxhall laid out a glittering path for me to follow, wrapped in my silks as I explored the satin-dark night. I was searching for adventure, and perhaps a companion to fill the hours until dawn. For, at last, I had met London at a time when a woman like me, who knew what she wanted and was brave enough to take it, might be considered scandalous, but would still be accepted, as long as she was sufficiently fashionable and interesting. This flirtatious, infatuated and deliciously vain city was my very favourite incarnation of her so far. She beckoned me on with her glittering eyes, daring me to dare a little more.

I had sensed the figure walking softly behind me some moments before, so when he reached for me and tried to pull me toward him my knife was already in my hand. The man froze, the blade at his throat, gleaming in the flickering light. Slowly he lowered his arms to his sides, palms facing out, taking great pains to show me that he meant me no harm. I observed him, noting the curl of his dark blond hair, the smile lines around his eyes, the full beauty of his mouth. I remember thinking that if he had only let me search him out, perhaps I would have taken him to bed. Then he spoke to me in Italian. Not just Italian, but in the old way; the way I hadn't heard since the places I knew had fallen into the past, and the language I'd grown up with had morphed into something different and new, time and again, always changing. He spoke to me from my past. I lowered the knife.

'At last, I have found you, Agnese,' he said, speaking my true name. 'I have been searching for you for centuries. So it would a terrible shame if you tried to kill me after all that effort. And besides, I doubt your efforts would be successful. I think you already know that.'

'Who are you?' I asked him, though somehow I already knew who he was. He was mine, and I was his one way or another.

'A friend, or rather, a friend of a friend,' he said. 'My lover made my portrait with the same mysterious method that he made yours not long before he left me. First, he left me for another man, and then he left me to die. Never once did he look back over his shoulder to see what he had done to me. I am like you, Agnese. Neither of us can die, and dear Leonardo is long, long gone, all his troubles far behind him. But ours, like our portraits, will never fade.'

'You are Salaì.' I whispered the name of Leonardo's lover and muse. I knew his face. I had seen it repeated in his work over and over.

'I am.' Jack smiled sadly. 'But please, call me Giacometti, or better still Jack. After he died, I found his secret notes about you. I wondered, I hoped, if there really could be another like me. I had almost giving up searching. You were difficult to find.'

'I have had to be careful,' I told him. 'People have tended to want to burn or hang an ageless, successful, single woman. Though times are a little more enlightened now.'

'And you have done well for yourself, Madame Bianchi,' he said, tasting my new name on his tongue with evident pleasure. 'Have your wealth and connections helped you discover what it is my dear Leonardo did to us? In all these years that I have been looking for you, I hoped to gain some understanding. I have visited with scholars and magi, studied ancient texts and pored over and over what I have left of Leonardo. And all I find is a trail of breadcrumbs that leads to yet another trail of breadcrumbs.'

'You've been looking too all this time, and yet we only meet tonight?' I shook my head. 'I have discovered a great deal, but not the answer to that secret. I determine to keep searching. Perhaps if we add the fragments we have together we might make a whole.'

'And if not, will you let me continue to search at your side?' Jack asked, and felt the longing in his voice vibrate in my chest. 'If we have one another then we will never know loneliness again.'

It wasn't until he had said those last words that I felt the weight of the years of loneliness that I had carried on my shoulders, heavy as the weight of the world. It wasn't until then that I realised how very much I would like to set that weight down.

'I believe I would like that,' I told him, folding him into a hug.

'Then it is done,' he told me.

★★★

'It seems impossible to think that you and I would never have had one another if it wasn't for Leonardo,' I say to Jack now as we make our last turn down the wide, leafy avenue towards the Collection. 'If it wasn't for the portrait. He brought us together, although we didn't know it at the time. Can you deny that it was meant to be?'

'I cannot deny that it feels that way.' Jack stops walking to turn and look at me. 'I cannot deny that without you I would have lost my humanity a long time ago.'

'Which is why,' I say tentatively, 'when I realised what Ben had to lose, and put that together with his expertise, I invited him to help me unravel the secrets in the painting.'

'Vita,' Jack says, 'why did you do that? You've put yourself – put *us* – in harm's way.'

'I haven't told him who or what we are,' I tell him. 'Only that I am searching for the secret and that I believe it is real, and that if he would like to, he can help me look. You said that perhaps I should see our meeting as an opportunity? And that is what I am doing. I'm being careful, I swear to you. But there is something about him that makes me wonder if…'

'If?' Jack prompts me.

'If he can help us finally see the secrets hidden in the portrait. Then we can save his life and all of this… it would have a purpose.'

'Vita, what do you mean?'

'I mean that since Dominic died I only wanted answers so that I could die. And now, meeting Ben, it's made me feel that perhaps I want to live.'

'Someone you have known barely two days has made you completely re-evaluate your entire sense of being?' Jack asks me.

There is hurt in his expression; too late I understand why.

'No, not him, but his longing to live. He's reminded me how precious life is.'

Jack turns in the opposite direction from the one we are travelling in.

'Are you sure you want to do this again?' Jack asks.

'What do you mean *again*?' I ask.

'Fall in love with someone who will die. Not in 50 years, but soon. Too soon.'

'I am not in love with him!' I laugh, incredulously. 'I met him five minutes ago.'

'And invited him straight into your most treasured secret – *our* secret –without asking me.'

'Only into the very outskirts of it; only what I am looking for, not what *we* are. And I told him that part before I knew that his life was in such danger.'

'I'm not sure if that makes this better or worse,' Jack says.

'You would like him,' I say. 'He's funny.'

Turning, Jack looks deeply into my face.

'You will suffer, Vita. If you go any further along this road the pain will cut you deeply enough to scar. Enough to hurt you, but not enough to kill you.' His smile is gentle, hopelessly sweet and sad. 'I don't know if I can stand to see you so broken again.'

'You are seeing complications that are not there,' I reassure him.

'You forget that I know you, perhaps better than any man has ever known any woman, and I have only ever seen that expression in your eyes once before. Even if you don't know how you feel yet, I do.'

For a long moment I look into the river. You can never know how cold the Thames is, or how terrifyingly strong the current until you've tried and failed to drown yourself in its sinewy depths. Until you have swallowed lungs full of foul water and yet still you breathe. Finding yourself, cold to the marrow and half-sucked into the black mud of its banks, staring at the leaden sky and knowing that is no way out of this existence. That death is a choice denied you.

Has Jack really seen something in me that I have yet to understand because it's still too far away for me to see it coming?

'I can't escape this life,' I say. 'So why not live it? With all my heart, as if there will never be enough time?' Jack turns his face away from me, and I realise I've hurt him somehow. I put a hand on his arm, and he leans towards me just a little.

'We have both almost lost our minds to this existence. Have you considered what you would be doing to Ben if somehow you were able to make him like us? Have you thought about what it means to bring someone into the world, reborn in a way that means they can never leave it? The loss he will have to endure? The responsibility that you can never walk away from? Have you considered any of that?'

'No,' I admit. 'I sort of thought I'd cross that bridge if we got to it.'

Jack sighs with exasperation.

'How is it that my dear, overthinking Vita has suddenly thrown caution to the winds after 30 solid years of being entirely sensible?'

'Aren't you a bit glad that I am?' I say. 'Jack, you and I are proof of the impossible. If I am the miracle that he longs for, if I don't at least try to help him, then am I still a human being at all? Or just this... this aberration, who has forgotten what it's like to feel mortality. What's the point of our existence if we can't do something with it?'

'Does there have to be a point outside of each other?' Jack sighs. 'You've thought you were an abomination for so long. Even in the early years. And after Dominic, I watched you try and tear yourself apart, Vita. That's what I'm afraid of. The horror and madness that comes with grief that you can never escape from. You can't go through that again and honestly, neither can I. I love you. When you are in pain, I am in pain.'

'Then you are telling me that I can never really love anyone again,' I say. 'And in the end, isn't that all there is?'

'Love me,' Jack says. He hesitates, then adds, 'The way you always have. Besides, the notion of romantic love is nothing but a sideshow. It's a distraction from what humanity really is. You still long to feel like a proper human, even when you know, better than anyone, that to be human is to be cruel, destructive, selfish and stupid.'

'And kind,' I say. 'And generous and brave. Inventive and creative. Tireless and hopeful. Love isn't a sideshow, it's what gives everything else meaning, and it's made all the more beautiful because it's all gone in the blink of an eye. And if I can't help him then Ben will be too.'

'And you will still be here,' Jack says. 'With me.'

'Perhaps,' I say.

'If not, then you and I are not enough anymore.'

He doesn't ask it as a question, but still, I don't know how to answer him.

***

When I arrive at the Collection, Ben is sitting in the courtyard garden among the roses. He leaps to his feet when he sees me.

'Hi,' I say, happy to see him 'We didn't arrange to meet, did we?'

'No.' His grin is rueful. 'I woke up, the sun was shining, Kitty is still hiding behind a *Do Not Disturb* sign, and I thought I'd say thanks for letting me be part of this – you know, before you go into work.'

I glance over his shoulder at the gallery, and I suddenly know.

'Maybe I'll skip work today,' I say. 'Would you like to skip my job with me? Our research needs to start somewhere, after all. Let's see if we can make a day of it.'

Chapter Twenty-Five

We stand side by side in the darkened manuscripts room of the Victoria and Albert Museum in front of the cabinet displaying two Da Vinci notebooks. I've never visited before. To see objects that were once in Da Vinci's hand moves me more than I am prepared for.

All the photos in the world don't do this place justice; all this swirling, arched beauty built just to house beauty. It's a wonderful folly, a testament to what makes us human: thousands of years of people creating the most magnificent thing they can, to hold it out to the universe and say, 'See what I can do?'

'When the museum first opened in this building in 1857,' Vita tells me, 'it was the first museum in the world to offer refreshments and to stay open late into the evening, to allow working people to visit after hours.' She smiles, picturing another age. 'Imagine this room, lit by gaslight. Walking down these great halls, seeing all these treasures glowing in the dark when ordinarily such extravagant things have always been out of sight to most people. Magical.'

'It must have felt like glimpsing the future,' I say.

'It really did.'

The room empties out soon after we enter, so we have it all to ourselves. Other distant voices echo through corridors, but our room is silent except for the ticking of my watch and the beating of my heart. In the moment it feels as though this room was made just for us.

Vita had told me on the bus that she was bringing me to look at some of the Da Vinci notebooks known as *The Codex Forster*, though only one or two are exhibited at a time.

'The ones we have at the Bianchi are about nature and art,' she'd told me. 'Studies of water and winds. *The Codex Forster* are rather more opaque. I've read them, of course, but maybe you will see something I can't.'

'I'm hardly an expert,' I say.

'You don't need to be,' Vita says. 'You just need a fresh eye. And in your line of work you're likely to spot something pertinent. We'll need to request to see them in the library. I think it's two weeks' notice.'

'Which might be too long to wait for me,' I say. She'd smiled gently, as her hand reached for mine briefly and squeezed my fingers.

'But the wonderful thing about living in London,' she'd gone on, 'is that some of the world's most amazing treasures are on view for anyone to see any time.'

As we'd travelled across London on the top deck of a red bus, she had looked out of the window, lost to her thoughts as the city-scape repeated in her eyes. I'd watched her and London slowly reveal themselves as the bus rolled along. I felt the heaviness of time passed in this city, traces of history slotting together in a chaotic puzzle, each a link in a chain that reached back to the very beginning. It was strange to find myself in a place I had never been before but that was so very familiar.

It's like walking on to a set that has been wating for me to make my entrance on to the stage for countless long and empty years. Now, at last, life begins.

'You can see by the way that some text disappears into the bind-ing that these were originally loose papers.' Vita brings me back to the moment, breaking the quiet as we gaze at the notebooks. 'And that someone – perhaps Leonardo, perhaps not – collected and bound them later.' She sighs.

I stare at Da Vinci's handwriting, marvelling at the way in which it feels like he just put down his pen and walked out of the room for a moment, leaving his notebook open. Miraculous concepts seem to appear on the page at the speed of thought, from the rap-idly forming ideas and illustrations to the inked thumbprint on a dog-eared corner. And yet he was just a human being who loved and struggled.

'Do you think the secret of *La Belle* is hidden somewhere in these notebooks?' I whisper.

'Not in these ones,' she says, her eyes fixed on the artefacts, so small that you could fit them into the palm of your hand, 'or the ones we have at the Collection – not in any of the known Da Vinci notebooks in the world. I've examined them all. He wrote all his notes backwards to make it harder for people to steal his ideas.'

'You've read all of his notebooks?' I am impressed. 'Surely you must be the most expert person on Leonardo in the world.'

'You could say that. I have examined them all in person, but you can buy a complete translation of his notebooks from pretty much any decent bookshop if you have the will and the time to read them. He also wrote in pictograms and puzzles, see?' Vita points to a page that looks like it's made up of hieroglyphs. 'We know he hid layers of information within layers of notes about something else completely. He was very good at keeping secrets.'

A thought occurs to me. I turn to look at her profile – her straight nose and frowning brows – and see her expression alter as she realises what she's just said, biting her lip. She's given away more than she meant to.

'You've been looking for the secret of *La Belle* for a long time, haven't you?' I ask her. 'Why does it matter so much to you?'

The dim lighting in the room throws her face into stark contrast. A worried expression is etched on there, caught between confession and concealment.

'It's hard to explain.' Before she can say more a group of art-school kids comes in, filling the room with noise.

Vita heads out of the gallery, glancing at me over her shoulder and nodding toward the exit. I follow her into the bright hallways, down a sweeping staircase, weaving in and out of people and exhibits, until we step outside in the warm sunshine and central courtyard, a secret oasis garden hidden away in the heart of the huge building.

There's a clear shallow pool in the middle of the square, where little children are slipping off their socks and shoes and running into the water, arms held out stiff to the side, enjoying the shock of the cold.

We take a seat on the steps that surround the pool. Vita removes her shoes and slides her toes into the water. Resting her palms on her knees, she tips her face up to the sun, taking a deep breath.

'There is the long story about me and *La Belle* and the short one,' she says. Turning to me she studies my face for a long time, searching for something she needs to see before she says more. 'One day I will tell you the long one. The short one is that I discovered the story that Leonardo had unwittingly found the secret to eternal life when I was very young, far from the people I loved and thought loved me. There was something about the story that gave me a purpose, something to follow, I suppose, when everything and everyone I had believed in had let me down. It was a story I could never stop telling myself or searching for the truth behind.' She stands up and takes a few steps into the water; ripples circle out from around her ankles as she draws her skirt above her knees. 'My life has been extraordinary in many ways. So much has changed around me and yet I am still that same lost girl. Curiosity saved my sanity then; reading and learning became my home and my guide, revealing my future to me in paragraphs, turning the pages of my life one by one. The more I read, the more I understood. But the Leonardo puzzle is the only one that I have never been able to solve. I have to follow it now though. I don't have a choice.'

It takes me a moment to take in what she's saying. I have a thousand questions that I want to ask her about this, about the extraordinary life she is alluding to, but something in the furrow of her brow tells me that, like when she didn't want to talk about Dominic the previous night, she would not be willing to answer them just yet.

'But how did you discover the secret existed?' I ask.

'Oh,' she looks at me. 'It was a long time ago. I don't recall exactly when or how. Just that once I knew about it, I had to follow it.'

'Wait, you don't remember how you found out about a legend that you are so fascinated by that you got all the Da Vinci portraits *in the world* to London?'

Just then a little girl splashes her feet in the water so hard she soaks through her shorts, much to her delight. Vita laughs as the child stamps and splashes around her and I sit perfectly still trying to take in what she is saying. This can't be real, not even if some- one as brilliant as Vita believes in it. It can't be real, but what does that matter? What can and cannot be? What does that matter to me when in this moment I can feel the beat of my heart and the cold water around my ankles. When I can almost see hope vault- ing overhead in the clear blue sky.

'It's so very hot, isn't it? Are you hot?' Vita says suddenly, a teasing look in her eyes.

'It is a bit warm,' I say, captivated. I watch, unable to move, as with a slow smile of pure mischief she kicks a splash of water over me.

'What the—?' I laugh.

'Come on,' she says, reaching for my hand. 'Come and cool down with me.'

I can sense the other people in the courtyard watching us, two grown adults behaving like children, but all my impressions fade to the sound of the cold water splashing round our ankles and the feel of Vita's hand in mine.

Chapter Twenty-Six

Having got up from the courtyard and strolled from one gallery to another, we eventually stumble out into the bright afternoon, blinking and stretching as if waking from a slumber.

'Well,' I say, measured, 'you have seen Da Vinci's notebooks. I suppose the next thing is to share with you all the research I've done. I have an office full of it at the Collection.'

'Hmm,' Ben squints up at the sky hesitantly.

'I've probably worn you out,' I say. 'I can get us a cab.'

'No, that's not what I mean,' he laughs. 'I just don't want *this* to be over. Can we carry on wandering about London?' he asks. 'I'm having a great day.'

It's hard to know how much longer I can balance on this tightrope. I was lucky today, lucky that Ben got distracted and hadn't followed through on his questions. I am careless around him, dropping fragments of the truth with willing abandon. I must be more careful, with his hopes and with mine.

'What would you like to do next?'

For a moment Ben screws up his face in thought, like a boy considering sweets.

'Oh, I know where I want to go!' But before he can tell me what location has made him so enthusiastic, his phone rings in his pocket.

'Hi, Kits!' he answers, turning slightly away from me. 'What do you mean where have *I* been? Where have *you* been?' His expression is one of distaste. 'OK, enough, I don't need details.' Shaking his head, he shrugs at me. 'Oh, I see. So now he's gone to work suddenly you miss me and worry about it? Got it. Yes, I'm out.' He walks a few paces away from me. 'Yeah, I talked to Mum. Yes. Yes.

Yep. OK. Well, try to remember that you worry about me the next time you go AWOL for hours.' He looks at me, rolling his eyes.

'Anyway, Vita's waiting for me, so... Yes, yes, I really do. I will, I swear. Cool. Laters.'

'Sisters,' he says fondly when he ends the call.

'So where do you want to go?' I smile, steadying my nerve.

He takes a breath, spreading his hands in the air.

'OK, I know this is very naff and exactly the sort of thing a tourist would want to do, but ever since we went to the Last Supper Club, I was thinking I'd love to go to...'

'The Tower,' I finish for him.

'Of London, yes,' he says. 'I want to see the carvings in the Salt Tower; the ones your Last Supper Club uses for their poster.' He notices I don't leap at the idea. 'Is it really that bad an idea?'

Little shadows seem to creep forward from their crevices on the sun-drenched street. I'm shuddering, despite the heat.

'No, not at all. It's been years since I visited. I'd love to go again!' His eyes light up and I push my misgivings away as we take the steps down to the long, cool underpass.

'When I was a little kid,' he tells me as we head towards the tube station, 'I never really wanted to go anywhere. Mum was always taking us places, and we were such gits to her about it. Every weekend, or whenever she had a day off during the holidays, she'd pack us up a lunch, and it would be, "Come on, kids, we're off to see a castle." And we were all, "But we want to watch TV with the curtains closed." I never really thanked her for that, for showing me how much there is out there that is so interesting, even when it was against my will. I've never appreciated that about her until now.'

'You should tell her,' I say. 'My mother was the opposite. She put so much effort into shielding me from the outside world that I was utterly unprepared.'

'For what?' he asks.

'Everything,' I tell him. 'If I had a daughter or a son, I would go out of my way to encourage them to discover anything and everything.'

'And to not put off living life like you can put time on hold – that there's nothing to fear.'

'There are things to fear,' I say.

'There are things to fear,' he repeats. Our eyes meet.

'But fear is one of the things that keeps us alive. Fear is something to be grateful for.'

A Circle Line train grinds slowly into the station and a press of summer travellers edges forward to meet its opening doors. We stand side by side, hands through the wrist straps, simultaneously swaying back and forth.

'There was a time when I was afraid of nothing,' I tell him. 'I took risks, made mistakes, led a chaotic and dangerous life for a while.'

'You led a dangerous life?' Ben asks, looking amused.

'Very.'

'Forgive me for saying this,' he adds, 'but you don't give off a very dangerous vibe with your swishing skirts and bright-green shoes.'

'Never judge a book by its cover,' I say. 'While you were busy inventing your lens, I was busy going out into the world, as far and as wide as I could. That's how I met Dominic. That was when I knew there was plenty to be afraid of; that when you care about something or someone, when you love them with all your heart and soul, you are *always* afraid. That's how you know you are alive.'

Chapter Twenty-Seven

Vita leads me past the tourists, school groups and organised tours with a kind of single-mindedness that is highly efficient but less romantic than I'd hoped for. Stout, moustached Beefeaters fade into a crimson blur as she walks briskly, whizzing past kings' towers, chopping blocks, armouries and treasure rooms, straight to the base of a modern, external metal staircase that leads up to the Salt Tower. I follow her as she trots briskly to the top, stopping abruptly outside the narrow door to the tower, all of London at her back.

'What is it?' I say, almost walking into her. Her scented hair touches my face for a moment.

'Just waiting to have the room to ourselves.' There's a tension running through her that wasn't there before when she glances back at me.

'Are you OK?' I ask her as the last of schoolkids file out, swearing and randomly thumping each other.

'Yes, I'm fine,' she says, although she doesn't sound entirely convinced. 'Well, here we are then.'

We step into the small room, empty for a few precious moments, except for us. I stand in the middle of the circular space, turning a slow 360 degrees as I take it all in. Significant portions of the walls are etched with the remnants of the room's former captives: archaic names, long-ago dates, all executed with precise care and a lingering pathos. Graffiti isn't the right word to describe it – these are *memento mori*, the last wills and testaments of the men who either died in this room or on the scaffold they would have seen being built from their window. These were men who knew death was coming for them one way or another, and who were determined to leave behind one final trace of proof that they had lived. That's a compulsion I understand.

Crouching down, I get my first ever in-person look at the mystical carvings left by Hew Draper, positioned low on the wall, about a foot above the floor.

'I wish they weren't under this plastic,' I say, touching my fingers to the Perspex surface.

'I think too many people wanted to do that.' Vita nods her head at my fingers, as she lowers herself next to me. 'All those fingertips were in danger of wearing it away.'

'Why did he carve it so low, I wonder?' I ask as I examine the extraordinary work, the careful table of astrological symbols, the three-dimensional rendering of the globe that I remember Dev telling me showed that this humble peasant man had cutting-edge knowledge of the science and physics of the time.

'This wasn't just a name or a poem,' Vita says. 'If Hew had been caught carving this he would have been executed on the spot. He used the space behind his bed so that he wouldn't be seen. This is exactly the sort of heresy he was imprisoned for.'

'Sorcery,' I say softly, relishing the drama of the word.

'No, *much* worse than that,' Vita says. 'He was a poor, low-born man who dared to be educated, who dared to be curious. He wanted to improve both his life and the lives of the people he lived with. Despite being no one, he made enough waves to draw notice. He threatened the Establishment because he was the sort of man people listened to, the sort of man who could make others stop and wonder why things were the way they were: why they were hungry, poor and living in filth and fear. The sort of man who could incite a rebellion and almost did.'

'You are an incredible historian,' I say. 'You seem to know everything about everything."

'There are so many old texts in the Collection that haven't been digitised yet. I've just covered Hew. I could spend 100 years in there and still not have done it all. He was a fascinating man.'

'You talk about him as if you were mates,' I say, teasingly.

'Well, that's the thing, isn't it?' she says, looking around the room once more. Outside clouds pass over the sun; the room is suddenly chill and dank. 'All these names belonged to beating hearts once. They were you and me, standing here wondering what tomorrow would bring. I suppose I always think of them as still living somewhere in time.' She shudders. 'Or worse still, trapped in moments of torture and torment.'

'It's hard to think of it as real,' I say, looking out of the tower door across the neatly manicured lawns, the quiet murmur of tourists in bright summer clothes strewn among the ancient walls like confetti. 'All the murder and the torture.'

'Oh, it was real,' she says, her expression drawn and taut. 'When they brought Anne Askey here in 1546 they threatened her with the rack to convince her to renounce her Protestant faith and give away any other outspoken women she was colluding with. Anne refused, so they racked her, slowly, over and over again. They brought in her maid as witness, in the hope that it would force her to betray her mistress, her friend. Anne was so brave, single-minded and determined. Far too clever for the men who feared her to allow her to live. Anne endured all of that and never revealed a single name. They burnt her alive a month later; she was 25 years old.'

A slow, single teardrop tracks down her cheek.

'Are you sure you are alright?' I ask her, rather bemused.

'I'm OK,' she says, wiping it away. 'I suppose I feel it more than a lot of people because I think about it more than most.'

'Think about what?' I ask her.

'The brevity of time between Anne's death, her screams echoing off the walls, and us standing here now. The chain of lives between then and now is so much shorter than you think it is. Anne is almost within touching distance.'

The wind drops suddenly, and for a second it seems we are alone in this great creature of stone, as if we have stepped out of time and the world is standing still just for us. A shiver runs down my spine as a plaintive cry splits the air and a seabird wheels overhead, diving for something the ravens have left behind.

Our eyes meet, then Vita laughs, zooming us back into the noise and bustle. The moment passes, but I feel it still – all of those who have passed standing at my shoulder, watching what I will do next. I will be one of them soon.

'You've just blown my mind,' I tell her, and she punches me lightly on the arm.

'Let's get out of here,' she says. 'It's too full of sadness. The air is thick with it.'

Once we are on the battlements, the breeze makes everything fresh and light again. 'So, can we have a look around?' I ask. 'The entry ticket cost me an arm and a leg – for that price ideally I'd like to stay here about a month!'

'Sorry.' Her expression is rueful. 'I did kind of rush us, didn't I?'

'Is it because of what you said in there, about the sadness? Are you psychic or something? Can you see dead people?'

'No,' she laughs. 'No, I can't see dead people. I look around here and I see all the living people who have passed through these gates. Or at least I remember them. A lot of history is concen-trated within these walls. So many people to remember.'

She's full of sorrow, I realise with surprise. She really does remember these people, more than she mourns them. She opens her heart to everything that has ever been and feels it all.

'Will you remember me, one day?' I ask her suddenly, daring to catch her hand and bring it to my chest. Her smile fades; her other hand gently touches my cheek.

'I will,' she says.

Chapter Twenty-Eight

I can't pretend I'm not glad to be outside the walls of the tower, out in the bustle and tumble of summer in the city again, where the long afternoon shadows of best-forgotten memories can't reach. We walk down to the river and look at London's skyline, sweeping outward in every direction, dotted here and there with cranes that punctuate the clear blue sky. This city will always be in an endless cycle of decay and renewal. Things fall apart and other things are born. And I might be around to see it for ever.

'Do you think Hew knew the secrets to eternal life?' Ben asks absently.

I look out at the river, wide and muscular. Early afternoon light glitters off the skyscrapers, while the older buildings sun themselves in the day's golden glow.

'I think he *almost* knew,' I say. 'I think he *almost* understood the whole of the universe, perhaps even glimpsed it a little and maybe even stumbled on something. There have been men and women throughout history who had this ability to conceive a whole that is much, much greater than the sum of all our parts, even if it was just for a moment before it escaped them again. We have a far greater understanding of the nuts and bolts of the universe now than we have ever had, but so much less intuition – or at least we've lost the ability to tune in to it. Imagine if modern man had the same willingness to embrace the unknown as their predecessors. What miracles might we find?'

'If I had more time,' Ben says, 'I'd try and find out everything. Last night, after we said goodbye, I couldn't sleep so I read up on the alchemists, who they were and what their methods were. They were pretty hardcore.'

'And women,' I remind him. 'You only ever hear about the men.'

'Bloody men,' Ben says with a wry smile.

'History forgets about Hypatia of Egypt, Christina of Sweden, Sophie Brahe, Isabella Cortese... Now she was an interesting woman, my favourite alchemist.'

'I admit I have never heard of her,' Ben says.'

'She was a sixteenth-century alchemist. She travelled the world in search of the philosopher's stone and thought most of the male alchemists were idiots and a waste of her time and money. She wrote *Isabella Cortese's Book of Secrets*. Collected all sort of arte-facts and documents in her search for the secret, but no one knows what happened to them.'

That's not entirely true. *I* know what happened to them.

There's something tugging at the corner of my mind: a thought that is just out of focus. I stare at the river for a moment, waiting for it settle like a butterfly deciding on a flower.

'Leonardo designed the portrait, so if he did indeed use it to test some theories of alchemy then he would have hidden them in the painting in the way that he did with *everything* interesting and mysterious to him. So, it has to be there, the answer *has* to be there somewhere. I've looked at it a thousand times through the eyes of an alchemist and an art historian and I can't find it.'

There's a thought that is hovering just out of my reach, but it refuses to form. 'I know everything there is to know about Da Vinci and alchemy – everything – but I know there is something I am not seeing, there has to be.'

'Could it be...' Ben begins hesitantly, 'that there is nothing there? I mean, wasn't this a court portrait? His bread-and-butter work, not the mystic stuff?'

Chewing on my lip I wonder if now is the moment to tell Ben that if I was anyone other than who I am, I would think he was right. But the fear that knots in my stomach tells me no.

'If it wasn't for the legend,' I tell him, 'you would be right. But the legend persists around that one court painting, quietly, obscurely. No one has written a blockbuster novel based on it and certainly most art historians would never acknowledge it as anything more than a fairy tale, but it persists in a way that rumours without a grain of truth in them just... don't.'

'Maybe it's like when I'm working on a project,' Ben says. 'When I was developing my lens there would be times when I would just hit a brick wall, when I could only see the problem and no solutions. The answer for me was to step back and get a set of fresh eyes on it. Why don't you talk me through it, the symbolism and techniques and everything else, like you are explaining it for the first time. Maybe I will see something you haven't seen before?'

I nod thoughtfully.

'The reason why most sensible academics dismiss the legend as pure fiction is because when Da Vinci *intends* mystery, it infuses the work,' I say. 'Think of *The Last Supper*, the *Mona Lisa* or *Salvator Mundi*: the three inclusions in the crystal globe that Christ is holding mirror the constellation of Orion exactly. He's saying, "Here is a riddle for you to solve," or "Here is an enigma for you to contemplate. Contemplate existence and your place within it." But there is none of that in *La Belle*, just the usual run-of-the-mill symbolism in her clothes and jewellery; so little, in fact, that no one can even be sure who she was.' An anonymity I have been ever grateful for – perhaps he intended that too. 'You could be right. I need your fresh eyes. If we go back to other alchemists and early scientists, to their work and artefacts, we might find something that will give us some inspiration at least.'

'What about Newton?' Ben suggests. 'I read last night that he was researching alchemy for a while too.'

'Not to blow my own trumpet, but I am confident there isn't anyone alive who knows Newton as well as I do,' I say honestly. 'But I can think of another famous alchemist who has always been quite hard to pin down, and whose most magical things we could go and see at the British Museum right now if we grab a cab.'

'Great,' Ben smiles. 'What are we going to see?'

'Dr John Dee's obsidian scrying mirror,' I say. 'If we hurry we might have about an hour before closing.'

'Brilliant,' he says happily.

Stepping on to the kerb I flag down a cab.

'I did read about one woman alchemist last night,' he says as we climb into the cab. 'Mary Herbert, also a member of Elizabeth I's court.'

'Well played, Ben Church,' I say. 'Very well played.'

★★★

'The speculum,' I say as we stand before the cabinet containing Dr John Dee's scrying equipment.

'A mirror used for seeing beyond normal realms,' Ben says, reading the description that accompanies the item.

We stand side by side looking at the small obsidian mirror about 15 centimetres across, sitting meekly in the glass cabinet alongside a collection of wax seals Dee used to secure his scrying table, where he placed the mirror to try and divine the future, a gold amulet and a small crystal ball. The mirror gleams darkly at us, looking oddly out of place among the objects that surround it.

'He really hoped he could discover the true fabric of the universe through this mirror and his crystals,' I say. 'That mirror was used by the Aztecs first. You wonder why he thought it would show him angels when it had been used by them as a portal to contact the dead. He really did believe that science would make it possible to talk to angels.' I glance up at Ben. 'He needed to believe it. Hope is a kind of madness, I think. It's a discovery engine.'

Ben leans forward, his forehead almost touching the glass as he gazes at the object, and I see in him the expression that I have seen in a thousand faces I have known. The look that hopes for the impossible and fears the truth.

'Just to prevail in this unknowable universe in which we improbably exist, we have to be a little mad to survive. To think past our own lives and deaths and try to reach into the unknown, we have to be full of hope. That's what Dee tried to do, and Leonardo, with varying degrees of success. To Dee there was no difference between the study of mathematics and the study of the spiritual realm. They were both sciences to be advanced.'

'Well, when I began this trip, I promised myself I'd find adventure, so why not ask the mirror like Dee would? Do you know how to scry? Can you peer into the mirror and ask an angel for a bit of advice?'

'No, I tried scrying, but don't have the talent for it,' I say, glancing sideways at him. Ben on the other hand has the need to believe. 'How about you try? Peer into the mirror and see what it shows you.'

Ben seems to think about it for a moment, and then nudging me gently aside, stands before the mirror and gazes intently into the reflective black surface. I watch him covertly: the frown of concentration that gathers his eyebrows, the slight twist of his mouth, how his long fingers rest against the glass as if bracing himself for discovery. Several seconds pass by and then his expression alters. His eyes widen, his face drawn closer to the glass, transfixed, his lips pursed. I see something in his expression that might be joy or grief, but both so closely aligned that I cannot tell which. Then in an instant he stands up abruptly, rubbing the back of his hand across his eyes, and steps back, turning to me.

'Nothing,' he says, taking a step back. 'Didn't see anything.'

'You seemed out of it there for a bit,' I say. 'Are you OK?'

'Did I?' he swallows. 'I might have had a small seizure – a petit mal, they call it.' He taps his forehead. 'It means my friend up here is on the move.'

'Oh god, Ben,' I say taking his hand before I can stop myself. 'What should we do? Should we go to a hospital?'

'No, it's fine,' he says. 'It has happened a few times over the last couple of months and I'm still here. No need to panic. Besides, I seem to have come to with a mystical-enlightenment-adjacent thought.'

'Go on,' I say, not so able to brush off the residual weight of the seizure as he is. I do my best to match his optimism. 'After all, where does inspiration come from if not from the gods?'

'You said at the Tower that you've looked and looked at the portrait and you don't see anything.'

'And?' I ask him.

'Well, this might be stupid, but it's the background behind *La Belle*, which is filled with unknowable depths that shift and change depending on your perspective and the light. It *could* be described as rather similar to obsidian. Maybe the answer isn't what is there in the painting. Maybe it's in what isn't?'

I look at him for several long seconds.

'I think you might just be on to something,' I say. 'You have given me idea.'

Chapter Twenty-Nine

'What now?' she asks as we walk out on to Great Russell Street. The air seems full of static and the world seems to glow and shine, but part of me has stayed behind in the museum, standing in front of that dull dark object I peered into, where I saw everything I'd ever wanted.

At first there had been only the quiet hum of the museum lighting, and the ever-electric thrill of being by Vita's side. I had stared past the glass of the display case until it felt as if it were just me and the scrying mirror. Then the shadows shifted and the room, Vita, time seemed to fall away. I saw myself, not now but years from now, staring back at me. Hair receded and grey; lines ingrained deeply around my eyes and mouth. My own blue eyes gazed back at me from this life-altered version of my face and I saw contentment there. I saw love and peace and a world where I had grown old in my own time and found for myself that the beauty of life is life itself.

When the present came snapping back it knocked the breath out of me. I made up the excuse of the petit mal and then regretted it when I saw the look of worry on Vita's face.

In every minute since then I can't help wondering if I looked into John Dee's mirror and saw the future. A version of time where I survive. No matter how I try, I can't exorcise this sudden certainty that somehow everything is all going to be OK.

'I don't think you have eaten properly all day,' Vita says, interrupting my reverie. 'Have dinner with me.'

'I'd love to,' I reply.

Within a few minutes we are sitting at a corner table in a restaurant that feels as if we have stepped back into the 1970s.

Thick stucco plaster covers walls that are set with faux beams and a variety of dust-dulled plastic greenery trails from above, drooping just a few inches over our heads. And yet the food is delicious – simple and fresh – and the wine she orders is smooth and soft.

'Thank you for today,' she says, looking at me over an old-school red candle jammed into a bottle, with remnants of candles past covering the glass in thick, waxy trails. 'For listening to me going on about all my geeky side interests.' Two miniature versions of the flame leap and flicker in her eyes and I am there too, reflected in the midnight pools of her irises. She continues. 'It's been a while since I've had this much fun.'

'I've enjoyed every moment,' I say. 'I haven't had this much fun in ages.'

'Shut up,' she laughs, conspicuously loud, so that other diners turn around to stare at her. 'You must have had more fun days than just trailing around London with me talking history at you.'

'Can't think of one off-hand,' I say, with a shrug. 'I've been focused on work for most of my adult life. I always wanted my own business, and I wanted to make things and invent things. And you can really do that and have a ton of fun at the same time, which makes me sound really sad. But the truly sad thing is that I actually enjoy what I do. Would I have done things differently, if I'd known I had a deadline? Yes, I suppose I would have liked to have travelled more, stayed up late at the weekend, tried an assortment of illegal substances, that sort of thing.'

'And what about... you know, girlfriends, boyfriends, whatever?' she asks, stirring a glass of iced water with her straw.

'There have been a few,' I say awkwardly. 'I mean literally a few. I am a very boring man to go out with. I don't get romance, or romantic gestures. I don't mind if I go out or stay in and there's never been anyone who...' I look at her and find the words sticking in my suddenly dry mouth, 'I have fallen in love with.'

'What about your first kiss?' she asks with a mischievous grin.

'No.' I cringe. 'Oh, god, it was mortifyingly terrible. I try never to think of it.'

'Career achievement?' she asks.

'Well, I'm patenting my lens system. I would love to see that come through and for it to start making some money, if not for me, for Mum and Kitty,' I say. 'It is nice that I'm genuinely interested in the work I do, and that my clients appreciate it, but being an optical engineer isn't the *most* exciting career. I don't go around trying to prove centuries-old mysteries every day, for one.'

'There must be one day you've had that has been a supremely happy day for you,' Vita says.

'Not a specific day,' I say eventually, 'but a collection of days with Mum and Kitty. My dad left us when we were little. I guess it was hard for Mum, but she protected us from it all as much as she could. Those were happy years – I realise that now, even if it didn't always seem it at the time. We were a tight little unit, always allowed to be exactly who we wanted to be, whatever that was that week. If I try to think of just one day I get a collection: dark evenings sitting around the dining table painting together, or long summer picnics or days at the beach. If you zoomed up into space and looked back at my life through a powerful telescope, those would be the days that shine the brightest.'

Vita says nothing, just watches me over the dancing flame.

'Did I bring the mood down?' I ask her.

'Not at all,' she says gently. 'I would have loved to have had that kind of family life.'

'I know it's hard to imagine, having lost Dominic,' I say carefully, 'but you are still so young. You might fall in love again one day and have a family.'

She sits back abruptly, her face falling into shadow. 'I can't have children,' she says at length.

'Oh, Vita.' I am mortified, dropping my head. 'I'm so sorry, I didn't mean to be so thoughtless.'

'It's OK. I'm at peace with it now,' Vita replies. 'There are hours when I long for that feeling again, the weight of my own child, safe against my heart. But it wasn't meant to be.'

'Again?' I ask her.

'I lost a son,' she says, her eyes downcast. 'I miss him.'

Slowly I slide the palm of my hand across the table towards where hers is resting. Her hand moves towards mine until our fingertips touch. Our eyes meet. We exchange a look of solidarity and sympathy.

'Now I've brought the mood down,' she says at length, glancing back up at me with a look that punches me hard in the chest.

'You know what?' I tell her with a carefully constructed shrug. 'It makes a nice change not to be the most tragic one in the room.'

Her mouth twitches into a smile.

I raise my glass, she follows suit. We look at one another across the candlelight. I could spend an age dwelling on the starlit depths of her gaze.

'You told me to stick a pin in perfect moments,' I say. 'Sitting here looking at you is one of them.'

Her gaze drops, a blush spreads across her nose and before I know it she is busy searching in her purse for her card.

'I didn't mean to make you feel uncomfortable,' I say hurriedly.

'You didn't,' she says, the fall of her hair and the sweep of her lashes obscuring her expression. 'I'm just not used to feeling this way.'

After we've paid, splitting it exactly down the middle as Vita insisted, we wander into Bleeding Heart Yard, dawdling our way towards Great Russell Street. The evening is warm, there's music drifting out of some high, open window. The air smells of trees and traffic.

'You know there's a great story behind Bleeding Heart Yard that my elderly neighbour Mariah loves me to tell her when she can't sleep,' Vita tells me as we come to a stop at the corner.

'You tell your neighbour bedtime stories?' Ben asks.

'I've known her for a long time,' I explain. 'I take care of her and she takes care of me. Mariah is my family.'

'That's really lovely,' I say. 'Tell me the story.'

'Well,' she smiles in anticipation of the pleasure of telling a good tale, 'legend has it that during a great and glamorous ball at Hatton House, the young and beautiful Lady Hatton made such an impact on the gentlemen that they were queuing for the chance to dance with her.'

'Been there,' I say. 'Women flock to me wherever I go.'

'But then into the room walked a devilishly handsome young man dressed all in black. He cut to the front of the queue, took Lady Hatton from her partner and danced with her for the rest of the night, eventually dancing her out into the garden. Well, the gossipmongers were on fire that evening. What had she got up to? Where had she gone? Her reputation would be in tatters, her character ruined!'

'And was it?' I ask, loving how her eyes light up as she recounts a story, always telling it as if recalling a memory.

'No, in a funny sort of way it was made,' Vita says, 'because the next morning Lady Hatton was found behind the stable block with her torso ripped open, her limbs torn from her body, but her heart still pumping out blood. They say she had been dancing with the devil himself.'

'Awesome,' I say, chills running down my spine. 'Is it true? I mean, that she was murdered?'

'Well, all the history books will tell you that it isn't true, and that she died many years later of natural causes in her bed,' Vita tells me. 'But don't you think it's a little strange that a London street name sprang out of something that *didn't* happen?'

'Yeah,' I say. 'Next they'll be trying to tell us that lambs didn't go down Lamb's Conduit Street.'

It feels like our laughter lasts until we are at the very moment of saying goodbye once again.

'So, I'd better actually go to work tomorrow,' Vita says. 'But if you would like you could visit me at lunchtime? I thought we could talk to our conservator – he knows so much about the chemistry of Renaissance art. Your comment about how the background of *La Belle* is a little like an obsidian mirror made me think about it. Maybe the secret isn't in the portrait of her, herself, but what she is made of.'

'Good idea,' I say, happy that we have a plan to meet. 'So, I'll see you tomorrow, about noon, OK?'

'Yes,' she says. 'About noon is perfect.'

The hour when I will see her again has a name.

★★★

'It's me,' I call to Kitty as I stroll back to the hotel. 'I'm on my way back. How are you?'

'I feel like a bad sister. I'm supposed to be looking after you but you have escaped my clutches. Are you OK?'

'Yeah, I'm good. And you are not a bad sister, you are a good sister. I'll be there soon. Want to watch a movie?'

'Yes, I do, and I want to order room service and stay up late overanalysing the text that Dev has sent me. I can't decide if it means he likes me or hates me.'

'What does it say?'

'Smiley face, smiley face,' Kitty says.

'I think it means he likes you,' I reply.

'OK. If you pass a shop, pick up chocolate and gin. Knock for me when you're back. And I'm going to want to hear all about what you've been up to today, even the boring bits.'

'OK then. Back in ten,' I tell her.

The night is warm, the buildings shine in the streetlights, the moon sails high over the rooftops and that unfamiliar feeling I have that makes every step seem so effortless is optimism. I don't know how much more of a future I have, but I feel like however long it is, it's going to be good.

Chapter Thirty

'Leonardo was different from many of his counterparts in that for him it wasn't really about colour but effect,' Fabrizio tells us as we sit at his tall table in his restoration room. The lighting and temperature of the room is carefully controlled, but Fabrizio has somehow made it seem as if we are sitting in his sun-drenched living room. Verdant plants trail from every available surface, he has an old and almost threadbare rug on the marble tiles, and in one corner an over-stuffed armchair, its broad arms piled with books. To one side of the door there is a dark-wood Edwardian hatstand on which hangs a battered top hat and a green velvet cap. And standing on every available surface are photographs of his wife and children.

'For certain, there are some rules he follows: a lasting true blue was made from lapis lazuli imported at great expense from Afghanistan, and as a result very rare. Because of that it was reserved for the Virgin. Red was created from beetle shells – very labour-intensive and expensive. As blue symbolised peace and serenity, so red symbolised vitality and power, and you will find it used in portraits depicting royalty or aristocracy.'

'What about the gold ribbons securing her dress?' Ben asks as I sit back on my stool holding my coffee. His face is alive with interest, his eyes bright with enthusiasm. 'What does gold mean?'

'In churches you would find a great deal of gold or silver leaf, because these were the sacred spaces where the finest materials were used. Gazing upon a work of art, from being on your knees in a candlelit church, with the light moving across the metallic surfaces created, was meant to be an intensely profound experience – art resurrecting Christ, if you will. But in this portrait

Da Vinci has created the *illusion* of gold, as there is no actual gold in this painting. He dismissed the work of the alchemists, yet he was a master at turning base materials into gold, was he not?'

'Wait, *La Belle* is wearing red,' Ben says. 'What does that mean? Could that mean that she herself is a symbol of vitality, or immortality?'

Here is where many historians would mock or dismiss the same question, but not Fabrizio.

'Most likely it means she belonged to a very wealthy and powerful man,' he says, clearly delighted at Ben's interest. 'A beautiful mistress was a status symbol, just as a Porsche or a Ferrari might be today. A large amount of an expensive pigment in a painting showed a man of great wealth, as we know the Duke of Milan was at the time this portrait was thought to have been painted.'

Fabrizio thinks for a moment as he looks at the image of the portrait. 'Having said that, it would not be unlike Leonardo to add his own meaning to the pigments he uses. He was a man who required some personal connection to everything he did, and there is something rather irregular about his choice of pigments in this painting.'

'Is there?' I ask him, wondering what there could possibly be about this work of art that I don't already know.

'It is perhaps nothing,' Fabrizio says. 'Vita, you will know that in the 1930s another version of *La Belle* came to light in New York. The owners, the Hahns, tried to sell it as a genuine Da Vinci, and went so far as to say that the version in the Louvre was a fake. The whole thing ended up in a month-long trial of the authenticity of each painting.'

'Are you saying this portrait isn't by Leonardo at all?' Ben says, eyes wide.

'Oh no, it most certainly is, and perhaps even both of them are. However, some interesting facts came to light in that trial, discoveries that were cutting-edge at the time. Principally that the Hahn version is painted with all the most expensive pigments, ones you'd expect to see in a work by Da Vinci, commissioned by the Duke of Milan. However, the Louvre one is not. It's painted in much cheaper, readily available, natural-earth tones and pigments, and the red in particular is... *elusive*. As to why *La Belle* doesn't contain the pigments that we'd expect, I don't know. But perhaps it has something to do with your myth – perhaps he was using materials ascribed to by the alchemists. I couldn't really say.'

'But it's possible,' Ben says, leaping to his feet.

'Anything is possible,' Fabrizio says. 'Only those who were there in the studio with him would know the truth for certain.'

★★★

'So, what next?' Ben asks as I walk him to the foyer.

'I need to review all the pigmentation research,' I say. 'I hadn't factored in the findings from the Hahn trial, because they have been updated with better technology since that first examination, but sometimes our predecessors notice things that we might miss. It's worth looking over.'

'You know if I could get my tech in front of the painting it would answer all of your questions,' Ben says. 'Do you think it could be possible?'

'I'm trying to work out how,' I tell him. 'I've not quite figured it out yet.'

★★★

Kitty is waiting for Ben in the foyer, kicking her toes against the tiles, her hands in her pockets.

'You didn't fancy a look round while you were waiting?' Ben asks her.

'Nope,' she says. 'Lot of old tat that belonged to dead people isn't really my bag.'

'I'm sorry. My sister is a philistine,' Ben says.

'It's probably much wiser to live your life in the present than in the past.' I smile at Kitty, who returns it with a shrug.

'Anyway,' she tells Ben, 'Dev's asked me to go to this party he's going to tonight. Turns out his cousin is like proper rich and getting engaged. And part of me is like, I've known you 20 minutes, love. It's a bit soon to be meeting in-laws. And part of me is, a Roaring-Twenties fancy-dress party at the actual Ritz? Yes, please! Obviously I said I couldn't come because I'm in London with my brother and I can't just abandon him, and he said why don't you ask Ben to come too? So I thought that maybe even though you don't traditionally like parties, we could go this once? For 10 minutes?'

'You go and have fun,' Ben says. 'I don't think I fancy being a gooseberry to you and Dev.' He glances at me. 'Unless you would like to come too, Vita?'

'I won't enjoy it without you,' Kitty says, putting her arm around his shoulders. 'I just thought maybe a really fancy party was sort of the order of the day? I mean when was the last time you went to a *really* fancy party? You didn't even go to your own prom.'

'But I'm not in an American high-school coming-of-age movie, so I don't really care,' Ben says. 'I'll go if Vita goes,' he says looking at me. I feel my insides churn at the very thought.

'I don't know,' I say. 'Parties aren't really my thing these days.' I can't help looking up at my portrait at the top of the stairs, thinking back to Madame Bianchi, the woman who lived my most hedonistic life to date. Now *she* would never have turned down an invitation. I can barely remember what it was like to be her any more. 'But I do have wardrobes full of vintage clothes. If you like, Kitty, I could bring some to the hotel for you after work?'

'Really?' Kitty says, her eyes widening. 'That would be amazing. Thank you, Vita.'

'I can't help with boys' clothes,' I tell Ben, 'but I think a standard dinner jacket will be easy enough to find.'

'Please come too, Vita,' Kitty says. 'for just long enough that I can get through the door and then decide if I've made a terrible mistake. Ben really needs someone he doesn't have to make small talk with and I feel like you two don't have that problem.' Ben flushes slightly at this. 'And believe it or not, he does scrub up pretty well.'

There are a lot of reasons why I would like to say no. A room full of strangers and noise are a few. But the reasons I should say no are the same as why I want to say yes. The idea of dressing up and spending time with Ben, without any talk of paintings or miracles, and perhaps even dancing, is one that appeals a little too much. Maybe there is a little of Madame Bianchi left, even now.

And yet, the longer I spend with Ben without telling him who I am, the more dangerous it could become.

'I shouldn't...' I begin.

'Come on. Live a little,' Ben says with a gentle smile, and all my fragile resistance melts away.

'It has been a long time since I've worn feathers in my hair,' I say.

'Yes!' Kitty gives a little hop, clapping her hands together. 'What kind of dresses do you have? Just because I'm weirdly really into this nerdy guy I just met and I'm worried about looking frumpy.'

'Don't worry,' I tell her. 'There was no such thing as frumpy in the 1920s.'

Chapter Thirty-One

Vita arrives at my hotel room with an armful of dresses which she drops on to the bed in a cascade of colour and slippery, sparkling material. There's a strange intimacy to her being in my bedroom. I know logically that it should have nothing to do with an item of furniture, and yet I feel as nervous as a kid.

'Wow,' Kitty says as she comes out of the bathroom to the rainbow of fabrics on the bed. 'Why do you have so many vintage party dresses?'

'Long story, but I inherited them in a way. They were in the house when I moved in,' Vita says. 'Everything that belonged to my great-aunt was still there and it felt wrong to get rid of it.' Vita fingers the hem of a soft, leaf-green dress. 'I think some of these might belong in a museum.'

'They are amazing!' Kitty says, with delight. 'Which one though?'

'You would look wonderful in this, Kitty, don't you think?' She lifts up an intricately beaded, sky-blue dress that matches the colour of my sister's eyes. Kitty greets the dress with an excited handclap and giggle, her deeply hidden girly side bubbling up with undisguised glee. I suddenly feel glad I agreed to go to the party.

'I love it!' Kitty says, taking the dress and holding it up against her.

'I have these too.' Vita empties a carrier bag of shoes on to the floor. 'They are all size 6.'

'I'm a size 6,' Kitty says happily, pulling out a pair of silver shoes. 'This is like Christmas. I'm going next door to get ready. Knock for me when you two are done doing whatever is it you do.'

'Oh,' I say as Kitty flies out of the room, shooting me a theatrical wink on her way out. Vita is standing there in her brown-checked trousers and cream top, the wave of her hair collapsing over one shoulder. 'I sort of thought she'd take you with her to get changed and do make-up, what with you both being – you know – *women*.'

'I think perhaps your sister is doing a not-so-subtle spot of match-making,' Vita says with a smile.

I have no idea what to say or where to look. The idea that I am a self-possessed, articulate grown man vanishes into thin air.

'I like that about Kitty,' Vita says into the silence. 'She loves you a lot.'

'And I love her,' I admit, the force of the feeling behind the word catching in my throat, remembering that one day there won't be a me and Kitty. There won't be me and Vita... or even just a me. Is that a reason to act on the way Vita makes me feel, or a reason not to?

Vita glances down at the dresses, frowning. 'Maybe I shouldn't be getting in the middle of you two. I could still just go home and leave you to it.'

'Please don't,' I say at once, taking a step towards her and then checking myself. 'I would really like to go to a party with you looking as beautiful as you do.'

'I haven't even put on a gown yet!' she says.

'You don't have to, you still light up the room,' I tell her. 'And I know that is the cheesiest thing a man has ever said to a woman, but it's all I've got right now. Please come, Vita. I didn't get to go to my prom, after all.'

'I thought you said you didn't care?' Vita smiles.

'I'm just going all out with the emotional blackmail in the hope that I can persuade you to stay,' I admit. 'I'm not very good at it.'

'I'll stay,' she says, touching her fingertips to my cheek. It's the briefest of touches, over in less than a second, but it sends a jolt through me that takes my breath away.

'I tell you what,' I say, thinking that some space and a closed door between us would be sensible right now. 'You take the bathroom. It's one of those huge fancy ones, with light-up mirrors and stuff. I've just got to get my suit on, clip on a bow tie and that. I'll watch TV while you get dressed.'

'Which one?' she asks, looking at the dresses. It gives me an excuse to look at her; to think about the way her dark hair frames her ivory complexion; how her eyes seem to contain the whole of the universe; that her curves seem to flow like the bend of a river from her breasts to her hips. Looking at the jumble of colours, I think of *La Belle*.

'I don't know anything about fashion,' I say, 'but maybe this one?' I hold up a burnt-orange number from the pile, crushed velvet fringed with rows and rows of dark, ruby-red beads.

'I think I agree,' she says, picking up the shiny dress, holding it against her body. 'I'll grab some accessories and go for this. Thanks, Ben.'

'Thank *you*,' I say, waiting until she closes the door before taking two pre-mixed gin-and-tonics out of the minibar and downing them in quick succession.

★★★

I think I've said about three words since we left the hotel, which is OK as it happens, because Kitty is talking for all four of us. My sister looks great, with a big feather in her hair and eye make-up like those women from silent movies. I could see how taken Dev was with her when we came out of the lift. His eyes lit up at the sight of her, and I have to say he didn't look half bad himself in his tuxedo. He greeted Vita with a hug and he and Kitty held hands like they had always been lovers.

The party is in a beautiful art-deco ballroom: black, white and gold from top to bottom, with balloons and streamers. Tall palms screen off tables set around a polished dance floor, lit from above by a glittering chandelier. On the stage a jazz band plays retro-arranged pop tunes as waiters in tails deliver cocktails and tiny bits of delicious food on silver trays.

I was doing quite well pretending I didn't find Vita so devastatingly attractive all the way up until tonight, but now all hope is lost. I mean, I always thought she was beautiful – it's not as if I didn't notice how great she looked in her summer dresses and baggy trousers, a pencil in her hair. But tonight her dress reveals the perfect curve of her back all the way down, and I feel like a mortal man in the presence of a goddess.

While Kitty and Dev dance to the jazz band playing covers of chart-topping tunes, she and I stand either side of a large potted palm, like a couple of wallflowers. Except that men in the room keep looking at her, and I am certain one of them will ask her to dance sooner or later. I want to ask her to dance, but even now with nothing to lose, I can't seem to find the words.

'We aren't doing very well, are we?' Vita moves a palm frond out of the way, and bends towards me, speaking in my ear. 'At being at a party, I mean.'

'You are,' I say, trying very hard not to show how flustered I feel when I look into her eyes. 'You look amazing, Vita. Like the whole world should fall at your feet. You should go out there and mingle.'

'I'd honestly rather poke my eyes out with rusty nails,' she says with a smile. 'And thank you, Ben. You look very handsome too.'

Turning, I look into her eyes to see if she is teasing me. I don't think she is. I'm not sure if this is a good or bad thing for my over-all plan not to fall in love with her, but I suspect it's somehow both of those things at the same time.

'I'm not anything special,' I say bashfully. 'I'm weird-looking.'

'You don't really think that, do you?' Her gaze searches my face. 'When I look at you, I think of a dancer: the way you move and talk is so eloquent, so expressive and full of feeling. You...' She turns her head away for a moment, affording me a view of her shoulder and neck. 'You are...' she clears her throat awkwardly, 'physically compelling.'

'Well, thanks.' I blush, realising how our conversation has drawn our heads close to one another. 'You're not so bad yourself.'

'Thank you.' She smiles.

'When I say "not so bad", I mean that I think you're beauti-ful, inside and out,' I add. Her eyes rise to meet mine, and I pick up her hand, bringing it gently to where my heart beats fast and furious. Her lips part slightly and I know with sudden, thrilling certainty that we are about to kiss.

That is until my sister decides this is the perfect moment to intervene.

'Come on, you two.' Kitty bounds over. 'Come and dance!'

'Shall we be brave?' Vita asks, holding her hand out to me.

'Do or die, I always say.' I take it and let her lead me on to the dance floor.

A few more martinis and it seems I don't actually care about how my arms flail around like an out-of-control windmill. All I can see is the laughter on my sister's face and the delight on Vita's as she tries to show me and Dev the steps to a Charleston. We are both terrible at it, but giggling, we spin and kick all the same and somehow find a kind of rhythm that works. Lights dance in Vita's eyes, her skin glows rosy and warm, her body tunes into the music with perfect syncopation. For once I feel part of everything: part of this crowd, of this party, of this world. For once I belong exactly where I am.

Then the music slows and the lights dim. Bodies move closer to one another, pairing off. Kitty flings her arms around Dev, and they are lost among each other's tonsils before I can look the other way. I catch Vita's eye, offering a small, questioning shrug. She nods and steps closer to me. Taking one of my hands, she rests it in the curve of her waist, and, wrapping her arm around my neck, takes the other in hers. Before you know it, we are dancing, old-fashioned style.

'What's this, a waltz?' I ask, trying to ignore the sensation of her body so near to mine.

'The technical term is more of a sway,' she replies, her voice low, her lashes lowered. 'You are very good at it though.'

'My speciality, swaying,' I tell her. The music swells, she leans into me. My arms tighten around her waist, her head nuzzles under my chin. Closing my eyes, I dwell on this beautiful moment, the night that I, Ben Church, held Vita Ambrose in my arms and danced with her. Or swayed, anyway.

The song ends and the tempo picks up, not that Kitty and Dev seem to have noticed.

'Ben,' Vita says, her expression suddenly very serious, 'I'm a bit tipsy. But that's not why I'm this…'

'Do you want some air?' I ask her, before she says anything.

'I do,' she nods. Bolts of lightning shoot through me. Arm in arm we walk together outside on to the street, where Piccadilly drapes her sequinned silk shawl around us in an array of sparkle and glamour.

'I want you to know,' Vita says after a moment, 'that I have thought you were marvellous from the first moment we met, and very attractive.'

'Thank you,' I say. Reality comes crushing in with the cool air and I remember.

'I haven't been with anyone, or even been close to anyone since Dominic,' she says. 'And… it's quite nerve-wracking. I feel like an idiot. You probably aren't having any of these feelings at all.'

'I have lots of them,' I say. 'About eight million per second at a rough estimate. But this is complicated. I couldn't stand the thought of causing you hurt.'

I thought being noble would feel better than it does. I have just looked the most beautiful last chance in the face and pushed it away. It hurts, like slowly peeling away a layer of skin.

Vita speaks before I can.

'It wouldn't be sensible,' she agrees, on a sharp inward breath. 'It wouldn't be sensible for you and me to be involved in anything that isn't purely platonic. Not for either of us.'

'Right,' I say, taking a deep gulp of air and a step back from her. 'Good. So, we're agreed. There are feelings here, between us. But that's as far as it goes.'

Vita closes the gap I put between us and takes my hand, bringing it to her lips.

'That's right.' Vita nods in agreement, her eyes searching mine. The city seems to burn with light. Galaxies appear to wheel in her eyes, as in one fell swoop, she topples all our resolutions.

'Or you could walk me home?'

Chapter Thirty-Two

'Or you could walk me home?' I ask him.

Right up until the second I take his hand I mean it as a simple request, to be escorted by a trusted friend late at night. But at the exact moment I make my resolve I toss it away again and lean on him as I take off my high heels to walk on in my stockinged feet.

'What if you tread on some cut glass?' Ben asks me, worried. 'Or a needle?'

'I'll be fine,' I say. As we walk up through Golden Square, I realise I want to invite Ben into my home. I never invite people in, but I want Ben to see it, for him to know more of me in little pieces until he can finally understand the whole picture.

Linking one arm through his, I let my head rest against his shoulder as we stroll side by side, deliciously slowly. The air is kind and mild, the streets busy and bright; I feel *happy*.

It takes a moment to truly understand that, to believe it.

It's been so long since I haven't felt as if every single breath I take is weighted down by lead-like melancholy. This airy sense of joy is heady, intoxicating. In this moment, it is *true*, it is *real*.

'I'm happy,' I tell Ben, turning to look at him. 'I'm really happy right now, with you, walking home through the streets of London. Knowing you these past few days has made me happy, Ben.'

'Me too,' he says. 'You make me feel the same way.'

It seems like the city is pleased for us. Everyone we pass is smiling. Car radios serenade us from open windows, flags flutter in the wind and the warm breeze makes the leaves in the trees twist and turn like confetti.

When at last we enter the densely packed streets of Soho, full of short shorts, sleeveless shirts and late-night shades, I feel a thrill of pleasure at the idea of bringing Ben into my private oasis in all this pulsating intimacy. Laughter peals brightly from busy bars and open windows. The scents of beer and perfume fill the air, mingling with the smell of sweat and sex. The night heats up as the day cools down, and tonight it feels like the streets of London are paved with passion.

We see a couple kissing intensely, leaning hard against a wall, bodies melded together. Another pair of lovers lie entangled on the grass of Soho Square, so lost in one another that the people around them have faded to nothing. They have made their own universe within their embrace. We turn and turn again to find two lovers entwined over an outside café table, hands and fingers in hair, knees interlocked in urgent need to fit into one other.

Tonight it feels like the whole city is in love, or in lust at least. Desire feels palpable in the air, and it's here too in the negative spaces our bodies make, building between us like static. With each touch of my hip against his thigh, every brush of his hand on the small of my back, the charge increases.

At last we plunge into the narrow, dark alley, and emerge into my shady little square, lit by a single Victorian-style streetlight.

'Here we are.' I nod at my narrow house that peers down at us benignly.

'This is like Narnia,' Ben says, looking around him. The sundial catches his eye. 'Wow. Your house is from 1770? And why have you got a sundial here?'

'I suppose when the houses were built it was all the rage,' I say.

'*Hunt the shadows if you will. Here's the place all time stands still.*' He reads the motto carved around the base of the dial, just visible in the lamplight. 'What does it mean?'

'Search me,' I say.

The air seems to thicken as he raises his eyebrows at me.

'I'd never have guessed there'd be two houses tucked away here,' he says, apparently determined to make small talk. 'Which floor do you have?'

'All of them,' I say. 'That's me on the left, and my friend Mariah lives on the right.'

'Vita, are you secretly rich?' Ben laughs with mild surprise.

'I suppose I am a bit,' I say apologetically. 'And it's old money, too. This house has been in my family since it was built.'

'Rich *and* beautiful,' he says. 'I should marry you quick.'

We look at one another; his eyes match the colour of the evening sky and they are filled with stars. My skin tingles to be touched.

I have fallen in love, and there's nothing to be done about it now.

'Will you come in, Ben?' I ask him.

'I want to,' he says. 'But there's a problem.'

'What's that?' I ask.

'The problem is how much I want to touch you.' His voice is very low, almost a whisper. His forehead dips to lightly touch mine. 'How much I want to hold you and kiss you. And that could be a bit awkward, given we decided about half an hour ago not to go there.'

'Only if I didn't want you to do all of those things to me,' I reply on a single breath.

'And where do you stand on that matter?' he asks, his voice tight.

My hands find their way to his face. I feel slight stubble under my palms as I draw him towards me and press my lips against his.

'I am all for it,' I say, skimming my cheek against his.

'What's all this then?' Mariah opens the front door of her house and peers at us. 'Who's this bit of stuff, Evie?'

Ben steps back from me, brushing his hair down, like a kid caught making out behind the bike shed.

'This is my friend Ben,' I tell her, reaching for his hand. 'He's staying over.'

'I don't blame you, my girl,' Mariah says. 'If my Len wasn't a jealous man I'd be all over that myself!'

'Come on now, Mariah.' Marta appears behind her. 'Leave the lovebirds to it.'

Mariah giggles as she closes the door. I press my hand over my smile and look up at Ben.

'That's Mariah,' I say. 'I'm not always certain which decade her mind is in, but I think right then it was all about you.'

'She obviously has excellent taste,' Ben says.

'Come on. I'll make you a drink,' I say, leading him up the steps. He stops suddenly.

'I want to,' he says. 'But Vita, you know this isn't a fling for me. It's only been a few days, but I… I think I could see myself falling in love with you. I think it's only fair that you know.'

For a moment I hesitate. Now is the time to tell him who I really am. But what if all this joy is snuffed out by the truth? What if a moment like this will never be ours again?

'Then I exchange my heart for yours,' I say, reaching for him, pulling his body against mine. I move my hand from his chest to mine, laying my lips lightly against his cheek. 'My skin is singing for you.'

Taking his hand, I lead him into my home.

IV

Soon comes night.

Traditional sundial motto

Chapter Thirty-Three

As soon as Vita closes the door we are draped in cool, balmy shadows that soothe my hot cheeks. Turning to face me, she pushes me against the closed door, her eyes fixed on mine.

'Can I kiss you, please?' she asks. I nod, dumbstruck.

Bracing her hands against the door either side of my head, she stands on her toes to bring her mouth to mine. Her lips are soft and warm and I feel the flutter of her lashes on my cheek, then the length of her soft torso melting into mine; the racing of my heart as my arm wraps around her waist and I pull her as tightly into my body as I can. There is just us, limb against limb, mouth against mouth, like the answer to a prayer.

Vita pulls back a little. A tangle of her hair falls across her forehead.

Her fingers walk down my neck to the top button of my shirt. One after the other she undoes each one, tracing her fingers over my chest as she goes, all the way down to my navel. Stepping back, she unzips her dress, and, pushing the straps off her shoulders, lets it drop to the floor and pool around her ankles. I am looking at a goddess: generous, creamy curves and soft flesh, from her shoulders to her rounded hips and the beautiful billowing white of her thighs. I want to drop at her feet and worship her inch by inch, kiss by kiss.

'Come on.' She takes my hands and I'm dimly aware of the steep, narrow staircase, of walls full of art and old photographs and the scent of dust and old books. Electric lights flicker and flare as we pass under them and she leads me into a large bedroom. A very old-looking mahogany canopy bed stands in the middle of the room, illuminated by the neon lights of Soho.

'Vita,' I whisper, 'you take my breath away.'

Turning her back to me, she stands at the edge of the bed, her dark hair flowing around her like a constantly moving shadow, her hand reaching for me.

Gathering her into my arms, we fall on to the mattress, a mass of kisses and fingertip touches.

'I can't believe I've found you,' I whisper into her hair.

'I can't believe I've been found.' She sighs.

All that follows is bliss.

***

She lies tangled in the sheets, her hair falling across her face, deeply asleep. The Soho lights that are illuminating the room through the open curtains turn her gold, white and pink.

I wish I could sleep now like she does, so heavily and completely. But my head is wide awake and alert. I don't want this day to end.

I get up to fetch myself a glass of water.

Her house is dimly lit. I suspect that it hasn't been rewired since the invention of electricity, but the barely punctuated gloom that gives the shadows free rein suits this house. It suits her, I think. Vita is like an orb of light in the age-old dark too.

A thickly fringed lamp flickers stoically at the top of the steep, narrow staircase – the one I remember climbing earlier in what seems now like an impossible dream. Descending slowly, I take in the various pieces of art and old photographs that line the wall: a sketch of a serious-looking, dark-eyed girl, drawn after the style of Leonardo in red and white chalk; a large, turn-of-the-century photograph of a group of about 20 women in massive round hats and sashes, holding a banner that demands *Votes for Women*. Peering at each one of the grainy faces, I search for traces of Vita, wondering if one of them might be a relative of her or her great-aunt, but time has worn away too much detail of their defiant faces.

Each step down brings someone new to look at. By the time I'm halfway down, it dawns on me that every image is some kind of portrait: some ancient, age-cracked oils of pale faces in lace collars; a pair of miniatures of a couple in powdered wigs and silk; portraits that could date from a variety of times over the last 500 years, including photographs ranging from the earliest kind of daguerreotype.

I'm stopped in my tracks by an image of a dour-looking young woman sitting neatly with her hands folded in her lap, and the most striking pair of luminescent eyes that seem to peer at me in the dark. I stare at her for a long time; she has to be a direct relative of Vita. Her hair is parted in the middle and drawn tightly back in a severe bun, her brows are knitted and her mouth turned down, but if she were to break into a smile at this moment and shake out her hair, she would be the image of the woman asleep upstairs.

I wonder if there is an old photograph somewhere in Mum's boxes of family stuff of someone who looks just like me. I hope that one day in the years to come there may be a future face that echoes mine; a distant grand-nephew or cousin – evidence that once I lived, coded into DNA.

It girls in furs and cloche hats kick up a heel for the camera. An impossibly suave gentleman in a trilby and pinstriped suit poses against a stone pillar. Finally, there's a Polaroid of a dark man in thick glasses, laughing as he raises a glass of wine to whoever held the camera. It's fuzzy and blurred, but judging by his collar I'd guess it was taken in the 1970s. Who is *he* then?

It takes me a moment at the bottom of the stairs to find my way to the oddly shaped kitchen at the back of the house, tiled in a sickly pink with freestanding cupboards that date to around the 1930s, I reckon, based purely on the fact that my great-nan's kitchen looked a bit like this. The fridge and the cooker seem to have been made this century at least, though the former is empty. Sliding open the corrugated glass front door on one cabinet, I smile to see neatly ordered rows of coloured tumblers and old-style champagne glasses. There's a neat row of gold-rimmed shot glasses and some red crystal wineglasses. I choose a blue tumbler and take it to the tap, which labours for a moment before bringing forth water in a juddering spurt.

Below, Soho is about as quiet as it ever gets, the streets all but empty bar a few figures lazily swerving home.

The calm of the city night seems to seep into my bones. I feel it run through my veins, sweetly exhausted and yet fizzing with feeling. For once all the parts of my body and mind feel like one. Each nerve ending is alert to every sensation and I am alive. So, this is what it means to be in love.

Taking my glass of water, I wander through the hall into the sitting room that faces onto the shadowy little square. In the window I see my own reflection looking back at me. We could have been set adrift from the earth. This house could be our ship floating in space, up among the stars.

Vita's sitting room is exactly what I would expect from this time-capsule house. The flick of a light switch splutters an overhead chandelier into life, revealing a room that would have been grand once, but is somehow more beautiful having sunk into decay. A large blue-velvet Victorian sofa squats regally in the bay window, its once opulent covers faded in places by squares of sun. Either side of the floor-to-ceiling mantelpiece are two large cupboards. Each depicts an intricate woodland created from expertly laid wooden veneers and mother-of-pearl. Each has a key in the lock, from which hangs a blue silk tassel. A huge painting of a stormy sea takes up most of the wall opposite the sofa, presiding over two exhausted-looking armchairs. In the middle of the room is a huge chest on which sits the box that Vita took to the Last Supper Club. I'm about to pick it up when I notice a black-and-white photograph on the mantelpiece, framed in a heavy silver frame. It's a wedding photo, a laughing bride, her veil swept sideways by a gust of wind, her new husband holding her hand as if they are both about to make a run for it.

Even though it breaks my heart in a hundred different ways, I can't stop staring at it. Vita as a radiant bride, her hair pinned back from her long neck, her eyes sparkling with joy. Her simple dress ends just below the knee. Dominic, in a casual suit and no tie, a shock of dark hair curling over his forehead, smiles triumphantly. White flashes of confetti rain down on them. It's a moment of perfect happiness. Picking it up, I feel a pang of regret and jealousy, but most of all sadness that Vita lost this love, and that if we become closer, she will lose me too before long.

So I sit down on this big, blue, dusty sofa, and take another look at Vita's mystery device.

And I decide to live every moment from now until then as if it were a lifetime.

Chapter Thirty-Four

I open my eyes to a room bathed in blue light and no Ben. Panic clenches my gut. Sitting up, I shake my hair out of my eyes and look for evidence of him. Relief floods me when I see his shirt on the floor, where it was last night. The door to my bedroom is slightly ajar and there are lights on downstairs. The luminescent green hands of Evelyn's old clock tell me it's just after three in the morning.

Grabbing my dressing gown off the back of the door, I pad down the stairs in search of him. What must he think of this strange museum of mine, all these faces of the long-ago lost and rooms full of artefacts that don't mean anything to anyone living anymore?

There's no original way to say that my heart swells with happiness at the sight of him – it just does. He's kneeling on the floor of the sitting room with that very specific angular grace he has, his torso glowing in front of a fire that's definitely about to burn out. He's sitting in front of my mystery optical device, gazing at it so intently that he doesn't notice me standing there, ogling him.

'Hello,' I say from the doorway after a moment. He looks up at me, starting a little. We smile at one another.

'I thought for a minute that maybe you'd gone back to the hotel,' I say, coming to sit behind him on the sofa. 'I'm glad you haven't.'

'I thought I'd let you sleep for a bit,' he says, turning to kneel before me.

'Thank you,' I say. I want to say so much more. I want to grab his face in my hands and kiss him until he sinks back on to the floor and we are lost in each other again, but I feel suddenly shy.

'Vita,' he says, 'last night…'

'It's not dawn yet,' I say, looking out of the dark window.

'Tonight then, it was… you are…' He falters.

'Finish that sentence, please,' I say. 'My heart can only take so much suspense.'

'I am ridiculously in love with you,' Ben says, taking my hands. 'All the way, deeply, truly, madly in love with you – that project *Just Good Friends* is irretrievable. I know it's too soon to say those words. You don't have to do or say anything about them, but I have to tell you the truth. I know it's complicated.'

'It's not complicated,' I say. 'It's the opposite; I am in love with you too.'

'Really?' he asks hesitantly. 'Even though I might be gone at any moment?'

'We don't have to think about that,' I say, pushing that darkness outside with the night. 'Whatever happens next it doesn't matter. This now, with you, is everything I want.'

'God, Vita.' His voice breaks as he wraps his arms around me, kneeling between my legs. We press together in a long embrace, clinging on for dearest life. Our souls cleave one to the other.

When he pulls away, he kisses me briefly before turning back to the machine on the chest. I let my hands run over his shoulders, up the nape of his neck and through his dark hair.

'You don't want to distract me,' he says. 'I think I might have figured out this thing while you were snoring.'

'First of all, I don't snore,' I say. 'And second, really?'

'Yes. Do you have any candles by any chance?' He gives me a look that suggests that might be a stupid question.

'Only about a thousand. I'll be right back.' I run into the kitchen and find three or four of varying lengths and a box of matches I keep next to the cooker. I scoop up an old pewter candleholder I keep on the windowsill and return, delivering my armful of goods.

'Great.' He looks up at the seascape that has been in this room for as long as I can remember. 'Can we take that down for a minute?'

'I'm not sure,' I say, going to remove the painting. 'I don't think it's been moved in about 200 years. It might be holding up the house.' Still, I lift it down. A soft snowfall of dust rains down as I tilt it and lean it up against one of the chinoiserie cabinets.

'OK.' Ben lights a candle, returning to its holder. 'This is very Wee-Willy-Winkie, by the way.'

'It pays to have some old technology to hand in this house,' I tell him. 'The wiring is essentially working from beyond the grave.

'So,' Ben says, 'while you were sleeping, I got out my handy pocket toolkit.' He shows me what looks like a large Swiss Army knife with the look of pride you might see in a Boy Scout. 'And I took it all apart.'

'You took it apart? It's 300 years old!' I sit back down next to him. 'What if you've broken it?'

'I probably haven't broken it,' he says. 'But staring at it wasn't getting us anywhere, so I dismantled it, and it's a good job I did, because then I could see what the problem was.'

'And?' I sit next to him, taking in the lines of his shoulders, the tilt of his head. His face is alight with the thrill of discovery. I wind my arms around his as he works, his muscles moving beneath my palms, and lean my head on his shoulder. It's been so long since I could be this close with anyone, it almost hurts to touch my skin against his.

'Someone, probably a very long time ago, judging by the dirt in the threads,' he says, working around me, 'had taken it apart and then put it back together.' He looks sideways at me. 'Wrongly.'

'Wrongly?' I let go of his arm, sitting forward to stare at the thing. 'Wrongly how?'

'This bit was upside-down.' He shows me a small component that looks something like a brass cradle or the base of a rocking horse that's holding a rectangle of metal about the size of a postage stamp. 'They put this in upside-down. Do you want to know how I know that?'

'I can hardly wait,' I say earnestly.

'Because if you turn it over it reveals this.' He moves it from one hand to another to show me its secret.

'It's a tiny mirror,' I say, catching my hair out of my face so I can get a better look. 'So that means that this thing isn't meant to be part microscope.'

'No, it's part telescope,' Ben says, inserting the piece back into the device. 'The lenses are designed to capture and magnify light. The mirror directs it through the prism which then separates it… in theory.'

'Huh,' I say. 'But using a prism to split the light spectrum was already being done back then, if not so elegantly. So what's it for?'

'I'm not a history nerd, so I don't know if this was rare,' Ben says, 'but this is not just a prism – it's a very artfully made double prism. See? Two pieces of glass have been joined together here.'

He holds the crystal in his elegant fingers, turning it over slowly so I can see.

Ben lights the candle and makes some adjustments to the device. Suddenly a rainbow of colours is thrown on to the bare wall.

'It works,' he says happily. 'What a really brilliant thing. Whoever made it was very clever and meticulous. I like them. Anyway, whoever it was, they were attempting to make a broad-spectrum analysis of *something* – we just don't know what or why. Of course, in the intervening centuries this has been solved a thousand times over with a million times more analytical power, so it's kind of obsolete. Cool, but obsolete.'

'So it doesn't hold any great scientific secrets,' I say, peering at it.

'Well that depends,' Ben says, turning to look at me. 'If you found it in a random junk shop, like you say you did, then it's a brilliant curiosity, but that's all.' I know where this is going. 'However, *if*, say, you had been fascinated by a certain painting all your life, and during your apparently exhaustive research into it were somehow led to this strange little object, *then* it could tell us something important.'

I sit back on my heels.

'Come on, Vita,' he says. 'Tell me everything.'

'I'm not sure I can,' I say. 'Not yet.'

'Did it involve a heist?' he asks with a wry smile. I hesitate, before settling on telling him a half-true, not-quite lie.

'It belonged to a brilliant man I knew in Cambridge,' I begin.

'A boyfriend?' he asks.

'No, just a friend. But he was brilliant; maybe the cleverest person I have ever known. For a while he shared my passion for discovering the secrets of *La Belle*. He had this in his laboratory, and he thought, like you said at the Last Supper Club, that maybe it was meant for trying to see what is not there. More than that there was a possibility – a pretty good one – that it might once have belonged to an alchemist who was looking into the legend of the painting.'

'Who?' Ben asks, curious. 'Maybe I read about him.'

I could tell him that my old friend in Cambridge was Isaac Newton, and that he was both the maker of the instrument and the obsessed alchemist that I persuaded to try and help me. But we are happy, and this moment is perfect. I want to preserve it.

'Oh, I can't off the top of my head. Isaac… my friend… dug up all sorts of obscure history. I'll have to check my notes when I'm back at the office.'

'You mean to say that there is something about the obscure history of *La Belle* that you don't know by heart?'

'It must be you,' I smile. 'You've rather flustered me.'

'Well, that's a mutual problem then,' Ben says.

He kisses me, and for a moment we are in danger of losing the point. But he eventually refocuses. 'The thing is, working this out brings us back to the beginning.'

'Oh,' I say.

'No, but that's good,' he says. 'If there was someone in the 1600s trying to invent a way of splitting light and seeing the invisible in *La Belle* then maybe they were following some information that has been lost to time since. It's not a huge clue but it means that we can do what this device could not.'

'Your lens,' I say.

'Yes. The lens that discovered the underpainting on the *Mona Lisa* was the most sophisticated broad-spectrum lens there has ever been, and that found nothing new on *La Belle*, right?'

'Right,' I say.

'Well, it *was* the most sophisticated broad-spectrum lens that had ever been… until mine,' he says, sitting back with a grin.

'My lens can look into the darkness and it can scry. If there is anything, *anything* there, it will see it.'

'Of course,' I say, wondering.

'I spent most of my adult life on this thing. I know that once it's out there it's going to change the industry. As things stand now, I have mixed feelings about that.' He frowns briefly. 'But if it can help you, and if, just maybe, it can help me stay alive, then maybe it was meant to be. Maybe I wasn't wasting time working so hard. Maybe I was saving my own life, I just didn't know it yet.'

It is so tempting to want to believe that all of this is fate playing the long game, waiting for exactly the right moment to reveal her reasons why at last. But I know fate, and I know that she lies.

'If we can get it in front of the painting somehow then maybe... well, at the very least we can know if there was ever anything to be found there. We just need to go to Yorkshire and get it.'

'That's easy. I can drive us there.' Pushing my misgivings away, I wrap my arms around his neck.

'You can drive and have a car?' he asks.

'Of course I do,' I laugh. 'And I've been thinking. Even though the board of directors and the Louvre would never agree, I do have the painting – sort of. I think I can find a way to have it taken out of the exhibition for one night. Maybe. Just for you.'

'That sounds risky,' he says. 'I don't want you to put your job at risk for me.'

'You wouldn't. I would.' I shiver, the house always at its coolest just before dawn. 'Besides, it's only half a plan right now. Let's go pick up your lens first while I work on it.'

Ben yawns, rubbing his hands over his face.

'You're exhausted,' I say, touching the back of my hand to his cheek.

'I'm OK,' he says, dropping his gaze from mine.

'Come back to bed and we can curl up and sleep until the alarm.'

'I... I don't like sleeping,' he says awkwardly. 'Since they told me I've got this thing in my head, I've been afraid that if I ever really sleep that... well, that I'll never wake up.' He glances back up at me. I take his hand.

'Come to bed,' I say. 'Come and lie down on my bed and sleep. I'll sit with you and keep watch until you wake up. I'll keep you safe.'

'I do feel safe with you,' he says, wrapping his arms around me as I pull him to his feet.

A little while later he sleeps, his arms flung over his head, his face turned slightly towards me. I rest my hand on his chest to feel its rise and fall. If there is a way to keep him alive, then I must find it, for his sake and for mine.

V

Grow old along with me!
The best is yet to be.

Robert Browning

Chapter Thirty-Five

Vita is cooking eggs in an ancient poaching pan. She stands in front of her cooker concentrating on the bubbling water, two pieces of toast under the grill. I found out the reason why her fridge is empty – it's because she has a pantry where she keeps her butter and cheese. Milk, she says, is for losers.

Watching her, silk robe tied loosely around her waist, is like watching a work of art in motion. I would never get bored of sitting here at the kitchen table and looking at her, except that I can almost feel my mum clipping me lightly around the back of my head and telling to make myself useful.

'I'll make tea,' I say, getting up. 'Where's your kettle?'

'Oh, it's one of the old whistling ones.' She gestures at a dull, metal, grey thing squatting resentfully on the side. 'You need to put it on the hob to boil. It takes about a hundred years.'

'Don't you ever feel like modernising this place?' I ask as I step round her to fill up the kettle. She pulls the slightly burnt toast out from under the grill.

'I have really good Wi-Fi,' she says, dropping the toast on to two plates and blowing the end of her singed fingers. 'Apart from that? No, not really. I feel at home here. It's a house full of memories.'

'Even if not all of them belong to you?' I say.

She shrugs in response.

'I couldn't help but notice your photo of you and Dominic – the wedding photo.'

She stops mid-scooping an egg out of the pan, the milky water draining back into it, and thinks.

'There's a lot of me in this house,' she says eventually. 'I wondered if I might feel strange about it, but you know he would have liked you. Is that weird?'

'A bit.' I shift in my chair as she spoons two eggs on to my toast.

'Don't get used to this treatment,' she says. 'Anna is OK with me taking some time off, but I will have to go back to work soon.'

'You can't help it that you're exhausted,' I say teasingly as she sits down opposite me, the front of her gown falling open just a little. Suddenly I can think of much more interesting things to do than eat breakfast.

'God, you're amazing,' I marvel. 'I've never seen anything more perfect.'

She freezes, crestfallen. She pulls her gown tighter around her.

'Sorry,' I say. 'I'm sorry. I didn't mean to freak you out.'

'You haven't freaked me out,' she says, frowning deeply, her shoulders drawn up as a barrier between us. 'No, it's not that. The thing is, I've let you get involved with me when you only half-know me. I should have told you everything about me before I let last night happen. I'm worried I've misled you.'

'Misled me?' I ask. 'You are a human being, not a house for sale. I don't need your whole biography to know that you are absolutely wonderful.'

'You know I've been married.'

'Yes, I do, and I respect that,' I say. 'In fact, knowing how much you love and miss Dominic makes what we have even more precious. I know you wouldn't choose someone else lightly.'

She nods. 'But there are things I haven't told you.'

'You don't have to tell me anything you aren't comfortable with,' I say. 'Or you can tell me everything. It won't make a difference to how I feel about you, Vita. Nothing can change that.'

She frowns deeply. 'The thing is, what I am trying to say is… I'm damaged. You don't have to look too closely to see the cracks.'

'All I see is an incredible woman,' I tell her, 'who has shown me that there is always something to be grateful for. I'm so grateful for you, Vita. I don't see someone damaged; I see someone strong, someone perfect.'

Vita turns her face to the window.

'Ben, I'm not. But I don't want to lie to you, so...'

'Vita,' I take her hand, sliding from my chair on to my knees on the tiles before her. I am not an idiot. I know there is something she has been keeping from me. But I don't want to know. All I want is this perfection, for as long as I can hold it in my hands. Nothing else matters to me. 'I don't need your confession. That's not why I am here at your feet. You have come through everything just as you are. If you weren't you then you would never have made me feel the way you do: like a man who can be loved and desired. We are equals in this, you and me.'

Reaching up, I push her hair off her face, and, seeing a tear trickle down her cheek, wipe it away with my thumb. She closes her eyes as my fingers trail slowly down her neck to the place where her gown gapes a little. Holding my breath, I pull at the knot in the belt at her waist. The robe glides silently off her shoulders. Reaching for me, she pulls me up towards her, her hand searching under my shirt, running over my ribs, as her legs wrap around my waist.

Entangled, we tumble on to the linoleum in a pool of slippery silk and soft dark hair. Our eyes meet and everything else disappears, as here on Vita's kitchen floor we remake the universe just for us.

Chapter Thirty-Six

His head lies on my breast, my arms around him, holding him close. It doesn't seem to matter that the floor is cold and hard, when he is so warm and brimming with life. I never thought the place I'd feel most content would turn out to be my kitchen floor. He says there's nothing that could change the way he feels about me. Maybe he's telling the truth.

At exactly the same moment that his phone starts buzzing on the table, someone knocks at my door.

'No one ever knocks at my door,' I say, without moving. 'Even the postman delivers my mail to the Italian.'

'Can't be good, then,' Ben says, nuzzling in closer to me. 'Can we just wait for them to go away?'

'No, sorry.' I roll him off me gently, kissing his forehead. Getting up, I pull my robe tightly around me. 'It might be Mariah.'

'I hope it's her. She's a legend,' he says. I smile as I see his hand appear on the tabletop groping for his phone. Seems like he unexpectedly liked the kitchen floor too.

It's Jack who is waiting for me to open the door.

'Jack?' I exclaim, feeling like a teenager who's been caught out by their dad. 'You never come round.'

'I'm sorry,' he says, gesturing at my state of undress. He seems flustered, out of breath and uncertain. Not like Jack at all. 'It's just you weren't answering your phone. I'd thought you'd be about to go to work and I could walk with you again. Didn't mean to catch you off-guard.'

'I'm off sick,' I say, touching my hand to my tangled hair, conscious of my rosy, stubble-kissed skin, guilty that I am hiding a secret man in my house.

'Are you OK?' Jack frowns. 'You're never sick.'

'I just need a break, after setting up the exhibition,' I say, glancing back inside to where Ben is talking to his sister on the phone in hushed tones. I don't know why I don't just tell Jack that Ben is here, as he's going to find out in the next minute anyway, but that means there're 45 precious seconds when none of this is a problem.

'Look, Vita, I've been thinking about the last time we talked. I made things difficult between us. You must wonder why I am trying to tell you how to live your life, and who to get involved with.' He stops abruptly, walking two steps away from me as he runs his hands through his long curls, before turning on his heel back to face me. 'The thing is – and I don't really know how to say this – it should be easy after everything we've been through together but—'

'Hi.' Ben appears behind me at the door and puts his hand on my shoulder. His shirt is still unbuttoned. 'All right, mate? I'm Ben.'

Jack's mouth hangs open as he looks from Ben to me and back again.

'Hello,' he says eventually. 'I'm sorry. I didn't think... I mean, I didn't mean... I didn't realise...'

'It's fine, Jack,' I say breezily. 'Ben, this is my best friend Jack. Jack, this is Ben. I've told you about him. We're... together now.'

I look back up at Ben and his smile agrees with me. I lock eyes with Jack, sending him a message I hope he can understand: *Please, don't make this awkward now. There's still time to get things straight with Ben. I'll make it right, I promise.'*

He gives me a look in return that I can't read.

'OK, well my thing can wait obviously,' Jack says, his devil-may-care persona returning in a flash. 'It was nothing really.'

'Seriously,' Ben says, 'please, don't mind me.'

It's clear though that Jack does mind Ben. He can't stop looking at him, almost as if he can't quite believe he is real.

Jack smiles at Ben, but there's no warmth in it. 'OK, thank you. In that case, Vita, could we just have a minute?'

'Cool.' Ben drops a kiss on the top of my head. 'I'll make more tea and check the fastest route to Hebden Bridge. Kits is hitching a lift too. Hope that's OK.'

'Of course,' I say, stepping outside and pulling the door to behind me.

'Going somewhere?' Jack asks, his smile gone.

'To Yorkshire. Ben has made a lens he thinks might be able to read *La Belle* in greater detail than ever before. It feels like it's meant to be, doesn't it? Meeting Ben right after he finds out he's only got limited time left. Ben, the only person in the world in possession of the technology that will be able to read *La Belle* in more detail than ever before, and at the exact moment when I have the portrait within reach? Everything feels like it's converging at exactly the right time. It's more than coincidence. It has to be.'

'Vita, what are you doing?'

'It's a bit late for a lecture,' I tell him, stung. 'Look, Jack, I'm happy and hopeful for once. I'm allowed that, aren't I? You want that for me, don't you?'

'I did. I do,' Jack says. 'But there is only heartbreak here for you, Vita. The chances are, you will lose him. Are you going to tell him the truth about us?'

'I think I am. I've thought about nothing else. I have to tell him, Jack,' I say. 'I need him to really know me. Dominic was able to accept it eventually. Ben will too.'

'Maybe he can,' Jack says, his tone low and taut. 'But...'

'But what, Jack? I don't understand where this is coming from. You were the person telling me just days ago that I needed to throw myself back into the pleasures of life! You know better than anybody that love doesn't come easily to me. Why should I turn away now, when I have found it?'

'You think it comes easily to me?' he says bitterly. 'Do you think I don't know what it feels like to love someone and know I can never have them?'

'Jack.' I reach for him, my hand on his shoulder. 'I'm sorry. I haven't been there for you. I know you've found it hard, having the painting here and all this talk about Leonardo.'

'That's not it,' he says, shaking his head.

'Then what is it?' I ask him, frustrated.

'Do you really not know?' he asks defiantly.

'I really don't know,' I say, searching for reasons in the thin air. 'You weren't like this about Dominic.'

'Dominic was different,' Jack says, his voice tight.

'Why?' I ask. 'Why was Dominic different?'

'Because I knew that even if you spent the rest of his life with him, you would come back to me eventually. That we'd be together again. But with Ben? Well, if you have your way it will be you and him for ever.'

'And you don't want that,' I say slowly. 'You want it to be just you and me.'

'Is that so wrong?' Jack asks. 'I waited for you, while you were with Dominic. We made a promise to one another on the night I found you: to always be there for the other. I let you go, to Dominic.'

'Let me go?' I exclaim, but Jack doesn't pause.

'You have never had to wait that long for me. If you have needed me, I have always been there at your side. I've never left you for 60 years to devote myself to someone else.'

'Because you devote your time to *everyone* else!' I exclaim. 'We are different, Jack. The only thing we have in common is what Leonardo did to us. If it hadn't been for that, our paths would never have crossed. You have always been able to embrace all this life flowing through your fingers like water in ways I never could. I have always wanted something I can hold on to. Someone.'

Jack frowns deeply as he looks at me.

'All this time and you don't really know me at all,' he says sadly.

'That's not true.' I take his hand. 'I don't mean to say you don't care, that you don't love but...' He gives a bitter laugh, pulling his hand from mine. 'You have never wanted anything that lasts.'

'Because nothing lasts but us,' Jack says. 'Unless you change that.'

'I have fallen in love with him, Jack. I didn't look for it, I didn't expect it, but it happened, and now thanks to Ben, I am closer to unravelling the truth about how we came to be than ever. If I can save his life, I will. And even if I can't, I don't want to walk away.' I hesitate. 'Not even for you.'

'Then you'd better make sure that Ben really knows the cost of living as long as we have, Vita, because it's a very long sentence with no reprieve.'

Something is broken between us, and for the very first time I don't know if it can ever be fixed.

'Everything OK?' Ben opens the door to find Jack and me toe to toe, our heads bent together, my hand clenched tightly on his arm.

'Everything's fine,' I say stepping back, smiling at Jack. 'Old friends bickering, that's all.'

'I don't know you, but I'm guessing that if you care about Vita then you're worried about Vita getting close to someone she can't keep,' Ben says, looking at Jack. 'That's fair. I'd be the same if I was her friend. But she's thought about this. She's going in with her eyes wide open, aren't you Vita?'

I nod, taking his hand, and giving Jack a look that tells him it is time to go.

'Well, as long as everyone knows exactly what the stakes are,' Jack said pointedly. He smiles at Ben, offering him his hand. 'You're a good man, Ben. I can see why Vita cares for you so very much. I'm here if you need me.'

Jack leaves, but an odd tension still floats in the air between Ben and me.

'Kitty will be round with my stuff in about half an hour,' Ben says.

'It's getting like Piccadilly Circus round here,' I joke weakly.

'What is going on with him?' Ben asks as I close the door. 'Does he fancy you?'

'God, no,' I say. 'Jack fancies everyone in the world *but* me. No, he's trying to be protective is all. But it's nothing to do with you. Don't worry about him.'

Ben nods and goes to gather his things from the bedroom, leaving me standing at the foot of the stairs, my hand against the door. Jack told me I didn't truly know him. The fear that I can't shake is that, if that is true, I don't really know Jack; that after living all these lifetimes I don't know anything at all.

Chapter Thirty-Seven

'Wow, you landed a rich bird,' Kitty says when I open the door to her. She's wearing shades and red lipstick, and hands me my rucksack. 'Maybe she will adopt me.'

'She does have a house,' I say. 'And it is worth a bit, I reckon. But apart from that she's basically just like you and me.'

'Apart from the entire house in Zone 1 and all the priceless antiques it's filled with,' Kitty says, gesturing around her.

'That all belonged to a relative. She just inherited it.'

'Such a burden.' Kitty walks into the kitchen, tapping me on the chest. 'Your shirt's buttoned up wrong.'

'Oh.' I look down to see that I am missing a button. 'That must have fallen off when—' I choose not to finish that sentence. 'Anyway,' I say, 'what's up with Dev?'

'He's OK.' She almost smiles. 'He's great actually.'

'Oh my god, you love him,' I tease her.

'I do not,' she says, giggling as she shakes her head. 'But I do like him. And I think he likes me. And he's coming up to visit next weekend, so...'

'Kitty's got a boyfriend!' I sing-song.

'Don't jinx it, OK?' she says. 'Anyway, you're one to talk, going AWOL with an aristocrat. She really let you have sex with her, huh? Wonders will never cease.'

'Kits don't be weird with her, OK?' I plead. 'I know the timing is strange, but she's nice. And she's... real.'

'It *is* a novelty for you to be going out with a real person,' Kitty says, grinning. 'Of *course* I'm not going to be *weird with her*, you muppet. I'm over the moon that you've found someone who will tolerate you. I would say it was a bit early to be taking her home to meet Mum, but needs must, I suppose.'

She opens her arms to me, and we hug, her half so tight it hurts my ribs.

'Seriously.' She punches me lightly on the arm. 'You look so happy. Even if she was a bitch, I'd totally fake liking her for your sake.'

'Hopefully I'm not though,' Vita says as she comes into the kitchen. 'Hi, Kitty. Sorry it took me a while to find the car keys.'

'Brought back your dress,' Kitty says. 'I had it dry-cleaned.'

'Why don't you keep it?' Vita laughs. 'It looks so great on you.'

'Really?' Kitty beams. 'Thank you. I will let you buy my affection.' She folds the dress back into her duffel bag.

'Where do you keep your car anyway?' Ben asks. 'There's nowhere around here to park.'

'In the garage,' Vita says, nodding across the courtyard.

'You keep a car in your own garage in central London?' I say.

'Where else would I keep it?' Vita looks from me to Kitty, genuinely perplexed.

'I mean, I don't know, but you could probably sell the garage to a developer for a couple of hundred thousand quid,' I say, smiling at Kitty.

'But then where would I keep my car?' Vita asks, and Kitty splutters into laughter.

'I love you, Vita,' Kitty says. And that's made my day.

★★★

Vita has stuffed a few things into my backpack, an act that makes me stupidly happy. We are a couple going on a road trip – one of those silly little things I thought I'd never get to do again, and now here I am, doing it. And despite myself, this makes me feel that if that out-of-reach wish can come true, then maybe all the other hopes and dreams can too. I'm feeling inclined to believe in miracles right now.

Vita's wearing those orange trouser-skirt things, with a bright-green silk shirt and yellow trainers, looking like the most beautiful thing I have ever seen. She leads us to the wooden, black-painted doors of the lockup that I assumed belonged to one of the businesses round here and begins to grapple with them.

'She is a bit temperamental,' Vita says as she unlocks a heavy padlock. 'But I give her a run out every couple of weeks, make sure she's still up for it.'

She pulls open one of the heavy doors as Kitty gets the other and flicks on strip lighting.

'*That's* your car?' I say, staring at it. She looks a bit worried.

'Yeah, I know she's a bit old, but she still goes OK... mostly.' Vita pats the hood. 'Don't you, girl?'

'That's a Jaguar Mark 2,' I say, 'manufactured between 1959 and 1967, with a 3.8 litre engine and a 125mph top speed.'

'He's a mine of useless information,' Kitty says to Vita, shaking her head. 'Stop mansplaining, Ben. Vita knows that; it's her car.'

'Yes, she's an old lady really, but I love her,' Vita says.

'*I* love her,' I say, running my hands along the car's flank. 'Do you know these were the favourite getaway car of the 1960s, because they could go a ton with five criminals in the back? Oh my god, Vita, have you got an Aston Martin squirrelled away somewhere too?'

'I'm afraid not,' Vita says, offering me the keys. 'Would you like to drive?'

'If I didn't already love you, I would now,' I say, taking the keys and kissing her so hard that Kitty makes retching noises until we stop.

'You realise we are now going to get bombarded with hours of geeky crap for the whole trip right?' Kitty asks Vita as she chucks her bag in the back. 'You're all right; he's still a novelty to you.'

'It's worth it just to see that smile on his face,' Vita says, and out of nowhere Kitty hugs her.

I slide in behind the wheel and Vita sits beside me. I turn the key and the engine starts with a perfectly tuned purr.

Then something I have been pushing away refuses to be ignored any longer.

'When we get there, I am going to need some time alone with Mum,' I tell them. 'I can't keep this from her anymore.'

Vita takes my hand and Kitty nods at me in the rear-view mirror.

'Right,' I nod. 'Let's see if we can get a speeding ticket.'

Chapter Thirty-Eight

Kitty catches up with me when we take a break at the service station.

'Hope the ride's not too uncomfortable for you,' I say as she falls into step beside me.

'It's fine. I'm sort of dreading getting home really. Dreading what this is going to do to Mum. The last couple of days, none of it has seemed real. Like nothing has changed at all.'

'Nothing has,' I say. 'You are all still the same people.'

She thinks for a moment and stops me with a hand on my arm, glancing around to make sure Ben is nowhere in sight. 'Vita, can I ask you something?'

'Of course,' I say.

'Ben loves you, head over heels straight away. If things were normal, I'd be telling him not to rush in, but I am glad that he's found you and you've found him.'

'I'm glad too,' I say. 'It makes him happy that you are OK with all of this.'

'And you're not afraid of... when it happens?'

'Terrified,' I say. 'But it is what it is. I choose love, that's all.'

'I want him to be deliriously happy for every second he's got,' Kitty says hesitantly, 'but can I ask you something? It's pretty selfish, but I need to ask it because my mum is too big a person to do it.'

'Go on,' I nod, knowing what is coming next.

'Just... please don't keep him all to yourself?' Kitty is both awkward and full of sorrow. 'Me and Mum and my son Elliot, we need him too, OK? We need to be around him while we can be too. Because afterwards... well, that's a very long time not to have him.'

The love in her words and the slight tremble in her tone stop me in my tracks. I hug her briefly, but very tightly.

'I know and I won't,' I promise. 'He needs you all too. He can't be happy without you.'

Kitty nods, hurriedly wiping away tears with the sleeves of her shirt.

'Here he comes.' She sees Ben and breaks into a determined smile as she waves. 'Pretend we've been chatting shit, OK?'

Inside the car we lapse into silence for the last hour of the journey, lulled by the noise of the engine, all of our minds, I suppose, turning towards the difficult hours ahead. Gradually the steelworks and shopping centres of Sheffield give way to the cities and complicated ring roads of Leeds and Bradford, until at last we're gliding through the hills and valleys. Up, up we travel on to the very top of the moor. The soft afternoon sunshine gilds the purple heather with edges of flame. The blue sky stretches all the way up to midnight stars. The air is clean and sharp, the road smooth and empty. The hills roll on for ever.

It's late afternoon by the time we approach Hebden Bridge, and I'm wondering why it is I haven't been back to Yorkshire for so long. London is my love and my home, but this landscape feels like poetry to London's prose.

Finally Ben takes us down through steep, twisted, woody roads into Hebden Bridge, a pretty, lively little town made up of rows of working-class houses that march up and down the steep inclines. We pass through a busy centre packed with cafés and shops, and out the other side to a high hillside lane of about eight terraced cottages that look out over the town and the woodland beyond.

'This is me,' Ben says, pulling up outside one of the cottages. He sits with his hands on the wheel, looking at the dark little house. 'A lot has changed since I last walked out that door.'

'And that's Mum's place,' Kitty says, pointing two doors down to a house where lights glow at the window and there's a wreath of sunflowers on the door. 'She's waiting for us all in there with Elliot and Ben's dog Pablo.'

'Should I go and get Elliot, take Vita into your house while you talk to Mum?' Kitty asks, her voice tight.

Ben thinks for a moment, his expression cloaked in shadow.

'No,' he says. 'You are my family. All of you. I love you all. We should all be together if that's OK with you?'

'Of course,' I tell him, putting my hand over his on the steering wheel. He looks at me and I see fear in his eyes.

★★★

The sunflower door opens. A kind of collie-looking dog races out and leaps straight into Ben's waiting arms, its whole body waggling with joy as it licks his scrunched-up face. That must be Pablo.

Pablo is closely followed by a little boy of about 4 who flings his arms around Kitty's waist, squishing his face into her tummy. Laughing, she picks him up and spins him round. In the doorway stands Ben's mum, a beautiful woman, tall and elegant like her son. Her long, reddish-brown hair is streaked with silver. She wears a cornflower-blue dress and has bare feet. There's paint on her fingers and the hem of her skirt.

'Well now, who's this?' She smiles at me, reaching out a hand that wants to hold mine rather than shake it.

'Mum, this is Vita. We met a couple of days ago,' Ben says.

'Well,' Sarah says. 'He is not normally one to bring lasses home. He must really like you.'

The front door closes and we are enveloped in the depth of warmth and light contained within the narrow little cottage.

'Mum,' Ben says, as he takes her hand. 'I need to tell you something.'

★★★

Sarah's art lines the walls: paintings of all sizes, all portraits of the landscape, composed of abstract, lyrical brushstrokes. Rugs she has made cover the stone flags, and the kitchen, Kitty tells me, was made just for her by a joiner she knows, out of bits of old wood she collected from skips.

She listens as Ben talks, with Elliot leaning against him, encircled by his arm. The muscles in her face contract as she begins to understand. Her hand never leaves his as she watches his face. Slowly and suddenly, anguish creeps into every shadow and angle of her body, and yet somehow she contains it with gentle strength.

'My boy,' she says at last.

'I'm sorry, Mum.' Ben's head drops. 'Maybe I should have come straight back.'

Sarah looks at me and shakes her head.

'No,' she says. 'You're here now. You did what was right for you.'

Pushing her chair back, she moves to him and pulls him against her chest in a mother's embrace, her arms winding around him tightly. Elliot goes to Kitty, climbing onto her lap and tucking his head into the curve of her neck. Her mother reaches for her hand, and grips it so hard her knuckles shine white. Pablo shifts at my feet, and I rest the palm of my hand on his head.

'I expect we could do with a cuppa,' Sarah says at length and Ben follows her into the kitchen. What happens between them there I don't know. I don't think I ought to know; there are some moments between a mother and her son that are just for them alone. The moments when they must hold on to one another tightest, the moments just before they must let go.

I wait with Kitty, and she holds her son in a hug that he instinctively understands is what they both want.

'Vita, meet Pablo,' Ben says, still fluffing the ears of his dog, who has fixed me with wide eyes as he gnaws gently on the toe of my trainer. Traces of tears are still visible, but he refuses to acknowledge them. Instead, he smiles determinedly as he looks at Pablo.

'Kitty calls him my emotional-support dog.'

'Pablo *is* your emotional-support dog,' Kitty says, sniffing as she follows his cue. 'The amount of sad Nineties rock he has to listen to, poor little pup.'

'And I'm Elliot,' the little boy says, easing himself on to my lap as if we were long-lost relatives. 'Would you like a hug too?'

'I would,' I tell him, as he winds his arms around my neck, pressing his soft cheek against mine for a moment.

Kitty smiles fondly at the boy, tousling his hair.

'I'm sorry, he doesn't really respect personal boundaries yet,' Kitty says as Sarah emerges from the kitchen and puts down a plate of freshly baked biscuits in the centre of the table, and I see that this is how this family copes. They pull together, quiet and unassuming, over cups of tea and biscuits, united and brimful of love.

Elliot takes a biscuit in each hand and a bite from each.

'Come here, kid,' Ben says, patting his lap to try and lure Elliot away. 'Let me see how heavy you've got.'

'Don't you dare.' I smile at Ben to reassure him that I'm OK. 'It's nice. I hardly ever get to hang out with children, or a family as wonderful as this one.'

'Well, you are one of us now,' Sarah says as she pours more tea. 'So you'd better get used to it.'

'I just wish you didn't have to go back again tomorrow,' she says, after a moment. 'You could stay up here for a bit, let me look after you both.'

'There's a work thing,' I say, looking at Ben. 'A way to try out Ben's lens.'

'Really? Well, not to worry – come back up after that,' Sarah says. I think about what Kitty said at the service station.

'I won't keep Ben all to myself,' I promise.

'Look at the way he looks at you,' Sarah smiles, making Ben blush. 'When he was a boy…'

'Oh god, let's not do the when-Ben-was-a-boy routine,' Ben says, reaching for a book from the shelf. 'Hey, look, this is the book that brought me to you, Vita. Mum's book about Da Vinci.'

'Wow,' I say, rather taken aback to see my face again, here in this little cottage.

'You look like her, you know?' Ben's mum says. 'It's quite uncanny.'

'Yeah, we should do one of those art museum memes for you,' Kitty says.

'You do, don't you?' Ben says, looking from the cover of the book to me. 'I hadn't noticed it before. How weird!'

'I've never really thought about it,' I say, feeling my heart race at the lie. 'I suppose we are both brunettes.'

Sarah smiles, 'Any one for any more tea?'

★★★

Ben goes out and gets fish and chips, which we eat on our laps watching TV. I feel like I've stumbled into a life I've never known; an ordinary family. Even my time with Dominic was never like this: we read books and ate meals at the table. Our life was full of love, just the two of us, but there was never this commonplace comfort. Every now and then Ben throws a chip at Pablo, who catches it every time. When we have all finished, he collects up the papers and takes them out into the kitchen. I collect up mugs and glasses and begin to fill the sink with warm water.

'No need for that,' Sarah says. 'I've got a dishwasher, see?'

'Oh, of course,' I laugh. 'I must be the last person on earth not to have one.'

'Still, nice manners of you,' Sarah says, leaning on the counter appraising me as I rinse out a mug anyway. 'Your mum must have taught you well.'

'Mum did teach me a lot about how to behave,' I say, thinking about that small, distant figure, veiled in unhappiness. She was worn-out and almost faded away at 30. Her chief purpose was to turn her daughters into obedient commodities. I don't blame her; it was all she knew or understood. Still, I wish I could have known her in the way that Ben and Kitty know their mum. I wish there had been fondness. 'To be quiet, always look my best, always do as I'm told; to submit to my father; to obey all men. I ran away in the end, and being willing to wash up pots got me my first job.'

I catch myself, and brace for a series of curious questions, but all she says is, 'My god, you poor girl,' embracing me. 'How hard for you and how brave to break free. Are you in touch now?'

'She died,' I say as she lets me go, retaining my hand in hers.

'And Ben told me you're a widow?' I nod. When she puts it like that, my life seems made of tragedy, and would be if it were crammed into the three or so decades that people assign to me. As it is, the tragedy and loss stretch out gossamer-like, over so many years, they become almost transparent. Almost. It seems like hardly any time since Dominic died in my arms, though it was more than 30 years ago now.

'Poor lass, you've had a lot of loss,' she says gently. 'And now you've gone and fallen for my boy, and you'll lose him too. Are you sure you're up to that?'

Glancing over her shoulder, I see Ben sitting on the living-room rug with Elliot on his shoulders, playing with Pablo.

'Honestly, I don't know,' I say. 'But that's not for now. Now all I have to do is love him, and that's easy.'

'He's a good lad,' Sarah says, turning from me suddenly. Lightly I place my hand on her shoulder.

'You are so strong,' I say softly. 'How are you still on your feet?'

'It is almost too much to bear,' she admits. 'All I want to do is to hold onto him and keep him close, but I can't. No matter how tight I hold onto him, I can't stop him from slipping away and that is… it's hard.'

'It's hard,' I repeat. 'But I'll be there for you all too, if you'll have me.'

'You're a godsend,' she says. 'I don't believe in God, because if there is one, he's a right bastard, but I'll say it about you, Vita: *you are a godsend.*'

She kisses me on the cheek and goes back to sitting on the floor with her son and grandson, pretending to scream when Pablo licks her. It's all so precious, this complicated, difficult, imperfect family life. Even if this, or some combination of it, is duplicated in all the other houses on the street, in this town or up and down the country and around the world, each one of them is precious and important. Each one of them is beautiful.

Chapter Thirty-Nine

It's almost midnight by the time I let Vita through my front door and straight into my front room. Pablo runs around in circles barking in greeting at his favourite things like the sofa and the snake-shaped draught excluder. Vita walks straight over to the mantel, where a framed print of *Starry Night* is hanging.

'I love this painting,' she says looking back at me.

'Do you? I always think I'm a bit naff having such a popular painting up.'

'Not at all!' Vita's eyes flash briefly at the idea. 'Just because art is beloved by many doesn't mean it is any less worthy.' She sees me smile. 'Sorry, touchy subject.'

'So, this is my place,' I say, gesturing round at the room, which now I come to think of it does look something of a bachelor pad. There's a battered old leather sofa that I rescued from a skip, four games consoles and a big telly, and that's pretty much it.

'That's the kitchen.' I gesture to the long, narrow room that leads off the sitting room. 'Bathroom's behind that. Upstairs, two bedrooms: one's my office. That's the extent of my property portfolio.'

'It's nice,' she says, circling slowly as she takes it all in. 'It's very you.'

'Do you mean boring and a bit run-down?' I ask her. 'I do have something pretty amazing though.' I take her hand and lead her through the kitchen, right past the washing-up I never did before going to London, and into my garden.

'Your shed!' she says, gesturing at the faintly luminous corrugated sides of my clean room that sits at the bottom of my long, narrow, steeply sloping garden. 'That is amazing.'

'Thanks.' Standing behind her I wrap my arms around her. 'But I don't mean that, I mean *that*.' I tilt her chin upwards so that she can see the clear sky, full of stars.

'There you are,' she whispers. 'It's been an age since I've seen the stars so brightly. London lights always blot them out.'

'When I'm feeling a bit down and hopeless I like to come out here and have a look up there,' I tell her. 'I like to think that that's where I'll be when the time comes. Not in heaven, but up there swirling around in cosmic dust with the stars. I reckon I'd like that.'

'We are all made of stardust,' Vita murmurs.

'Are you tired?' I ask her.

'Why, what do you have in mind?' she asks, turning in my arms.

Well, I know it's late, but do you fancy a walk and a bit of a pilgrimage to teen-Goth me?'

'Lead on, Macduff,' she says. This woman cannot help herself.

★★★

The full moon rides with us as the three of us walk through the village, up the steep, zig-zagging lane that leads to Heptonstall.

'Sometimes I'll be driving back from somewhere early in the morning and the valleys are covered in mist,' I tell her as we labour up the steep incline. 'It's like driving over the clouds, no landmarks at all except for the village of Heptonstall rising up like it's Brigadoon – a magical place visible only once in a hundred years.'

'I'd love to see that,' Vita says as we reach the cobbled main street, lined on either side by tightly asleep cottages, the faintly glowing embers of dying fires lighting their windows. Here and there Pablo plunges towards a cat poised on a wall or curled on a windowsill, all of whom regard him with aloof disdain.

'I hope you're not easily spooked. I'm taking you into a graveyard,' I tell Vita, as we come upon the old church, stretching up into the darkness as if it's trying to drag itself free of the earth.

'Fortunately, I've got nerves of steel,' she whispers, taking my hand as I lead her into the ruin.

'This is beautiful,' she says, looking up at what remains of the church, set against the starry sky. 'Creepy as all hell, of course, but beautiful. What happened to it?'

'It got blown down in a gale in the 1840s,' I tell her. 'They built a new one and that was struck by lightning. Personally, I think it's the curse of the Heptonstall Witches, getting revenge on the parish for being taken to trial in 1646.'

'Oh no. What happened to them?' Vita asks me with the same amount of concern as she might if the trials had taken place last week.

'Well, it wasn't too bad. They got blamed for sickness, as women often were back then, and beaten half to death by the villagers. In the end the judge decided they had suffered enough and dismissed the case, telling them not to do it again. Which, all things considered, was pretty enlightened at the time.'

'All those who suffered because of such ridiculous fear...' Vita mutters, her hands against one blackened wall of the old church. 'So many innocents murdered for being too clever, too beautiful, too different.'

'Yeah, I don't know if we would have done very well in those days,' I say.

'We would not have,' she says. 'I can see why teen-Goth you liked it here so much – it's like the set of a horror movie.'

'I thought a lot about death here,' I say. 'Suddenly I had to try and figure out what it meant to exist, what the point of me was. Although I have to admit that now I'm nearly at the end, I wish I'd spent less time trying to second-guess what it would be like and more time just being alive. Like now.'

Vita steps into my arms and we kiss in the moonlight. It feels almost as if stardust is falling around us, coating our bodies in the heavens. The scent of the trees, the call of the night animals, the feel of her warm and alive under the palms of my hands. This is life, this is aqua vitae; I could drink a case of this and still be on my feet.

'Hey,' I say, pulling back as a thought comes into my head. 'Your name means life!'

'I was aware of that.' She smiles.

'I think you are the Holy Grail,' I tell her. 'You are the cure for all ills. At least, for right now.'

Vita peels her body away from mine, a rush of cool air separating us. I wonder if I've said too much.

'There's one other place I want to show you, if that's OK?' I ask her, relieved to see her relax and nod. She holds out her hand to me.

'Sylvia Plath.' Vita kneels on the damp grass in front of the small grave. 'Isn't it something wonderful that a life as short as hers can be so incandescent?' As soon as she says it she turns to take my hand. 'I'm sorry, I didn't mean—'

'No, it's fine. My life has not been bright and shiny – I get that.'

'That's not true,' Vita tells me, climbing to her feet and pulling me into an embrace. 'All lives shine bright. Some reach a little further than others, that's true. But every single person who has ever lived has been loved by someone, has loved someone. They have remembered those they've lost and been remembered in turn. That's what we are, we humans. We are a great tapestry of finely woven connections, each one interlaced and constant. Even when there is no one left alive to remember our names, we still remain somehow.'

'You never forget anyone, do you?' I ask her.

'No,' she says. 'There's not much I can do with my life but remembering those who have passed through it seems like something worthwhile.'

It helps to know that even when I'm gone from this body she will carry the traces of who I was in her heart for as long as she lives.

VI

Time, like an ever-rolling stream,
Bears all its sons away.

Isaac Watts

Chapter Forty

'Home at last,' Vita says with a sigh as we walk back through her front door. She flicks on a few faltering lights as she walks through the house.

Pablo shoots past me, darting in and out of rooms and up the stairs, performing a standard securing of the perimeter in his capacity as head of security while also checking for snacks. When he returns he dances around my legs, anxious that I might try and leave without him. Taking a seat at the kitchen table, I let Pablo climb on to my lap, even though he is far too big a dog for that.

'If your working-dog mates could see you now, fella,' I say, rubbing his ears so that he leans his head against my chest and sighs happily.

I hadn't known I'd wanted to bring him back to London with me until he'd leapt into the passenger seat of the car and given me a look that said, *Where are we going, Dad?*

'God, I'm a terrible father,' I'd muttered out loud. 'Sorry, mate. Still, another sleepover with Granny, hey? She'll spoil you rotten.'

'Or we could just bring him,' Vita had said at once. 'Look at his face. And I bet Mariah would love him too. Let's bring him. Every decent adventure needs a dog.'

Impossibly, I fell in love with Vita a little bit more.

'Shall I hop in and try my luck too?' Mum had only half-joked, dismay at my departure imprinted on her face.

'Why not?' Vita had said at once. 'It'd be a bit of a squeeze, but you can all come if you like. I've got spare rooms, and I *think* there are beds in there, under all of the things stuffed into them.'

Mum had exchanged glances with Kitty, who had stood with her hands on Elliot's shoulders. They'd thought about it for a second, and then Mum shook her head.

'No, I don't think so,' Mum had said. 'You get off. Come back in a couple of day when you've done whatever it is you are doing with that lens. Both of you, OK?'

Vita had hugged Mum hard and climbed in beside Pablo to give us a moment.

'See you later, loser,' Kitty had said.

'Not if I see you first,' I'd replied, and we'd fist-bumped as we always did.

'Seriously though,' she'd muttered as Elliot ran inside. 'I love you and shit.'

'I love you and shit too,' I'd replied. 'And thanks for coming to get me.'

'Any time.' She'd hugged me hard and gone inside with her boy, giving me just one backward glance, one last, low-key wave goodbye.

'You take care of that girl now,' Mum had told me when it was just us, buttoning up my jacket like it was the first day of school. 'There's something special about her. And you take care of you, you hear me?'

'I will, I promise, Mum. I'll be gone a few days and then I'll be home.'

She'd put her hands on my cheeks, scanning my face as if imprinting it into her memory.

'I'm so proud of you,' she'd said.

'I literally haven't done anything,' I said with a smile.

'You have,' she said. 'But even if you hadn't, you're my beautiful boy, and I'm proud of you whether you like it not. And I love you. Never forget that. Even after we can't be together on this earth any more. Wherever you are in the universe, I will still be with you.'

'You are making this sound like a last goodbye,' I'd said, trying desperately to be light. 'It's not, I promise. I haven't even had a twinge for days. I feel good. Everything's OK.'

'Of course it is, and it doesn't have to be a last goodbye for me to tell you how much I love you, does it?' she'd replied, her voice as bright as glass.

'No, Mum. And I love you too,' I'd told her.

She'd kissed my cheeks, my forehead, my closed eyelids, just as she always used to when she was tucking me into bed.

'I'll see you soon, kid,' she'd said.

'Count on it,' I'd told her.

***

'Are you having a moment?' Vita asks as she comes into her kitchen and finds Pablo in my arms. 'Should I come back later?'

'He's just worried I'm going to go and leave him with a strange woman who doesn't seem to have a tin of biscuits in the house,' I tell her. 'What have you got against snacks?'

'Nothing. That's why there aren't any in the house. I never really do a shop,' Vita says apologetically. 'Sorry, Pablo.' She reaches over and kisses his head. 'I've got some chocolate liqueurs somewhere.'

'Best not,' I say. 'Dogs and chocolate don't go so well together. Plus, I think he'd be a maudlin drunk. Thanks for letting me bring him though.'

'I've always wanted a dog,' she says, leaning her chin on her hand as she watches Pablo and me fondly.

'Why don't you have one then?' I ask her.

'They don't live long enough,' she says. 'I decided not to fall in love with anyone who wouldn't outlive me.' She realises what she's said just as the last word leaves her lips.

'I'm sorry, I didn't mean—'

'No, I'm sorry,' I say, as Pablo climbs off my lap. 'It's all come as a bit of a surprise to me too that we've fallen so fast into this thing together. I can't be sorry that you love me, but I'm sorry that it will cost you. The last thing I want to do is cause you pain.'

'Meeting you has made the opposite true. You soothe my pain,' she says, reaching for my hand, her expression still and serious.

'It's only the absence of you that will cause me pain, and I'd bear a hundred years of it and a hundred more willingly for right now.'

We kiss, until Pablo tries to get in on the action by licking Vita's ears.

'And you never know,' she says carefully as she rubs Pablo's chest, 'perhaps we will find the secrets they say Leonardo hid in the painting. And if we do, well then perhaps we will have all the time we need. Can you imagine what that would look like?'

'No,' he says. 'I have decided to only think about now. It seems safest. I look at you and I think I sort of believe I've had more than my fair share of good fortune.'

'You haven't,' she says, as if she is certain. 'The answer is in the painting, I know it is. Tomorrow there's a chance we will find out. At the very least it will be an adventure. Even if I might go to prison for it.' She looks at me proudly. 'I've worked out how I'm going to get *La Belle* out of the exhibition for one night,' she whispers, as if we might be overheard.

'I'm scared,' I confess.

'I feel like your mum would prescribe tea for that,' Vita says. 'All I have to offer is wine and a pizza from over the road, but there is no need to be scared. I'm the perp, you're just an accomplice, barely even a sidekick really.'

She arrives back from her cellar a few minutes later and I get glasses out, revelling in every little domestic moment. The way we move around each other with ease, my dog curled up under the table. Oh, for a lifetime of this familiarity and yet it could all be gone in an instant.

Vita senses my fear.

'It's exciting, not scary,' she says, pulling her chair next to mine and leaning her head against me, 'and I think it will work. It's been ages since I've done anything so daring. I'm quite looking forward to it.'

'I can't imagine it,' I tell her. 'Not you pulling off a heist, I can imagine that easily. I mean the reality we will have to face one way or another and all too soon. I can't imagine not existing, not being in this body, not seeing or holding you ever again, and that is terrifying enough. And then I can't imagine existing forever. I know I want it right now. I want more time, more than anything. I want the time that is owed to me. But then, I can't imagine wanting to live without Mum and Kitty, Elliot and … you. Or feeling more and more out of time until nothing is recognisable anymore. I suppose if it came to it, I could just jump off a bridge or something.'

Vita is still for a long moment, her face masked by hair.

'First, let's see if we can find the secret,' she says at last. 'Let's not worry about anything that isn't real yet. Deal?'

'Deal,' I say, happy to push away fear for a few precious hours. 'So, tell me, when was the last time you did something daring?' I ask her, somehow heartened by the idea that she's done really stupid and highly likely to fail things before.

'Oh, before Dominic,' she says, shaking her head.

'You don't talk much about your past,' I say. 'I mean you do – you tell me important and difficult things – but … I don't know. What about university? Tell me about what you got up to at uni.'

'Oh, not much,' she smiles. 'We mature students are very sensible, you know.'

'Before uni then,' I say. 'Before Dominic, what were you like?'

She thinks for a moment.

'Afraid of everything, and excited about everything.' She smiles. 'A bit wild and reckless. Travelled a bit, tried on a lot of different versions of myself until I found one that fitted. Nothing stayed the same until Dominic, and then all I wanted was for nothing to change. I suppose I wanted to settle down.'

'I would like to settle down,' I say with realisation. 'And if this works out, I'd like to whirl around the world with you, adventuring.'

'We will do both,' she says. 'Maybe I can take you to see the northern lights in the Arctic, or the rosy glow of the sunset on the Taj Mahal. Or maybe we can go to Florence and Milan and revisit the works of the Old Masters. I would love to show you all the things I've seen.'

'And would you come and live with me in Yorkshire?' I ask her. 'I'm not sure London is for me.'

'London is for everyone,' she says. 'And she is my constant companion. But perhaps I would, or perhaps we can divide our time among a series of grand and eccentric homes dotted around the world.'

'Filling all of them with children,' I laugh, biting my lip as I catch my blunder. 'Sorry.'

'There's no need to be,' Vita says. 'You would be a beautiful father, Ben.'

'Well, I can be a beautiful uncle instead,' I tell her. 'I wish I had done all the things you have before 30,' I say, shaking my head.

'I didn't tell you my age,' she laughs.

'You don't even look 30,' I tell her. 'Not that it matters to me how old you are.'

'I'm older than you,' she says, with a small frown.

'It's only a number,' I say, kissing the crease between her brows. 'And were you ever in love, before Dominic, and before me?'

She tilts her head in thought. 'The answer is no, I realise now. I thought I had fallen in love plenty of times, but those feelings weren't real. They were ideas and dreams – most of them weren't even mine. If I think about it, I have only ever really been in love twice,' she smiles. 'I've had lovers, of course. I've had some really wonderful lovers and some fairly average ones. I've had lovers that stayed a long time, some that stayed for a night. There was one that wanted to keep me, like a bird in a cage, and one who only wanted me because he... hated me. One that would have hurt me.' Her expression darkens as she says this. 'And that made me wary.'

'You really have experienced all that life has to offer,' I say. 'And all while I was sitting at my desk.'

'Does that offend you?' she asks.

'No,' I tell her honestly. 'No, you belong only to yourself. It's one of the reasons I love you.'

'After my childhood it took me a long time to heal enough to really be able to feel what it means to love someone else; to know I'd give up everything I had for them.' She pauses for a moment, sipping her wine. 'I'm grateful I got there; grateful for Dominic and for you, Ben. Real love is rare, it's delicate. To know it once in a lifetime is a blessing – twice is a miracle.'

'I had begun to think it would never happen for me,' I say carefully. 'I was living my life like that, like the notion of love was something that happened to other people. I tried a couple of times to sort of get into it, but it never took. I didn't know what I was missing until now. Until you. And that makes it so much harder to know that unless something incredible happens, unless there is something there for my lens to see, then I won't have years with you. And it is hard to have that hope and fear all at once. But at the same time, I'm glad I know. I'm glad I know what loving you feels like.'

Our hands entwine, our faces drawing close, so that all I can see is the reflection in her eyes, and all I can feel is her skin against mine.

'I'm scared about tomorrow,' I tell her. 'That it will be like waking up from a dream and discovering that nothing is real.'

'I'm not afraid,' she says just before she kisses me. 'The best adventures begin with the unknown.'

★★★

Later Vita dozes on my chest and Pablo is curled up at the foot of the bed on an old quilt that she found for him. All this seems surreal somehow, like a fever dream, the risk of failure so high that I should be out of hope. What if somehow this works, and we stop the clock on my life for ever?

I allow myself to dream that future for a little while. What it would be like to let go of the fear that has wrapped itself around every sinew, always there even in my happiest moments, to never know uncertainty again. And is it right to claim that prize just for me when there are so many people facing so much loss? Maybe it could be the beginning, the dawn of a new age that could help the whole of humanity. A discovery that could somehow bring an end to disease, if not death. To never die, to never know an end in sight does fill me with a kind of dread, but not one I am going to dwell on. Not when my full stop might be just a few sentences away. That is the shadow that threatens to blot out everything now.

This is all madness; I know that. It's all a beautiful, crazy, inconceivable quest that I am doomed to fail at, but that doesn't matter. Not when there is even the tiniest germ of hope remaining that tomorrow could be the day when forever finally begins.

VII

Let others tell of storms and showers,
I'll only count your sunny hours.

Traditional sundial motto

Chapter Forty-One

There are not many ways to get a painting out of an exhibition during its run. In fact, short of the owner of the painting demanding it be withdrawn, or an insurance issue, there is only one way. The thought of it plunges me into icy dread, and I try to recall the person I was in those dangerous years during the war, when I'd creep through the forest at night, intent on blowing up Nazi supply trains with consequences far more dire – and for many more people – than now, when all that is threatened is myself, my job and perhaps the imminent arrival of a criminal record.

I must cause damage to *La Belle* in some small, temporary way that will result in it being taken down to Conservation overnight. Then, when the studios are empty and everyone has left except for security, I will sign in Ben and his equipment as an 'insurance assessor', and we will have until dawn to unlock her secrets. There's no way to do this without putting myself and my job at risk, but then again both of those things have only existed to get to this moment, this hope of discovery. I can't imagine life beyond that yet.

I have had to wait until late in the day.

Anna cornered me at my desk the moment I walked in this morning.

'Hello, are you feeling revived?' she'd asked me.

'So revived,' I said. 'Had a lovely little break.' I'd found it hard not to talk about Ben. When I wasn't with him, I wanted to say his name, to think of his face and body, to remember his long limbs stretched out on my bed, his body arching under my hands. I'd nodded and tried not to give away my joy in my carefully composed, deadpan expression.

'I sense romance,' she said with a smile. 'You've got that look about you.'

'If I say yes, will you not ask me any more questions?' I said. 'It's new, you know.'

'Oh, to be young and in love again,' she said. 'I won't pry... for the rest of today at least.'

I will miss Anna when I have to leave, which I'm sure I will, at least for a few more decades, but I've had to come and go for most of my life. From the time when I built this house and called myself Madame Bianchi, until the day after tomorrow when someone will have to lose their job and I will insist it's me. But as I would have said when I was Madame Bianchi: *It's adieu, my love, not goodbye.*

I have often wondered whether someone might look at the portrait of my previous incarnation that hangs in the grand entrance hall and say, 'You look just like her.' But apart from that one time with Ben's family, they never do. Not even when I stand next to *La Belle*, and Ben looks at her and then at me, does he see the truth. When the truth is so hard to believe it becomes invisible. Strange how humans prefer palatable deceit.

I'd spent the rest of the day at my desk finishing reports, tying up loose ends for the next person who bags this dream job. I'd always thought it would only be about finding one answer, but I have loved all of this job. I love steeping myself in so much beauty and knowledge. I even love my ordinary little corner of the curator's room; my bog-standard desk, placed hard against one long elegant window in a room where I used to entertain dukes and princes, a little like a chambermaid who has made herself queen. Madame Bianchi was her own kind of revolutionary, but how pleased and proud she is now to have set aside her silks and jewels and earned her way to sitting in this humble revolving desk chair. The woman I am now was made here, and this small corner has been just as much a home to me as the whole of this great mansion. Now it's almost time to say goodbye again.

One more night and then I'll be done with the gallery. It has been my haven and refuge and one of a handful of places where I've felt at peace. But the time has come to move on, as it always eventually does.

★★★

There's a small can of water-soluble spray paint concealed in my pocket. I've timed this as carefully as I can, waiting until the exhibition is at its fullest during the after-work slot. I weave in and out of the press of people as they peer around one another to look at the paintings. I nod at the security guard on duty as I pass by and dive head-down into the crowd, offering up silent prayers of forgiveness with every step. It's not the first time that paintings have been attacked in the gallery, I tell myself. Suffragette Mary Richardson stabbed *The Rokeby Venus* in protest at the treatment of Mrs Pankhurst. She never was afraid to shy away from violence and controversy. I need to channel her spirit. And then there were the climate-change activists, throwing soup at Van Gogh. I could think of better targets for their ire, but they knew from the start that they would not permanently damage a masterpiece, in the same way that I do.

Because what I'm planning is much less destructive than soup and entirely temporary. It feels bad – it feels *terrible* – but it might just save a life.

Yet just as the moment arrives, I find all my self-justification melts away. I turn and walk hurriedly out of the exhibition, out of the gallery, into the hot, dry, exhaust-filled air of Trafalgar Square, where I gulp it in as though it's nectar.

What am I doing *really*: dragging Ben along with my obsession, looking for answers I have never found before after so much searching? If I fail, for me nothing changes, but for him? The age when magic and science collided for a few brief decades is long past. The legend was real once, but what if it just isn't any more? When I left Ben this morning he was so full of the hope that I have given him without telling him the reasons why. If I let him down I won't be able to live with myself. And yet I won't have any choice but to do just that.

Before Ben showed up in my life, I had no thought of a future, just the now, getting through every day with just enough will to see the next one. If I give up now and go back home, tell Ben I've changed my mind and that I can't go through with it, what would he say? He'd be sweet, he'd understand. He'd throw everything he has left into whatever time we have left together, pretending in every second that he can't hear the tick of the clock counting down.

And yet I can already hear the endless echoes of all that time empty of him.

I suddenly realise that I can't give up. I would do anything to try keeping him alive, even something as hopeless as damaging the portrait that means so much to me. Taking a deep breath, I walk back into the crowded rooms of the exhibition.

People congregate around each portrait in little knots, determined to spend time in front of each work, to dwell on each painting. This kind of exhibition might be their only chance to stand face to face with a Leonardo. But it's also competitive and claustrophobic: there's no time to linger or to stand and stare. This constant movement makes things all the more difficult, and as I look around I can see the multiple CCTV cameras covering every angle.

Keeping my hands in my pockets I let myself be carried by the slow current of the crowd, waiting for exactly the right moment. Hovering at the back of the throng, half-listening to the tour guide, Rita, explaining each painting to her group.

As my portion of the people gathers in front of *La Belle*, I turn my back to her as if I'm watching the guide, and just as I sense the group passing I take a step back and squirt a short, sharp burst of paint behind my back, straight from the hip.

Walking on, I wait for the shouts of horror, but nothing happens. Rita moves on and the crowd moves on. No one has noticed what I've done. Heart racing, I glance back casually at *La Belle*, relieved to see the paint has mostly hit the panel she is mounted on and a little of the frame. But there is enough – just enough – to have her removed from the exhibition for tonight.

I complete the circuit of the exhibition at an excruciatingly sedate pace and finally emerge through the exit. I go into the bathroom to check my hands for paint, and, after wiping the canister, drop it into a sanitary-disposal unit.

As I'm washing my hands, I meet my reflection, my eyes glittering with adrenalin.

'I'm doing this for us,' I tell the girl that found herself trapped by time half a thousand years ago. 'Please tell me that it will work?'

She does not reply.

There's still no activity coming from the exhibition room, except for the typical low murmur that hovers above the crowd as they travel through. Perhaps it was too subtle to cause a stir. After all, most of these people wouldn't know the difference. It seems I'll have to do it myself. But how, without looking suspicious? Everyone saw me take my usual daily route. If I go to the bathroom and come back and discover the splatter, then I am basically handing myself in.

As I stand outside the entrance, caught in indecision, Rita hurries over to me.

'Vita, something's happened,' she says in a low, urgent voice, her eyes wide with worry.

'What?' I ask her.

'Someone sprayed red paint on *La Belle Ferronnière*,' she whispers. 'What should we do? Shall I call the police?'

'Oh, my god.' I hate how good I am at lying. 'No, not yet. We need to stop the next round of visitors. Go and tell Mo to hold them at the door and I'll call Anna. And can you get everyone out a bit quicker without alerting them to the problem? I need the room empty in ten minutes, and we don't want this to get out. If the Louvre hears about it before we've assessed the situation, we're fucked.'

'I'm on it,' Rita says, her eyes wide with the intrigue and excitement.

Anna arrives in minutes, all but running up to the painting, her mouth falling open with a sharp inward gasp of dismay.

'Who would do such a thing?' She looks at Mo. 'How could this happen?'

'I'm so sorry, Anna.' Mo looks gutted. I realise suddenly that he is probably worried for his job now. I feel sick. 'The team had cameras on every painting.'

'OK. Deep breath. Let's think this through.' Anna stares at her feet for a moment, gathering her thoughts. I feel stuck to the spot, unable to speak.

'Right.' Anna takes a deep breath. 'Mo, get someone from Restoration up here now and all the CCTV for today.' She puts her hands on his arm. 'Don't worry, we'll figure this out. If anyone is on the chopping block, the buck stops with me. I sign off all the security protocols.'

'But I designed them,' I said. 'If anyone has to go, Anna, it should be me.'

Her eyes fill with grateful tears and she hugs me. I have never hated myself more.

'You aren't going anywhere,' she says, composing herself.

'Wait a minute,' I say, taking a bottle of water out of Rita's hand. 'There's something simple we can do to see what we're dealing with here. I tilt the bottle on to the hem on my skirt and wipe away a spot of the paint on the exhibition board. Smiling, I show Anna the resulting stain.

'Looks like it's water-soluble,' I say. 'Whoever did this must not have known what they were doing.'

'That is good,' Anna says. 'Excellent news,' she says as Fabrizio arrives, stroking his beard and peering at the splatter over the top of his glasses. 'Vita thinks this is water-soluble. What's the best-case scenario?'

'Hmm.' Fabrizio ponders this question for several seconds, during which Anna nearly explodes. 'I'd say Vita is right. We can get this cleaned up tonight and back on show tomorrow. I'll have to make a report for the Louvre.'

'Oh dear,' Anna sighs. 'I suppose it can't be avoided?'

'We have to.' Fabrizio straightens up. 'It's a matter of good practice, as you know. We have a duty of care to ensure that all restoration done to a painting is catalogued.'

'Of course,' Anna says.

'I'll do the paperwork,' I tell her. 'This is my exhibition and you have let me take all the glory for it. I certainly should be allowed to take the blame when things go wrong.'

'At least we keep it out of the press. Agreed?' Anna says.

Fabrizio nods.

'It should be fine,' I say. 'We'll take it down at closing and it will be back by tomorrow. I don't mind going with it and waiting for the work to be done. I'll stay until it's back. I'll oversee it all.'

'Vita, you're a brick,' Anna says. 'OK, let's get the painting removed now. Move some stuff around and say it will be back tomorrow. Give anyone who notices another ticket, gratis. And, Vita, you stay down here until the last person has left. Don't leave her side until she's in Restoration, poor thing.'

'I won't,' I promise.

I nod, and, seeing the strain on her face, my stomach churns with guilt.

'I'd better go and see the director.'

'Vita,' Mo approaches me, glancing at Anna as she leaves, before going on in a low voice, his eyes meeting mine, 'we've reviewed the CCTV.'

'And?' I ask, holding my breath.

'It's impossible to see anything. There are so many people. We have cameras everywhere, but somehow this person knew what they were doing. I'm so sorry.'

'OK, well, we need a security review,' I say. 'A new plan and new cameras need to be in place by opening tomorrow, whatever it takes.'

'I'm so sorry,' Mo says. 'I feel like this is my fault.'

'No,' I reassure him. 'This isn't your fault, Mo. You won't get the blame for this, OK? I'll make sure of it.'

'Thanks, Vita.' He is so grateful.

Nausea washes over me again and again as I stand next to *La Belle*, waiting for the conservation team to arrive with everything they need to move her. I feel her eyes on my back, implacable, serene.

Panic rises in my chest at the thought of what I've started here, and the terrifying dizzy fear of not knowing how it will end.

Chapter Forty-Two

Since Vita left I've been pacing around the kitchen table while Pablo watches me from under it, wagging his tail uncertainly. Feeling the need to do something, I grab Pablo's lead, to a great yelp of joy, and we venture out into the narrow streets of Soho. I know that if Vita manages to take the painting out of the exhibition that my lens will be able to analyse it in much more detail and with much more nuance than ever before. But what am I hoping to find there? A spell? A mathematical equation? Vita believes in the magic of the painting, and I believe in her. But suddenly the idea that it contains some tangible information that might somehow not only save my life but also make me immortal? That's madness. I know that's madness. And even if it wasn't, what would happen to me, after everyone I loved has gone, Mum, Kitty, Vita? That's an unendingly bleak future that I can barely contemplate, not even standing right here, under the shadow of death.

Everything has to end. Everything *should* end… including me. Just not right now.

In my heart I know it's nothing. I am prepared for it to be nothing. I don't even know what would happen to me if I really did live on for ever, but I *know* that I do not want to die. I want to cling on to every breath and every heartbeat in case it is the last.

'I know Vita loves London,' I tell Pablo, determined to push these thoughts out of my head, 'but why would anyone want to live in this city, where there aren't moors and woodlands, and only little squares full of small dogs wearing jackets and bow ties?'

I plan to take us straight back, so I can resume my pacing and counting down the hours, but somehow we get lost in less than 1,000 square metres. It's almost as if the entrance to Vita's secret square really is at the back of a wardrobe or something. We go right and right, searching for the entrance to her square, and twice pass a bright, orange-fronted juice bar that I'm sure I would remember having seen before but have no recollection of. But that is definitely the pub at the end of the road, isn't it? Increasingly amplified anxiety needles its way under my skin and I feel my chest tighten. Maybe all the happiness of the last couple of days has distracted me from the little signs I'd noticed before.

Could it be that I'm not noticing I'm about to die?

The thought stops me in my tracks, literally. Strangers swear under their breath as they swerve around me, and Pablo yips at me to get going, but I don't move. Maybe *all* of this has been a dream, that final explosion of neurons easing me from life to death with a fantasy that feels like days to me, but is really only seconds. If it is, do I care? What can I do about it anyway? Maybe I dropped dead that first time I met Vita and took her with me into brain death as a final comfort. That seems terribly plausible. Because if I was ever going to conjure up something to take away the fear of death it would be her; it would be this bright morning with the promise of a completed quest waiting at the end of the day.

Fear roars towards me at 1,000 miles a second. I don't want to go. I don't want to die. My heart races, my breath comes quick and sharp, and all of a sudden, tears are pouring down my cheeks.

What if there is nothing? What is there is nothing after this?

In the middle of the street, I stare up at corners of blue sky.

Please don't take me. Please let me live. Please. Please. Please.

Whatever pain comes with living too long, I will take it gladly.

Pablo jumps up at me, scrabbling his paws against my stomach. I look down at him and see all the people walking by, pretending not to notice me. A sudden shuddering inward breath reminds me that I am not dead yet, and that is the best I can expect. I got lost. I stopped paying attention, but I'm not dead. I then see the entrance of the alley that leads to her square and the sundial that never sees the sun.

'Sorry, mate,' I tell Pablo as he yips again. 'I was just having a small breakdown. It's over now.'

★★★

Vita's neighbour Mariah is standing on her front step smoking like a Fifties movie star, if Fifties movie stars wore flannel nighties.

'Fancy a smoke?' She offers me a cigarette. I haven't smoked since I was 15, but that moment on the street has shaken me, so I take one and let her light it. It won't be nicotine that kills me, after all.

'Now isn't this fella handsome?' she says, creaking down to take a seat on the step and make a fuss of Pablo, who decides immediately she's his new best friend on the basis that she's got something that smells tasty in her pockets. 'Look at you, with your lovely face and your waggy tail – nearly as good-looking as your dad, you are!'

She laughs delightedly at my blushing and pats the step next to her.

'Sit down here and flirt with me a minute,' she says. 'Don't get any funny ideas, mind. I love my Len, and he'll be back from work before long. I just like to keep my hand in, you know. So, you are Evie's young gentleman, come to visit at last. I thought she'd stay in France for ever after the war, but I'm glad she's home – I've missed her.' She stamps out one cigarette under her foot and lights another. 'When I was a kid it was always Evie who'd keep my pecker up, during the bad times, you know. Bombs were falling from the sky and everything was rationed, but she always had sweets and a song for me. Nothing scared Evie, not even Hitler.'

'She sounds formidable,' I say.

'Well, you ought to know, Dominic,' she says, murmuring into Pablo's ears. 'What a silly chap he is, hey Kip?'

'How long was Evelyn in France?' I ask.

'She went in '44. Oh, I cried, I did. I begged her not to go, but she had to, she said. Said she'd been drafted into a munitions factory up north. Course she couldn't tell us where she was really going, that was all secret. But I worked it out after the war, when she wrote to me from France to tell me she was married. Took her so long to come back, and here I am 20 years old and married! Len wants us to get our own place – he can't stand living with my mum. But I told him. I said, if the Nazis can't get me out of this place neither can you, Len Walker. That shut him up.'

'So was Evie a spy?' I ask, fascinated.

'Well, she never told me in so many words, but I reckon it's a dead cert,' Mariah says. 'That's where you swept her off her feet, after all. She doesn't talk about it. It's not the done thing to make a fuss, is it? But we know what you were doing out there. Blowing up Nazis!' She glances at me as she giggles. 'Here, talk some French to me, would you? I do love to hear it.'

'I can do a spot of Yorkshire for you?' I offer.

'Seriously now.' She leans towards me, threading her slender wrists through the railings that divide us, to put her hand on my knee. For a moment I'm a bit worried about what she's going to suggest next. 'You take care of my Evie. She's been through a lot and none of it's her fault, you remember that. None of it's her fault.'

'I will,' I promise.

'Don't you go dying on her. She's had enough of that. I said to my doctor, I said, I'm not moving into no home and I'm not dying. I've got Vita to think of.'

Her words punch me in the gut and I draw in a sharp breath.

It seems like Mariah is back in the present for a moment. Her pale-blue eyes search out mine and lock on.

'You feeling quite all right, son?'

'Just a bit...' I can't explain the fear that has just shot through me. 'I just really care about her.'

'Good. Because I'm watching you, fella,' she says. I'm glad I took a cigarette now. 'You hurt my Vita and I'll be after you. I might not look like much, but I have my ways.'

'Mariah, I need to tell you something.' I know she might not remember what I say and that it probably won't matter to her, but she means so much to Vita that it matters to me to know what she thinks. 'I'm terminally ill. I am going to die soon,' I tell her. 'I love Vita so much, and we both know that it will be her who pays the price for how happy we are now. She told me that's what she wants, and I believe her. But should I just walk away now and save her the pain later?'

Mariah thinks for a moment, sucking on her cheek, her eyes never leaving mine.

'No, I suppose not,' she says eventually. 'I could see when she introduced you to me that you've brought a light to her, and she needs it, even if it's only for a little while. The memory of you will keep her going for another lifetime. Like the memory of my Len does me. Oh, I know he's dead and long gone, 20 years ago now.' She frowns. 'Or is it 30? Anyway, to me he's still just in the other room, you see? And even though his body's gone, his love is still here.' She taps first her chest and then her forehead. 'You won't know this about me, Dominic, but my mind goes AWOL from time to time, and then I don't have to imagine Len in my arms any more, because there he is, and it's wonderful. I suppose it will all get a bit messy one day, but I don't mind it so much now, coming and going like I do. People are kind to me. Vita is kind to me. She takes care of me, just like Evie did. And when I'm so far gone that I don't know how to breathe or eat any more, well, I'll be off somewhere with my Len, and none of that stuff will matter to me, will it? We're the lucky ones, you and me. It's those we leave behind that suffer.'

Unexpected tears blur my vision, and I have to look away as I wipe my eyes on my sleeve.

'Mariah.' A woman emerges from the house. 'Stop flirting and come in now, your lunch is ready.'

'Sometimes I get why Len doesn't like living with Mum,' Mariah mutters as I help her up. 'And as you for you, young man, you should know better. I'm a married woman!'

After that the temptation to open drawers stuffed with papers and look through them is strong, because I can't think of a better distraction to keep me occupied between now and when I leave to meet Vita than learning about the story of a Resistance heroine. But that would be a betrayal of privacy – of Vita's and Evelyn's, and whoever lived here before her. I scan every one of the portraits and photographs that line the walls again, hoping to come across a photograph of heroic Evelyn. I pick up book after book and put them all back, then eventually I go into the sitting room, and look at the big, fancy Chinese cupboards.

Opening one of the doors wouldn't be prying, would it? That would just be art appreciation.

When opened, the doors reveal about two dozen beautifully decorated drawers, like an actual treasure chest. When me and Kitty were little, Mum would read us *Pippi Longstocking*, and I'd dream about what it would be like to have a pirate dad who left me with a huge chest full of treasures. This is exactly what I imagined.

Brushing aside any misgivings, I pull each drawer open in turn.

There seem to be only one or two objects in each one. In the first I find smoky glass and gold beads, threaded on to a very fragile ribbon that might once have been scarlet and gold, and a small smooth oval of amber set in gold and strung on to a fine chain. Both look very old and delicate. In the next there is a pebble that fits nicely into the palm of my hand, and is a pleasing, soft brown, the colour of Pablo's eyes, set with little flecks of crystal. I wonder if it was Vita or her aunt who picked up this stone, and where they were. Perhaps on a beach somewhere, maybe with someone they loved. Perhaps this ordinary-looking brown stone used to be a symbol of something – of love lost or found – and it still goes on holding on to that memory even when there is no one left to remember.

Then I find a strange, square object that I deduce is a compass, even though it's covered in Chinese symbols. The needle turns to the north as I rotate it gently. Carefully I put it back, afraid of breaking something that has been pointing one way in the dark for so very long. I open and close drawers and find things that seem so mundane: an empty bottle made of thick glass; a pocket watch stopped at midnight or midday. In the next drawer, though, there is a very old-looking piece of paper – parchment, I'm guessing.

There are letters written on it in a language I don't understand, and strange drawings of people and symbols. A shudder runs through me, and I close that drawer quickly, glancing over my shoulder as if I have just let something out.

Catching my breath, when I open the next drawer I find a revolver. Carefully I take it out. I'm no arms expert but it looks old to me. Was this Evelyn's service revolver, the weapon she kept at her hip as she worked with the Resistance?

Next, I find a posy of dried flowers that looks as if even a strong breath might reduce it to dust.

And then, in the bottom drawer, there is something so small I almost miss it. It's a button, a light-blue button – the button from my shirt that came loose that first night with Vita. She has added it here, to this strange collection of memories that stretches way back before either of us was born. She picked up this little piece of plastic and placed it here. Oh, how I want to stay with her for ever.

***

Finally, it's time to leave. I give Pablo my sweater to sleep on and fill two china cereal bowls with water and food.

'Won't be long, mate,' I tell him.

It all gets to me a bit, just as I'm about to open the front door. This is it. Fear knots my gut. To believe in Vita, to have faith in her and her quest has been the most beautiful distraction from the terrifying dark. Tonight I get to examine *La Belle* for myself, to be close to her, next to her; to look into her eyes and ask her what she knows at last.

I know in my heart that the secret she is chasing *has* to be impossible. And yet, I find I am unable to give up that last shred of hope. But tonight, one way or another I will have an answer, even if it is that there is no answer. And I have to prepare myself for that to be enough. To be glad for every good thing the last few days have brought. To be alongside the tragedy. Tonight, I take down the windmills.

I open the door and find Jack standing on the other side, hand raised to knock.

'All right, mate?' I say, taking in his turned-up linen trousers and sandals. 'Vita's at work.'

'It's you I came to see,' he says, taking off his aviator shades and twisting them in his hands.

'Oh. Right.' It would be good to get to know Jack, as Vita's oldest friend, but his timing is terrible. 'The thing is, I'm running a bit late to meet Vita.'

I close the door behind me, edging past him down the stone steps. He follows me.

'Please can I just speak to you before you go to see her?' he asks. 'I'll make this quick.'

Suddenly I look past the clothes and the hair and see a man who looks anguished – in fact, who looks like he hasn't slept in days. 'OK. Is everything all right, Jack?'

Jack takes a deep breath, and I realise he's been rehearsing this speech all the way over here.

'You think you know Vita,' he says, 'but you've only known her a few days. You think you are in love with her, but you can't be, because you don't know the whole of her. You don't really know the first thing about her – what she's lived through, what she's seen.' He looks away as he says this, his words coming out with difficulty. 'And I worry that if you did, you would feel differently about her. That you don't really know what you are getting yourself into.'

Suddenly, the reality of the situation dawns on me. 'You are in love with her, aren't you? Is that what this is about? Because, mate, I won't be your competition for very long.'

'You don't understand. There's a lot at stake here. More than just now. However you decide to live the rest of your life, however long that happens to be, you deserve her honesty and she deserves... to be sure of what she is choosing. That's why I'm asking you, for your sake *and* hers, not to go to meet her tonight. Just go home, go back to Yorkshire and forget you ever met her. You don't know what you're getting yourself into.'

I frown. What does he mean, I don't know what I'm getting myself into? I should press further but I don't want to know. I just need to keep believing for as long as I can.

'Look, I'm sure you mean well, but I can't talk about it now. I've got to go.' I try to walk past him but he stands in my way. 'Jack, you clearly need to tell Vita how you really feel about her. Get it off your chest. If that's the choice you want her to make, then she can't do anything about it unless she knows. But I think she will choose me, because maybe we only met a few days ago, but I believe that what we have is real. Now, please get out of my way. I need to go.'

'When she realises what she's done to you she won't be able to live with herself,' Jack tells me. 'Except she will have no choice but to do just that, and it will drive her mad. If you really believe you love her then the kindest thing you could do would be to leave her.'

'What is it that you think Vita is doing to me?'

'She's…' Jack struggles to say more. 'She's not being honest with you.'

'Look, I don't have time for this now,' I tell him. 'So please, let me go.'

'Ben.' He grabs my shoulder. As I try to duck, I find myself somehow off-balance and stumble backwards.

Smack. The back of my head hits the stone steps with a sickening thud. Fuck! This would be a very stupid way to die.

I lie perfectly still, afraid to move.

'Oh, god, Ben, are you OK?' Jack's at my side. 'I'm sorry. I didn't mean to. I'll phone for an ambulance.'

'I'll be fine in a minute,' I say. Seconds pass and the world doesn't seem to end. I sit up very slowly and touch the back of my head. No blood, no cut. Perhaps it wasn't as bad as it felt.

'How do you feel?' Jack asks. 'What can I do?'

'I think I'm fine,' I tell him. 'I just need to go.'

Jack puts his arm under my shoulder to help me to my feet.

'I'm sorry,' he says as he steadies me, taking a step away. 'Do you really love her, Ben? If the stakes weren't so high, would you still love her?'

'I love her,' I say; the truest thing I ever have. 'It's only been a few days, but I know that I always will.'

'Right, I'm sorry.' He hesitates a moment longer before adding, 'Look, for both your sakes, just ask Vita to tell you the truth.'

He walks away briskly.

Suddenly it hits me; Jack is trying to tell me there is no legend; no miracle cure-all. That Vita believes in something that doesn't exist. Of course, it makes sense. I have fallen for a woman swept up in a delusion.

And yet, I realise in the same breath that nothing has changed. I will follow her dream as far as it will let me, no matter whether it's real or not.

Alone now in the dark little square, I sit and wait for the world to stop spinning and for my stomach to drop out of my chest. It was just a bit of a bang, that's all. I've had worse.

Pablo barks at the door, scratching to get to me.

'Everything is OK, boy,' I tell him. 'I just need a minute to—'

The dark drops out of nowhere.

Chapter Forty-Three

I sit on a stool beside Fabrizio as he meticulously removes the paint from *La Belle* with nothing more than a series of cotton buds, a jar of clean water and a great deal of patience. It's soothing to watch him at work. The room is imbued with his calmness, as if his concentration alone can slow down both hearts and time into something close to slumber.

'A terrible thing to happen,' he says softly as picks up a new cotton bud. 'But not permanent, thank god. She will be fully restored, every trace of today's incursion completely removed.' He glances up at me. 'What a strange thing to do. And for what purpose?' He sighs. 'You know, I don't think I understand this modern world, Vita.' Through his magnifying glass he examines the corner he has cleaned. 'There, she is restored.'

'Thank you, Fabrizio,' I say with a sigh of relief. Even though I had selected the paint with great care, the thought that I might have altered the painting in some lasting way had terrified me. 'What a day, eh?'

'Pah, I've had worse.' He banishes my stress with a wave of his hand. 'At least I have had the privilege to sit before the work of the master and wonder at his genius. For me this has been a very fine day.'

'You make an excellent point,' I say. 'So, will she be reframed tonight?'

'No, no rush. Maggie has cleaned the frame too. She tells me she will be able to reframe *La Belle* first thing tomorrow. She will be back in her place in the exhibition before the doors open, and all will be well.' He folds his arms, smiling fondly at the portrait. 'Yes, she is a priceless work of art, but still underneath the magic there is just oil, pigment and wood. All that is required is great care and respect.'

'Oh, Fabrizio, I wish you'd adopt me,' I say, having to resist the urge to weep on his shoulder. 'You always make everything better. You've saved my life today. How can I repay you?'

'Come home and have dinner with Clara and me?' He offers. 'My wife has at least five suitors she would like to match you with, including our son, but don't tell his wife.'

'Oh!' I laugh. 'I'm taken, Fabrizio. Sorry to disappoint you.'

'The young man you brought to see me?' he asks, as he stands up, going to fetch his jacket from the old-fashioned coat stand he keeps down here. 'Come. I'll lock up after us.'

'Yes, that's him. It's new, but I like him a lot. And don't worry. I've still got a ton of paperwork to do, half of it in French. You go. I'll lock up and liaise with the security guys before I leave.'

'Very well. I must break the news to Clara that you are no longer available. She will be heartbroken.' He smiles as he closes the door behind him.

I check the clock on the wall. Ben should be here any minute. Leaving Fabrizio's room, I pick my way through the basement labyrinth, noting that the lights are off in the discovery lab and that we should have the whole floor to ourselves. Reaching the fire door, I disarm the alarm, unlock the barred metal gate that covers the door and leads to a set of dank, concrete steps, and then the grille that covers the recess from the street. The air is warm and the narrow strip of late-evening sky that slots between the rooftops is ultramarine blue. I can see one star faintly glowing despite the city lights.

Sitting down on the top step I wait for Ben, trying to unwind my mind from the tangle of this strange day. When he arrives, we will be alone with the painting. I try to bend my mind to all the possibilities the coming hours will hold.

I imagine him focusing his lens on her, and suddenly revealing miraculous, impossible secrets from the painting. I see him picking me up and twirling me around in joy.

It seems impossible that before the dying sun rises again, all of this will be over and we will know.

But Ben still isn't here. He's 30 minutes late, and though I haven't known him long, it doesn't seem like he would want to be late for something so important. When I call him, his voice-mail picks up. I repeat the call three times and get the same result. For a moment I think about calling Sarah or Kitty, but I know the moment they see my name appear on their phone screen they will fear the worst. But what if it is the worst?

I stand up, making myself breathe through the fear. Ben is only a short walk away. He will appear around the bend in the alley at any moment. And if not, he will be at my house. His phone prob- ably ran out of charge, or perhaps he fell asleep on the sofa and didn't wake up.

And didn't wake up.

A cold wash of fear threads ice through my veins.

My fingers stiff and fumbling, I relock the grate and the door, stuffing the keys into my pocket, as I hurry up from the basement back to the security office.

'Hi, Sam,' I say, a little too fast as I all but run into the jun- ior security guy's desk. 'I'm waiting for a guy from the insurance company to look at *La Belle* – his name is Ben Church. Have you seen him?'

'Nope,' Sam says, tapping his Biro on the desk. 'Been all quiet since we closed. You all right? You look a bit strung out.'

'Well, it's been quite a day. Maybe he's lost.' I do my best to smile when I want to cry. 'I know what. I'll pop out and have a quick look for him. Don't be surprised if you see me turning up again later with him – all the admin has got to tied up by tomor- row.'

'Yeah, don't worry, Vita. We got you,' Sam says reassuringly. 'Hope you find him. I'll give you a shout if he turns up here, yeah?'

'Thanks, Sam.'

★★★

The house is dark, the square empty. Inside I can hear Pablo bark- ing and scratching at the door.

Where is Ben? I know he hasn't left me. If he'd left me, he would have taken Pablo with him, and in a way that would be a relief, to know that he had just changed his mind about me but was safe.

What has happened? What—?

Pablo scrambles into my arms as I open the door, clawing anxiously at my chest as if he's trying to burrow into me.

'Where is he, boy?' I ask the dog. 'Where is he?'

Pablo bolts out of the open door. I watch as he darts around our little shadowy square, his nose to the ground as he searches for Ben. He repeats the same search three or four times, and then inexplicably he curls up on the second step outside my house, whimpering and shaking, his tail over his nose.

Ben's trail stops right where it started.

Terrified, I knock on Mariah's door.

'Hello, Evie, love,' she says. 'We're just going out, me and Len.'

She gestures into her sitting room, and for a moment I think I'll see Ben there, cast in the role of her beloved husband, reluctant to leave her until her night carer arrives. But the chair she gestures to is empty.

'Mariah, it's Vita,' I say carefully. 'Have you seen Ben?' I ask desperately. 'I was supposed to meet him almost an hour ago now. Pablo's upset and I can't think where he would be.'

'I don't know anyone called Ben, Evie,' Mariah says. 'Have you got any sweets for me?'

'Here,' I pull a couple out of my pocket and drop them into her palm.

'Green ones,' she says, disappointed, as she peers at them. This is 8-year-old Mariah, not the Mariah I need now. Taking a deep breath, I try again.

'Mariah, it's me. It's Vita. Think now, because it's important. I need to know if you have seen my friend Ben today. Remember Ben? Tall and skinny, nice, kind Ben?'

'Oh, I met your Dominic,' Mariah says, popping one of the sweets into her mouth. 'He spoke to me in French.'

'Mariah!' I find myself grabbing her slender arms. Her eyes widen in fear, and I back away at once. 'I'm sorry.' I let her go, 'I'm so sorry. It's just I don't know where he is, and I'm scared. I'm so scared that I'll be too late.'

'Vita?' It's Seba from the restaurant, looking up at me from the bottom step, his face full of concern. 'Are you looking for your friend?'

'Ben, yes. Have you seen him?'

'Yes, Ben,' Mariah says, as if a lightbulb has just switched on in her memory. 'I remember him. He dropped dead right on my doorstep!'

'What?' I gasp, as the street falls away from under my feet.

'No, no,' Seba reassures me. 'He was unconscious, yes. We thought maybe a fall. Viv called the ambulance. She didn't want to tell you over the phone, knowing that... well... She waited as long as she could to tell you in person, but she had to go home so she asked me to tell you. He's gone to the Royal Free.'

My knees buckle and Seba catches me just before I fall.

'I told her we should have called you,' Seba says. 'I said you'd want to know, but it was only just an hour ago.'

All the time in the world.

'I'll make some tea,' Mariah announces.

'No, thank you, I need to get to the hospital right away. Seba, thank you.'

'I'll take you,' he says decisively, nodding at his motorbike. 'I've got my bike and a spare helmet. Much quicker than a taxi.'

'Thank you.'

I turn back to Mariah as Seba goes to get his stuff.

'I'm so sorry,' I say gently. 'I am so scared but that's no excuse to frighten you. Please forgive me.'

'You haven't frightened me, Evie,' she says. 'Have you got any sweets?'

'No, not today, but...' I look at Pablo curled up on the step. 'Will you look after Ben's dog for a bit? I don't think he wants to be alone.'

'Really?' Mariah claps her hands together in delight. 'Come on, boy. I've got a chop you can have, yes I have.'

It takes until Seba returns for Pablo to be coaxed inside with a bit of ham. Mariah sits down on her sofa, and he climbs to sit at her side at once, resting his head and paws on her lap.

'You're a good boy, aren't you, Kip. Aren't you a good boy?'

'Ready?' Seba asks me kindly from the doorway.

'No,' I say.

Chapter Forty-Four

I wake slowly and painfully, as if I've been stuck naked to a piece of flypaper. Everything hurts and yet somehow, I feel disconnected from my body, as if I've already moved out. Distantly I remember reading about near-death experiences. Is this me looking down on my own demise?

With great, nauseating effort, I can raise my hand to touch my face. I am still alive.

The room seems to move and fall apart, reconnecting in all the wrong places. I can't tell which way up I am. I need to get up, let gravity figure it out.

Sitting up, it feels as though my brain is trying to escape out of the back of my head, and my stomach lurches. Bitter fluid floods my mouth and I fall backwards or forwards, I'm not sure which. I'm supposed to be somewhere. I'm supposed to be doing something. Vita.

This is a hospital room. I know hospital rooms. Closing my eyes, I reach down for the familiar weight and shape of a call button.

'I need to go,' I tell the nurse that comes to my side.

'Not a good idea,' she tells me as she takes my obs. 'The doctors wanted me to page them as soon as you woke up. They'll be here soon.

'Right.' My heart sinks. Whatever it is they have to say, I know I don't want to hear it. I need to shake off this heavy drunken feeling. I need to get to Vita.

When he arrives, the doctor introduces himself as Mr Perrera, and tells me that he and his colleagues have already been in touch with my consultant in Leeds. As he recites the history of my condition right up until the discovery of the aneurysm, he seems to know more about me than I do.

'So,' he says, 'you are a rare bird. It's not often we see something of that size and complexity involved in so many important structures of the brain.'

'I'm really sorry, but I don't want to talk about my aneurysm. I just want to go, please.'

'We took a CT scan of you while you were out, compared it to your last one, and there's no movement or bleeding that we can discern in your brain, though you have got a lump the size of a small avocado on the back of your head and we'd like to keep an eye on you for a couple of days. What happened? Did you have any pain? – a blackout? A fit? Any nausea leading up to the event?'

'I just fell over,' I say. 'Look, with the best will in the world, I need to go.'

'I see,' he says.

'I mean basically, it's no worse than it was yesterday. That's what you are saying? If the prognosis is still the same and I might drop dead at any given moment, then I don't want to waste any time here.'

'Yes, well, more or less.' He smiles at his flunky as though they are all in on some private joke that I'm not privy to.

'I know.'

'Reading your notes, I see your consultant didn't think surgery was advisable. I can see why – the risks of causing permanent brain damage, paralysis or death are very high.'

'That about sums it up,' I say.

'Have you had any symptoms? Blurred vision, headaches, nausea, hallucinations?'

'Yes,' I say. 'But not too badly, and not for long. I assume that means that things are OK, at least for now. Which is why I'd like to go and live however much life I've got left.'

'Ben,' Mr Perrera hesitates, 'Mrs Patterson was completely right to rule out surgery and to keep a close eye on you instead – that's absolutely the sensible call. However, we have a specialist AVM clinic here. We've been trialling advanced techniques for almost a decade, and given your prognosis without intervention we would, with your permission, be willing to attempt a surgical solution.'

'What?' The room tilts off centre and doesn't come back.

'We could try to shrink it with a laser knife. Because of the location the odds of success are not great, and if you were to survive all the normal risks of brain damage, etcetera, would apply, but we would be willing to try, with your permission. There is a chance – a very slight but real chance – that we could remove the risk it poses entirely.'

'You mean you could cure me?' I sit up too quickly, causing everything to spin in a kaleidoscope of pain.

'Cure is a strong word. The AVM would still be in place but if everything went according to plan we could bring about a solution that would significantly lower your risk of a further intercranial bleed and give you the same life expectancy as any man of your age. We calculate that there is a 12-per-cent chance of success. Although this is the first procedure of this kind that we will have carried out here, we are world-renowned experts in this field. We can give you your best chance, if you are prepared to take it.

'Oh.' No words arrive. 'Oh.'

'It's a lot to take in,' he says. 'Look, let us keep you in for observation tonight. Why don't you rest up and tomorrow we can talk through the procedure in greater detail; give you a chance to assimilate all the information. How does that sound?'

'Nah, you're all right, thanks,' I say. The thought of Vita waiting for me is the only clear thought I have. I push myself out of bed despite the pain that shoots down my spine, causing the room to split into infinite versions.

'Mr Church... Ben,' he persists. 'I really don't recommend you leave us now. Things look good, but you never know with something like this. We really need to keep an eye on you overnight to be on the safe side.'

'I've got somewhere to be,' I say. 'Where's my bag? Have you got my bag?'

'You didn't arrive with a bag.'

'Bloody hell,' I say. 'I need it. I need my bag. What's the time? I'm late already. Where's my bag? I need it. I haven't got another one!'

'Ben, I have it. Mariah kept it safe for you.' I hear her voice and turn towards it, relief rushing through me as she appears, parting the medics as she comes to my bed, takes my hand and kisses it. 'I've got it. Everything's safe. What about you?'

'Vita, I'm so sorry I'm late.' I begin. Vita puts her arms around my shoulders and gently kisses my temple. I relax into her arms.

'It doesn't matter,' she says. 'It doesn't matter.'

'I beg your pardon. We haven't been introduced,' Mr Perrera interrupts.

'Vita Ambrose,' she says. 'Ben's girlfriend.'

Our eyes meet, Ben nods slightly, our fingers interlock. We are together.

'OK, well, Vita,' he says, 'perhaps you can persuade Ben to stay in for observation and he can talk through some of the things we've discussed. And Ben, tomorrow we can go through it all in detail. Is that acceptable?'

'Yep,' I say, giving him a thumbs-up and leaning back on my pillow.

Once he has left the room, I sit up again.

'Come on. Let's get out of here,' I say, reaching for the plastic bag that has my clothes in it.

'Ben.' Her hand stops mine. 'He said you needed to stay in.'

'I'm fine. I have a headache, and a bump on the head, but nothing's changed,' I tell her. That's basically true.

'What happened?'

'It was stupid. Jack came by as I was leaving your house, and then after he was gone I slipped down the steps and banged my head, blacked out. Good job your neighbours are so nosy. But I'm fine – sore, but fine.' Whatever it is, it can wait until after I'm dead. 'How did it go at the museum?'

Her shoulders slump.

'I did it,' she says, as if she can hardly believe it herself. 'I feel sick. Poor Anna, poor Mo. But it worked and I'm going to resign tomorrow. That way everyone else can keep their jobs.' She closes her eyes for a moment. 'But it worked.'

It suddenly hits me exactly what Vita has sacrificed for me and I feel guilty that I ever doubted her.

'I'm sorry, I never should have let you do this. You love your job.'

'You didn't let me do anything. I do love my job, but I'll be OK. Anyway, none of that matters now. What was he talking about when he said you should tell me about *the things you've discussed*?'

'The usual stuff,' I say.

Vita's expression as she gently kisses each cheek and my forehead is one of beautiful sadness. The truth is I'd rather know I could have even just a few good hours with her than take the risk of losing them for a lifetime. I've lived so long in my head that now I've finally found out how to exist in the moment, it's too wondrous to want to go back.

'I love you,' I say, reaching for her hand. 'And you basically pulled off the crime of the century this afternoon. All I want now is to know the answer, to know if the legend is true. That, and I don't want to waste any time here.'

'I don't want to do anything that will put you in danger.'

'You won't,' I tell her. 'I'm in exactly the same amount of danger now as I was this morning, and we will never get this chance again. Let's just go. I promise it will be fine.'

Vita studies my face for a while, and as she is thinking I realise the room has stopped tilting and my vision is clear. My head hurts like there's no tomorrow, but I suppose that is to be expected, and besides, maybe there won't be a tomorrow.

'OK,' she says. 'Did you drop your bag when you fell? What if the lens is damaged?'

'It's fine. It's in a protective case. If you have my bag, I have everything I need,' I say.

'This is it,' Vita says, her complexion pale as she takes my hand. 'No going back.'

Never before has an expression felt so true.

Chapter Forty-Five

I let us in through the basement entrance, waving at the security camera as I lock the door behind me. Sam nods up and down once to signify he's seen us. The phone is ringing in the conservation lab as I let us in. Ben hesitates in the doorway, catching his breath. The lights are low but *La Belle* seems to glow in the dark, shining out from her corner of time with renewed intensity, as if she is expecting something to happen at last. I know exactly how she feels.

'Hi, Sam,' I say. 'Is it OK if we do the signing in and out paperwork on the way out? Really keen to just get cracking with the assessment.'

'OK, but don't forget, yeah?' Sam cautions me. 'I don't need trouble from Mo. He's right shook about all this.'

'Promise I won't,' I reassure him, worrying about how I've traumatised Mo. When I hand in my resignation letter I must make sure to point out that Mo was not at fault in any way. 'We'll be down here a while, probably until dawn, so don't worry about us.'

I hang up the phone and look at Ben, who is looking at *La Belle*. And I don't mean just standing before her. He's pulled up a stool and is sitting inches away from her face, almost nose to nose. She meets his gaze steadily.

'Sorry to interrupt, but where do we start?' I ask, making him start a little.

'It's just seeing her out of her frame. It makes her seem more real somehow.' Now would be a good moment but I let it pass in silence. He pauses to take her in again, studying every detail of her face. I wait until he breaks away. He doesn't look at me as he unzips his bag. 'I've got all the software I need on my laptop, and my lens, which I designed to fit over an LAM camera just like the one you use for imaging here.' He looks around. 'Wait, where is it?'

'Next door,' I say. 'We'll have to take her into the lab.'

'That means we'll be on CCTV, right?' Ben says.

'Yes, but only in the hallway, and then I'll have to log into the system there for you to upload your software,' I say. 'Look, someone is bound to ask what we were doing, what your credentials are, why I was logged in on this system and uploaded new software. They might not notice right away but they will notice eventually. Maybe if we stopped right now and went home then we might get away with it, but probably not even then. So let's just do what you have worked so hard for, and deal with the consequences later.'

'Are you sure you really want to do this?' Ben says. 'We could just stop now and nothing would have changed.'

'We've come this far,' I say. 'And don't get it into your head that this is all just for you. It's for me too.'

'Right then.' He looks at *La Belle*, sitting there watching us. 'Do we just... pick her up and carry her?' he asks.

'No!' I exclaim. 'We wheel her round on her easel. The less we actually handle her the better. She is 500 years old, you know! You get the doors. I'll move her. I'm insured, at least. Though I'm not sure if that still applies under these circumstances.'

The lab phone is ringing as we position *La Belle* in front of the LAM camera. Sam is obviously paying good attention tonight. I pick up the phone as Ben goes back to get his equipment.

'Dude, what are you doing?' Sam says when I pick up the phone. 'You can't just roll that thing around the hallways like it's nothing, bro.'

'We need high-res photos for the insurer,' I explain, 'so they can be satisfied there is no lasting damage. It's all good, Sam. Don't worry. You know me. Would I do anything to risk a Leonardo?'

'No, otherwise I'd be down there keeping an eye on you in the labs where the CCTV don't go. He's your favourite painter, isn't he?' he says. 'I prefer that Artemisia bird.'

'He's special to me. I won't do anything to put this painting at risk.' The lies I'm telling are coming at increasing velocity. I'm in too deep to do anything else now.

'If you say so,' Sam says. I take the phone out into the hall to give him a cheery, reassuring wave before I hang up. I will make sure that there are no consequences for him or Mo or even Anna – that is one thing I can do to salve my conscience, at least.

'I'll start setting up,' Ben says, going to the fixed camera as I log into the system. He takes a square black box out of his backpack and I watch as, after putting on cotton gloves and carefully removing his lens, he fits it over the camera.

'I just need to get the focusing right and upload my software and then we'll be ready. It will take a while to complete the imaging, and then we'll have to wait for the software to sort out the light frequencies and make sense of them, and then...' He shudders visibly, suddenly hugging his arms around himself, staggering back a couple of steps.

'Are you OK?' I cross to his side at once, putting a steadying arm around him and guiding him to a seat.

'I'm OK. Just a bit tired and cold. Is it cold in here?' I turn his face to me. He looks pale, grey almost. This is all too much for him. I shouldn't have let him leave the hospital.

'These rooms are temperature-regulated, but they're not cold.' I take his freezing hands and rub them between my palms. 'You are probably feeling the after effects of shock. Let me take you back to hospital, please.'

'No.' He is adamant. 'No. I don't want to go back there. I'll be fine. I just need something to eat probably. I've got a cereal bar in my bag. Mum has been secreting them about me since I was 16, in case I forget to feed myself. Can you turn the heat up a bit? But not if it will harm the painting or anything.'

'I think I can a little,' I tell him. 'There are parameters that are centrally controlled but they do allow us a little bit of leeway.'

Before I can move he pulls me into a hug, kissing me with such tenderness that it's as if it's me who is the fragile one and not him.

We linger in the embrace, his body drawing heat from mine as he holds me against him.

Regretfully he draws back, scanning my face. 'These last few days with you have been the best of my life,' he says simply. 'No matter what happens now, I wouldn't change anything. Make sure you remember that.'

'High crimes and hospital visits?' I smile as I touch his cheek. 'Are you sure about that?'

'Completely sure.' He nods, straightening his shoulders. 'Now, to work.'

***

'So, what we are able to do with my new and improved Layer Amplification Method is to use a series of intense lights directed at *La Belle* to give us measurements of the light's reflection. Basically, it enables us to look inside the layers of paint and, through a series of minute comparisons, determine any underpainting, even if it is invisible to X-ray and infrared.

'Sorry.' He looks up at me, and I shake my head, confused.

'I don't mean to geek out. I'm more reminding myself what I'm doing. This is mostly stuff I've taught myself. So, anyway, it's your job to keep an eye on the monitors. You're familiar with the kinds of images that previous tech throws up. It isn't always clear if you don't know what you are looking for and this technique is controversial as it is, as a lot of people think it's all smoke, mirrors and Photoshop.'

'Well, we'll find out soon enough.'

Sitting in silence I watch as Ben goes through his settings and positions the equipment precisely with an almost balletic ease and confidence. The tension that has shaped his guarded limbs since I found him at the hospital drains slowly away. The pleasure he takes in doing what he does shows in his expression of concentration that softens with a slight smile and shining eyes. Even with the underlying unease of what we are doing here and all the trouble that will come, I find myself basking in his beauty. Picking up a pen and a notepad from the desk, I start to sketch him. Each stroke of ink is a long limb, a dextrous hand, the tilt of his head just so, the muscles moving under his shirt here.

I thought I'd be on a knife edge. After all, we are at the now-or-never point of both our stories: if there is nothing there hidden in the painting, what next? I've been searching for the answer to how I exist to find a way out. Now all I want is a way to allow Ben to stay. I've been fixated on the consequences of not finding anything, but for the first time I find myself wondering what will happen if we do.

But that thought fades to abstraction in the comfort of watching him work, and I wish to myself, *Just let me just live a lifetime in every second that's ticking by.* All the life-and-death questions can wait for now.

And anyway, this isn't the first time I've had to contemplate the death of someone I love.

***

Until this day I am not sure exactly how the man from the ministry found me, or how he knew I spoke French and Italian fluently. I had been working at the Collection, under my third incarnation since I had bequeathed it to the nation, helping record and pack up our priceless works of art before they were to be taken by train to spend the rest of the war under a mountain in Wales. During the day I sifted through everything I had collected, searching again for answers to my existence, and at night I would take care of Mariah while her mum worked the graveyard shift. Jack had joined up at the first opportunity, keen to fight Mussolini, and I was left behind, frustrated and restless. So, when a well-spoken gentleman in a dark-blue suit asked me if I would be interested in 'playing my part' for the war effort, I agreed before I even knew what I was signing up for. Within two weeks I was a fully trained special operative, ready to be deployed undercover to France.

It was a dark, cloudy night when I parachuted into a wheat-field in rural France. For a moment, when suspended in the sky, looking at the landscape below me, I knew with a sudden certainty that something that happened here would change me.

I didn't know it yet but it wouldn't be fear or violence that would alter me for ever. It would be love, flowering in the midst of destruction and evil. Dominic.

Walking alongside death every hour made everything seem richer and more intensely coloured; the black-and-white photos that are left behind never really capture what it was like to live through it. I knew that though I might endure pain, terror or torture, I would survive to see the war end one way or another. But my comrades did not, and they filled every minute with the same energy I could see in Ben now, conscious that at any moment everything they loved, everything they were, could be consigned to darkness. In the evenings we would walk to a riverside café, drink wine and smoke, while the coloured lights that were strung out overhead turned into Van Gogh stars. I thrived there, among the lust for life that came with constant fear; it almost made me forget my beloved London completely.

Dominic walked into my life on the tenth night. He appeared out of the back of the restaurant somewhere, dark hair a little too long, hanging over his downcast eyes, white crumpled shirt shoved into his trousers, hands in his pockets, a cigarette hanging from his lip. He didn't look like he could get out of bed, let alone mastermind an operation to disrupt ammunition supplies.

'Hello. Pleased to meet you,' I'd said in perfect French, offering him my hand. His response had been to roll his eyes and ignore me. I was so infuriated by this snub that for the rest of the evening I hardly took in what anyone else said. Dominic just slouched in his chair, drinking cheap brandy and scowling at his feet.

'He doesn't do well with change,' a woman called Bridget explained to me when she noticed me watching him covertly. 'He had a soft spot for Thierry, the one you have come to replace.'

'Oh, I *see*,' I'd said.

'Not like that!' she laughed. 'Dear Dominic is very much into the female of the species – a little too much, if you ask me. No, it was more that they were good friends. Dominic thinks he should have done more for Thierry. He's taking his guilt out on you.'

'I see,' I'd said, a good deal more gently this time.

'He is crazy, but clever and brave.' She smiled. 'Just don't, whatever you do, fall in love with him. He will break your heart without a second thought.' She sighed wistfully at this, in a way that made me suspect that she knew this first-hand.

The moment I fell in love with Dominic is still as vivid and bright in my memory now as it was in the first seconds that I lived it. Deep in a valley, surrounded by the tightly laced, freezing forest, the ground beneath our feet was frosted solid. Our breath misted in the air and there was a blanket of silence just before the explosives we had set along the railway tracks tore through the night in a spectrum of violent orange and thunderous noise. Every one of us flinched, ducked and covered our ears. All, except for Dominic, that is. He alone stood tall and perfectly still, smiling triumphantly as the reflection of the raging fire burnt in his eyes.

Soon after that I understood that I wanted him with a hunger I had never really known before in all my centuries of living. Before that war desire had always been something controlled by parameters set by men. Decades had passed in which I had always attempted to protect or construct an acceptable reputation. Even Madame Bianchi with her wild and indulgent parties had never been seen to take a lover. Even the girl who danced until dawn at the Ritz with rouged knees knew that to keep safe she had to play by the rules.

Before Dominic, desire was always a transaction in which, even when it was filled with affection and pleasure, I had been a passive participant. The world before had always ensured that it was that way for women; that we were the knowing temptresses who must be kept out of sight, screened from the male gaze by corsets, veils and modesty in order to earn the prize of chastity. The world after the war would try and reimpose all that once again, but in those years, the war years, I felt completely free to feel every impulse as my own. And the one thing I wanted more than anything was to take Dominic to bed. For years after his death I would think about him in every quiet moment, of running my tongue slowly over the Adam's apple of his throat or slipping my fingertips under his unironed shirt to explore the taut, tanned torso that lay beneath. I had known every inch of him and made it mine.

Life was very dangerous after we sabotaged the train. We were obliged to stay apart from one another for several weeks, keeping our heads down, watching impassively as suspects were dragged in for interrogation for our deeds. That was the way it had to be. We'd have glimpses of one another, polite smiles and casual waves from across the street. We'd even sit in the same bar, but not together. We couldn't be seen together too much in case we looked like we were in cahoots. Then one evening, when things seemed a little safer, he caught up with me as I left the bakery for my lodgings. Neither one of us said a word as he accompanied me, head down, hands in his pockets, smoke from his cigarette winding into the evening. Every step on that short walk was taken without speaking, with the moon shining on the rain-soaked cobbles and a current of silence acknowledged between us. He lingered in the covered doorway as I searched for my key. Once I had it he caught my hand, looking at my fingers as he spoke.

'I would like to kiss you,' he told me. 'I have wanted to for a while, and I think you might like to kiss me too?'

I wanted nothing more than to slam him against the wall right then and devour him, but I held back, enjoying the moment of anticipation.

'I'm not sure it would be a good idea,' I said. 'Not when we have to work together. Wouldn't it make things difficult? Put us all at risk?'

'If you were anyone else I'd agree.' He had smiled, his midnight eyes full of mischief, 'but I can't seem not to think of you.'

'The trouble is, if I fall in love with you,' I'd teased, 'you will break my heart one day. I've heard this first-hand from those who know you better than me.'

'Perhaps,' he'd said with a shrug. 'But I promise it won't be today or tomorrow.'

I'd tugged him into my arms then. I remember the heat of his lips and the length of his body cleaving to mine, hot and urgent. We'd stumbled upstairs before collapsing on to the bed. Here, at last, was an equal union. We loved and wanted one another in exactly the same measure.

After that first night we repeated the first hesitant conversation many times, in leisure, in lust, in love.

'You will break my heart,' I'd say fondly.

'Perhaps, but I promise it won't be today or tomorrow,' he'd reply.

And that was true, right up until the day he wasn't able keep his promise any more.

The day I told him my secret it had rained overnight, and in the morning the river was shrouded in mist. Across the wide river the towers and spires of the town rose from the gloom like a huddle of ghosts longing, crying for rescue. I could not have him think I was a hero like Bridget was, like he was. There was no weapon or will that could kill me, no matter who wielded either.

Dominic had come to stand behind me, wrapping his arms around me. His hands roved over my thin cotton nightdress, making me shiver with delight as I surrendered to him. He'd turned to me, and I'd lifted my face to his, expecting to be kissed. But his expression was serious.

'I love you,' he'd told me, simply and swiftly but with such gravity I knew it wasn't something he would pronounce lightly. 'I always thought of myself as too cold for such a thing, but there it is. I love you, and because I do, I am weakened, I am vulnerable. I am afraid, not for me but for you.'

'You don't need to be afraid for me,' I'd told him. And very quietly, almost in a whisper, I'd told him all my secrets, showed him the small amounts of evidence I carried with me: a sketch, a very old photograph in a travelling case. Looking back, of course I can see how it was too much too soon, but once I had begun I couldn't stop. I'd shocked him to his core, shaken everything he thought he understood about me, us, everything. He called me a liar and cursed me, shouted and railed, before fearing that I had gone mad, he told me he was going to get me the help I needed. Then he left me, saying I should go back to England because he was done with me.

But he came back just a few minutes later, soaked through to the skin, his dark hair running into his eyes. He cried as he held me. We never talked about it again after that – not even on the day he died. He'd decided to love me anyway. He kept on loving me right up until the end of his life. And even then he wasn't afraid for himself. Only for me.

★★★

Perhaps I should have told Ben everything all at once, before he was even near to feeling how he thinks he does about me now and before I knew I had fallen for him. Yet I chose a few days of bliss instead, and I still don't know what the price for that choice will be.

Ben switches off the overhead lights, and with a few taps on the keyboard starts the equipment. He walks over to me, his arm snaking around my shoulder, pressing his lip to my ear.

'I'm scared,' he says.

'Me too,' I say. And we hold one another close, each other our only defence against time.

Let me live a lifetime in every golden minute until the very last one is gone.

Chapter Forty-Six

We spread a long, black-wool coat we found hanging on an old-fashioned coat stand out on the floor in a shadowy corner. She lies there now, her head on my chest. Her hair is spread out across my shirt, silken and dark. Her palm rests on me lightly, her fingertips stretching to just beneath my collar bone. My hand trails lazily up and down her back, and if I didn't keep reminding myself about what we are doing here I would very easily drift off into sleep.

Since arriving here I've managed not to think about what the doctor told me in the hospital. That conversation feels as if it happened in another world to another man. I don't need to make that decision because I have Vita, I've had tonight, and perhaps by the time the sun rises, I'll have until the universe dies and the stars return to nothing

I'm not sure how much time passes before the quick succession of three beeps and the rhythmic slide of the scanning system coming to a halt signal the end of the imaging, but I know it's not long enough.

'Is that it?' Vita asks, sitting up at once.

'Not quite,' I tell her as I climb up too. The aches and pains are beginning to return to my bruised back and sore head. Weariness suddenly threatens to overwhelm me again. 'Now we wait for the software to make a basic interpretation of the raw data. What we will know fairly soon is if it has discovered anything new or not because it will be flagged up in the images. Then we download everything and take it back to yours so we can really assess the data.'

Vita screws her face up.

'So is this a pivotal moment – or not – then?' she asks, smoothing her hair behind her ears.

'Let's say it's one of them.' My guts tighten as I approach the computer.

Vita has always believed there is something hidden in *La Belle*; that for some reason Leonardo chose this, his most modest of portraits, as the hiding place for all his secrets, safe from warmongers and invaders, safe from the future – at least as much of it as he could foresee. I have hoped for it for just a few days, but it still feels like a lifetime. I cannot imagine what knowing for certain will feel like.

'It's processing the first image,' I tell Vita as a new bar appears on the screen. 'Five minutes remaining.'

Vita stands behind me, a hand on one of my shoulders, her chin on the other, and we wait. And wait. Then all at once the first image fills the screen.

And there is nothing.

No secret writings, no underdrawings or corrections. Nothing.

'What does that mean?' Vita asks me. 'What am I looking at?'

I don't know how to tell her.

'There's still a long way to go yet,' I say. 'That image doesn't show anything, but now it will repeat that process hundreds of times. We just have to wait and see.'

For the first time in my life I want time to speed up.

★★★

We sit in silence, looking at each other.

'So that's it?' she says. 'There's nothing there?'

'It's not conclusive,' I say numbly. 'Not yet. We need to take it home and analyse the data. But I can't see anything, and I'd expect to. Something... anything. There's not even any other underdrawing.' I think for a moment, still trying to catch up with this anticlimax. 'Maybe it's my software or my lens.'

'Do you really think it could be either of those?' Vita asks me.

'No,' I say sadly. 'I've spent years developing this tech. I know the equipment inside out, and this is the thing I do, the thing I'm really good at. So I don't think so.'

'I don't think so either,' she says. 'We can just take it away and get advice, get it checked, get all the data reviewed.'

'That will take months,' I say.

I knew that this could happen. I'd thought I was prepared for the fact that this would be the most likely outcome. The truth is I believed it would work; that the stars had aligned, that this was meant to be, that fate had put me and Vita together at exactly the right moment to save my life. Under all the pragmatism and rational thinking, my surface courage about being prepared to die, I thought something miraculous would step in and change the universe just for me.

The cold reality dawns on me that there is no grand design, not here, not on that canvas, not anywhere. I am frozen in fear.

Suddenly Vita leaps to her feet.

'But this is impossible,' she says, placing her hands on her hips. 'It's impossible because I *know* that's where Leonardo hid his secrets. I *know* it is. It is there; it has to be.'

'It's not there,' I say, with a hard edge. I had let myself get swept up in Vita's world and mind, because I so wanted it all to be true. Jack had come to warn me about her. Was this what he was so desperate to tell me? That all of her ideas and theories were just fantasies? The thought hangs within me like a cold shard of ice.

'Vita, I think… I think we have to let it go.'

She stands there in front of the painting looking at me as if she's waiting for me to come to some brilliant conclusion.

'You said the images don't show anything new,' she says, 'but that's impossible. We know Leonardo was a man who changed his mind frequently as he worked, that he was rarely completely satisfied. That's why he struggled to finish a portrait, why he kept the *Mona Lisa* with him until the day he died. Pascal Cotte's work found results. Even if they are controversial, they were there. So we should have found *something*. Could it mean that he has somehow blocked it from sight? Not that he anticipated this technology, but that he used something to ensure his discoveries were preserved, but well hidden? Better hidden than we anticipated?

'I mean, as Fabrizio told us, the chemical composition of *La Belle* has been analysed to the nth degree. All the years that people have argued over whether or not she was a Da Vinci mean that we know so much about her, but nothing came up as being out of the ordinary.

'So, could it be something *ordinary*? Something somehow hidden in plain sight? The cheap everyday pigments he used?'

The edge of a thought nudges somewhere at the back of my head.

'Maybe,' I say. 'We know he was testing alchemical methods, seeking to disprove them. The alchemists of the day were pioneers of modern chemistry, right? They were all combining vast ranges of different ingredients, trying desperately to hit on the correct formula for the philosopher's stone and our favourite cure-all – the elixir of life.' I take Vita's hand as the idea gradually gains traction. 'Look at the case of Hennig Brand, a seventeenth-century alchemist in Germany that I read about the other night. Hennig devoted months to collecting, storing and boiling down stale human urine because he figured that human beings were made up of all the elements of the universe, so maybe the secrets of the universe lay within us. He wasn't totally wrong. So he'd boil vats of pee and wait until they burst into flames, then syphon off the resulting syrup.'

'That's very unpleasant,' Vita says.

'Then he'd heat it again until he got a red oil that he could skim off, which he'd... Well, there were lots of other disgusting steps, but anyway the gist is that he'd end up with this black, rocky stuff, and when it was heated it glowed in the dark. He must have thought that he'd discovered something that would take him close to solving the mystery the alchemists were pursuing. It must have seemed magical – gross, but magical. He truly believed he was well on the way to knowing how to turn lead into gold. And in a way he had, because he'd accidentally discovered phosphorous.

He went on to sell the recipe and made quite a lot of money. So he turned wee into gold, sort of.'

'Are you saying that...?' She frowns deeply. 'What *are* you saying?'

'I'm saying that Leonardo da actual Vinci was doubtless combining endless ingredients, and that he could have made some concoction as part of his experiments, using materials that we'd expect but in unexpected ways. I don't know anything more, except that phosphorous glows when it's heated.'

Then it comes back to me – me and Mum painting magic t-shirts on a Saturday to sell to tweens at the market on Sunday.

'There are a few natural dyes that change colour when heated. We need a hair dryer.'

'A hair dryer?' She shakes her head. 'We've got two hours until dawn and you want me to find a hair dryer and then point it at a Da Vinci masterpiece?'

'Yes, really close up, to get results the quickest.'

'Ben...? Her whole body is a question. 'You want me to point a hair dryer at a Da Vinci?'

'You believe there is something hidden here. You have made me believe too. This may be our last chance, Vita.' I pause, my eyes holding hers. 'Or mine anyway.'

Vita chews her lips as she thinks for a moment.

'There's a hair dryer in the staff showers,' she says after a moment.

'So we can try?'

'Wait for me here,' she says. And then she is gone.

Vita comes back with the hair dryer, an extension lead and a stony expression, her lips drawn into a tight knot.

'Are you OK?' I ask like an idiot.

'We have 30 minutes, and if that's not enough, then...' Her eyes are wide. 'I'm so scared. I thought I'd got past the endangering-priceless-works-of-art stage.'

'I know.' I take a step towards her, but her expression stops me going further. 'It's priceless – it's precious. I know that. It's been your friend for a long time, and I know I fell for her the moment

I set eyes on her. She means so much.' I run out of reassurances. 'Look, let's just try it in the top corner, and if we get nothing there...' I'm reluctant to say out loud that we will give up. I'm beginning to realise I would tear this painting apart if it would only answer my questions.

'OK.' She hands me the hair dryer.

I begin to heat the corner we agreed on, and yes – seeing the craquelure buckle and strain under the heat makes my stomach lurch. But then, faintly – just faintly – it looks as if maybe something appears underneath in dull, dark-brown marks that could be something.

'Take a video, I say, holding the heat on the area for another 30 seconds.

'Yes,' she says. 'Yes, that's Italian. That's his handwriting.'

'Are you sure?' I turn to her, turning off the hair dryer. The marks fade almost at once. 'Is this that thing that brains do when they want to make sense out of nothing?'

'I think I'm sure,' she says, playing back her video. 'This really looks like the word *impasto*, meaning "dough" or "paste". I mean, I don't know, but maybe?' She looks up at me.

'OK,' I say. 'Focus your camera as close as you can to the painting without losing definition. We'll do one-inch squares, left to right, 30 seconds on each. Enough to get a reading, but not enough to damage her. Yes?'

'Yes,' she agrees, and we begin.

Within minutes our doubts are fading as fast as the hidden symbols in the paint emerge.

'You found it, Ben,' Vita whispers in awe.

I found it.

I found it, and I'm terrified.

Chapter Forty-Seven

Pablo has clearly enjoyed his short stay with Mariah, though he has been renamed Kip, handfed tinned Spam and tuna, and seems to like being wrapped up in a crocheted blanket.

'Hello, Evie,' Mariah says as Marta lets us in, noticing but not commenting on our dishevelled state. 'Got any sweets for me?'

Fortunately I find one at the bottom of my bag, making a mental note to buy some more later, as it's my last one.

'An orange one,' she says happily, cupping it in her palms as if it were a precious jewel. 'Here, do you know where Mum is? I can't find her.'

'Night shift at the factory, I think,' I say. 'Marta's just leaving, and Viv will be here soon. Is it OK if we take Pablo now?' The dog has dragged himself out of his swaddling and is doing his best to climb into Ben's arms. Ben picks him up and cradles him a like a baby, screwing up his face as Pablo covers him in kisses.

'He likes you!' Mariah smiles, but then her face falls. 'Mum said he had to go too. She said that rations mean we can't have a pet no more, and that he has to go and live on a farm with the evacuees. Would you take him to the farm, Evie?'

'Yes,' I say, taking her hand. 'He'll be happy there and well fed, and when the war is over, he'll come back.'

'I'll miss him so much.' Mariah holds out her arms for Pablo, who sweetly allows Ben to put him down and trots over to her, where he lets her weep into his fur for a little while.

'I miss my mum too, Evie,' Mariah sobs, 'and my Len. Where did everyone go?'

'I'm still here,' I say, sitting next to her. 'I'll always be here, Mariah. Don't you worry about that.'

'Yes, you always have been, haven't you?' she says, leaning into me. 'You have always been here. Tell me a story? The one about the heiress?'

I glance up at Ben, who nods slightly.

'Madame Bianchi?' I ask, and Mariah nods.

'Tell me about her dresses and her jewels,' Mariah says, her eyes wide.

'Well, Madame Bianchi was something of a mystery,' I say. 'She arrived in London in a bit of whirlwind, and no one knew where she came from, who her people were or how she came to have such a vast fortune. There were rumours that she and her brother were former pirates, but no one cared if that was true because Madame Bianchi was rather brilliant, and she set the social scene on fire.'

'Tell us what she did,' Mariah said.

'She built the most beautiful *palazzo* right in the heart of London,' I tell her. 'Paid three times as much as anyone else to have it built in the space of a year, and at the same time, she built houses all over the city for the rich, the ordinary and even the poor. Madame Bianchi designed and built your house, Mariah, and mine, and she must have done a good job of it because they are still standing. But it wasn't her good works that the jet set liked best about her. It was her parties. Her parties were famed all over Europe. People would fight to be invited. And at every party she wore a new gown, of the finest silks and satins, all the colours of the rainbow, and so many precious jewels they say she was in danger of outshining the royal family. They say that there was no one as radiant, witty, clever or as wonderful as Madame Bianchi. And best of all, she left everything she was interested in, everything she collected during her lifetime, to all of us. So in a way all her lovely gowns and jewels belong to you now.'

'And you work in her house, don't you?' Mariah asks. 'Will you bring me home a tiara?'

'I'll see what I can do,' I say with a smile, kissing her forehead.

The front door is unlatched, and Viv comes in from where she and Marta have been exchanging notes in the hallway.

'Morning, Mariah,' Viv calls out cheerfully, filling the room with sunlight. Her smile broadens when she sees us. 'Oh, Ben, so nice to see you up and about. We were all so worried about you yesterday. What a relief.'

'Thank you for everything,' Ben says. 'I'm so grateful you were there to step in.'

'No problems, my darling,' Viv laughs, and so does Mariah.

'So, will you be staying to take breakfast with us?'

'No, we can't,' Ben says. 'We've just come to get the dog.'

'Well, I know that Mariah would like eggs on toast,' Viv says.

'Yes please, Mum.' Mariah settles back into her armchair, her gaze travelling off somewhere we can't follow.

'How is she doing, do you think?' I ask Viv as we are about to leave. 'Do you think she is still OK here? I'm used to her time-travelling but calling you *Mum* is new.'

'There's bound to be deterioration, but home is still the place for her,' Viv says. 'Doc says she's in good health physically. And she certainly keeps me and Marta on our toes. It's a good thing what you're doing: you know... covering all the costs so she can stay in her home. I'm not sure if she realises how lucky she is to have a friend like you.'

'I do it for selfish reasons really,' I say, glancing at Ben as he takes in the news. 'Mariah means a lot to me.'

Viv sees us out and I hear her singing 'We'll Meet Again', Mariah joining in at once as she closes the door behind us.

'That must cost you a lot,' Ben says as we walk down Mariah's steps and back up mine.

'I have a lot, remember?' I say. 'More than I want or need. Makes sense to use it to help other people.'

'You are such an amaz—'

'I'm not, Ben.' I stop him as we stand before the front door, my finger on his lips. 'I'm not amazing. I'm lucky. Everything I have – the house, the garage, the money – comes from blind luck, even though sometimes it feels like more of a curse. I'm lucky, and

Mariah's all alone in the world. Taking care of her matters to me, and that's it. So, we'll say no more about it, OK?'

'OK,' Ben nods, adding quickly, 'I still think you're amazing though.'

I have never been so glad to be in my little house, or at least I can't think of the last time I have been this glad. I'm exhausted but buzzing with excitement too. It feels like static is fizzing through my veins instead of blood.

Ben flops on to the sofa, and at once Pablo climbs on to curl up into a ball in the bend of his legs.

'You should sleep,' I say, pressing my palm to his cool forehead. He looks drained after a night dozing on the museum floor. 'There's nothing more we can do for now. I'll go to the print shop and get the photos printed as large I can with good resolution. I expect it will take a few hours, so I'll go to work, see what the lie of the land is.'

'Yes, OK,' he says, one hand over his eyes, the other resting between Pablo's ears. 'Sounds like a plan.'

'Ben?' I sit on the edge of the sofa. 'Are you feeling all right? No more after effects we should be worrying about?'

'I don't really know.' He drops his hand to look at me. His face is pale: shadows bruise the underside of his eyes and a growth of dark beard softens his jawline. 'I'm still trying to get my head around everything that happened last night.'

'Me too,' I say, 'but at least *La Belle* is back in the exhibition and looking just as she did yesterday morning, although that feels like a hundred years ago now.'

'Can't you skip work again?' he asks. 'You must be worn-out too.'

'I'm OK. I'll go in as soon as I've dropped this off.' I show him the USB stick I've transferred the photos to. 'I'm going to write my resignation letter and give it to Anna, so if it's at all possible I'll try and sneak off early.'

'You need sleep too,' he says, taking my hand. 'Can't you just lie down here with me for a minute?'

'I'll be there all day if I do,' I tell him. 'I'm OK. Coffee and sugar will get me through.'

'I'll miss you,' he says, his blue eyes bleary. 'I feel better about sleeping when you are here.'

I sink to my knees in front of him, pressing my face into his chest.

'I will miss you too,' I tell him. 'But you need rest. Pablo will keep an eye on you,' I ruffle the dog's ears as he does his best to get in the middle of our embrace. 'I won't be long, I promise.'

He's already asleep as I leave the room.

***

Work seems like a waking dream. The whole world has an unreal sense about it, as if everything is a little altered from the way I know it, remade to be almost but not quite the same.

La Belle is back in the exhibition. Visitors file in and out of the museum just as they always have, many going straight to the Da Vinci, but just as many bypassing it completely to visit just one room or object. I like to see them, the regulars. For them the Collection is more than a museum; it's an extension of their homes and themselves; a place where rarities can become familiar wonders, just as they always do. That's how I feel about it too.

Mo is back on shift, scanning the exhibition room with extra scrutiny.

Even Anna's composure seems fully restored. I sit beside her in a meeting and she shares progress with the directors on a future exhibition we are planning around the Collection's hoard of objects that were once considered magical. No one has asked me to resign yet, and I haven't had a chance to write the letter I had planned because Anna has needed me at her side all day and I haven't had the heart to leave her. If I wasn't so tired, I'd be hysterical with the irony of it all.

At lunchtime Jack meets me in St James's Square where he has been keeping a bench free for us. Sheepishly he hands me my favourite double-shot, extra-hot coffee and smoked salmon and cream cheese bagel.

'I wasn't sure you'd still be talking to me,' he says, which catches me off-guard before I can tell him anything about what has happened over the last 24 hours.

'Why?' I ask him, bewildered. 'Ben mentioned that you came over.'

'He didn't tell you?' He seems surprised.

'Tell me what?' I ask him, frowning.

'I fucked up,' Jack confesses. 'I wanted to warn him, prepare him. He didn't want to listen, he just wanted to get to you. And… well, he fell. Hit his head pretty bad. He seemed OK though. I made sure he was OK before I left.'

'Jack.' I shake my head. 'He blacked out in the street, and had to go to hospital. That could have killed him!'

His eyes widen. 'I'm so sorry about that. I thought he was OK. I promise you it was an accident.'

'If you hadn't been there meddling, he would not have hurt himself.' Anger ignites in my chest. 'Jack, what the hell are you doing? This is nothing to do with you.'

'Vita, it is to do with me when you aren't thinking straight. How can he make a decision when he has no idea what's at stake?'

'I am going to tell him,' I say. 'I'm waiting for the right moment.'

'And when will that be, Vita?' Jack asks me. 'Before he walks into an endless life with no idea what that's like? Or after he's died?'

I slap him hard across the cheek, drawing my hand back in horror at once.

'I'm sorry. That was wrong of me,' I stutter. 'I can't talk about him like he's an experiment: like if he dies and I can't save him there's no harm done.'

'I know that,' Jack says, holding a hand to his face. 'I didn't mean to sound cruel. It's just that this whole situation has made a lot of things clear for me. I suppose I thought that you and I would go on for ever just as we were, and nothing would ever change. But everything changes eventually, whether we want it to or not.'

'Is that what this is?' I ask him, feeling the fragile truce between us stretch and snap. 'That you don't want me to have anything that is just mine, so that I can be there for you forever? I'm not like you, Jack. Or if I was once, I'm not any more. I can't treat the world like a trinket or a toy. I want to live in it, be part of it. Unlike you, I want to care about something other than myself.'

'You are making this impossible.' Jack stands up abruptly, running his hands through his hair in frustration. 'I know I am selfish, vain, but I have always been there for you. I need to know if you are certain this is what you want. If Ben is. Does he know he will see everyone he loves die? Does he know that you have *hated* it ever since Dominic died, Vita – that you hate this life with all your heart? So much so, that sometimes I think you hate *me*?'

'Sometimes I think that too.' I spit the words out before I realise what I am saying and to whom. Jack and I stare at one another aghast.

'I don't mean that,' I say, too late. 'I'm exhausted and I just want to save him, Jack. Of course I love you – you are my dearest friend. I just want the best for you, which is why I don't understand why you don't want that for me.'

'I know,' he replies stiltedly. 'So, what did you find? You told me you found something. Was it the secret to eternal life?'

'I don't know yet,' I say, wondering if there is any way back from this hole that I have punched into our relationship. This is not how I pictured this moment, with Jack and me sitting at opposite ends of the bench feeling worlds apart. 'I found Leonardo's words hidden in the portrait. I haven't had a chance to study them yet, but perhaps. Don't you want to know them too?'

'I just want *us*,' Jack says, 'but that's not enough for you.'

'It's not that,' I tell him. 'It's not that you are not enough. It's that I need all of this, all the life that we have lived, to mean something. If I can save Ben then it will have meant something. It will all have had a purpose.'

Jack looks at me for a long time and I can't read his expression. It's as if this face that I have looked upon a million times has become a stranger to me in a matter of minutes.

'Then don't you think it's about time you tell him the truth?' he asks. 'Before you save him, before you even try? Tell him exactly what Leonardo's gift of immortality means. If you love him, isn't that the very least he deserves?'

'And isn't the least I deserve to choose how I live?' I ask him as I get up and start to walk away. 'Or will you try and control everything I do for the next 500 years too?'

'Vita!' Jack calls after me. 'That's not what I want. I am just trying to tell you, to explain to you, that I—'

I turn around.

'Jack,' I tell him, 'if you loved me you would let me go.'

★★★

Leaving work early was impossible when Anna needed me, and if I am honest I didn't want to hurry home, not with my fight with Jack still circling my exhausted mind. So I kept hanging on, waiting for the long arm of the law to clap its hand on my shoulder, but nothing happened. The CCTV was inconclusive, the room so busy and dark that nothing useful could be made out. All that was left of the whole sorry incident was a mountain of paperwork. We had even managed to keep it out of the press.

Somehow that seemed more unlikely than a set of secret notes made in heat-reactive dye being hidden in one of the world's most famous works of art.

Finally I arrive home with a weighty folder of A4 prints of each photograph I took of *La Belle*. Ben greets me at the door smelling clean and looking much better. He puts his arm around me as I walk in through the door. Leaning into him, I let him direct me to the sofa, which I fall on to like a rag doll.

'I've not been arrested,' I say as he removes my shoes and lifts my feet on to the seat. 'So far even the rumpled coat hasn't been commented on. I'm almost disappointed. Being a criminal genius isn't much fun these days.'

'There's still time,' he says pulling a large silk shawl over me. 'I'm expecting a police helicopter and a SWAT team at any minute.'

'Are you OK?' I ask, catching his wrist and pulling him to me. I can feel my body giving in to the exhaustion at last. All I want to do is to roll over and sleep.

'I'm fine. Don't worry about me.' He kisses my forehead. 'Is this folder the prints? Can I pin them up on your stormy sea wall while you sleep?'

'Hmm,' I mumble. 'Yes, take your time. Whatever.'

★★★

'Hey, Vita. Hey.' Ben's voice slowly rouses me from the deepest of sleeps.

'Already?' I mutter. 'Five more minutes.'

'You've been out for six hours – it's midnight!' he says, stroking my cheek. 'And I know you'll want to see this.'

'Will I?' I roll over to face the opposite wall and there is *La Belle*'s face blown up to fill most of the wall, covered in the briefly visible writing that really does look like Leonardo's hand.

'Fuck,' I say, sitting up.

'My thoughts exactly,' Ben says.

VIII

Be as true to each other as this dial is to the sun.

Traditional sundial motto

Chapter Forty-Eight

'I need wine and food, in that order,' Vita says as she sits on the rug crossing her legs. She opens a notebook on the chest in front of her, searching for a pen in her bag.

'I went out and bought stuff,' I tell her proudly, pouring a glass of wine I bought from a Tesco Metro. Earlier I had thought about venturing into her cellar to get a bottle before realising that I would probably end up opening something worth thousands of pounds, so instead I went to the shops while she slept and bought the most expensive bottle of red they had.

'Oh, this is nice,' she says after the first sip. I am proud of my accidental sommelier skills.

'While you translate, I will be making you fresh pasta with tomato and basil, dressed with parmesan, garlic and truffle oil. Carbs, but also good for you.'

'Sounds delicious. Will you marry me?' she says absently as she jots down something in the notebook.

'Name the day,' I say lightly. She looks up at me with a smile, and I can feel between us the almost physical presence of impossible hope that one day, perhaps, with world enough and time, we could have a future laid out before us. Suddenly, the promise of possibility seems like a living thing, like that very mercurial magic that the alchemists were searching for all along.

'Well,' I say, finding it hard to break the hold of her gaze, 'I'd better get the pasta on — I'm making fresh tomato sauce. It will be nice for you to eat something that hasn't been delivered for a change.'

'Not sure my body will be able to stand the shock,' she says, returning to her notebook. But as I leave the room her words follow me like a whispered vow. 'I love you, Ben Church.'

Pablo sits at my feet as I chop and sauté, occasionally stopping to take a sip of the very expensive wine that, if I'm honest, tastes exactly like all the other wine I've ever drunk. The lights flicker and hum overhead, comfortingly monotonous. Out of one window Soho leaps and pumps like a hardcore trance track, and out of the other all is silent and swiftly growing dark. I ought to be feeling happy. And yet, nagging at me are the things I haven't told Vita since she came home.

Like the fact that when I woke up this afternoon there were four missed calls on my phone, all from the hospital, urging me to come back to discuss a treatment plan with them, so at least I'd be walking away fully informed. Or that ever since I hit my head there has been a new persistent pain at the back of my skull. A new dark spot floating in my field of vision.

We are so close to a miracle. All I need is a little more time. Just a little more time.

'How's it going?' I ask her when I come in, sitting on the floor next to her and putting a bowl of pasta in front of her.

'It's coming along very slowly,' she says. 'A mixture of text and pictographs, and of course it's written back to front. Once I have worked out the key it will come quickly, but that will take a bit of time looking at reference sites. As far as I can gather, he is reflecting on fate: why some are chosen for luxury and riches and others are condemned to misery. You realise that if we ever tell the world about this, they will definitely conclude it's an elaborate hoax?'

'I don't care what the world thinks,' I say. 'I care what you think. Do you think it's really him, or some crazy nineteenth-century Parisian getting carried away?'

'Oh, it's him,' she says. 'I recognise his voice.'

Another hour quietly dwindles away until, eventually, she gets up, taking her notebook with her to stand in front of the wall-sized *La Belle*.

Her faltering overhead light doesn't seem bright enough, so I switch on a lamp and light some more candles on the mantelpiece. Somehow the fluid light brings the portrait to life, making her seem like a living thing who might blink and smile at any minute.

'I've finished,' she says softly, still facing the wall.

'And?' I ask her. Vita's hands – one still clutching her notebook – fall down by her side.

'Vita, and?' I repeat. 'What is it?'

'It isn't a recipe for eternal life,' she says, turning back to me. Tears are rolling down her face. 'It's a testament. It's the story of the woman in the portrait.'

I try to take in what that means and find I can't quite yet.

'Will you read it to me?' I ask. I don't know what else to say.

Vita takes a candle down from the mantel and sets it on the chest. Kneeling, she picks up her notebook and begins to read.

'This is the story of a young woman who was made to sit for this portrait by her master the white monk. Her name is Agnese, and I have heard that she has never aged a day in the 20 years since I completed this portrait. When I met her Agnese had lived in the court of the Duke of Milan for four years from the age of fourteen. She had been given to him by her father as payment for a debt. He rarely had use for her, having another favourite mistress, a fact that she was immensely grateful for. However, one evening he came upon her when he was in a rage. He visited all his fury upon her person. Some months later at the allotted time she gave birth to a son, who was then taken from her to be raised away from court. I was called to mark the occasion with this portrait. How moved I was by her grace and dignity, her intelligence and thoughtfulness. I sketched her multiple times and we became friends of a sort. We talked of fate and God's plan for us all, why some lives matter so little and some so very much when each of God's creatures should be equal. I wished with all my heart I could give her some freedom from the cruel shackles that she had been bound with from childhood. But only time can grant freedom to the enslaved, and time is not a kind mistress. I thought perhaps I could give her time. Time to outlive those who kept her captive. During the execution of this portrait I used the methods and materials of the alchemists, using the geometry of the stars and the secret of the Egyptians as I had been taught them by my friend Luca. Never would I have imagined these methods to be more than

a fruitless charade, and yet in the years that have since passed, the duke has died, the court has fallen away, my beard has grown long and grey, and she remains exactly the same. They told me she had retreated to a nunnery where the sisters wonder if she is a miracle. I sought permission from the king and went to see her. She was indeed unchanged. It is possible that I made her unnatural. After our meeting I located the portrait that was hanging in her mother's house, and under the guise of repairing it hid her strange story here so that perhaps one day it may be understood. When we met, I asked what she would do if all she knew crumbled to dust around her and she remained frozen in time, bound to eternal youth. She told me she would leave this place and roam the world for ever, seeing everything there was to see, and when she was done she would begin again. As I write this I do not know more, for since my last enquiry she has vanished from the earth.'

She closes her notebook, the light of the candle illuminating one side of her face, and knots her hair into a ponytail at her nape. After a moment she looks up at me with an expression of such hope and such sadness that my tears echo hers.

'Ben, don't you understand?' she says. 'You must surely see it now? I'm so sorry. I really thought we'd do it, I really thought we would.'

'Understand what?' I ask. 'See what?'

All I can do is try and focus on the numbing realisation that the quest is over, and we failed.

Before Vita can answer there is a frantic hammering at the front door.

'Who's that at this time?' I ask, going to the door. Vita joins me as we find Marta, barefoot, her dressing gown pulled tight around her on our doorstep.

'What's happened?' Vita asks at once.

'It's Mariah – she's gone,' Marta says. 'I checked in on her at two and all was peaceful. Then I got back just now and her bed is empty, the front door open, her shoes gone. I don't know what to do. Where will she have gone, Vita?'

'There are so many places she might have gone,' Vita says, pulling on her boots at once. 'It depends how she is feeling, where in time she is. She could be going to find a barge to hitch a ride on, or to dance at the French House. It's impossible to know. Marta, you stay here in case she comes back, and call the police. I'll go and check some of her favourite places.'

'I'm coming,' I say. She nods and takes my hand tightly in hers.

Vita is just as afraid as I am in this moment, I can feel it. But I am not certain it is only to do with the fact that we may, finally, be running out of time.

Chapter Forty-Nine

'If she's gone to the river, towards the main roads...' I hold on to Ben tight as we thread our way through the still-busy streets of Soho.

'If she's gone that way someone will find her and help her,' Ben says. 'Try not to worry too much. Think of some familiar places that she might be drawn to.'

'St Anne's,' I say, heading towards the church. 'After the war she liked to take her lunch there in the summer and sit and eat it under the trees.' Letting go of Ben's hand I rush across the street to where the Regency church reaches skyward, as if it might take off towards the moon at any minute. Its gardens stand more than 6 feet above pavement level, and I have to stand on my tiptoes to peer through the railings and make out if Mariah is somewhere there among the shadows, imagining herself on a sunny afternoon with a jam sandwich wrapped in brown paper.

'You're taller than me.' Urgently, I press Ben forward so he can look for her, since the base of the wire fence that surrounds the church is so high above street level, the graveyard built up high to accommodate plague victims. 'Can you see her in there?'

Ben hoods his eyes as he searches the dim garden for a few minutes.

'I can't see anyone,' he says, turning to me, 'and besides, she'd have to be a ninja to get over that fence. Where else?'

'The French House, the Coach and Horses – she loved to go there for cocktails and flirting with theatre folk, though they'll both be closed at this hour.'

'Well let's head that way anyway,' Ben says. 'Maybe she will be somewhere around there trying to get in.' His calm in the face of my anxiety is reassuring.

We were almost there. I felt so certain. And then, it all came at once – the moment I knew I couldn't save him and the urgent need to tell him the truth; all the life we will not have together. And yet here he is, with me, searching for Mariah like it's the most important thing in the world, because he knows that for me it is one of them.

We call out her name as we peer into alleyways, looking into closed shops and restaurants. A couple of lads a little worse for wear come staggering up the road towards us.

'What a silly old bint,' they are complaining as they walk past. 'All that bloody fussing and screaming. Cops should stick her in a home.'

'Who?' I grab one of them by the arm. 'Who was fussing and screaming?'

'Hey, watch it.' He shrugs me off, and spotting Ben behind me, backs off a step or two. 'What you on about?'

'Who were you talking about?' I ask. 'Look, an elderly woman with dementia, my friend, is lost somewhere around here. You said you'd seen a *mad old bint*?'

'We didn't mean nothing by it,' one of them says. 'She was just down at the tube – Leicester Square – shaking on the railings, trying to be let in. There were people filming her, but we never.'

'The tube,' I say, looking at Ben. 'She's looking for shelter in the air raids.' I break into a run, Ben at my side. We race down Charing Cross Road to where a small crowd has gathered around the entrance to the tube. I hear her shrieks and cries before I see her.

'My mum's in there. You've got to let me in,' she says, rattling at the metal doors that secure the entrance. 'Don't leave me out here. I'll be blown to bits, I will! Let me in. Please, let me in. I just want my mum!'

Pushing my way through the crowd, I almost fall over as I'm ejected on the other side.

'Go home,' Ben says, waving them away. 'Go on. You're scaring an old lady. What's entertaining about that? Get off with you. Now!' I flash him a grateful smile as I turn my attention to Mariah, her fingers laced through the meshed metal, her head leaning on the door as she cries pitiful tears.

'Mariah?' I say her name softly. 'Mariah, it's… it's me. Darling, you're safe now, OK? I've come to fetch you home.'

'Evie?' Mariah turns to look at me, her face ashen and streaked with tears, her fine silver hair standing up on end in a halo. 'I can't find my mum, Evie. I heard the sirens and I ran here, but they won't let me in. We've got to get in, Evie, else we'll die. I don't want to die.'

'There, there, love. The raid is over,' I say holding out my hand to her. 'Didn't you hear the siren sound the all-clear? Everything's OK now.'

'Are you sure?' Mariah asks uncertainly.

Very carefully I take another step towards her.

'Your mum is on a night shift and she sent me to bring you home so you wouldn't be scared. I'll make you a drink of Oxo and we can have a sing-song. How about that, Mariah? Would you like to sing, and I'll tell you a story?'

'Mum's down there.' Mariah rattles the door once again, but this time with a bit less urgency. 'I think she's down there, Evie.'

'Come on,' I say taking her hand in mine and rubbing it. Gently I begin to sing to her as I start to lead her home.

'Run, rabbit, run, rabbit, run, run, run.'

'Don't give the farmer his fun, fun, fun,' Mariah sings back, her spirits seeming a little lifted. 'Here, Evie, have you got any sweets for me?'

'I have at home,' I promise her. 'Come home and I'll give you all the sweets you want.'

'I want sweets now,' Mariah cries. 'Mum saves me a sweet for when the raids come.'

'I promise you, as soon as I get you home,' I say again, searching vainly through my pockets.

'Here you go, love.' An exhausted-looking woman in her London Underground uniform hands me a couple of wrapped toffees. 'I always have some on me.'

'Thank you,' I say. 'Here we are, Mariah. Toffees!'

'I haven't had toffees for a long while,' Mariah says, delighted.

She begins to walk with me. The last stragglers who were watching melt away.

'Who's that bloke, Evie? And where's Dominic?' Mariah asks, looking at Ben. 'You went to France and met Dominic and you didn't come back, not for years and years. I got married, I got old, I got so lonely and you didn't come back until you did. And then Dominic was gone – he'd got old and ill and died, and you came back looking the same as the day you left. Where'd you go, Evie? Why are you called Vita now?'

'I know that is silly, isn't it?' I say, brushing the question off as Ben frowns deeply.

And finally, he sees the truth entirely.

Chapter Fifty

When I let myself in the house is quiet.

From the hallway I can see Ben standing motionless in front of the huge image of *La Belle*, his hands at his sides, his eyes scanning her features. In his hand is my wedding photo.

'I don't know how I didn't see this before,' he says without turning to look at me, his voice troubled. 'Of course, it makes sense. I'm so stupid. I've been such a fool. It's been right in front of my face the whole time. You believe in the legend because you *are* the legend.'

'Ben…' I begin.

'I understand it all now.' He turns back to me. 'Mariah keeps mixing you up with Evie because you *are* Evie.' He tips over the silver photo frame so that the photograph falls out, the glass clattering to the floor where it cracks into two pieces.

'Paris, 1945. Evelyn and Dominic. Wedding day.'

'Let me explain.'

'What I don't understand, Vita, or Evie, or whatever your name is, is why you didn't tell me who you were? I thought you and I were so close, so open. That from the moment we met we had been able to say anything. And yet for every hour that I have known you, while we've been talking again and again about whether the legend was true and I've been daring to hope for a miracle, you have been hiding the biggest lie of all. That you are the proof.'

I take a breath. This has all unravelled in an instant and now I am lost in the middle, uncertain how to explain. Taking a step into the room I start to talk, unable to keep the desperation from my voice. 'I didn't tell you because I didn't know. And I felt ashamed of all this time I have and didn't want, when you don't have enough. I thought that if we could have saved you, then... '

'I can't get my head round this. It just makes no sense. You've been searching for a secret that you knew was real? Then why not tell me?'

'Because I don't know how it happened. I could make no promises.'

'You need to explain this to me from the very beginning. Who are you, Vita? What are you?'

'At the time the portrait was painted my name was Agnese,' I begin. 'Since then I've had many names, most of them as lost to history as my first. Agnese, Beatrice, Isabella Bianchi... Evelyn until Dominic died and now, Vita. I don't know how long that will be my name, but I have learnt that there's always a moment when I have to say goodbye to everything and start again before people start to notice that I never change. I hold on to who I am for as long as I can. As long as they will let me.'

Ben's expression is implacable. A quiet anger radiates from his stillness.

'I am 531 years alive,' I tell him. 'Time moves on around me, but think I exist in one moment – the one I lived on the day I was painted. I think somehow Leonardo incorporated his pity for me into his experiments and this is the result.' I gesture at my body. 'I don't imagine he ever thought it would work, it was a flight of fancy for him. An imaginary way of setting one pretty caged bird free. I'm sure that if he had been certain that there was true power at the heart of alchemy, he would have asked for my consent. He would have asked me if I wanted so much... time.' My hands drift outwards, drawing the endless years that I have breathed in one long, all-encompassing gesture. 'But then again, he had his faults. He could be vain, grandiose, cruel even. Just ask Jack.'

'Ask Jack?' Ben says, setting down the frame but still holding that one precious photograph in both hands. 'What do you mean? What's Jack got to do with it?'

I gather my courage.

'Jack's full name is Gian Giacomo Caprotti da Oreno,' I tell him. 'Better known to history as Salaì. He was Leonardo's partner, his lover for 25 years. We didn't know about one another for more than a century. And then when he discovered I existed, he searched for me. He found me when I had just arrived in London as Madame Bianchi. We've been together ever since.'

'Together?' Ben says. 'You and Jack, together?'

'Not like that; *never* like that,' I tell him. 'It's never something we have come close to. I think we knew at the beginning that we needed each other too much to risk it all for—'

'For love,' Ben finished for me. 'I don't know when, but I think that Jack might have changed his mind about that sometime in the last 50 years or so.'

'No,' I shake my head. 'We promised each other at the start not to risk it all for—'

'Love?' Ben says again. 'Then what does that say about us?'

'For sex,' I finish. 'Not that we have ever... Look Ben, this is silly. I have known you for a few days. I have known Jack for 400 years. We are bonded together. How can we not be? We are the only two people in the whole world we can count on. You don't need to be jealous of Jack. He's a good man.'

Ben nods, looking down at the photo again.

'This is a lot to take in,' he says finally.

'I know,' I say.

'Why not tell me at the start?' he asks me again.

'Would you have believed me?' I ask him.

'Maybe not at first, but if you'd shown me this photo, if you'd explained... I love you, Vita. I trusted you. And now I don't understand what's happening. I don't understand what you want with me.'

He sways on his feet, his knees buckle as I rush to him, supporting his weight on my shoulder just in time. Slowly I help him to the sofa.

'I want everything,' I tell him gently. 'I want everything with you.'

Kneeling on the floor before him, I sit back on my heels.

'Before you, the only reason I was looking for the answer to what happened to Jack and me is because I had had enough of living. Because I was so *tired*. Aside from Jack, I have lost everyone I ever loved, Ben. My husband, my family, my son, my friends. And I will lose Mariah before long, the woman I have always loved as if she were my daughter. I have tried and tried to end it, Ben, and it never works. I always survive. I have wanted it all to be over for so long. Until I met you. And now I want everything I have for you. For us, together. Always. But I didn't know if I could make that promise. So I... kept one secret from you. Just one.'

'Just one,' Ben drops his head into his hands, laughing bleakly.

'Perhaps you should rest,' I say, touching my hand to his cool cheek. 'We can talk again later once you've had time to think.'

'I don't have time,' Ben says, moving away from my touch. 'There is no time for me, Vita. Keep talking.'

'I don't know what else to say. I've been trying to understand it for centuries, but after I lost Dominic, that's when I really wanted to know how to escape.'

'When did Dominic die?' Ben asks, his eyes closed as if he is in pain.

'In 1992,' I say quietly.

'You went to France and fought alongside the Resistance?'

'Yes,' I say. 'I was that woman once long ago, and part of me always will be. But now I am the woman who is in love with you. It's you, Ben, who has made my heart beat again. Who has made me want to discover the secrets Leonardo knew – not to die any more, but to live. With you.'

Ben sinks into the cushion, his arm wrapped around himself, Pablo is at his side in one bound, leaning hard against his shoulder.

'There were so many times when I thought you would look at her and see it,' I say, my hands clasped in anxiety. 'Perhaps not right away, but eventually. No one has ever looked at me the way you do. I thought you'd see it, and I thought you of all people might be able to understand.'

'I want to understand,' he says, and I hear tears straining his voice.

'I never lied to you,' I say. 'Everything I told you about my life is true.' I look back at Agnese's face, and all the horror and hurt that lie behind that implacable expression. 'The portrait was ordered because I had just given birth to a son. Sons, even illegitimate ones, were always celebrated.' I tear off another square that frames that firmly closed mouth. 'My baby was taken from me when he was one day old. I didn't see him again for 60 years, though I always knew where he was. I stayed as close to him as I could and watched him grow old from afar. When I heard he was gravely ill I went to him, sat beside him as he died, and it rained. He didn't know who I was.' The scent of sodden earth, the sound of the rain. The feeling of my little boy's hand in mine, twisted and withered with age as mine never would be.

'I've lived through lifetimes of persecution, abuse, assault. Lifetimes of growing freedom, desire, hedonism. Lifetimes of adventure, danger, and discovering that I am allowed to be exactly who I am without apology. All of those lifetimes have made me into the person you know. This person who you love and who loves you.'

'Just stop,' Ben says, covering his face with his hands for a moment before staggering up from the sofa. 'Please, it's too much. I need some time, to work all this out. I think I should go.'

'Please, Ben, don't. You don't look well. You need rest. Stay here. Stay here and I'll go.

'Because you are invincible,' he says bitterly.

'Because I love you,' I say. 'I want to take care of you.'

Ben presses his lips together, as if trying to stem a tidal wave of grief, and I see it all suddenly. That I showed him magic was real and yet I still didn't save his life. No wonder he wants to go far away from me now.

'I'm going to go,' he says. He moves to walk past me, and I let him, watching as he hooks Pablo's lead on to his collar.

As the front door closes the photograph of me and Dominic flutters to the floor.

I am alone again.

Chapter Fifty-One

Pablo and I walk into the night with no idea where we are going.

Even at this dark-purple time of the morning, London is busy with people. We weave in and out of the crowd with the same single-minded determination, as if we too have somewhere to be. If only.

They might know where they are going, but all I'm trying to do is get out of my own head and escape my own fatally flawed body. Only there is no eject button. The only way this ends is by going down in flames.

I walk without seeing where I am going. People flow around me and I get the sensation that even as I put one foot in front of the other, I am not moving.

I began this journey hoping for magic, I ended it not only witnessing the impossible but falling in love with her. Even now, as I cross the same busy roads around Trafalgar Square where I first met Vita, I still don't understand the way I'm feeling, the hurt and the sense of betrayal.

I wanted it to be real, and it is. But not for me.

The final blow was struck when we deciphered the letter in the painting and I realised there was no hope. That loss doubled and trebled when Mariah made me understand finally that the woman I love has years and years in which to forget me, and I have only moments left to love her. In just a few days Vita has become the biggest, most important love of my life, yet I will only ever be a fragment of hers.

Somehow we have made our way down to the river, Pablo picking up pace as we walk, his head down as we walk along the

Embankment, nose to the ground. We walk up on to Waterloo Bridge as the full force of 9–5 London reaches its peak. When we reach the centre of the bridge I stop, looking out over the river, with London's metallic and concrete skirts arranged around the silvery steam like the petals of a flower. If I look one way I see the city thrust upwards, the glass of the skyscrapers catching fragments of sky in their net. I turn the other way and the Houses of Parliament dominate the riverbank, spires and crenellations that speak of another age long since gone.

Vita has seen all of this rise and fall. She's seen the river turned to ice thick enough to hold fairs on, and the Blitz rain fire down over St Paul's. She's woven herself into the history of this place in a thousand different coloured threads, and somehow she seems present everywhere I look, embroidered in glimpses. All that life, so much of it stretching back as far as the Thames all the way to its source, and forward into the future where oceans of time are waiting for her.

The thought of all that time makes me swerve and sway, as if I'm standing too close to the edge of a very high precipice.

Pablo tugs at his lead and we walk on over the bridge, taking the steps that lead down to the South Bank, turning left and heading towards the London Eye. Staring up at it I imagine it's a wheel, and if I only knew how to spin it backwards I could replay the last few days with Vita again and again, and then it wouldn't matter how it ends, because we'd always have those few sweet days before magic and reality parted ways so sharply.

We find our way into a strange little park with winding pathways cutting through grassy mounds. A pigeon lounges on the open pages of a discarded newspaper. A squirrel races up a tree making the leaves shimmer. Around me there are people, all kinds of them from every corner of life, coming together here through this conduit, joined in this moment before travelling on.

This city is beautiful, and so are all its people. This life is beautiful, every minute of it. Even the ones that break your heart. Even the ones that kill you.

Vita has endured that for half a thousand years, and despite that magnitude she chose me. She let herself love me.

Wearily I sit down on a bench, dropping my aching head into my hands. For most of life I was half-asleep, waiting for it to begin. It was the touch of death that taught me how to live. It was Vita, taking my hand and showing me what lies beyond this everyday world.

Perhaps there isn't much time left for me, but there could still be a miracle. Just not the one I planned on. But if there is a way I can grow old looking at the gentle curves of her remarkable face, then I am ready to risk whatever I have left for that chance.

I know what to do.

Taking my phone out, I make a call.

'Mr Perrera? It's Ben Church. I'm ready to come and talk about surgery.'

IX

I am silent without the sun.

Traditional sundial motto

Chapter Fifty-Two

'So,' Jack says, breaking the sorrowful silence between us at last. 'He knows it all now?'

'Yes.' I bow my head. 'You were right, I should have told him sooner. It seemed too hard, but seeing him like that, so shocked and bereft… that was worse. I'm so worried about him, Jack, out there with nowhere to go and no friends. I found him at the worst time of his life and put him through all this pointless hope. And now, I think that perhaps he hates me.'

'He doesn't hate you,' Jack says, looking up at me from under his curls. 'Trust me on this. He loves you with every cell of his body. Whatever he is feeling – shock, despair, confusion – it isn't hate. Give him time.'

'He doesn't have time, though, does he?' I feel the catch of tears in my throat. 'I'm leaving the Collection,' I say, forcing my thoughts away from the look on Ben's face before he walked out of my door. 'I emailed this morning. Anna has asked me to think about it but I can't stay.'

'You don't really want to be kept away from your Collection for another 20 years, do you, Madame Bianchi?'

'I honestly don't think I care,' I say wearily. 'I've searched every part of the Collection for answers time and time again, always thinking that a new decade might bring some new way to make sense of this, yet I've never found a way to escape. And just when I thought I might have a reason to want to live for ever, I discover that Leonardo didn't have a clue either. It's the worst of both worlds.'

Jack shifts in his chair.

'I didn't mean…'

'I know.' Jack smiles at me. 'I have always seen the possibility in you and I will until the end of the universe. I know you lost that after Dominic. And found it again with Ben.' He pauses, his expression implacable. 'I should have understood what you were going through sooner.'

'How could you, when I didn't really know myself?' I reach for his hand across the table. I am glad he's at my side once more.

'So, what did the painting tell you?' Jack asks at last, as if he's been dreading the moment.

'He wrote a letter, I suppose you'd call it – or a testament perhaps – recounting the time that he came to visit me in the nunnery. At some time after that he must have gone back to the painting and amended it. But whatever he did to make me like this, it wasn't revealed in the painting – just a sort of footnote, really.'

'That's so bloody like him,' Jack says. 'Wanker.'

'Only you would call Leonardo da Vinci a wanker,' I say.

'Only I'm allowed to.' He laughs.

'I'm sorry, Jack,' I say. 'I've been so wrapped up with Ben. I should have listened to you. He was overwhelmed, frightened, hurt and angry. By the time he walked out on me I think he had accepted the truth.' My head drops. The tabletop blurs with tears. 'But he left. I don't know where he has gone, and I don't know if he will come back.'

'Oh, Vita.' Jack comes around to my side of the table, puts his arm around me and leans my head on his shoulder.

'You will always have me,' he says. 'I will always love you.'

'Yesterday Ben tried to tell me he thought you were in love with me.' I sniff and smile. 'As if you would ever feel that way about me.'

I expect Jack to snort and laugh and make some off-the-cuff comment. But he is silent and still. Holding his breath still. Sitting up I look into his face.

A dozen puzzle pieces fall into place. 'Jack?'

'I didn't expect it either,' Jack says with a small sad smile. 'It rather took me by surprise. I didn't know I had fallen in love with you, Vita, until the day I watched you marry Dominic. I saw how you looked at him, and I realised I'd live another thousand years for the chance that you might look at me that way one day. I don't think you know how remarkable you are. Yes, we have been through this together, but it was always easier for me than you, because I am a man. You have endured terrors, yet still you hope, still you fight, still you love. You are impossible not to fall for.'

'But—'

'I wasn't going to say anything about this revelation on your wedding,' Jack says. 'I'm not that crass. I could wait until the time was right. Fill my days with beautiful people and experiences, while you were happy and married, and afterwards, when you were in the depths of grief. I could wait until you had had enough time to grieve and to realise that life is worth living, is always worth living, if you have love.'

'Jack...'

'And then just at the moment I thought I could finally tell you that sometime in the middle of the last century I fell in love with you, you met Ben. It was something of a blow.'

Jack drops his arm from mine, reaching across the table for his coffee.

'I didn't realise,' I say. 'I'm so stupid. It just never even occurred to me. I'm so sorry. I love you, Jack, but I ...'

'Stop,' Jack quiets me with the palm of his hand and a wry smile. 'I haven't lived this long to be friend-zoned by you. I don't want to go over it. And you don't owe me an apology for not feeling the same way about me. It is what it is, and you know I'll get over it. Eventually. After all, I've an eternity available for therapy.'

I fling my arms around him, and he returns the embrace, pulling me tightly into his arms for one moment before determinedly untangling my arms from around his neck and moving his chair back an inch or two.

'I think it must have been after he visited you in Milan that he made a portrait of me,' he says, changing the subject with some finality. 'I was already past my prime then in his eyes, and perhaps he thought, having seen you, that he'd be able to make it so that

I kept the last of my good looks. "Ah, Salai," he'd say, "you are the most beautiful being I have ever known." Not quite beautiful enough for him to love me to the end though. Twenty-five years together, and even when he trapped me in amber I stopped being beautiful enough for him.'

He sighs. 'I just wish he'd asked me, asked you,' Jack said. 'I mean, at least with you he had no expectation of it working, but with me? He must have known there was a chance – he had proof of it working before.'

'And what would you have said if Leonardo had offered you forever?' I ask him.

'I would have said yes then,' Jack admits. 'And yes now, I suppose. I still love this strange, wonderful life: I can't imagine ever being tired of it, even given certain... *disappointments*.'

'I'm glad about that,' I say.

'And despite my own issues of the heart,' Jack says, 'I want you to know that I will always be your friend. I want you to be happy, Vita. That's the most that I want from this world.'

'I know,' I say. 'You are a good man, Jack.'

'But not the right man,' he says with finality. 'The man you love, the man you belong with, is Ben.'

'If I could have him back, even just for a little while, then perhaps the prospect of another five centuries might be bearable.'

'And if he doesn't come back?' Jack asks.

'I'll keep looking for an escape hatch,' I tell him. 'I need to know that one day this will end as it should do, naturally; as it did for Leonardo; as it did for my son. As it should for me. If I knew I would be returned to the stars once again, to be with my boy, Dominic, eventually Ben... all the people I have loved and lost, then I would have peace.'

There's a long silence. Even the busy city all around us seems to have fallen quiet.

'Vita,' Jack says at length, his expression suddenly afraid, 'you will be angry, but please just listen to me and try to understand why I did what I did.'

'What do you mean?' I ask warily. 'Why?'

Jack bows his head, and I can tell he is choosing his words carefully.

'Jack, why would I be angry?' I ask him. 'What have you done?'

'It's not what I've done; it's what I haven't… yet.'

'Just tell me, Jack,' I say.

'When Leonardo died, he left me half a vineyard – *half* of one, mind you – and many of his works of art, sketches and notebooks all loaded up into this great chest.'

I nod. I know this. I've seen Jack's collection more than once. 'You know how it went. After Leonardo, I was a drunk, lost and in chaos. There was no kind of trouble I couldn't get into and it came to the point when I had to let it be known that I had died in a suitably dramatic fashion.'

'Death by crossbow was impressive,' I say.

'It was a long time before I realised what was happening to me – or rather, what wasn't. By the time I realised that I was like you, Leonardo was dead and I had no one. Until I found you, that is.' His smile is full of sorrow. 'You know how every now and then I let one of the least interesting bits be *discovered* and made a little money? Like that time it got us out of that fix in Paris?' I nod with a shudder. It had been called 'the Terror' for a reason.

'So, what haven't you told me?' I ask him. He's reminding me of all the things that we have been through together. Whatever this is, it's bad.

'About 30 years ago – seems like yesterday – you were in Dorset with Dominic and I was in Berlin. You loved your life with Dominic, and I loved it for you, but it was hard for me. Harder than I admitted to.'

'I understand,' I say.

'Anyway, one day I was going through my chest, having a look to see if there was anything in there I could turn over. For once I'd taken everything out of it and laid it all out on the floor. It was a lovely hardwood mahogany floor in that apartment, do you remember?'

'Jack.' Whatever expression he sees on my face he takes it as a warning.

'Well, I noticed there was this catch on the bottom of the chest, designed to look like a joint. Of course, there was – Leonardo loved secret compartments. Anyway, it didn't take much to open it, and there it was.'

'There what was?' I asked him, sensing the answer in the plummet of my heart.

'I swear to you, if I'd known about it before then I would have told you,' Jack says. 'But by then Dominic was already old and sick.'

'What did you find, Jack?' I ask, my voice rising.

'A packet, sealed with wax,' he says. 'I opened it, and inside were powdered pigments, a vial of oil and the smallest fragment of a red, waxy rock, as big as my thumbnail, that he had called a *philosopher's stone*. And his notes on the processes he went through when he painted you and then me. I found the answer to immortality, Vita, and there are just enough of his materials left for one more portrait. One more portrait that will freeze the sitter in time.'

His words punch the air out of my gut. I stare at him.

'Vita, listen,' Jack persists. 'I didn't tell you then because I knew you'd want me to use it on Dominic. And I had no idea if it would work, and if it did, it seemed like...'

'Like what?' I ask him.

'Well, as you say, Dominic was very ill then.' He sees my shock. 'To keep him stuck for ever like he was at that time would have been unfair to him. This wasn't about me. You must believe that. I was trying to protect you *and* Dominic. I was there with you those last months, remember? He asked me to take care of you once he had gone. He told me that he couldn't let go unless he knew you would be loved and cared for – that's what I promised him. He wanted an escape, Vita, just like you do. I didn't tell you then because it would have been too hard on you.'

Closing my eyes, I let the world steady, and everything he has just told me fall into order.

'You were right not to tell me about it then,' I say, and he breathes out a long sigh of relief. 'It's just you know that I have been looking for this for so long, Jack. And you had the answer all along.'

'No, you haven't. And no, I don't,' he shakes his head. 'You've been looking for a way to *end* it. This only tells you how to begin the process. Leonardo says nothing about how to end it. That is still a mystery to us both.'

It takes a moment for that realisation to sink in, and the smallest glimmer of light to shine through the darkness.

'And why have you decided to tell me this now?' I ask him, hardly daring to hope.

'Because, whatever you may think of my choices back then, I love you. All I want from this world is for you to be happy. And because there is just enough for one more portrait. Enough to save Ben, if it works, and keep him at your side for ever.'

Chapter Fifty-Three

There are 15 missed calls on my phone when I leave Mr Perrera's office with Pablo at my side. I told him I wasn't going anywhere without my dog, and he let me break the rules at once.

When I walked in there about an hour ago, I told him I wanted the surgery and that I wasn't going to change my mind, so I didn't need to hear all the gory details. Of course he made me listen to them anyway.

They are going to use the scans they took of my brain to make a computer simulation so they can practise the procedure over and over again. I listened as he talked me through all the plans and contingencies they had made on the off-chance I would change my mind and get in touch. He tried to get me to check in to a ward right now so that they could monitor me, but they wouldn't be ready for the surgery for three days, and I said I wasn't going to spend 72 hours hanging around a hospital. He didn't like it, but he understood.

I want to be excited and grateful about the prospect of a surgical cure – or even nervous or frightened – but all I am is numb. It's the same numbness that washed over me on the day I left Leeds looking for the meaning of life, like an idiot who thinks it can ever be so simple. For a while Vita pierced the low, thick, grey cloud that seemed set on defining my last days on earth, and filled it with a rainbow of colour. But now? Now I have no idea what I think or feel or believe any more. I'm not even sure which way is up.

This unveiling of a secret universe makes me angry. I know that it shouldn't, but it does. And yet I miss her so very much that it hurts in every cell.

Fifteen missed calls, and all of them from Vita.

She doesn't leave a message until the last call. Tapping my phone on to speaker I hold it up to my ear and listen.

'Ben, please call me,' she says. 'I have something really important I need to talk to you about as soon as possible. Please. I am at home. I'll be here all day. Please come. I need to talk to you face to face. It's urgent.'

There is an edge to her voice, something I can't interpret. I don't know if I have the heart to try.

So, instead, I FaceTime Mum, who picks up on the second ring,

'What's wrong?' she asks, looking at my expression. 'Ben, what's happened?'

'Is Kitty there?' I ask, and a second later the two of them peer at me from the screen of my phone. Best to get right to the point.

'There's a surgeon down here, who thinks he has a shot of clipping the aneurysm, and I've decided to go for it,' I tell them. 'Will you two come down? I want you to be here with me.'

'But Mrs Patterson thought it was too dangerous,' Mum says.

'I am not going to lie, it is really dangerous,' I say. 'The odds are a bit better than Mrs Patterson thought, but not much. The thing is, it's a chance. And I want to take it. But not unless you are here with me. I need you both.'

'What does Vita say?' Mum asks.

'I am about to tell her now,' I say. 'Look, my mind is made up, Mum. I just want you guys here.'

'We're coming,' Kitty says. 'I'll sort tickets out for tomorrow.'

'We're on our way,' Mum says before pressing her hand over her mouth to stifle a sob.

We just look at one another then, our gazes magically connected over hundreds of miles by technology that Doctor John Dee would have thought was delivered by angels. Perhaps a last chance to look at their faces, and save their image in my heart.

'See you soon,' I say as I sign off. Please don't let that be a lie.

The moment the call ends, I wonder whether I should just give up trying to stay alive and go home. Forget Vita, forget surgery, just get the next train home and spend whatever time I have left with people I love, in places I know. I came down here to define what my life has been and who I am. I expected something earth-shattering to happen, I willed and wished for it. And it did. And I just feel numb.

But if I never see her again, never touch her again, then the rest of my life will be hollow.

'Come on, boy,' I say to Pablo. 'There is somewhere we need to be.'

***

'Ben.' There are tears in her eyes as she opens the door, but she is smiling. 'I was so afraid you wouldn't come.'

'I nearly didn't,' I say. 'I am struggling, to be honest.'

She steps back into the shadows of her hallway and makes way for me and Pablo to enter. I let him off the lead and he trots into her sitting room, hopping straight on to the sofa like it was made for him.

Leaning against the sitting-room door I see that all the print-outs have been taken down.

'It's a bit much looking at my own face blown up to the size of a house,' Vita says, nodding at the pile of fragments on the coffee table. 'Look, I understand why you are so angry with me,' she says in a rush. 'I wanted to tell you – I was about to...'

'I know,' I tell her. It's hard to be this close to her and not feel able to reach out and touch her. 'I don't need to forgive you. I was hurt, but I'm not even angry anymore.' I walk into the front room and fold down on to the sofa next to my dog. 'I don't know how I feel about anything. Before I thought I understood it. I had this notion that we were all in it together: we all live and we all die. Sometimes fate is a bastard and people die too young. It's a roulette wheel I played, and I lost and it sucked, but I could deal with it. But now I know it's not a level playing field, that you and Jack exist. Nothing I thought I had come to terms with makes sense any more. There's a whole different, secret version of this world to the one I understood, and I don't know how to deal with that.'

'I know, it's not fair,' Vita says. 'It's unnatural by definition. Jack and I cheat death every day and we don't know why. We are lucky. Endless time has allowed so much good fortune to fall into my lap. But we suffer too. I have suffered through centuries of a world that hated and feared me even if it didn't know why. So if you hate me I understand why. I can't bear the thought of it, but I understand. If the rest of the world isn't ready to understand what has happened to me yet, then why should you be?'

Her words shake me out of my slumber.

'I don't hate you, Vita,' I tell her, leaning forward, preventing myself from opening my arms to her with a huge force of will. 'It would be easier if I could. But I love you.'

'Still?' she asks, her voice small and quiet.

'Probably always,' I say sadly.

'And I love you,' she tells me, tears tracking down her face.

I nod, my throat too tight to speak. We sit across the room from one another, just a few feet apart, and yet it feels as though universes fill the void between us.

'It is hard, this life,' she says. 'You have seen how hard it has been for me. It can be gruelling, confusing, frightening and painful. I lose almost everyone and everything I love, time and time again. And it doesn't matter how much I try to insulate myself against caring, love always seeks me out again in the end. Life will always makes me determined to feel, even if that is the last thing I want. But it can be full of joy and wonder too. In the midst of the worst of times I have seen how humans still hope, how they still strive to be good and to love one another.'

I look at her, not sure how to respond.

'But it is hard, and forever is a very long time, Ben. A long time to live with regret.'

'I can imagine,' I say.

'Can you?' she asks me. 'Can you imagine what it would be like to be there when your mum and Kitty die? When Elliot grows old and passes away? Could you stand that? Because

I need to know you are sure you could withstand that and not hate yourself. That you are sure that you will give up the life you have now, which is safe and kind, even if it is too short, for one that may never end... and millennia of me. It might feel like a dream come true, but there are sacrifices. You need to be certain you are willing to make them.'

'What are you talking about?' I ask her, trying to stop my mind from racing to conclusions.

'Jack... Jack has found the secret. It seems he had it in his possession all along, although he only found out recently. He knows how to do what Leonardo did to us.'

'Are you being serious?' The room shifts and warps. I reach for something to hold on to and find her hand as she crosses the few steps to my side.

'I am,' she says. 'We know how to repeat the experiment.'

The possibility behind what that means is too much to take in, so instead I root myself into the old reality, the one I understand.

'When I got taken into the hospital, the consultant who saw me,' I tell her, 'he said he would operate on me, to fix me.'

'What?' she gasps.

'They think there is a 12-per-cent chance of success, of a cure. Well, not a cure for the Marfan syndrome, but for the aneurysm.'

'And if it isn't successful?' Vita asks, ashen.

'Death or brain death,' I say, hearing the tremor in my voice. 'I already told them to do it. Day after tomorrow. If it works it will mean we have more time together. I don't think I knew it until just now, but if it works I'll come straight back to you as soon as I can.'

'But the risk?' she says. 'The risk is so high. What if I lose you tomorrow?'

'What if you don't?' I say. 'It's a chance. One I never expected, and somehow it feels... fair.'

'So, you are sure?' she asks. 'You want the surgery? You don't want a life like mine, with me?'

For a long moment I don't know how to answer her. When it was all hypothetical, I wanted nothing more. Now I understand it a little better, as much as my small mortal brain can, I sense the great weight of all that time. I can almost feel the burden of it; living for so long in a world that never pauses for breath. I'm not sure I do want that, yet she has no choice.

'The thing is, I didn't think it was a possibility until about 10 seconds ago,' I tell her. 'And I still don't know if it actually is, because you haven't said it is.'

'Oh, god,' Vita lets out a long shaky breath. 'Sorry, sorry, sorry, I'm so desperate for you to agree that I am rushing ahead. I'm trying to tell you that Jack will help us, Ben. If you want it, he can make you immortal, just like me. If that is what you want. But you have to be sure.'

'For ever,' I say, wondering at the true meaning of the words. Vita was alone when forever happened to her, she had nothing. I have everything: a family that loves me, a home, places I feel safe. To agree to this would mean letting all of that slowly rot away and decay before my eyes. The thought of losing Mum and Kitty, Elliot and even Pablo hurts more now that I realise there is no way out. I'd be caught like this for ever. There is only this though. This a surgery that is almost certain to kill me. Leave them now or endure them leaving me. In the end it isn't a choice at all.

'As far as I know,' Vita says. 'We can't know for sure that the process will work – the ingredients are old and might be useless. But we do know that it has worked before.' She leans towards me so that our foreheads are touching. 'I am certain of one thing; that if you say yes, I will love you for as long as the world turns and beyond.'

It's not a question of what I have to lose; I have so very much to lose. But if it works then this peculiar miracle will keep me on this earth long enough to appreciate all that I have, and more. And there will always be Vita.

'For ever it is then,' I tell her, bringing her hand to my lips. 'I want for ever, with you.'

X

Our last hour is hidden from us so that we watch them all.

Traditional sundial motto

Chapter Fifty-Four

'Perhaps we should wait for Kitty and your mum,' I worry as Ben, Jack and I stand across the street from the Bianchi Collection. 'They should be here for this. You should discuss it with them, see how they feel about it. As far as we know you are the first person in history to choose to do this, so it's important to do it right.'

Ben stares at the building as if he is seeing it for the first time. I greet it as an old friend, my one constant among decades of change, one that has stood sentinel over the phases of my life from the night when it glittered with torchlight right until this moment when it stands silent, shrouded in dark, waiting for me to come home.

'Choosing life means living through everything, but also outside of it. Witnessing history but never truly becoming it.'

'Are you trying to talk me out of it?' Ben asks.

'No, I just want to be sure that I haven't talked you *into* it – that this is your choice.'

'It is my choice,' he says. 'And as far as we know there is nothing to discuss with them yet. Let's see how this works out. They are coming down in the morning anyway, for the surgery, so we'll cross that bridge when we come to it. Agreed?'

'Agreed, except how will we know if it works?' I ask him. 'Jack and I didn't realise for years.'

'The surgery,' Ben says. 'If I survive the surgery then stay alive for a few months... we'll know there's a good chance that I can't die.'

'May I suggest we get to the breaking-and-entering part of the evening?' Jack suggests. 'There are an awful lot of CCTV cameras in London.'

'It's not breaking and entering when you own the building, Jack,' I say.

'Wait, what?' Ben asks. 'You still own it? How?'

'We *are* the Bianchi Collection, Jack and I. I was Madame Bianchi and Jack was my brother. We wanted to understand what had happened to us, how it had happened. So we travelled and we collected everything that might have given us an answer, or even part of one. This is *our* collection. When the original Madame Bianchi, whose portrait still presides over the grand entrance hall, died quietly in the countryside in 1781, her descendants – Jack and I, of course, with different identities – kept up the house for as long as we could, but the world changed and people didn't live that way anymore.'

'And besides, we couldn't get the one thing we really wanted, which was access to the Da Vinci portraits,' Jack says.

'So we bequeathed it to the nation in 1920 in the hope that one day its reputation as a world-renowned cultural museum would enable us to bring the paintings to us.'

'That's what I call forward planning,' Ben says.

'This life is all about the long game,' Jack adds.

'And quite often serendipity,' I say, smiling at Ben. 'Anyway, we are – or rather, versions of us are – still on the board.'

The lights turn red and we cross the road together.

'But then why are you working in a job that you had to get two degrees for, in a museum you own?' Ben asks.

'Because Vita has never believed in taking advantage of her unique position,' Jack says.

'After Dominic died, I went back to university,' I tell him. 'I have collected degrees like baseball cards, but of course most of my qualifications don't fit my appearance for very long. So every now and then I start again.'

'And a few years ago she decided she wanted to go back through the Collection with the benefit of more recent technology, so she went back to university, armed herself with knowledge, and when a position came up, she applied just like anyone else.'

'Well, I did have a bit of insider knowledge that probably gave me the edge,' I admit. 'And there are some advantages to living a very long time that you can't avoid – the accumulation of wealth being one of them.'

'What if you hadn't been successful?' Ben asks. 'What would have happened then?'

'That never really occurred to me,' I say thoughtfully as we walk up to the main entrance.

'And while Vita was at university I went back to Florence and brushed up on my artistic skills, thought I must say no teacher I have ever had was as brilliant as Leonardo himself.'

'It must have been amazing,' Ben says in awe, 'to have known Leonardo so well?'

'Though never as well as I thought,' Jack says quietly.

'Anyway, it just so happens that a fabulously wealthy donor has arranged to hire the entire building for a small private function tonight, complete with their own security, so we will have the whole place to ourselves.'

'What about the wealthy donor's party?' Ben asks me.

I give him a long look.

'Oh, *you* are the wealthy donor. Wait, why didn't you do that before when we were trying to photograph the portrait?' Ben asks.

'I am immortal, not perfect,' I say. 'This was Jack's idea – he's much more Machiavellian than me.'

'Now there's a man who wasn't as bad as history paints him,' Jack says lightly.

★★★

Since this is a momentous night and it's been such a very long time since I have had this place almost to myself, I let us in through the front door.

The grand entrance is fully lit and it still takes my breath away to see our works of art lining the emerald-silk walls, our beautiful furniture and belongings displayed for other people to look at.

'Home, sweet home,' Jack sighs. 'I miss the eighteenth century; I think it's been my favourite so far. The outfits, for one thing.'

'It feels really wrong to use this expression,' Ben says, walking into the centre of the hall and turning around very slowly, 'but all this is making my head explode. I mean, who else have you met? Where else have you been?'

'There will be time to tell you all of that later,' I tell him, taking his hand and kissing it. 'Jack, what now?'

'Well, first of all I need to make sketches of Ben,' Jack says. 'I suggest the courtyard. Leonardo says the portrait must be completed under starlight. He doesn't mention that for the pre-paratory sketches, but I don't suppose it's worth taking the risk.'

We follow Jack through the old drawing room and ballroom and out into the covered yard, where a glass dome sits over a pool with a fountain, lined with the ancient statues that we brought back from Rome and Greece.

I hold Ben's hand, watching as Jack sets up his easel and pins several sheets of brown paper to it. He opens his bag and takes out the brand-new box of chalks I bought him.

'Will those chalks do?' I ask him anxiously. 'They aren't exactly Leonardo's, are they?'

'No, but chalk is one of the few things that has not changed in 500 years,' Jack tells me. 'Chalk is chalk. Now stop bothering me and my muse, otherwise I'll have to ask you to leave.'

It takes a lot of effort, but I know Jack hates to be watched when he works, so I do as I'm told. I'd read the instructions Leonardo left before we came to the Collection tonight. He'd written that he'd completed the portrait of me between two and four in the morning over a period of weeks. We don't have weeks for Jack to perfect his portrait of Ben, to work on the *sfumato* or pin down that particular expression in his eyes. We have to hope that the materials, the act, are enough to save Ben for good. We have to hope – and I do. With every beat of my heart I hope as hard as I can, until it strains every muscle and my whole body is wracked with a fever of wishes.

'Is that *it*?' Ben peers at a little nugget of dull, reddish material that Jack had set on the table before we left tonight. 'That's the philosopher's stone?'

'According to Leonardo,' Jack says with a shrug. 'It could just be pigeon poo for all I know, but this is what we have to work with.'

'I mean, if it does work, shouldn't we send it to a lab, have it analysed? Share this with the whole world?' Ben asks.

'I can't think of a worse idea,' Jack says. 'And neither could Leonardo. Which is why, after he realised what he'd done, he did his best to hide it. He knew what man was capable of. He knew how something like this would upset the balance of creation if it was discovered before humanity was ready. I'll save a tiny amount, enough to be analysed one day a long time in the future, if the day ever comes when civilisation is advanced enough to know how to use it – though the last 500 years have not given me a great deal of hope.'

'Do *you* understand how it works?' Ben asks.

'I do realise this is potentially a life-altering moment for you,' Jack says, 'but I'm afraid I have to confess that on this occasion all I know how to do is to follow instructions and paint. Exactly how the process alters the actions of time and space is a mystery to me.'

'It's just all so low-key,' Ben says. 'It feels wrong that something so momentous can take place so *quietly.*'

'Leonardo didn't really understand it either,' Jack says. 'In the instructions he writes about striving to create a perfect balance, a harmony of atoms; of moving us, his subjects, Vita and me, and now you, into complete synchronicity with every other atom of the universe, existing as we are in the moment the portrait is completed, but as part of the fabric of the whole too. And he writes of capturing the spirit of creation that flows through everything and making a kind of dam to contain it. I am not a scientist, but I think perhaps he was talking about dark matter.'

'The God particle,' Ben says.

Jack completes his first sketch and lifts it up for Ben and me to see. He's captured him perfectly, with care, even affection. I look at Jack, thanking him silently from the bottom of my heart. He smiles a little and nods in return. 'The proof of the pudding is in the eating. Are you still willing to try this, Ben, before you try suicidal surgery?'

'I am,' Ben says.

'Go and ready yourself then,' Jack says. 'Do your hair, brush your teeth. You want to look your best.'

Once Ben has gone, I take Jack's hand.

'Thank you,' I say simply. 'For giving Ben this chance. I know how much it must cost you.'

'Giving you a chance at happiness costs me nothing,' Jack says, kissing me lightly on the forehead. 'I just hope it's enough. Now leave me to it. I'll send him to find you when I'm ready to begin painting.'

Leaving him in the courtyard, I wander through the hallways, stopping here and there to revisit old friends. Turning into the Da Vinci exhibition I find her, *La Belle*, waiting patiently for me.

I drag a chair to sit in front of her and watch her watching me. I wish I could go back to that moment and tell her that no matter what comes next, one day she will be happy.

'You are safe now,' I tell her, the girl I once was, the brutalised, lost soul who was robbed of all of her joy and almost broken. 'Agnese, you don't have to be afraid any more. You don't have to despair any more, because I have you now. You are safe.'

Perhaps it's just a trick of the light, but I think I see her smile.

Chapter Fifty-Five

'I just wanted to say that I realise the weight of what you are doing for me and Vita,' I tell Jack, after we have passed at least an hour in a pretty awkward silence. 'I think I understood the way you feel about her even before she did.'

'No point crying over spilt milk,' Jack says with careful lightness. 'I missed my chance, if I had ever had one. I will always love her, but the pain will pass in a hundred years or so. It turns out time can be a great healer if you have centuries to spare.'

'You are a pretty amazing man,' I tell him.

'I know,' he says with a shrug.

'I am so grateful that you are here tonight, for her and for me. I will never forget that.'

'The thing is,' Jack says, measuring me with the length of his brush, 'Vita was never going to love me that way, whether you had come along or not. I know that now. I tried hard not to tell her at all, but... well, I'm only human. Look, don't feel sorry for me. I'm devastatingly handsome and irresistibly charming. Soon enough some beautiful person will captivate me into a grand passion and I'll be back to my old self again.'

'I won't feel sorry for you,' I promise. 'Just... thank you.'

'Vita has saved my sanity more times that I care to mention. She has kept my feet on the ground, kept me human,' Jack says. 'I owe her more than I can ever repay.'

'I can see how that would be important,' I say. 'That you might be at risk of losing that when you have seen as much history as you have.'

'How do you think you will deal with all that history?' he asks me. 'So much of it passes us by. Sometimes we are swept up into the whirlwind, thrown around while we watch people we care about suffer and die. And then sometimes we are spat out to begin again. To learn *how* to be again. To try and operate a sodding mobile phone. How do you think you will cope with that?'

'I don't know,' I say, trying to picture it. 'Before all this I never appreciated how little time we have on this earth to do something with our lives. Now I know I want to use time to do something that matters – that will make life better for everyone. It has to give you a unique perspective, right? Because there's no passing the buck to the next generation when you *are* every generation. You and Vita have fought in wars and stood up against the worst kind of evil. You've done your bit more than once. Maybe I can solve climate change or something. And also, I want to go everywhere, do everything and try it all. If we pull this off, I'm never going to take one minute of time for granted ever again.'

'I like your ambition,' Jack says with a wry smile. 'You know there might be times... no wait, strike that. There *will* be times when you and Vita are not lovers, or even in love. When you tire of each other, annoy one another, or circumstances will pull you apart. What then?'

'My nan and grandad were married for 60 years,' I say. 'After he died, my nan told me she'd hated him for the whole of the Eighties. I mean, she loved him, but she hated him too. She was sick of the sight of him. They stuck it out, stayed married, because that's what people did then – working people, anyway. And then one day, after about 10 years of being miserable, lonely and resentful, they just looked at each other and all of that hurt and misunderstanding fell away. She said it was like they had fallen in love yesterday, and that it was like that until the day he died. I believe that love endures, and even when those times happen I know we will find our way back to each other eventually.'

'You had better live up to everything she believes about you,' Jack says lightly, 'because while I won't be able to kill you if you don't, I will be able to make your life a misery on an extended basis.'

'Noted,' I say.

'Well, I think I have enough sketches to begin the portrait,' he says. 'Fetch Vita.'

★★★

'The sky is clear,' Jack says, looking up at the glass roof. 'Hard to see any stars in central London, but they are up there, and that's the main thing.'

'They are,' Vita says, looking at the sketches of me that Jack has pinned up around the courtyard. 'These are amazing, Jack. You've captured him exactly.'

Taking a look at one of the sketches I see a portrait of a man who is just about to smile; a man who is afraid, but who has hope; a man in love. Somehow Jack has managed to capture all of that and more in these sketches. He is a great artist after all.

'So, is that it?' I ask him nervously, trying not to think about the enormity of it all. 'No rituals? Incantations? We don't need to sacrifice something?'

'No,' Jack says adding a drop of oil to his powder. 'To be honest I'd feel better about our chances if there were some mumbo-jumbo. But I have prepared the board, made from yew as prescribed. And I have mixed the paint. But neither you nor I were present when this part happened, Vita, so I don't think you and Ben need to be here. Go and spend some time together. Finally make some use of that lovely four-poster in the State Room.

'Come and find us when you are done,' Vita says.

She pauses for a beat and then runs to hug Jack, who returns her embrace.

I offer Jack my hand and he takes it.

'Thank you is not sufficient to cover what this means to me, to us,' I tell him. 'Even if it doesn't work, that you were willing to try is everything.'

'The look on her face is thanks enough,' Jack says.

★★★

'Well.' Vita's eyes are glittering as she prepares to lead me through the Collection. 'We are in the museum at night. What do you want to do?'

Suddenly fear rushes up behind me and takes hold. I'm frozen to the spot by terror and all I want to do is to go home. To my little cottage in Hebden Bridge, to get in my bed and pull my duvet over my eyes and sleep.

'Ben, are you OK?' Vita asks.

'I'm scared,' I say, simply. 'Scared if it works. Scared if it doesn't. I think I've been scared since I found out about my head and...' I look at her.

Vita opens her arms and I walk into them, letting her wrap herself around me, and hold me close enough to feel the beat of her heart.

'I'm scared too,' she admits. 'Scared of losing you. Scared of forcing you into making a choice you might live to regret. Scared of what we are doing here.'

'Life is terrifying,' I whisper into her hair.

'Yes,' she replies. 'If you want to we can just turn around and go home now. I'll tell Jack to stop painting and we'll go for the surgery and—'

'No,' I say, pulling apart from her a little so that I can see her face. 'I'm really scared, but what kind of an idiot would turn his back on a miracle like the one you and Jack have offered me? I'm certain this is what I want. Terrified, but certain. Now show me your beautiful home. Take me to your favourite thing.'

Vita looks into my eyes for a moment, then kisses me, hard, determined, hungry.

'Or to that big bed Jack talked about,' I say with a smile.

Taking my hand, she begins to lead me up the grand central staircase as a new insistent worry wends its way up with me.

'Vita,' I ask her as we reach the top, and she waves her hand to turn on a succession of lights that illuminate an opulent landing, 'what if this doesn't work? Have you thought about what then?'

'Honestly, I haven't thought about much else. But if it doesn't we still have the surgery.'

'And if that doesn't work?' I ask her. 'What will happen to you then? You have to promise me that you won't give up on living, that you won't go back to trying to die.'

Vita is still, her chin drops, her hair sweeping across her face in a dark curtain.

'I can't think about that. Not tonight. Tonight, we need to believe in what we are doing.'

'But I need to know,' I say to her. 'I need to know that you will be OK if things don't work out the way we want them to.'

She looks up at me, her arms hanging at her side.

'Do you remember what I told you, when you asked me if your mum and Kitty would be OK when you died? My answer is still the same. If I lose you, Ben, my heart will be broken. I will be broken. Time will pass – perhaps aeons of it – and I will always remember you. I will always miss you. And when the world ends and I am finally set free, I will be saying your name. So, no, I won't be OK, but I will still keep living, the way you have reminded me to. How could I do anything else?'

Taking her face gently in my hands, I kiss away the tears on her cheeks. Tonight is not a time for fear. If these are some of our last hours together, some of my last hours on earth, then they must be filled with courage, joy and love.

'You know,' I say, taking her hand, 'I think it will be fine. It's bound to be fine. We'll watch the sun coming up tomorrow together in a few hours, and all that will lie ahead of us is a future that we will be able to fill in any way we like.'

'Do you really believe that?' Vita asks me.

'With all my heart,' I say. 'And whatever happens, remember that Mum and Kitty are your family too now, promise me?'

'I promise,' she says.

'Then take me to what you were going to show me – your favourite thing.'

'Oh this.' She unlocks a glass cabinet with her thumbprint and brings out a little, unassuming gold ring set with a green stone. 'I don't know if it is my favourite, but it is the most personal. My mother gave me this ring.'

'This ring?' I take it from her and look at it in my palm.

'Yes, I was 12 years old,' she says. 'Mother called me to her chamber and put this ring on my finger and kissed me. I hardly knew her; in lots of ways she was a stranger. But on that golden afternoon we sat together side by side and I remember feeling so loved.'

I take the ring from her, looking down at the simple gold circle, a gift of love that continuously completes itself even when those who gave it are long gone. Swallowing, I take her left hand and look at her.

'You know, if we had been ordinary people, who'd met in ordinary times, I would have waited to ask you to marry me. I knew that pretty much from the moment I met you.'

Silently Vita nods.

I slip the ring on to her finger. 'From now until forever.'

'From now until forever,' she echoes.

We stand there for a while, looking into one another's eyes, knowing that whatever might come we will always belong to one another.

'Now I can tick that off my bucket list,' I say.

'I didn't think you had one,' she says.

'Neither did I until just now,' I tell her. 'Won't someone notice the ring is missing?'

'Probably, but it does belong to me after all. What would you like to share with me next?' I ask her as she leads me over to a large sofa.

'Well, all that I am I give to you.'

★★★

'Are you happy?' she asks me a while later.

'I seem to always be happy when I'm half-dressed and on a sofa with you,' I murmur into her hair. I'm so tired that my body aches and tingles with exhaustion. Underneath it all is a sensation I have waited my life to feel: contentment.

'And yes, I am happy – truly happy.' I turn my face to hers, kissing the tip of her nose. 'Your love has made me safe, Vita. Even if there was no magic, no miracle. Even if I only had another hour to live. Your love has stopped me being afraid of anything at all, because I know that these last few days with you will belong to me, for ever, wherever I am.'

'I love you, Ben,' she whispers, her lips against my eyelids as they finally close.

I feel the beating of her heart, the rise and fall of her chest. I feel perfect happiness.

XI

The time to be happy is now.
The place to be happy is here.

Robert Green Ingersoll

Chapter Fifty-Six

Slowly early morning light sifts its way into my sleep and I open my eyes. The library is still and quiet, outside the streets are almost silent. Ben slumbers deeply next to me, one arm thrown across my waist. Gently easing myself out from underneath him, I smile as I look down at him. His hand trails off the edge of the sofa. The tips of his fingers just graze the worn-through rugs. The first light of a summer's day streams in through the window, pale gold, casting dappled shadows on his face. He is smiling. Bending down, I kiss his temple lightly. Noting the coolness of his skin on my lips, I find a coat to cover him with, then I go and look for Jack.

He is sitting in the courtyard, on the edge of the koi pool, his head bowed in exhaustion. He looks as if he has always been there, cast in bronze. It was here we'd sit and talk into the night, making plans for our next adventure, back before the weight of all this time started to feel like a burden. That changes today. From today Ben will be at my side. I can't see Jack's easel, or his paints. His head weighs so heavily in his hand I think he is sleeping. It's no small thing he's done for me tonight. Not only has he given Ben the gift of a future, but he has also let me go to him, knowing that nothing will ever be as it was again. It's a true gift of love.

Gently, I place my arm on his shoulder.

'Jack, are you OK?'

He looks up at me with bleary eyes, and smiles.

'I will be,' he says, stretching his arms wide, and encircling my waist, pulling me down to sit next to him.

'Do you think it worked?' I ask, allowing myself just the very edges of joy.

'I think it worked,' Jack says, smiling. 'It feels like it worked. I made a really beautiful portrait of Ben. The more I worked on it the more I realised why you had fallen for him. He has this delicate beauty. Such grace and poise. And I think… I really think I could feel something else happening around me, in the air. Like the build-up of static just before a storm. Perhaps it was the stars aligning to my command.'

'Oh, Jack, do you really think it was?' I ask him. 'I so want to believe that it was.'

'It felt like it used to,' Jack said, with a small smile. 'The sheer force of love I had for Leonardo lived once more; it *breathed*. And as it did, I felt colours running through my veins, returning me to the man I was when I was in his arms. I think I had forgotten what it meant to be truly human, but somehow last night it all came back: the joy and passion, the exhilaration of just being near him; the sweet tenderness we shared, and the still, silent moments. It was as if with every touch of the brush I painted myself back to life. Leonardo was close, Vita, I know he was. In spirit and touch. I felt…' He dips his head. 'I felt his love again, Vita. Just as it used to be. He was returned to me for a little while.'

He weeps quietly, even as he smiles.

'How do you feel?' I ask him.

'I feel wonderful,' he says. 'I feel healed. I'm sure I'll be cursing his name for all eternity again by teatime, but for now I feel the peace that you've been going on about for so long. It feels good.'

'I'm glad,' I say, leaning in to kiss his cheek.

'I just put the finishing touches to the portrait as the first rays of light reached over the horizon. It was kind of miraculous actually.'

'It *has* to have worked,' I say. 'How can it not have? And now life begins again.'

Jack laughs as I get up, dancing round the pool.

'It's only because I love you so much that I am not offended that you thought of life with me as a living death,' he says.

'That's not what I mean,' I say, catching his hand and pulling up. 'You know that I—'

'I know, Vita,' he says. 'You don't need to say more. Besides, it was all worth it just to see you like this again, my Madame Bianchi, poised to take the world by storm.'

'Everything's new now,' I say, spinning him around as he laughs delightedly. 'Everywhere we go, and everything we do will be like living it all for the first time. I'm going to take Ben around the world, at least ten times. All the wonderful sights of this glorious world are his too now, and we will never run out of time.' I release Jack, who twirls to a laughing stop. 'And I promise you will never be alone. You will always have me.'

'Until I grow bored of you anyway,' Jack says with a smirk.

'We can build a home together,' I say softly, as the possibilities grow before my eyes. 'I don't mean I'd leave London for good, of course not, but this time…' I look at Jack. 'Jack, this time it will all be about the future, instead of holding on to the past. Everything we dream we can make come true.

'Can I see it?' I glance around to search for the portrait.

'Let's fetch Ben and we can look at it together, the three of us,' Jack says.

Racing ahead of him I take the stairs two at a time, running at full tilt across the lone marbled tiles and back into the library.

Ben has not moved an inch. Still that dear sweet smile on his lips.

I kneel down in front of him. 'Ben?' I whisper, rubbing his shoulder. 'Wake up, Ben. It's time.'

He doesn't stir. I press my lips to his cool cheek.

'Come on, sleepyhead, it's time to rise and shine.' I shake him a little. His head falls to one side.

'Ben?' My face close to his. A flutter of disquiet. 'Ben?'

Jack walks into the room as I sit back on my heels.

'I think something's wrong,' I say in a very small voice. 'Ben's not waking up. Do you think he might have concussion or something, from when he hit his head?' I look up at him desperately. 'Jack?'

Jack moves quickly to his side, putting his ear to Ben's mouth. I wait as he listens.

'He's not breathing,' Jack says, his voice calm but taut. 'But that's impossible. It worked. I know it did.'

'What do you mean not breathing? Are you sure?' I shake Ben a little harder, my voice catching, panic rising. 'Ben, wake up! Wake up!'

Jack lifts Ben down on to the polished floor and puts his ear to his chest.

'Ben,' I plead. 'Ben, come on now, it's time to wake up. Come on.'

Jack sits back on his heels, his face white with shock. His hand is trembling as it reaches for mine.

'Vita,' Jack says. 'There's no heartbeat. He's cold. I think... I think he's been this way for some time.'

'No, that's not right. He's warm, see?' I tell Jack, rubbing Ben's hand between mine. 'I just woke up and he was sleeping. He hit his head and maybe he passed out but... We need to get help. Jack, call for help.'

'Vita,' Jack whispers. 'He's gone. He's left us. I'm so sorry, but we weren't in time. Ben is dead.'

'No.' I shake my head as I collapse on Jack. 'No, you're wrong. It's too soon. Call for help! We need to get help.'

Jack takes his phone from his pocket, fumbling with it. I hear his sob as he turns away from me and places the call.

I lay my head on Ben's chest, hot tears streaming on to his shirt. Beneath my hands I feel the familiar contours of his body, strong and still. Holding my breath, I listen. I will his heart to beat, to feel the rise and fall of his ribcage, but there is nothing but empty echoes.

Everything is nothing now.

Chapter Fifty-Seven

Everything that follows happens at a distance. I sit on the floor holding Ben's hand to my cheek for I don't know how long.

The paramedics perform CPR three times before looking at one another and shaking their heads. They try to take him away but I won't let go of his hand until a young woman gently unwraps my fingers and tells me where they are taking him, and that I will be able to see him again. 'But you must be wrong,' I tell her. 'He can't be dead. He was just here. We just got married.'

The police are talking to Jack in low voices, glancing over at me. I don't know what he is telling them, or how he will explain what we were doing here, but I don't care. When the paramedics begin to carry Ben down the grand staircase I follow them, one careful stair at a time, all the way to the threshold of the building where an ambulance is waiting. They tell me once more that I have to leave him then, but I will be able to see him again. They tell me someone will call me.

When the doors are shut the vehicle pulls out quietly into the flow of morning traffic. I watch it for as long as I can, until it's lost in the hum and mayhem of a summer rush hour.

We didn't have long enough.

All the years left in the turning of the earth would never have been long enough, but we never got to try.

When there is nothing else to do I turn around, walk back into the beautiful palace that was once my home and has become my refuge for a short while more. I shut and bolt the door.

'The board has closed the museum for the day,' Jack tells me. 'I told them that there was a tragedy at a corporate event. I'll deal with everything. Don't worry.'

'We were so close,' I say faintly. 'We were almost there.'

'He must have died in his sleep before the painting was finished,' Jack says. 'He was in your arms, Vita. He died loving you and being loved. It's no consolation, I know. But it's something.'

'It's not enough,' I say.

'Let me show you the painting,' he says. 'I think it will help.'

I let him lead me by the hand into the muted gallery where his work is set up beside Da Vinci's portrait. A mirror image of a painting made 500 years apart. Their bodies are turned toward one another, their faces look out from the canvas. A perfectly matched pair.

Jack has captured Ben beautifully. The slight hopeful smile, the warm light in his eyes. The gentle tilt of his brilliant head. In her expression there is sadness and loss. In Ben's there is love and hope. Together one makes a promise to the other.

Jack puts his arms around me. There is nothing else to do but cry my heart out.

***

'I need a way out.' Hours have passed, though I'm not sure how many. When my eyes were hot and dry and my body ached with pain, Jack suggested we go to the roof, where he poured us both a glass of whisky from his flask.

It's sitting here, on the edge of the roof with my legs threaded between the balustrades, that I make my confession. It's not a new revelation, but it's heartfelt. And now I mean it more than I ever have.

'I want to get old, Jack. I want to know that each minute is special because it will never be repeated. That I won't be left behind by the people I love ever again.' We sit side by side looking down on the city that gave us shelter and let us call her home. 'If we had been in time, if we had saved Ben, then perhaps I could have lived another hundred lifetimes, but not now. I need a way out. I need it so much it hurts.'

'What would I do without you though?' Jack asks, squeezing my fingers. 'Who would I have to tell all my secrets to?'

'You'd cope,' I tell him. 'You live in the moment – you always have – and that's why you are so much better at this than I am. For you there is no past or future, there is only now. And there can never be too much of that. You'd live an infinite number of nows without me, and after a while I'd just be a fond memory.'

'Vita, I love you, and I can't bear the thought of you not being here with me.' Jack's voice breaks a little. 'All these years and I only ever really loved Leonardo and you. But if this is what you need, then I will help you. I think I've figured out how to break the spell. How you can make yourself mortal again.'

'You have?' I raise my gaze to meet his and see the conflict in his eyes.

Jack sighs, pulling his hand from mine and running it through his curls.

'I realised how simple it was last night, when I was making the painting,' he says, his eyes fixed on the horizon. 'Creating a portrait using Leonardo's method fixes a soul in one moment of time while everything else goes on. It's like a rock planted in a riverbed; all of time continues to flow around it. Now, I can't say I know for sure, but it seems logical to me that to kick the rock loose would turn it back into the current, where it would travel along with the rest of creation. My magical portrait is lost somewhere, but wherever it is it endures for now. I have no choice in who I am, and I'm at peace with that. But your portrait, Vita, is right there.'

'You mean if I destroy it I'm free?' I ask, turning slowly to look. 'Destroy a Da Vinci and my clock begins to turn again?'

'It's only a theory,' Jack says carefully. 'But yes, I think so. Strange, isn't it, how the most complicated mysteries so often have the simplest of solutions?'

'But to destroy a Da Vinci?' I say, looking into the face of the girl I once knew.

'Could you do it?' Jack asks me.

'I don't know.' An alarm goes off on my phone, making me start. My glass tumbles down, glinting in the light for a moment before it shatters on the ground. 'We have to go. Kitty and Sarah are about arrive.'

***

We stand under the vaulted heights of King's Cross and wait for the flow of travellers to disembark from the train. I had asked the police to wait for them to arrive so that it could be me who told them about Ben. I see Kitty first, Elliot bouncing along on her hip. Then her mum, just behind, wheeling a suitcase. They are smiling right up until the moment they see my face.

Kitty drops her bag. Sarah stops in her tracks.

I run to them, arms open. We hold one another in a tight knot, anchored by our grief as the rest of time flows all around us, travelling to a distant ocean of stars. Each of us loves him, and that will always endure.

XI

Carpe diem

Chapter Fifty-Eight

There was alchemy in the air that night. It just wasn't the kind we had anticipated. And though it will never change how much I miss Ben, miss all the people I have lost, it does give me a reason to live.

Four months have passed since we lost Ben. Four dark months where I began again, though I thought it might kill me to try. That was until one morning I felt something moving inside me like a flutter of butterflies. I knew I had felt that before, though it took me a minute to place the sensation. Then quite suddenly I realised I had been given the most beautiful gift. In the same moment as one life was taken from me, another was bestowed.

Now I am sitting on the bathroom floor with Pablo outside scratching at the door, watching as the pregnancy test turns positive. Laying my hand over my belly, I close my eyes and wait for movement under the flat of my palm that tells me that life grows there. Mine and Ben's baby, preparing to unfurl into the waiting world where she will be so loved.

'Hello, little one,' I whisper. 'It's your mummy here.'

'Well?' Kitty asks from where she is waiting at the top of the stairs.

Climbing to my feet, I open the door and smile at her and at Sarah, who sits three stairs down.

'You are going to be an aunt,' I tell Kitty. 'And Sarah, you are going to be a grandma again.'

With a joyful sob Sarah holds her arms out to me and somehow the three of us, and Pablo, find ourselves tangled in a complicated hug halfway up and down the stairs.

'It's a miracle,' Sarah says, though she will never know the half of it. She doesn't need to, now that I am mortal once more.

★★★

The painting – *my* painting – is now listed as stolen by mysterious art thieves, lost to some private collector's vault. No one in the world, except for me, knows if they will ever see it again. I know they will not.

When the time was right, I took the painting on to the roof of the Bianchi Mansion, where Jack was waiting for me with a box of matches, and we set the painting on fire. We watched it burn, sunset embers floating up into the dark sky like lanterns, until there were only ashes. I scooped up what little was left and took it to the river where we scattered the ashes into the water. And I knew then that though it would take a few more decades, one day I would once more be with all those I have loved and lost. I would be with Ben again.

The gift of my mortality has been returned to me.

But in the years between now and for ever I will teach our child everything Ben taught me about what it means to truly live with all your heart.

Every moment is singular, it is precious. It can never be repeated.

This is life.

Acknowledgements

My heartfelt thanks to all the people that I could not have written this book without, especially Lily Cooper, Hellie Ogden, Ma'suma Amiri, and Emily Randle.

Thank you also to my dear friends, particularly Julie Akhurst and Steve Brown, whose son this book is dedicated to. Noah lives on in our hearts forever.

And finally, to my wonderful husband Adam for his endless support, my brilliant, funny, amazing children and my marvellous dogs, Blossom and Bluebell.